the BOYS of SUMMER

⊣ RICHARD COX ⊢

Night Shade Books + NEW YORK

Night Shade books may be purchased in bulk at special discounts for sales promotion, corporate gifts, fund-raising, or educational purposes. Special editions can also be created to specifications. For details, contact the Special Sales Department, Night Shade Books, 307 West 36th Street, 11th Floor, New York, NY 10018 or info@skyhorsepublishing.com.

Night Shade Books® is a registered trademark of Skyhorse Publishing, Inc.®, a Delaware corporation.

Visit our website at www.nightshadebooks.com.

10 9 8 7 6 5 4 3 2

Library of Congress Cataloging-in-Publication Data

Names: Cox, Richard, 1970- author.
Title: The boys of summer / Richard Cox.
Description: New York : Night Shade Books, [2016]
Identifiers: LCCN 2016012889 | ISBN 9781597808781 (hardcover : alk. paper)
Subjects: | GSAFD: Bildungsromans | Suspense fiction.
Classification: LCC PS3603.O925 B69 2016 | DDC 813/.6--dc23
LC record available at https://lccn.loc.gov/2016012889

Cover design by Claudia Noble

Printed in the United States of America

Permissions: Pages 24-25, 124, 142, 169, 210: "The Boys of Summer," Words and Music by DON HENLEY and MIKE CAMPBELL © 1984 WOODY CREEK MUSIC and WILD GATOR MUSIC. All Rights For WOODY CREEK MUSIC Administered by WB MUSIC CORP. All Rights Reserved. Page 340: "Crazy," Words and Music by THOMAS "CEE LO" CALLAWAY, BRIAN BURTON, GIANFRANCO REVERBERI and GIAN PIERO REVERBERI © 2006 WARNER/CHAPPELL MUSIC PUBLISHING LTD., CHRYSALIS MUSIC LTD. and BMG RICORDI MUSIC PUBLISHING SpA. All Rights for WARNER/CHAPPELL MUSIC PUBLISHING LTD. in the U.S. and Canada Administered by WARNER-TAMERLANE PUBLISHING CORP. ("Crazy" contains elements of "Last Man Standing" by GIANFRANCO REVERBERI and GIAN PIERO REVERBERI, © BMG RICORDI MUSIC PUBLISHING SpA). All Rights Reserved. Reprinted with permission of Hal Leonard Corporation and Alfred Music.

For Kimberly

Acknowledgments

This novel would never have seen the light of day without the steady and challenging insight from my good friend and agent, Matt Bialer. I would also like to express gratitude to Jeremy Lassen, Cory Allyn, and Mark Tavani for their constructive and passionate editorial guidance.

Special thanks to Don Henley and Mike Campbell for their unwitting contribution to this project.

Finally, I would like to thank my wife, Kimberly Cox, whose support helped breathe new life into the characters you'll soon meet. I sure do love her.

Author's Note

The opening scenes of this novel depict an actual weather event that took the lives of more than forty citizens of Wichita Falls, Texas and remains one of the most devastating tornado strikes in U.S. history. While every effort has been made to capture the reality of that day, dramatic license, as one might expect, has found its way into the version of the event you'll read in the upcoming pages. A detailed analysis of the weather conditions of the day, and the tornado outbreak that arose from them, can be found at: http://www.srh.noaa.gov/oun/?n=events-19790410.

The forecasts in the novel have been modeled after formatting employed by the National Weather Service, and have also been fictionalized. Also, some of the language and procedures of the NWS have evolved over the years, but for the sake of simplicity all forecasts have been formatted to today's practices.

I leave it to you, the reader, to discover what else in this story is real.

You're either reading a book or you're not.
—Jonathan Franzen

f you believe legend, the city of Wichita Falls was doomed from its first day. Erected near a small waterfall on a muddy tributary of the Red River, where white settlers displaced a tribe of Indians known to them as Wichita, the community was officially named on September 27, 1872. Just before sunset, as new landowners celebrated their good fortune, the revered chief named Tawakoni Jim recalled an old Caddo legend about a boy bestowed with the Power of the Cyclone, which enabled him to summon black clouds and bring their powerful winds to the ground. Tawakoni Jim did not recognize Texas claim upon tribal land and implored any white man in range of his voice not to make a home upon land stolen from his people.

"The Power of the Cyclone enjoys a long memory," Jim is believed to have said. "You may build a settlement here that thrives for many years. But someday, when you have long forgotten our people, the boy will enact vengeance. Build your homes from the strongest wood bound together by the strongest iron, and still no white home will stand against his power. The boy will erase your town from the land and many lives will be lost. To avoid tragedy, I ask you kindly not to settle upon this site."

Being Christians by birth, if not necessarily by nature, the new landowners considered this story a silly pagan myth told by a well-spoken, displaced savage. They built their town at the site of the falls and for many years it flourished. The Fort Worth and Denver Railway arrived in 1882 and oil was discovered nearby in 1911. By 1960, the city's population had swelled to 100,000. And except for one small tornado in 1958 that killed a farmer, Wichita Falls avoided nature's wrath. By that time, anyone present when Tawakoni Jim spoke his infamous prophesy had long since passed away. Even in 1964, when an intense stovepipe tornado raked across the city's north side, only seven people were killed. New radar technology allowed weather experts to see storms in more detail than ever before, making it possible to warn the population of an impending tornado strike. Surely Jim could not have foreseen such scientific advances.

But you can know something terrible is going to happen and still not be able to get out of the way. On April 10, 1979, a massive tornado churned through Wichita Falls, a multiple-vortex, mile-wide monster that demolished schools, businesses, and displaced 20,000 people from their homes. Pictures and video of the aftermath shocked viewers across the country. Damage was so widespread and costly it was not equaled by another tornado for over twenty years. And while the storm did not erase the town, as Jim had prophesized, it did set in motion a chain of events that led to a far worse disaster twenty-nine years later.

What happened in Wichita Falls on June 2, 2008 has been described as "biblical," though Wichita Indians know the Bible had nothing to do with it. Careful readers of the story that follows, however, will find clues to a mysterious book that *did* contribute to the demise of a Middle American city and a number of characters contained herein.

PART ONE
April 10, 1979

ZONE FORECAST PRODUCT
NATIONAL WEATHER SERVICE NORMAN OK
TXZ086-111000-
WICHITA-
INCLUDING THE CITIES OF ... WICHITA FALLS
155 PM CST TUE APR 10 1979

... TORNADO WATCH IN EFFECT FROM 230 PM UNTIL 700 PM CST ...

.THIS AFTERNOON ... MOSTLY CLOUDY WITH SCATTERED THUNDERSTORMS. SOME STORMS MAY BE SEVERE, WITH DAMAGING WINDS, LARGE HAIL, AND TORNADOES POSSIBLE. HIGH IN THE LOWER 80S. WINDS SW 10-20 MPH AND GUSTY. CHANCE OF RAIN 70 PERCENT.
.TONIGHT ... CLOUDY AND TURNING COOLER. LOW AROUND 45. WINDS NW 10-20 MPH. CHANCE OF RAIN 40 PERCENT.
.WEDNESDAY ... PARTLY CLOUDY. HIGH IN THE MID 60S. NW WINDS 10-15 MPH.
.THURSDAY ... MOSTLY SUNNY AND WARMER. HIGH IN THE MID 70S. WINDS LIGHT AND VARIABLE.

1

The day was electric, charged with possibility. Bobby Steele could feel it in the humid air and freshening wind, the power of the world. Ahead of him the sky was a gathering darkness. He was ten years old and had the strange feeling something important was about to happen, something that would alter the story of his life forever. At the moment Bobby was headed south toward Jonathan Crane's house, and by the time he crossed Midwestern Parkway it was barely five o'clock.

His feathered hair bounced against his head, blonde and thick and sculpted by the wind. His smile was magnetic. It was the second day of Spring Break and his mom didn't expect him before dark. She would have let him stay out longer if it weren't for his dad, Kenny, who was unreasonable when it came to Bobby spending time with Jonathan. But his dad framed houses during the day and played cards in the evening, and he never walked into the house before eight. That was three hours from now. Three hours was forever.

The streets in this part of town were wider than those in his own neighborhood, the houses bigger and solid and made of brick. Anybody could take one look at Bobby's banged-up, garage-sale Huffy and figure out he didn't live around here. Anyone could see he was far away from home. But he rode how he pleased anyway—relaxed, no hands— because even as a kid he knew the best way to get on in a place was to act like you belonged there.

It was a long ride, and by now he was inhaling and exhaling great breaths of air, but if it had been a contest he could have gone on for a lot longer. He was a strong boy, after all. A competitive boy. He was a winner, he had to be, because his dad was pretty fond of saying how he hadn't raised a loser.

Such was life for young sons born to legendary football stars. In 1966 Kenny had quarterbacked the Olney Cubs to the 1A Texas state football championship, where he rushed for five touchdowns in a lopsided victory over what Kenny liked to describe as "a team full of Mexicans." On the game's final play, however, with victory well in hand, his dad elected not to take a knee near the opponent's end zone and had instead run a naked bootleg. The way his dad liked to tell the story, Kenny Steele had been a poor kid from a small town hoping to impress a bunch of big-time college coaches, and everything had been ruined by some long forgotten Mexican. But in reality the old man had been showboating, and Bobby supposed the angry linebacker who denied that sixth touchdown brought a little karma to the goal line. The collision shattered his dad's kneecap as if it were made of glass, and that was the last time he had ever run a bootleg, naked or otherwise.

Bobby loved football and knew he would someday follow in his dad's footsteps, but he also suspected there was more to life than sports. Lately he had been playing at Jonathan's house more and more often because he could enjoy things that would never happen at home. Take chess, for instance. Where his own dad thought board games were pointless, Jonathan's father liked watching the boys play and sometimes taught them strategy. Strategy was a concept foreign to Bobby until he started playing chess. It was like winning with your brain instead of your body. Sometimes he wondered what would happen if he approached football as if it were a chess match, like if he combined athleticism with strategy, but his dad didn't much care for the idea. Specifically he explained how football was a game of speed and power and intimidation, that chess was for pussies, and if his son wanted to grow up to be an Ivy League wimp he could go live somewhere else. After that Bobby didn't say anything more about chess and promised not to visit Jonathan again. He wasn't proud of himself for being dishonest, but sometimes his dad was too unreasonable for his own good.

When he parked his bike in Jonathan's driveway, Bobby noticed the clouds in the southwestern sky had grown even darker and were moving in a way he'd never seen before. Like someone was up there stirring them on purpose. The sound of the doorbell was louder than he expected and reverberated in a way that seemed loaded with meaning. By the time Jonathan appeared, Bobby was ready to get inside.

"Hey, man. I didn't think you would stop by today."

"Can I come in?"

"Yeah, sure. Is everything okay?"

"I don't know," Bobby said. "It feels weird outside."

"Yeah, there's bad weather coming. Maybe you should have stayed home."

Jonathan's house smelled great like it always did, as if someone were frying chicken and boiling potatoes and baking cookies all at the same time. Sometimes Bobby wished Mrs. Crane could be his own mom.

"What kind of bad weather?" he asked.

"There was just a tornado in Vernon. My mom's watching TV and they keep showing the radar."

"Where's Vernon?"

This question prompted a look of contempt on Jonathan's face so evident that Bobby was tempted to punch him in the gut. But he didn't. After all, the whole reason he had made friends with this guy was so the smart would rub off on him.

"Vernon is northwest of here," Jonathan explained.

"So the tornado is coming this way?"

"Not that one. The guy on TV says another storm is coming up from Seymour."

Bobby nodded as if this made complete sense, but in reality he didn't have a clue where Seymour was, either. He was starting to think there would be no chess today.

"So what do you want to do?"

"Let's go watch the radar with my mom. My dad's still at work and she's pretty worried."

Jonathan started toward the back of the house, where the bedrooms were, and Bobby followed him.

"You don't think a tornado is going to hit here, do you?"

"You never know," Jonathan said. "They're saying it's pretty bad. Like there might be a bunch of tornadoes."

He led them into a room where the TV was on. Mrs. Crane was sitting on the edge of the bed, staring at the screen, close enough to change channels without having to get up.

"Hey, Mom," Jonathan said. "Bobby's here."

Now she looked up. "Bobby? Why aren't you home?"

"I didn't know bad weather was coming."

"He could have dinner with us tonight," Jonathan suggested. "He'll never get back before it starts raining."

"I don't know. Bobby, can you call your mom to come get you? She'd probably feel more comfortable if you were there with her."

"We just have the one pickup. My dad drives it to work every day."

"He might get off early, though," Jonathan said. "Since he can't work in the rain."

Bobby hadn't considered this, and now he realized the decision to come over here had been a big mistake. If his dad showed up early looking for him, tornadoes would be the least of Bobby's worries.

"Maybe I should go," he said. "I might be able to get back before the storm hits."

On the television, a man was explaining where to take cover and be prepared to do so at any time.

"Now that you're here," Mrs. Crane said, "it's probably better that you stay unless we can get your parents on the phone."

"But my dad—"

"We'll call and let them know you're staying, all right?"

"All right," Bobby said. And while it was easy to blame his dad for what happened next, the truth was Bobby's presence here was a product of deliberate deceit. Even worse, he'd wished (plenty of times!) that Mrs. Crane were his own mom. He hadn't meant this literally, of course, but whoever was in charge of such things must not have understood. And when the tragedy was over, when his mother had been counted among the dead, Bobby felt he had no choice but to assume responsibility. It was a burden too onerous for a ten-year-old boy, especially a boy already saddled with the expectations of a disapproving father who had blown his own chance at greatness. But Bobby shouldered it anyway, and carried that burden until a strange night twenty-nine years later, when he would give his life to make amends for this and all of his mistakes.

On the television, the radar remained covered with angry splashes of orange and yellow that for some reason made him think of fire. As if the storms approaching were not made of rain and wind but great monster columns of swirling flame.

A moment later, the tornado sirens began to sound.

2

The trees were thick by the river. Ten-year-old David Clark lived in one of Tanglewood's newest homes, but he could walk down here where the construction stopped and take a few steps past a barbed wire fence and immediately be swallowed by wilderness. He loved the feeling of isolation, the palpable sense of stepping into the past, as if he were Tom Sawyer or Huckleberry Finn. In fact he spent so much time in the woods that several months ago he'd built himself a fort using two-by-fours and plywood and fence planks given to him by the house builders. Some of his friends were surprised at how easily the workers had given over the raw material, but not David. He'd learned from his father that people would do all sorts of things if you could summon the nerve to ask.

He'd intended for the fort to seem as remote as possible, like so far into the woods you could forget where you were, but the raw materials were difficult to carry through the trees. In the end he'd built his structure only thirty yards outside the barbed wire fence. What he really needed was a place to hang out closer to the river, which was where he spent most of his time.

Today was a perfect example. He'd been down by the water, watching for beavers and alligator gar, when the skies grew dark and threatened rain. Since David didn't feel like being soaked, he turned and started back home, working his way through the trees and vines and watching for poison ivy. He was maybe halfway to the barbed wire fence when raindrops began to fall, large and fat.

Then David noticed how the ground, with each step, was sliding perceptibly beneath his shoes. He noticed how the trees swayed. Raindrops pelted branches above him, raindrops thumped the ground, and some of them must have been huge because the sound was louder than he would have expected. Now the trail bent around a thatch of mesquite trees and ascended a small red cliff. Thick, exposed roots were like steps that his feet used to propel him upward. They were slippery, though, and he nearly fell, and—

I can see you . . .

—the world seemed to flip somehow, as if down was up and up was down, and for a moment David thought he heard a guitar. As if someone had played a burst of music, a song he'd never heard before but somehow recognized anyway. Then he was on his back and looking at trees towering like skyscrapers. The raindrops pattering around him were percussion, the wind whistling through branches was music, and he imagined these sounds were the opening bars of the song he'd just heard. For a while he just lay there on the ground, listening to the forest and its music, and he might never have moved if something hadn't hit him in the face. Something sharp, something that hurt. Something that felt like a rock.

Was someone out here with him? Had someone been watching him?

Then another rock landed nearby. And another. Except they weren't rocks. They were hailstones. Falling around him, little marbles of ice. Another one crashed into his shoulder.

"Ouch!" David yelled at no one. "Stop that!"

The forest was not playing music. It was in turmoil. Trees bent this way and that. The wind shrieked. Raindrops and hailstones poured down around him. David pushed himself off the ground and started toward his house again. Again he felt a chilling and real sensation of being followed, of being watched. In the grass he noticed something white and irregular. It looked like a hailstone, but it couldn't be, because the thing was the size of a tennis ball.

More of them were falling.

David took off, flying down the path as fast as his legs would take him. There was no point in trying for the house now; even if he made it out of the trees safely, there was a fifty-yard stretch of backyard lawn where he would be completely exposed to the sky. His only option was to stop at the fort and hope the roof could protect him.

Most of the hailstones were small, cold and hard, but the bigger ones might crush bone with a direct hit. Broken branches fell to the ground, branches and hailstones that pounded the earth with unreasonable force. One of them fell into the path directly before him, a chunk of ice that thumped the ground so hard he could feel it in his feet.

The sky was darker now, as if the sun were on its way down. David could see maybe fifty yards ahead and that was it. For the first time in his life a terrible and inconceivable thought occurred to him.

What if I die?

David was familiar with death like everyone was, but until today he'd never really imagined it for himself. Now the idea seemed as real as the hailstones falling around him. He could die. He could be gone forever and never know another thing or think another thought. What would that be like? How could he be here and then not here?

A flash of light turned the sky to fire. Deafening thunder shook the forest. Branches were falling everywhere now, branches and leaves and hailstones so massive that he could barely credit what he saw. He ran as hard as he could. He ran for his life. And now he thought he could hear footsteps following his own.

As if someone were behind him.

In his mind he heard his dad's voice, or what he assumed was his dad's voice, cheering him on. *Don't look back, you can never look back.* Except what it really sounded like was someone singing, like he was hearing that mysterious song again. *I thought I knew what love was . . .*

And then, through the trees, he finally saw the fort. Hailstones bounced off the roof looking like marbles and golf balls and the occasional baseball. When he reached the door he fumbled with the latch but could not get it open. Any minute now the footsteps were going to catch him, and still David fumbled with the latch. Thunder exploded above him. It sounded like a gunshot and he nearly screamed.

Just as he figured out the latch, a hailstone slammed into his ankle, striking the knot of bone there. Heat and pain flared up his leg. He gritted his teeth and crawled underneath the work bench even as his ankle threatened to crumple beneath him.

From here David thought he might be able to relax, but when he looked between slats of wood at the storm outside, he imagined he was looking out the window of an airplane. Like he was taking off and watching the ground below him, which was pretty strange considering he'd never flown before and the only planes he'd ever seen were on television. He could not connect the storm to the vision of being airborne, of flying away, yet for a few seconds both realities were so vivid that he felt suspended between them. As if he were flipping a page of his life from one scene to the next.

Eventually the assault of hailstones returned David to clarity. He closed his eyes and squeezed out tears and wordlessly begged whichever gods were listening to spare his life. He promised to be good and generous and do right by everyone, to be a giver instead of a taker, to be thankful to have survived the storm.

His ten-year-old self couldn't know that later versions of David would not live up to such standards, that over time his character would gradually veer in the opposite direction. Four years would pass before he met Todd Willis, before he heard the mysterious song again, and even then its significance would be lost on him. He would not fully comprehend the strangeness of this stormy evening for another twenty-nine years, after his father's murder and a series of devastating fires that signaled the city's eventual demise. By then his fate had already been written and rewritten and all he could do was watch helplessly as his life began its ferocious descent.

Eventually the hail began to taper off and then stopped completely. David stood up, protecting his wounded ankle, and opened the door. Through the trees loomed the blackest cloud he'd ever seen. He hobbled toward the barbed wire fence, climbed through it, and ran like a madman toward his house. He was almost there when he heard the ominous ringing of the tornado sirens.

It was a sound that would soon come to haunt his dreams.

3

The way Jonathan Crane's life changed forever began with a loud banging on the front door of his house. The source of the noise was

Bobby's father, Kenny Steele, who was demanding to be let in. Jonathan's mother, Carolyn, refused and had just hung up the phone after a frantic call to his father.

"Dad didn't answer," she explained. "He's probably on his way home already."

Bobby's face was the color of paper. He opened his mouth as if to speak but nothing came out. Jonathan's mom put her hand on his.

"Don't you worry. Sometimes adults get upset for no good reason. Hopefully we'll get this straightened out without having to call the police."

Jonathan, who had never seen his father belligerent, wondered how Bobby could live every day with a man like Mr. Steele in the house. Of course later, when all this was over, he would regret having foreshadowed such a notion into existence.

The banging was so violent it rattled the door in its frame. The whole house seemed to shake with each blow and Jonathan could tell his mom was growing more frightened by the second.

"I think I'm going to call the police," she finally said.

But Bobby was hysterical at this idea.

"Please, Mrs. Crane. My dad already had some trouble with the cops last year. Please don't—"

Carolyn was reaching for the phone anyway. She was about to start punching numbers when the banging abruptly stopped and Jonathan heard his father's voice outside the door.

"Can I help you?"

"I'm looking for Jonathan's daddy," Mr. Steele replied.

A moment of silence followed and then Jonathan heard his father's voice again, this time farther away.

"I'm Michael Crane. What's going on here?"

Jonathan didn't make any sort of decision about opening the front door. He did it automatically, helpless to stop himself.

"Honey!" his mom cried. "Don't go out there."

"But Dad might be in trouble!"

In fact his father and Mr. Steele were standing on the front lawn, face to face, so near each other their noses almost touched.

"What's going on here," Mr. Steele said, "is your boy is trying to turn *my* boy into a pussy."

Jonathan rubbed his eyes and wondered if this scene was really happening. That's what it looked like: a scene someone had written in a book. When you loved to read as much as Jonathan did, it was natural to wonder if you could write a story of your own, and lately he'd been trying to picture the events of his real life as written scenes. In this one, Bobby's dad was wearing a flannel shirt and torn jeans and hadn't shaved in days. He was upset because he seemed to believe Jonathan had corrupted Bobby in some way. But what, exactly, did he think had occurred? And did he honestly plan to fight over it?

Ominously, the tornado sirens began to wail again. It was the second or third time he'd heard them in the past twenty minutes. Jonathan felt someone behind him and realized his mom and Bobby were watching from the door. The wind began to pick up and gusted so suddenly that it was difficult to hear what the two men were saying.

"Look," his dad yelled. "I don't know what you think my son has done to yours, but whatever it is I'm sure we can work it out. Right now we should—"

"Right now you're going to tell your little pussy son to stay away from my boy. That's what you're going to do right now."

Jonathan didn't understand why Mr. Steele was calling him names. And he could tell his father didn't either, who with each passing second appeared to be growing more frustrated.

"Listen," his father said. "You hear the sirens. You know what they mean. Let's talk about this another time when there's not a tornado about to—"

"There ain't going to be no *tornado*," said Mr. Steele.

Until now Jonathan had barely noticed a white pickup truck sitting in front of their house. Presently the passenger door opened and a woman, Bobby's mom, lurched toward her husband.

"Kenny Steele!" she yelled. "I told you not to start a fight. We got to take shelter!"

Jonathan sensed his father was weighing options on how to proceed. He looked angry enough to hit Mr. Steele, but he also kept glancing at the sky and the swirling clouds above.

"I see where he gets it," Mr. Steele said. "That streak of yellow in your son, I see where—"

That's when his father seized Mr. Steele by the throat. Jonathan could barely believe it was happening. All his life he'd been taught that fighting was more often the cause of problems than the solution, but now he understood that sometimes it was necessary to fight. The security he felt watching his father physically defend him was as powerful as the storm swirling overhead. Jonathan had never loved him more than he did in that moment.

The security, however, was short-lived. Mr. Steele's hands reached out and grabbed his father's own neck, and soon they were both on the ground. It didn't take long to see who was going to win the fight and who was going to lose.

Jonathan ran forward, desperate to help, but Mrs. Steele stepped in front of him and jumped on her husband's back. Michael rolled away from them, choking and reaching for his neck. Carolyn rushed to his side and tried to lift him off the ground.

"Jonathan," she said. "Come here and help me."

But his dad was already climbing to his feet. He wasn't looking at either of them. He was looking at the sky. Pointing at the sky.

"We have to get inside. We have to go now."

Jonathan looked up and saw clouds, swirling and black, so low they seemed close enough to touch. Beyond them, not far away, something was roaring.

"Oh, my God," Carolyn said.

"Tornado!" Bobby screamed from behind him.

The roar deepened, rumbling and unmistakable, like it was some kind of real life monster. Jonathan turned back to his dad, not knowing it was the last time he would ever make direct eye contact with him.

"Run, son! Run inside."

"But I can't leave you!"

"Your mom and I will be right behind you. Run inside. Now!"

Jonathan glanced at Bobby and his parents. He wanted to be angry for what had happened. After all, if the kid wasn't such a moron, if he had any idea about the storms, Bobby would have stayed home and none of this would have happened. Still, there was no way for anyone to have known a real tornado would come right at them, and it certainly wasn't Bobby's fault his father had started a fight.

The swirling mass approaching them wasn't a weather event. It was a nightmare that had found its way into daylight. There was no hope for it to miss them. It was too large and it was coming right at them.

"Come on!" Michael said. "Let's all go inside before it's too late!"

His father made it to the door and took Jonathan's hand. Together they ran toward the kitchen and more specifically the pantry.

"Squeeze in there," Michael said. "Carolyn, you too. Mrs. Steele—"

His dad turned around and reached for Bobby and his mom.

"You guys, also. Mr. Steele and I will have to hide in the guest bathroom."

"What?" Carolyn screamed. "We can all fit! Don't leave us here alone!"

"You won't be alone. You'll all be together. We'll be right around the corner."

"Mike!"

The sound of the tornado had changed. Now it sounded like a piercing shrill that made Jonathan think of water swirling down a giant drain. He didn't think a person could be more frightened than he was now.

"Let's go," his father said to Mr. Steele. "We're out of time."

"Mike, no! Please!"

His dad shut the door. The light wasn't on and the four of them were thrown into darkness. With nothing to see, the only available sensations were the terrible sounds of the storm, and honestly the shrieking of the tornado was more than sound. It seemed to be draining oxygen from the air. Bobby and his mom were both crying. Jonathan himself was silent, straining to hear signs that his father was still out there, that he was still alive.

"The bathroom is this way," Michael shouted. "Come on, we can—"

But his voice was severed by a world-ending crash of wood and glass, and a great weight drove Jonathan to his knees. He heard a terrible scream. A woman's scream. He hoped it wasn't his mother. He hoped his dad had made it to safety. He reached for his own body, hands searching for wounds or blood or some kind of signal that he was either hurt or okay, but he found nothing. His body didn't seem to be there at all. And when he tried looking for a sign of what had happened, of where he was,

Jonathan realized he couldn't see anything. Everywhere he looked there was nothing.

Nothing but white.

4

Alicia Ulbrecht was just nine years old, and there were many things that confused her, but one thing she knew for sure was her daddy could protect her from anything, especially thunderstorms. In her estimation he knew more about the weather than anybody in the whole world.

The problem was, whenever bad storms came, her dad would take their car and his camera and drive out into the countryside to see the weather up close. That left Alicia and her mother to stay home and fend for themselves. Later he would return and tell stories about the amazing and terrible things he had seen, like uprooted trees, cars tossed around like toys, and houses leveled to their foundations. Sometimes he even shared photographs with her, images that never failed to send shivers up her back. Her favorites were the slender tornadoes, dark and sinister, framed against yellow skies.

But today the storms weren't out in the countryside somewhere. They were rolling into town, so close the weatherman on TV was explaining how this was a LIFE THREATENING EMERGENCY FOR WICHITA FALLS. And her daddy was nowhere to be found.

Later in life she would wonder if her inability to sustain relationships was borne out of a fear of abandonment that had been seeded at this moment. Maybe she had come to expect that even men of the highest character were cursed with an instinctive, nomadic need to hunt, to run away. This suspicion would eventually be reinforced when her mother took ill and required constant care, because even then her dad could not bring himself to stop traveling for work or hire someone to look after her. He would expect Alicia to assist, and naturally she did. She would never be able to turn him down for anything.

At the moment her mother was frantic. She kept running into the yard to look for her husband, and then returning inside to check on Alicia. It would have been funny to watch her if it weren't so dark outside, if the wind weren't shrieking and the tornado sirens weren't wailing like giant ghosts.

"Where is he?" her mother cried. "He said he would come back if the storms got too close. Where is he?"

Alicia knew, when a tornado was on its way, that she and her mother were supposed to climb into the tub and cover themselves with a mattress. But since no one was enforcing this directive, she was instead standing on her bed to look out the window. From here she could see the storm approaching, and also her daddy's car if it ever turned onto their street.

The sky looked like it had fallen to the earth. Black clouds danced and rolled at a speed that made them look unreal, like she was watching a movie in fast forward. Trash was landing in their yard, silver tape and cardboard boxes and papers, papers everywhere. A strange sound began to swell around her, like a long, powerful train speeding toward some unknown but prewritten destination. She imagined a boy, or boys, cowering before the storm. One of the boys thought he might be dead, but she knew he wasn't because one day she would fall in love with that boy. Over the tops of houses, maybe two streets over, she could see the violent, swirling monster. The tornado wasn't like any picture her dad had ever showed her. It wasn't a tube or a funnel. It was a many-limbed monster, a giant spider twirling in pirouette. A car spiraled into the air. Blue-green light flashed near the ground, rapid pulses, one-two-three. The roof of a house was swept into the air and disappeared. Now the boy's father was dead.

"Alicia!" her mother screamed. Her voice was desperate, ragged, as if she were dying. But they weren't going to die. It was obvious from watching the tornado that it was now moving away from them.

"Alicia! Where are you?"

"In my room, mom."

Her mother appeared and tore her away from the window.

"Mom, what are you doing?"

"We have to get into the bathtub!"

"But the tornado passed us already. They don't go backward."

Her mother wasn't listening. She pushed Alicia toward the bathroom and into the tub.

"Mom, this is stupid! The tornado isn't coming this way!"

Her mother climbed into the tub with her and pulled Alicia into a sitting position. Threw her arms around her. She was crying.

"Mom, it's okay. Dad always says—"

"Your dad's not here! He left us alone!"

"But—"

"You hush, Alicia. Your dad may think he knows everything about the weather, but I *know* you don't. This time we're going to do what *I* want. No one ever asks me what I want!"

Later they would learn her father had been stranded in the countryside near Seymour when a different tornado he was chasing damaged the car so badly it couldn't be driven. In the madness that followed the day's outbreak of tornadoes—twenty-four of them, in fact—it would be hours before he was picked up by a highway patrolman, and days before he could retrieve the car. By then the city of Wichita Falls was beginning to comprehend the effort that would be required to recover from such a catastrophe, and Alicia had understood for the first time that adult relationships—like her parents' marriage, for instance—weren't themselves impervious to collapse.

5

Adam Altman couldn't understand why his mother hadn't returned from the store. She'd left maybe thirty minutes before to buy medicine, and since no one in the family was ill, the kind of medicine she probably meant was the liquid his parents liked to pour into their sodas or into glasses so tiny they held only one swallow. And anyway it seemed like an odd name, calling this stuff "medicine," since typically when his parents drank it they felt sick the next day.

His mother had left in a rush, not bothering to turn off the TV, so Adam and his sister, Christi, passed time watching the weatherman talk about how tornadoes were threatening the entire city.

Which was pretty confusing when you considered how close his parents were to God, and how they had explained—many times—that no tornado would ever strike down a family who honored the Lord and His only son, Jesus Christ. Every spring, in fact, Adam's mom and dad gathered the four of them in the front yard to glorify God and ask for protection against the stormy Texas weather. For years this appeared to work because the only tornadoes Adam had ever seen were in books. Now the guy on TV was advising everyone in town to take cover immediately.

"Climb into your bathtub and cover yourself with a mattress," said the weatherman. "Or go into a closet and close the door. Whatever you do, do it now. This is a large tornado coming straight into Wichita Falls."

Adam hadn't planned to do anything of the sort since he believed, truly, that God was watching over their house. But then the power went out and the two of them were left staring at the dark television set, and their mother still had not returned.

"I'm scared," said Christi. She was five years old, frightened of everything, and Adam typically felt obligated to poke fun at her every weakness.

But in this case he said, "Remember what Mom and Dad taught us. We pray to Jesus so this sort of thing won't happen to our family."

"But the guy on *TV* said—"

"Mom will be home any minute and she'll tell us what to do."

"But what if she doesn't come home?"

This was an outcome Adam refused to consider. What kind of mother would leave two children home to face a terrible storm alone? And why would God send a tornado toward a family that glorified him?

Adam walked to the front door, the clear storm door, and looked out. The sky was black. The wind was howling and screaming. The trees in their front yard thrashed like they were in agony.

"Let's get in the coat closet," he said to Christi. "I'm sure nothing will happen, but it can't hurt to be careful."

Soon the two of them were standing between jackets and coats in the claustrophobic darkness. His sister was clutching the pockets of his jeans, shaking, almost crying. She tried to put her arms around him, but he pushed her away. He didn't enjoy being this close to her or anyone.

"Adam, please hold me!"

But he couldn't. He wasn't like other kids. Everything had changed one evening, long ago, when a girl named Evelyn had tricked him into doing something awful. His parents didn't love him anymore. They loved Christi, who was their favorite, who remained pure because she had not committed the unforgivable sin.

The storm was growing louder. It growled like a giant and angry monster. Beneath the growl it sounded like the world was ending, like cars were crashing and walls were collapsing and the monster's great feet were scraping across the ground as it approached.

In New Orleans, the night Evelyn betrayed him, Adam had never felt so abandoned, so alone. It was a terrible feeling he would never wish on anyone. But now, when his own sister required his support, Adam resisted. He couldn't understand why she would want to be held, or why he should be the one to hold her.

"Adam!" Christi screamed. She grabbed his arms, his legs, she choked his stomach. He did not hold her back.

And now the growl was deafening, all around him, everywhere. The house creaked. It made a sound like splitting pants, like nails being hammered, like nails being pried free. Glass shattering, wood tearing. Loose earth. Suffocation.

Inexplicably, beneath all the noise, Adam imagined he could hear music. He imagined a boy was playing this music for him, for all of them. It was hot outside. It was summer.

"Adam!" his sister screamed. "Make it stop! Please!"

They were his friends, these four boys. It was summertime. The sound of the storm was deafening. Adam couldn't understand where God was. Why had the two children been left all alone?

Then the closet disappeared, or half of it did, and suddenly he was outdoors. The rest of the house, everything but two walls of the closet, was gone. The wind whipped and whistled around them. He could feel the sting of shrapnel on his face and arms, like leaves and twigs and pieces of wood, and his sister was screaming in his ear, and he couldn't stand it anymore, the guilt. Here was the bare concrete slab of their house, which seemed wrong, wrong and somehow familiar, and he wouldn't understand for a long time how these flat rectangles would come to define his life.

The tornado plowed onward. Adam could see its backside, swirling and fat from the houses it had devoured. Somehow it had left them behind, had left them alive. God was glorious! God was good!

"Christi?" he said. "Are you okay?"

Even before Adam looked he could tell something was wrong. At some point Christi's grip had weakened, and she was no longer clutching him the way she had before. In fact he could barely feel her weight at all.

When he looked down at his sister, the world seemed to change somehow. Adam's head swelled, inflating like a balloon, so expansively he was sure it would burst. His body suddenly weighed less than it ever had and seemed to float into a space where *up* and *down* were arbitrary, where all directions were arbitrary, and for a while all he saw was a plane of pure, formless white. In this space he floated for a while, it was impossible to say how long. He may or may not have heard people talking. Or screaming. He couldn't be sure because everything was obscured by the veil of flat white nothingness.

Eventually Adam returned to find people all around. His next door neighbor, Mrs. Merrill, was kneeling in front of him. She appeared to be speaking, but Adam couldn't hear what she was saying. Maybe he didn't want to hear.

Because Christi was gone. She was never coming back. Adam had refused to hold her, had chosen not to cover her body with his own, and in this way he had failed her as a big brother. He couldn't imagine how his mom and dad would react when they learned their favorite child was gone forever.

Later he would pray to God and offer himself in place of Christi. Not only because he was sorry, but because he didn't really want this life. Nine years was enough time for him to understand that things weren't someday going to improve. They were just going to keep on getting worse. Eventually the world would go up in flames, and since Adam didn't want to be around when it happened, he prayed and prayed for God to spare him, to extend this tiny bit of mercy.

But all he received in return was silence.

6

To Todd Willis, the white void wasn't frightening. It didn't generate any emotional response at all. It simply existed, and he now he existed within it.

Just before he arrived here, Todd had been trying to forge his mother's signature on a school progress report while she was on the phone with his dad, who was still at work. Apparently the two of them had discussed something about windows, because after she hung up his mom jogged frantically from room to room opening every window in the house. This behavior of his mother alarmed him more than the approaching tornado, because he'd never seen her run anywhere for any reason.

On the television, the weatherman made loud noises and had himself seemed frightened, which in Todd's estimation was also a first. Once the windows were opened, his mom grabbed some blankets from the linen closet and took him into the bathroom. They lay down in the tub and she shivered, telling him not to worry. She told him everything would be okay.

But then the winds came, and the roar, and when his mom began to cry Todd knew she was as frightened as he was. He reached for her hand just as everything began to shudder violently.

Then all the sounds and noise disappeared so suddenly it was like they had been playing on a giant tape player that someone had turned off. Like someone with a giant finger had pushed a giant STOP button, ending the sound of the world.

Now there was just this white void. He couldn't see anything or hear anything and he wondered if he were dead.

After some time passed, he couldn't say how long, Todd imagined he could hear something after all. Like someone tapping their fingers on a desk, or maybe striking the ground with a stick. At first he thought he'd imagined the sound, but later he heard it again, a little louder, and finally he realized what he was hearing was music.

Somewhere, someone was listening to this music. A rock song, something he'd never heard before. When he looked around at the white void, still seeing no shapes and no colors and no shadows of any kind, Todd couldn't imagine where the song might be coming from, or how he might find the source of it. If someone was listening to this song, then it followed that someone else must be here with him, someone he could conceivably talk to . . . if he could only figure out how to find them.

The haunting lyrics, however, seemed to dispel any hope of company:

Nobody on the road
Nobody on the beach
I feel it in the air
The summer's out of reach
Empty lake, empty streets
The sun goes down alone
I'm driving by your house
Though I know you're not home

At nine years old, Todd had spent little time thinking about his own mortality. Death was something that happened in the movies, and even then it wasn't well understood. Darth Vader had swiped Obi-Wan Kenobi with his red light saber, something that should have cut the old man in half, but there had been no blood and no body or anything you would normally associate with death. Where had Obi-Wan gone? To a place like this? Was Todd himself dead?

And still he kept hearing that song.

A little voice inside my head said
"Don't look back. You can never look back."
I thought I knew what love was
What did I know?
Those days are gone forever
I should just let them go, but—

Maybe he was a ghost, trapped between the living world and the dead. Maybe, if he waited long enough, the white void would disappear and reveal something wonderful. Maybe his arrival here was a test of will, a way to determine if he was worthy of eternal life. He wondered if the song in the background was a clue of some kind.

I can see you
Your brown skin shining in the sun
You got that top pulled down and that radio on, baby
And I can tell you my love for you will still be strong
After the boys of summer have gone

If this place was a test of will, Todd was up to the task. As nine-year-old kids went, he was one of the stronger ones. He was a patient boy and could wait a long time if he had to.

But in the end the wait was much longer than he or anyone could have imagined.

PART TWO
May 26–29, 2008

ZONE FORECAST PRODUCT
NATIONAL WEATHER SERVICE NORMAN OK
TXZ086-271000-
WICHITA-
INCLUDING THE CITIES OF ... WICHITA FALLS
355 PM CST MON MAY 26 2008

.REST OF TODAY ... MOSTLY SUNNY. AFTERNOON HIGH
NEAR 95. WINDS SW 15-25 MPH AND GUSTY.
.TONIGHT ... MOSTLY CLEAR. LOW NEAR 66. SOUTH WIND
10-15 MPH.
.TUESDAY ... SUNNY. HIGH IN THE MID 90S. SOUTH
WINDS AROUND 20 MPH.
.TUESDAY NIGHT ... CLEAR. LOW IN THE MID 60S. SOUTH
WINDS AROUND 15 MPH.
.WEDNESDAY ... SUNNY. HIGH IN THE UPPER 90S.
.THURSDAY ... SUNNY. HIGH NEAR 100.

7

H ad Alicia Ulbrecht realized how fundamentally her life would change
in the span of seven days, she would have skipped her date with
Stuart Pride. Even now, before the fires and the inexplicable music and
the storm, Alicia realized it had been a mistake to have dinner with
him. Stuart was short, somewhere between muscular and plump, but
she could have looked past his appearance if he were friendly or witty
(or both). He spent a lot of time talking about himself, but that was true
of many successful people, as well as nervous men on first dates. What
Alicia could not tolerate from Stuart or any man was blind persistence.
He was the kind of guy who invented arbitrary goals for himself and
then relentlessly pursued them no matter how unreasonable the goals
or what it might take to achieve them. This quality was so fundamental
to his character that he might as well have been wearing it on a T-shirt.
Four words inscribed in an anxious font: I AM A STRIVER.

Stuart was in charge of what he called Strategic Recruiting at
Feldman Golf, a manufacturing plant halfway between Wichita Falls
and Burkburnett on I-44. Alicia was curious about his work, because
she hoped to move to a bigger and better city and start a real career
sometime before she turned fifty. But when she inquired about what
sort of training he called upon to select talent, Stuart's answer revealed a
predictably narrow world view.

"Why would I need training?"

"You know," she said, smiling. "To be able to recognize the 'best and
brightest.'"

"I think I know who is promotable and who isn't. I was a salesman
in the field before this job at headquarters. That's all the training I need."

Alicia smiled and laughed and handed control of the conversation to him again. Somehow it seemed like she was always doing this on dates, smiling at men, laughing at their lame jokes, agreeing with their baseless opinions, and she knew she would never meet someone in Wichita Falls. The few intelligent fellows she had encountered over the years, Brandon aside, were boring or religious or both. And even when she made it to a second or third date, when she invariably stopped smiling and agreeing, her first instinct was to challenge, to understand how curious the guy was. Maybe the reason she'd been so attracted to Brandon was that he had been raised in Pennsylvania, that even though his field of study was physics, he still knew more about history than anyone she'd ever met. And it didn't hurt that he'd been nowhere near Wichita Falls when the tornado had ruined the town and everyone who lived here.

Stuart droned on. She tried hard to focus on what he was saying, but since he rarely paused to ask her a question, her attention waned again. She lost interest even in her chicken fajita salad, and for some reason the smell of fried food was making her queasy.

"I'm having a great time this evening," Stuart barked. "How about you?"

"Sure," Alicia said. "Chili's is a great restaurant."

Her date seemed to accept this and went on to complain how network television could use more programs that appealed to real Americans, like "Home Improvement" and "The Dukes of Hazzard." He also believed the liberal media was tearing the country apart, except for the local news, which he enjoyed. Alicia smiled at his pauses and began to imagine a studio apartment in Manhattan. It would be microscopic, barely long enough on one side for her to lie down at night, but that wouldn't matter because she really wouldn't be there that much. She'd be at corner bookstores and in Central Park and in little cafés where she could read real literature without people shaking their heads, where someone might actually want to have a conversation about books that didn't begin with a plane crash or a tornado on page two.

As if on cue, Stuart said, "So next year is the thirtieth anniversary of Terrible Tuesday. I can't believe it's been that long."

Terrible Tuesday was the name given to the massive tornado that in 1979 had left 20,000 people in Wichita Falls homeless. It was one of Alicia's earliest and most visceral memories.

"That's right," she said. "I guess there will be some kind of memorial. Maybe a parade?"

Stuart didn't seem to find this funny.

"Did it hit your house?" he asked.

"It missed us by two blocks. But my dad is a storm chaser. He saw the tornado when it was still outside of town and his car got hit pretty bad. He almost died."

"Shit," Stuart said. "A storm chaser in the 70s. I didn't know they existed back then."

"Yeah, he was so into it that he got a new job that didn't tie him to an office. I don't know how he could stand to chase after what happened back then, but he loves it. Was your family affected?"

"No, we lived up near the Air Force base, so it wasn't close to us. Thankfully."

She couldn't think of anything else to say about the tornado, and apparently neither could Stuart, because for a few moments they sat there staring at each other.

"You want to get out of here?" he finally asked.

"I don't think I'm going to eat any more of this salad." Her stomach made a sound angry enough that she wondered if Stuart had heard it. "For some reason I'm not so hungry this evening."

Another quiet moment passed, and even though there was no chemistry between them, it seemed to Alicia like something incredible was about to happen. She wasn't sure what, exactly. But it had been a permanent fixture of adulthood, this idea that something big would eventually come along and alter the story of her life forever. Maybe another reason she had loved Brandon was because his work at the particle accelerator had seemed so exotic, like it might someday change the world. But he was gone now and she was still here and Alicia wondered if all along she had been wrong, that nothing about her life would ever change. Every day in Wichita Falls was the same as the one before. The same people wearing the same clothes all dining at the same chain restaurants. If the definition of insanity was to expect a different result from unchanging behavior, then it was time for someone to lock her up. Maybe she was already locked up. Maybe right now she was being watched from beyond some giant, one-way mirror that to her looked like life.

Stuart was mustering the nerve to ask her something.

"So I hear there's this new cover band playing over at Toby's," he said, finally. "They play a lot of 80s music. They're supposed to be pretty good."

"Oh, yeah?"

"Yeah. Didn't you say you liked 80s stuff?"

"I don't think we talked about it," Alicia told him.

"Do you want to go over there for a little while? Have a drink or two and check out the band?"

"I appreciate you asking, but I think I should call it a night. This is going to sound so lame, but I don't feel well."

"Oh," Stuart said.

She felt guilty turning him down, really she did, but a storm of some kind was developing in her digestive tract.

"You do look a little green," Stuart said. "I could take you to the drugstore, get some Pepto maybe."

The apartment didn't have to be in Manhattan. She could probably live in Brooklyn, where it was cheaper, there was always a way if you wanted it badly enough, right?

"Alicia?"

"That's okay. Probably better if I just went home."

"Sure," Stuart agreed. "Okay."

In the parking lot she began to feel worse, and the noise was almost too much to bear. Chili's was located on Kemp Boulevard, where every weekend teenagers in oversized pickup trucks shook the street with loud, throaty mufflers and thunderous speaker systems. Traffic barely moved as the kids threatened and cajoled and made lurid advances upon each other, and normally it amused Alicia to watch this ancient mating ritual, since in high school she had cruised the strip all the time. But at the moment she was sweating, shivering, and someone appeared to be doing chemical experiments in her stomach. She thought how silly she must look, how much of a whiny, high-maintenance bitch he probably thought she was. Alicia felt like laughing. She felt like crying.

Stuart, walking alongside her, seemed to take offense.

"What's funny?"

"Nothing," she said.

"What? Me?"

"No. Of course not."

"I'm sorry. I just thought we might go do something else tonight."

"I told you I don't feel well."

Alicia stopped next to her car.

"This is me," she said. "Thank you so much for dinner."

Gas ballooned in her stomach. The night air was uncomfortably humid and warm. Stuart took her hand in his.

"I enjoyed being with you this evening," he said.

"Yes, dinner was fun."

"Would you like to go out again soon?"

Alicia didn't know what to say. She couldn't bring herself to shoot him down right here in the parking lot.

"Call me," she said. "Let's talk again, okay?"

"Okay."

He stood there, maybe trying to decide if he should kiss her. Alicia leaned forward and hugged him instead.

"I'm sorry I don't feel well. Give me a call, okay?"

"Okay."

In the rearview mirror Alicia saw herself as Stuart had just moments before. Her forehead was damp. Strands of hair were stuck there. Her face was pale and punchy-looking, the whites of her eyes bloodshot. She had been trying to grow out her hair for several months now, but it was still in that awkward, between stage where she couldn't do a damned thing with it. The blonde hair of her childhood had turned dark long ago, but lately she'd been thinking of bringing back the lighter color, reconnecting with her past.

Traffic on Kemp was barely moving, and Alicia thought she might die right here in the car. Or at least vomit her salad out the window. This was quite an existence, she thought deliriously, that she had settled into while waiting for fate to light a fire on her doorstep.

During her teen years Alicia had hoped for a storybook life, like marry well and maybe become a doctor. But when she left town for Texas A&M, unexplained depression seized her almost at once, and the only way she could cope was by drinking. It made no sense that going away to college should be so stressful, because Alicia had been waiting for years to escape her hot and dusty hometown. But night after night she found herself unable to sleep because of a nagging sense that she had left something unfinished behind, that something immense and unreal was out there watching her. Waiting for her. The only way she could banish these thoughts was to have a drink or two or ten, and in this compromised state she could make no sense of electron shells and atomic weights. Along with Chemistry, Alicia gave up any hope for undergraduate pre-med, and in her second semester she entered Blocker, home of the College of Business. Here she found android students stalking the halls in search of an easy degree and entry into the tedious world of market penetration and core competencies and customer delight. Her depression intensified.

After graduation the only job offer she received was from The American Heart Association in San Antonio. She gladly accepted and prepared for the obligatory U-Haul move. But then the phone rang, the day before she was to leave, and Alicia learned her mother had been diagnosed with Multiple Sclerosis. Her father, a regional sales manager who spent two weeks every month on the road, asked Alicia in a broken voice if she would consider coming home for a little while. He couldn't bring himself to admit what he meant by "a little while," but he didn't have to—retirement was still ten or fifteen years away.

Alicia had cried for days afterward. Cried with her mother and father, cried by herself. But strangely, once the initial shock of the diagnosis had worn off, Alicia found her depression had evaporated. Maybe this was because she had finally found real purpose in life— to care for her mother—but an insistent voice deep in her subconscious whispered that the real reason for her recovery was the return to Wichita Falls. That something here was waiting for her. Something here needed her.

By the time she emerged from the glut of traffic on Kemp, Alicia's stomach had begun to calm itself. She was sitting at the intersection of

Southwest Parkway when she noticed a flicker of red in her rearview mirror. At first she thought a cop might be behind her, but as the flashing lights approached she realized they belonged to a fire truck. It rushed past her in a blur just as the traffic light turned green, and once the truck was a safe distance ahead she started forward, essentially following it. Since her neighborhood was only a few blocks away, she naturally watched to see if the truck would turn in that direction.

It did.

But there were many houses in the neighborhood. Scores of them. It was easy to fear the worst, but what was the likelihood that her home was the one on fire? If any of them were? Maybe someone's cat was stuck in a tree.

Ahead of her, the fire truck turned onto her street.

Okay, this made the odds different. There were maybe twenty houses on her block, and now it seemed certain one of them was on fire. She could smell it in her car even with the windows rolled up—a smoky, chemical odor.

As she approached her street, Alicia's palms began to sweat. Any second she would know for sure. Hers was the third house on the left.

Before she even made the turn, Alicia could see her house was an inferno.

There were actually two fire trucks on the scene. One of them was already set up and shooting a jet of water at the roof. Alicia couldn't understand why they were aiming there when flames were shooting out the front windows. Her valuables were not on the roof. They were in the rooms where the flames were brightest and angriest. She stopped her car and approached one of the firefighters.

"Oh, my God!" she screamed. "Oh, my God!"

"Ma'am," responded the fireman. He looked both bored and determined. "You need to get back. Go stand across the street."

"But this is my house!"

Now his expression softened.

"I'm sorry to hear that, ma'am. Is there anyone inside the house you know of? Any pets?"

Alicia hated to cry, especially in front of people she didn't know, but right now she felt helpless to stop herself. Flames were shooting out of a gaping hole in the roof. Storm clouds of smoke rose above the flames. The heat was scorching. And the worst thing of all was there was no one to call, no one immediately available to help her. Her father was scheduled to be out of town all week, and who else would she ask?

"No. It's just me. I live here alone."

Up and down the street, neighbors watched the spectacle from porches and front yards. Neighbors she hardly knew. Almost everyone (including her) spent most of their time indoors, and if they ventured outside it was to mow the yard or walk a dog. On a typical day she didn't even see many kids around, which was vastly different from her own childhood, when Alicia had spent half her time at the houses of friends or exploring the neighborhood on her bicycle. Back then it seemed like everyone knew each other. Today, many of the parents she knew were afraid to let kids out of their sight.

Images from her childhood made Alicia think briefly of the year she had met Jonathan Crane and David Clark. Arson had been a problem in the summer, first a house down the street from hers and later a restaurant owned by David's dad. The kid blamed for the crimes was named Thomas or Todd and had been friends with both Jonathan and David. Alicia had been thirteen that summer, and it was the first time she could remember feeling special, as if life had something unique in store for her. But now she was thirty-eight, she lived less than three miles from her parents, and there was no standard by which her life could be judged as anything but ordinary.

A crash inside the house startled her. Sparks shot out of the hole in the roof like fireworks. A teenage girl squealed. Or maybe it was Alicia herself squealing. She knew there would be a moment soon when the reality of the fire would seize her, and she would mourn the loss of her home and the years she had spent accumulating the things contained within it. But at the moment all she could do was watch. And cry. And wonder what on earth could have caused it.

Was this the incredible thing that had been lying in wait all these years?

Was this the way her life would change forever?

8

There were times when Adam Altman feared his life was an illusion. He was thirty-eight years old, yet sometimes it felt as if the hours and weeks and years of his adult life had crept by almost undetected. Had it been only yesterday when he crouched in the hall closet, enduring the roar of the killer tornado, or had it really been twenty-nine years? The empirical answer and the reality he felt in his bones did not match. It was true that Adam was a married adult male, father to a five-year-old daughter, but on a morning like this one he could recall almost nothing of the many years that were purported to have elapsed between the death of his sister and today. For that matter, he could not be entirely sure yesterday had occurred. He knew it must have, because he had just stepped out of the shower, presumably to wash away the oils secreted after a night's sleep, and he planned after breakfast to visit his project in Tanglewood. The project was a new home being constructed upon the site of an old home that had fallen into disrepair. Adam himself was the builder, and while he didn't physically build anything, he did manage the various smaller projects that equaled the construction of a residential home. Taken together, these details about his work and life were clues that his existence was not an illusion. But they were hardly enough to allay the sense of mounting dread he had felt all morning.

Beyond the bathroom door, in the bedroom, someone was stirring awake. That would be his wife, Rachel. It was a little before seven o'clock and time to get Bradie ready for school. Here were more details of an authentic, ongoing life. Rachel would dress their daughter and feed her frozen waffles and brew a pot of coffee. Adam would kiss them both goodbye, climb into his pickup, and drive off to begin another day.

When he went into the kitchen, the television was on but no coffee was brewing and no waffles were cooking. Off-schedule mornings usually meant Rachel had encountered some difficulty with Bradie. Common problems included clothing disputes and unruly hair, and indeed as he approached his daughter's room, Adam could hear she was crying.

"I hear tears," he sang to Bradie. Rachel was sitting next to her on the bed.

"She had another nightmare, Adam."

He joined them on the bed and took his daughter's soft and small hand into his own.

"Was it the bad kid again?"

Bradie nodded. "He comes after me and I know he's there but I can't see him or hear him. It's so hot in there and all I see is white."

Bradie reached across Rachel and clutched his waist. Adam looked down at his crying daughter and felt a sense of déjà vu so staggering that he put his hand on the bed to steady himself. It was no surprise that Bradie bore a striking resemblance to Christi, who had died many years ago in the tornado, but from this angle the resemblance was unnerving. Adam stood up and brought her into his arms and she held on desperately. Christi had been the same age when she died as Bradie was now.

"Listen to me," he said. "No bad kid is ever going to get you. Do you understand? Your Mom and I will protect you from anything. You'll always be safe with us."

"I know," Bradie said. "But in the dream you can't help me. No one can help me."

"But you're awake now, see? There's no bad kid around."

"Maybe you could sleep with me, Daddy? And if I start dreaming, maybe you'll have the same dream and you can keep the bad kid away?"

"I don't think it works like that, Honey. But Jesus is everywhere and He wouldn't let you get hurt in a dream. When I can't be there to help you, He will be. Okay?"

"Okay," said Bradie doubtfully.

Adam left them to get ready and went back into the kitchen. He made coffee himself and found half a bagel in the bread box. The national news was on and they were talking again about the burst of the housing bubble, a topic that had been the lead story on the morning shows for what seemed like months. Adam didn't need the television to tell him the problems with real estate prices, because he lived with the reality every day. Right now he was managing only two new construction projects, and there was nothing behind them in the queue. Even remodel business had dried up in the past year. During the spring months Adam had nervously joked with Rachel about the possibility of another tornado, something small that wouldn't hurt anyone but that *would* create demand in town for new construction. Rachel hadn't found this funny. Tornadoes were funny to no one in Wichita Falls. But neither was the desperate state of his family's personal finances.

The national news went to break while the local station discussed weather and a few top stories.

"Investigators have said arson may be the cause of a devastating house fire two nights ago near Kemp and Southwest Parkway," said a deeply serious news anchor wearing a dark suit and a powder-blue tie.

"The home belonged to thirty-eight-year-old Alicia Ulbrecht, who has lived at the residence for eight years. She says she has no idea why someone would have set fire to her home."

Adam stopped chewing his bagel and closed his eyes. He saw flames devouring walls and carpet and ceilings. Sparks shooting out of the roof. Smoke rolling toward the sky like thunderclouds. A pair of eyes in the darkness, eyes he had not expected to see, that none of them had expected to see.

"I'm just devastated," said a female voice. "Why would someone do this? Maybe it was an accident but they're telling me someone poured gasoline around my house and set it on fire."

Adam opened his eyes and realized Alicia Ulbrecht was onscreen. It was difficult to reconcile this face with the girl he had known many years ago. She was still attractive but not quite the starlet who had been an object of fascination for the boys in Tanglewood. He hadn't seen her since high school graduation, twenty years ago, and now here she was on television, her home a ruin of cinders behind her.

Seeing the burnt skeleton of Alicia's house robbed Adam's legs of their strength. He wobbled slightly and grabbed the countertop to steady himself. Behind him, Rachel and Christi were laughing. No, Rachel and *Bradie* were laughing. Apparently the nightmare had been forgotten and now they were braiding her hair, and this was amusing them for some reason. Adam braced himself against the countertop and closed his eyes again. He saw Alicia riding her bicycle past his house. Todd was imploring Jonathan to call her. There was music.

I can see you, your brown skin shining in the sun . . .

No, it wasn't music. It was his phone ringing, thrumming in his back pocket. He retrieved it and saw Juan Romero was calling.

"This is Adam."

"Hey, Boss. You awake?"

"Of course I'm awake. What's up?"

"I think you better come out here."

"Where? The job?"

"Yeah, the job. Something's happened."

"What's happened? Spit it out, Juan."

"We're gonna have to start all over. The framing's gone."

"What do you mean it's gone?"

"Someone torched it, Boss. The studs, the sill plates, all of it's ruined. We're gonna have to pry it all up and start again."

For a moment Adam imagined that even the countertop itself was not steady enough to hold him upright. He imagined the very floor was trembling beneath his feet. And if the earth itself could not be relied upon for stability, what was there to do but tumble?

"Musta been vandals," Juan added. He seemed amused by what had happened. "I don't know why anyone would want to burn down a bunch of drywall studs. Do you?"

Adam wasn't sure how to answer that.

9

At thirty-nine years old Bob Steele could no longer call himself an athlete, or even healthy, which was a shame considering how he had once aspired to greatness. And if there was ever a reason to recall those ancient days of glory, to channel them for something productive, it should have been tonight. Instead, Bob felt as if every cell in his body, from the strands of his thinning hair to the tips of his arthritic toes, was crying out in exhaustion. When he looked into the rearview mirror, yellow eyes stared back. Something was wrong with him, something awful, but he couldn't say precisely what. The hallucinations—haunting him almost daily now—distorted his consciousness so profoundly that at this point he could hardly tell dreams from reality.

Despair was not uncommon in this forgotten part of the world, but sometimes Bob felt like his particular failures and disappointments had been intentionally inflicted upon him by some outside force. His guiding ambition, for instance—which he had chosen at a very early age— was to live a better life than his asshole father, to succeed where the old man had miserably failed. And yet in almost every way Bob was the one worse off. His football career had proved inferior. His shitty job as a car salesman barely kept Darlene out of the welfare line, which made him a worse husband. And though the elder Steele was an alcoholic who had worked in the brutal Texas heat his entire adult life, he would probably outlive his own son.

"Not sure about that last one," Todd Willis said from the passenger seat. "The word *outlive* implies a life, and we both know that isn't true in your case."

Through the pickup's dirt-stained windows, Bob stared warily at the building before him. Lone Star Barbecue was a squat, tan building with a fence-enclosed pit room appended to its western wall. Even now, two hours after the restaurant had closed for the night, smoke drifted out of the pit room like rising cumulus clouds, smelling of brisket and mesquite.

It was in this place, twenty-five years prior, that Bob had learned a strange secret about the world. Back then he had been young and stupid and unable to comprehend the implications of Todd's revelation. He'd also been distracted, because a few minutes later the five of them had burned the restaurant to the ground. In the intervening years Bob had tried to put that summer behind him, had done his best to live a halfway-decent life, but he could see now his efforts had been doomed from the beginning. This was not a life. The totality of his existence had simply been a prelude to this scene, this night, when he would finally be forced to confront the pages of his past.

For sixteen years Bob had been married to a fat woman who had once been a high school bombshell. Darlene's guiding ambition had been to bear children, and when it became clear she was medically unable to do so, his wife had retired to the couch, where she immersed herself in soap operas and reality television. This behavior of hers was how Bob rationalized his cheating. Lately it was this redhead receptionist at the dealership, a twen-ty-three-year-old tart named Sherilyn who had white, freckly skin and an ass that wouldn't quit. Two hours ago he'd been in her apartment, listening to window screens rattle in their frames, trying to ignore the collection of teddy bears she kept on three white shelves above her bed. But it wasn't easy to ignore them when prominent streamers of lace were pinned to the shelves like bunting. As Sherilyn tiptoed to the bathroom, Bob half expected the bears to produce miniature brass instruments, strike up "The Star Spangled Banner," and march off the shelves like lemmings. He didn't know if he was losing his mind or feeling guilty for cheating on his wife again. Probably both. He hated those fucking bears.

"Those bears are like you," Todd said to him. "Sitting on their asses, doing nothing, while the world goes on without them."

Bob turned away from the restaurant and looked into the passenger seat, where Todd Willis sat staring at him.

"You were the hero," Todd said. "The quarterback who took Old High to the state quarterfinals. Every guy wanted to be in your shoes and every girl wanted to fuck your brains out. When did you give up your dreams for this?"

Bob couldn't remember when exactly that had happened. At some point he had started in on the meth and nowadays his memories were pretty hazy. But worse than any lost memory was the idea of his mother, somewhere in Heaven, looking down on the mess he'd made of himself. She had lost her life in the tornado and he had actively squandered his own. It was unfairness like this that made Bob hate himself a little more every day.

"Why did you come back here?" he asked Todd.

For a long time the only answer was the memory echo of his own voice, and Bob was afraid he knew why: because he was talking to him-self. For the past few days he'd spotted Todd in unlikely places, like at the dealership, or on the street in front of his house, and once in a white Ford Focus on Southwest Parkway. These sightings didn't sound like much of a problem until you considered Bob hadn't seen or heard from Todd in twenty-five years. When you considered that detail, it made you wonder where he had come from so suddenly, and why he seemed to be following you around everywhere.

The memory echo repeated itself, again and again, like a recorded loop of music. This made him think of Todd's childhood penchant for writing songs, how he had carried his Casio keyboard with him everywhere, always tapping out some new and amazing melody for them.

"I'm here to tell the story again," Todd finally said.

"What do you mean? What story?"

Todd laughed, and the sound of his voice in the truck was eerily flat, no reflections or reverb at all, as if it had been spoken in some kind of endless space. In that moment Bob felt frightened the way childhood nightmares had once frightened him.

"We were The Boys of Summer," Todd said. "Remember?"

"That was a long time ago, man."

"You must be an idiot. Or a coward."

"Big talk for a little kid. You better watch yourself."

"Is that what you see when you look at me, Bobby? A kid? You're one crazy redneck, you know that?"

"I am not crazy," Bob said automatically. But Todd had a point. If this person in his pickup had been a kid twenty-five years ago, how could he still be one?

"If you're not crazy," Todd said, "tell me what you plan to do with the five-gallon can of gasoline in the back of your truck? And the box of wooden matches between your legs?"

Bob couldn't see his truck bed from here, not with the toolbox in the way, but when his right hand felt the seat between his thighs, there indeed was a cardboard box, one with a striking surface on either side. He couldn't remember having put it there.

"We were The Boys of Summer," Todd explained, "and now it's time to continue our story."

"What story is that?"

Todd gestured out the window, where the restaurant loomed, but Bob suspected he meant something more.

"This town has reached the end of its useful life. What greatness could possibly arise from this place? Any future Nobel prize winners, any bright pupils who might someday become President? No, the only thing you people have to root for are athletes who seem talented compared to each other but not when measured against other, better communities.

And you're the perfect example, Bobby. Everyone wanted you to follow in the footsteps of your legendary old man, but you simply didn't have the talent."

"That's bullshit. Those refs at L.D. Bell called a terrible game. They gave us no chance to win."

"Bobby, please. By now you must understand the best gift you were born with is your name. The only reason you ever started for Old High was because your dad talked Coach Tyler into it."

Of all the insults Todd could have hurled at him, this was far and away the worst.

"I wouldn't blame your dad, though," Todd added. "He wanted to believe as much as anyone."

Bob was unwilling to consider that the glory days of his life, however unspectacular, had not even been earned. Fury bubbled up inside him.

"Shut up. You're lying."

"Your dad wanted to believe his son was a winner in his own image, instead of a loser who would never measure up."

Bob lunged at Todd then, his hands reaching quickly for the kid's throat, but all he came up with was air. By the time he realized what had happened, Todd had somehow climbed out of the truck and was headed for the pit room door. Bob followed him, limping and breathing heavily, but he could not catch up to the kid before he disappeared into the darkness of the pit room.

It was then that the world seemed to undergo some kind of shift, a resampling of reality, because what Bob expected to see when he entered the shadowy pit room was not what he actually saw. What he planned to do was not what he actually did.

A man was standing in front of one of the cylindrical barbecue pits. He was broad across the shoulders and round in the gut. His receding hair was steel colored, his skin bronze and crisscrossed with a network of deep wrinkles. He wore black oven mitts and tight Wranglers held together with a giant silver buckle. Engraved on the buckle were the initials "KS." Bob appeared to have interrupted him unloading briskets from the pit.

"Who the hell are you?" the man demanded.

"He doesn't even recognize you," Todd whispered from the shadows of the pit room. "If that's not the ultimate insult, I don't know what is."

Bob could not comprehend why his dad would be working at this restaurant or how he had put on so much weight in the three weeks since they had last seen each other. Still, there he was standing less than ten feet away.

"I'm only going to ask you once, mister," his dad said. "Get the fuck off my property. *Now*."

Todd's voice was low. Urging. "I don't think that's how a father should talk to his son, do you, Bobby? Especially one who forced his kid to play football when he was never going to excel at it?"

"You're right," Bob replied. "He shouldn't talk to me that way at all."

"Maybe you should shut him up, then," Todd said. "Like maybe you ought to make sure tonight, right now, he knows exactly how you feel."

It was difficult for Bob, despite a lifetime of resentment, to imagine hurting his own father. But it had never been easy to disagree with Todd. As kids, Bob and his friends had been both fascinated and frightened by Todd and his four years of walking sleep, and by the end of that summer it was easy to dismiss the kid as mentally ill, as an infection that had spread to all of them. But now, when Bob thought of those hazy, sweltering months in 1983, he sensed something was wrong. Really wrong. Like what he remembered about that time could not have occurred during that time.

I can see you, your brown skin shining in the sun. You got your hair slicked back and those Wayfarers on, baby . . .

He heard this music the way he might hear it in a nightmare: echoing, distant, dissonant. Understanding this music was the key to understanding why his life had turned out the way it had.

"Your life turned out this way because of that man," Todd reminded him. "What are you waiting for?"

Bob saw his father had reached behind his back to retrieve what turned out to be a large meat fork.

"I asked you to leave," he said. "Now I'm going to make you."

Kenny Steele stepped forward, brandishing the fork. But his movements were hesitant, unsure, and Bob saw how even in a compromised state he could easily dominate this confrontation. He closed the distance between them and immediately his father reversed course. This shift in momentum allowed Bob to grab Kenny's arm, the one holding the fork, and slam it against the brick exterior wall of the restaurant.

"What are you gonna do now, old man?"

Bob pinned his father against the wall with both arms. The elder Steele's breath smelled of barbecue and fear.

"What do you want?" Kenny cried. "I've got money! Just take my wallet and leave."

"I don't want your money, you murdering sack of shit."

Bob brought his knee violently forward. Kenny Steele made a guttural sound and crumpled to the ground.

"You killed my mother, do you realize that? You killed your own wife."

"I don't know what you're talking about," Kenny croaked.

"You drove her to Jonathan's house so you could fight with his dad, and for what? To stop me from playing chess? Which was really smart of you since *our house wasn't even hit by the tornado.* And did you, even once in your life, regret what you did? Did you ever say, 'Hey son, I'm sorry I killed your mom. I sure am an asshole for doing something so stupid.'? No, you didn't. You were selfish then and you are selfish now and I wish you were dead. I wish I could trade you for Mom. She was a decent woman and you are everything wrong with the world. I fucking hate you."

Bob was crying now and could barely see through the glistening distortion of tears. His father writhed on the ground. It sounded like he was struggling to breathe. Bob knelt beside him.

"And maybe I wouldn't have been such an average football player if you had taught me to use my brain a little. Everything doesn't have to be a big-dick contest, you know?"

From the darkness Todd said, "Why don't you go ahead and finish him off?"

"Finish him off?"

"You just said you wished he were dead."

"Well, right, but I can't actually—"

"Why not? *He* did it. He killed your mother."

"But he didn't *intend*—"

"And anyway you've got nothing to lose. You only have weeks left to live."

"What do you mean I'm going to die soon?"

"Come on, man. Your eyes are yellow because your liver is fucked. You drink too much and do way too much meth. I would be shocked if you were alive a month from now."

"Yellow eyes don't mean I'm going to die."

"It's the same thing with your skin. And you've been getting sick to your stomach lately, have you not?"

Bob noticed the meat fork was in his right hand. In his trembling right hand, held high above his father's chest. It was true he had thrown up three times in the past two weeks, that he generally had been feeling like shit for more than a month. Even Sherilyn this afternoon had complained that he smelled weird.

"You've got nothing to lose and your father has everything to gain. Are you going to let him be better than you forever? Are you going to keep letting him get away with that?"

On the ground, Kenny Steele's eyes were becoming lucid again. He looked nervously at the meat fork and then up at Bob.

"Wait," he said. "You're one of my son's friends. The football player."

"Shut the fuck up," Bobby said. "I was never any goddamn football player. Not a real one, anyway."

"Just do it," Todd implored. "Just kill him. He doesn't respect you and you'll be dead long before any trial."

"Wait!" his father cried. "You're Bobby Steele! I know your dad! He comes in here all the time and he loves the brisket po' boy. Please!"

"What is he talking about?" Bob moaned. He was pointedly not looking at his father's face, desperate not to see the terror that was surely there. "Why is he saying this shit?"

"He's desperate," Todd explained. "He'll say anything that will get him out of here alive. But if that happens, he'll call the police. Your dad will win again and you will lose. Like you always do."

"Please, Bobby," his dad said. "You and my son grew up together. You're a good guy. I know you are."

"He thinks he's better than you, Bobby. He always will."

"Please!" Kenny Steele cried.

"*Kill* him."

In the end Bob brought down the fork primarily to silence the voices. His right arm (his throwing arm) swung in a wide arc and the twin silver tines sank deep into Kenny's chest. The old man's mouth opened involuntarily, but instead of a scream he choked up blood and growled something unintelligible. Bob rocked backward on his heels and sat down with a thump.

Revenge twenty-nine years coming was as strenuous as it was fulfilling. He'd earned a little break.

On the floor next to him, Kenny Steele made gagging sounds and gamely reached for the meat fork lodged in his chest, which did not appear to move. His blue shirt was soaked red. Blood pooled in his mouth and trickled down his cheek.

The barbecue pit was still open. It was a ten-foot cylinder stood on end, six feet or so in diameter, fire at the bottom. Left unattended, with all the doors open, the fire inside had begun to grow. It climbed the perimeter of the cylinder, and watching this reminded Bob of the night twenty-five years ago when they had burned the entire restaurant to the ground.

It also reminded him that Todd Willis remained in the pit room.

"Todd," he said. "There's something I need to ask you about the night we burned this place down. Something you told us that I can't remember."

Beside him, on the ground, his father's mouth opened, as if he wanted to say something, but instead he appeared to choke. He coughed out a mouthful of blood and then stopped breathing altogether. So that was done.

Maybe he should have been sorry, but instead Bob wondered where the silver belt buckle had come from. He'd never seen his dad wear anything monogrammed before.

And the initials, well, something about them wasn't right. From here, instead of "KS," they looked like the letters "FC."

Bob wondered again how his father could have gained so much weight in the past month. He'd been a strong, thin man his entire adult life. Now he looked like some random redneck with a beer gut.

"Todd," Bob said. "Can you come over here and look at my dad? Something isn't right."

Again, no answer from Todd.

Bob couldn't sit here forever. He'd done a terrible thing and now he would have to figure out a way to cover his tracks. His truck had been parked in the restaurant lot for a while now and someone would eventually notice.

With great effort of will, he shifted his gaze from his father's midsection to his face.

But it wasn't Kenny Steele on the ground. It was Fred Clark, owner of the restaurant. Father of David Clark, Bobby's childhood friend who was now an Internet billionaire.

He thought maybe he had known the entire time. It should have been obvious to everyone watching the situation unfold what was really happening. Yet Bob had done it anyway, killed a man who was not his father.

In a way it wasn't really surprising. In a way this outcome had been written long ago.

The night of the restaurant fire, when they were kids, Bob had learned something he could not fully remember now. But he did recall that something was wrong with the world, and his place within it was particularly wrong. His father was not in this pit room, and Bob couldn't be completely sure Todd was here or if he had ever been here.

I will never forget those nights. I wonder if it was a dream . . .

Bob stood up. He walked out of the pit room and back to his truck. From the bed he grabbed the can of gasoline, and from the front seat he picked up the box of matches. He walked back toward the restaurant with purpose. When he reached the pit room, he shoved the matches into his back pocket and unscrewed the lid of the gasoline can. With casual strokes, as if he were an artist tossing paint onto a canvas, he began to coat the ground with gasoline. He splashed it liberally over the body of Fred Clark and moved gradually toward the building itself. The door was unlocked, and he splashed gasoline in the dishwashing room, the kitchen, and throughout the restaurant proper. He made a complete loop back to the exit and found himself in the pit room again. By now his feet were soaked with gasoline. It was probably on his clothes. Bob reached into his pocket anyway and retrieved the matches.

This was it. Once he struck the match, once the fire was lit, everything would be over. All his failures would be erased by this one action. All he had to do was play his part.

Bob opened the box and retrieved a single match. He held the match before his eyes and wondered if he possessed the nerve to actually go through with it.

I can tell you my love for you will still be strong after the boys of summer have gone . . .

The way he finally summoned the nerve to light the match was to imagine seeing his mother's face after all this was done. He hoped she would understand. He hoped she would still love him.

"You there!" someone yelled. "What the hell are you doing?"

The voice had come from behind him, and for a moment Bob was sure it was his mother here to admonish him. But what he saw when he turned around was a man. A police officer stood in the doorway of the pit room, a portly fellow whose uncertain expression did not match the intensity of his voice.

Bob pictured his mother's face again, her caring, gentle face. He could not wait to see her, to feel her arms around him again.

He held the matchbox up where the officer could see it. He presented the match.

"Drop that! Hands out where I can see them!"

The officer reached reluctantly for his gun. Bob could tell by the uncertainty in his eyes that the guy didn't want to shoot him. He was afraid the way almost all humans were afraid. But he did point the gun in Bob's direction.

"Don't do it!" the officer yelled. The gun shook violently in his hand, as if it were an animal struggling to get away from him.

And then, at the last possible moment, Bob remembered what had happened in the pit room when they were children. He remembered exactly what Todd had told the four of them. The occasion of this memory infused him with an unexpected sense of accomplishment and humor so overwhelming that laughter began to roll inside of him, rumbling and rushing toward the surface of his mouth like a gusher of oil that was about to make someone a very wealthy man.

"I'm sorry," Bob said to the officer, and before he could stop himself, the laughter erupted from him, powerful gales that overwhelmed the quiet space of the pit room. The officer looked confused, even horrified, but Bob could not remember a happier moment in his entire life. After years of trailing in his father's shadow, Bob Steele was about to step into the light and be recognized as the better man.

"I'm sorry," he said again. "Todd said it ends like this."

Bob lit the match and tossed it into the air. The tiny stick of wood seemed to float before him, turning over and over in slow motion, and when the first bullet hit his chest, Bob felt something like ecstasy.

Flames appeared from nowhere, danced in front of him like a swirling vortex. Bob fell to the ground and was swallowed by fire.

He died smiling.

10

David Clark's home in Carmel was a two-story Spanish-style mansion floored with Macassar Ebony hardwoods and Pietra Firma tile. Large plate windows presented movie theater views of the bay and evening sunsets over the Pacific. Kitchen appliances were industrial quality. There was a chummy billiards room. A powerful and calibrated home theater. On the second floor were six bedrooms, including the master suite, which commanded a spectacular ocean view through a single, room-size window. The bed was a custom Hästens Vividus, six inches longer and five inches wider than a standard King, which had cost him $68,342.88, an unreasonable price by any standard except the exospheric.

His golf playgrounds were Pebble Beach and Cypress Point, two of the most spectacular courses in the world. He dined regally. He owned twelve cars, including the newest addition, a Bugatti Veyron, having paid a thousand dollars for each of its 1,001 horses. And last year he'd purchased his newest and most extravagant vehicle yet—a Gulf Stream

G550 personal jet for the rock bottom price of $48,350,000, which didn't include a $27 million retrofit to further soundproof the interior.

The opulence of his life wasn't limited to the west coast. He played four rounds of golf each year at Augusta National in Georgia. He'd accidentally stepped on Jennifer Aniston's foot at Rao's in New York and—already three cocktails into the evening—convinced her to accept a drink in return. She found him funny. He found her sexy and accessible. They had dinner three times, but then she met an actor who was (presumably) funnier.

His was new money and so it had limits, but David could do pretty much whatever he wanted. Go wherever he wanted. He had fled like an escaped convict from the incarceration of Wichita Falls, was as far away from that cultural hellhole as a man could be, had shed his Texas accent and sheath of Middle American fat and his antiquated social conservatism.

But something was wrong. Something nearby yet invisible, something that followed him everywhere, something he could sense in his peripheral vision but could not see when he tried to look at it directly. It had come for him that day in the trees as a storm of giant hailstones, and even now, at night, it haunted him as a ghostly sound he could hear beyond the ringing of his own ears, a distress signal he was sure, if amplified, would resemble a tornado siren.

David had never admitted this feeling to anyone, but the people who knew him best seemed to sense it about him anyway. He played his part as a relaxed and carefree millionaire: perpetually tanned, impeccably groomed, dressed daily in custom-fit clothing, but he never spoke about his childhood in Texas, never mentioned his family. He ignored the questions until they stopped being asked, which inevitably created distance that made it difficult for him to maintain close relationships. Particularly of the romantic variety.

It was easy to blame his discontent on the perfect cliché, that as a wealthy, single man David saw no satisfaction in a conventional life. For the typical American man it was time to marry, time to have children. Everything is different when you see that head pop out, says everyone on earth, when you hear that first cry. Priorities reorganize themselves. The existential fog lifts and life becomes clear. *You'll see*, his friend, Jim

Thain, told him once. Or rather a hundred times. *Millions of fathers can't be wrong.*

If David believed his anxiety could be silenced by fathering a child, if a storybook family life were the antidote to fear, he would have married long ago. Any one of his serious girlfriends would have made a decent wife and mother. But deep down David knew the problems with his life could only be exacerbated by allowing someone else to share them, which meant, no matter what her arguments, a woman who insisted upon settling down with him was asking for trouble.

It was just after midnight, and he was in bed with his current girl-friend, Meredith. Her blonde hair was a starburst on the pillow beside him, the hair of a sleeping angel. David was sitting with his back to the headboard, reading through the *New York Times* on his laptop, trying to decide if he should break up with her.

He'd met Meredith almost a year ago in the Pebble Beach pro shop. He was immediately drawn to her sharp eyes, to the pony tail that poked out of her white Nike golf cap. She was there by herself, she told a staff member, had just moved to the peninsula, and hoped to join a group that was already scheduled to play. The staff member looked dubious. He explained how tee times were hard to come by and suggested she try another time. David looked the girl over again and wondered if the guy behind the counter was gay.

"I have a tee time in the morning," he said to her, because it was almost ridiculous, this good-looking woman hoping to find a golf part-ner at a lavish course frequented by the richest, most eligible men.

The girl turned and looked at him. Her eyebrows were naturally arched and her makeup was light. She wasn't model gorgeous, but her athletic frame was a sight to behold, and David required great effort not to stare at it.

"You can join me if you like," he told her.

"I would really appreciate that. Do we have a partner, or is it just the two of us?"

"I did have a partner," David said, "but he won't be joining us."

In her smile he saw a relationship, and that's exactly what happened. He took her to dinner, to stage plays, to Sundance in Park City. Soon she was staying at his house for days at a time, and eventually David began to hear the familiar ticking clock, the countdown to a confrontation about their prospects for a long-term relationship.

The hour had grown late and he realized his eyes were closed. He could barely keep them open. At this point a normal person would set aside the laptop and turn in, but David was a poor sleeper. Even on nights like this, when his eyelids felt like there were fishing weights tied to them, his mind raced as soon as his head hit the pillow. When, he wondered, was this fictitious existence in California going to end?

Six weeks ago, to prove he was not a prisoner to his former life, David impulsively purchased a 4-carat Neil Lane diamond engagement ring. But he had planned and failed to present the ring to Meredith no less than five times since, and now he wasn't sure if he ever—

Beside him, on the nightstand, his iPhone pulsed. David picked it up quickly, hoping the noise hadn't awoken Meredith. He slid out of bed and padded into the hallway before he answered. The number, area code included, was unfamiliar to him.

"David Clark."

"Mr. Clark?" said a voice that sounded both brusque and tired, like someone charged with an important task they'd grown weary of completing. "Mr. David Clark?"

"Yes. Who is this?"

"My name is Detective Jerry Gholson. I'm calling from Wichita Falls."

There was a hiccup in David's consciousness where for a moment he thought he might have passed out. It seemed he could hear his name being called from some faraway place, the sound of it echoing and cavernous.

"Mr. Clark, are you there?"

"Yes," David said. "I'm sorry. You're calling from Wichita Falls?"

"Yes, sir. I'm afraid I have some bad news. Your father, Fred Clark, was killed this evening."

David heard a sound nearby and realized his eyes were closed. He opened them to find Meredith standing next to him.

"How?" he said into the phone. "What happened?"

"It appears he was murdered, Mr. Clark. I'm sorry to say."

"What? How? Do you know who did it?"

Meredith was tugging on his shirt. Her eyes were large and concerned.

"Something's happened to my dad," David whispered to her.

On the phone the detective said, "We're pretty sure, yes. The primary suspect is Bob Steele. He seems to have broken into your father's restaurant and engaged him in some kind of confrontation. Then he set fire to the building. Fire crews were on the scene quickly, but Steele apparently poured accelerant throughout the establishment. It's pretty much gone."

David swallowed and turned away from Meredith. His eyes closed again, as if to blot out the world, but the darkness only made things worse. Now he could see smoke thick like fog. He could see fire dancing in Todd Willis' faraway eyes.

The idea of insulating himself with luxury in Carmel, that a wall of money could somehow shield him from the reality of his life . . . it was stupid. It had always been stupid. In 1983 he had walked into a house with four other boys, splashed gasoline into the bedrooms and bathrooms of someone's home, and lit the entire place on fire. He had done this at the suggestion of Todd Willis, a confident kid who had suffered a strange injury during the tornado of 1979, who had influenced them in ways David still didn't understand. But it was the memory of the second fire, the one at his father's restaurant, that really worried him. Not because he intentionally burned down the building where his dad had built a business. The old man deserved that. What drove David's anxiety was the memory of Todd's eyes that night, the mystical and faraway look in them, and the extraordinary secret he had shared. A secret David could not remember but that troubled him deeply.

"This obviously has caught me off guard," he said. "I'm not sure what to do now. Does someone need to identify the body? Have you charged Bobby with a crime?"

Saying his friend's name aloud brought forth other memories from that time. The five of them—Todd, Bobby, Jonathan, Adam, and David himself—had been the only members of a club called The Boys of Summer. They'd played football and video games and explored the woods together. On the night of the house fire, a boy named Joe Henreid had somehow discovered what they were doing, had found them in the house even as flames were devouring its interior. Their response had been to run, to leave him in the house alone, and after that no one had ever seen or heard from him again.

David had spent his adult life not thinking about Joe or Todd or basically his entire childhood, and now he felt like all of it had happened yesterday.

"Identification will need to be ascertained formally with dental records. The fire was severe. And there will be no case against Bob Steele because he perished on the scene as well. But there are legal issues to take care of, and since your father listed you as his emergency contact, and since we don't know any other family members or next-of-kin, it would be helpful if you could come to Wichita Falls sometime in the next few days. If that's possible."

"Uh," David said. "Yes, I can do that. I'll arrange to be there in the next day or two."

"That would be fine. Let me give you my contact information, and you just call me up when you're in town."

The two of them exchanged phone numbers and email addresses and David ended the call. He realized he had wandered into an adjacent bedroom, and when he turned around he nearly ran into Meredith again.

"Honey," she said, and put her arms around him. "I'm so sorry. So very sorry. Do you want to talk about it?"

"I don't know what there is to say. My dad's dead. It seems he was murdered. I have to go take care of his affairs."

"Oh, my God!" Meredith cried. She grabbed him by the arms and pushed him out where she could see him. "Oh, my God! By who?"

"By this guy I used to hang out with. He was the quarterback of our high school team. I hadn't spoken to him in like twenty years."

"Oh, David. You must be devastated. I'm so sorry."

She embraced him again, and David let himself be held. But he didn't know what to think or how to behave. His mind was a blank page, a white void waiting for someone to type how he should feel and what he should do.

"I know you don't like to talk about him," Meredith said. "I know you guys weren't close. But you're allowed to feel sad, David. Or angry. You keep your emotions to yourself and maybe that works most of the time, but whenever you're ready to talk, I'm here to listen. Okay?"

He appreciated what she was saying. Really, he did. But in this case Meredith didn't know what the fuck she was talking about.

Because David had known his dream life would eventually come crashing down around him. He wanted to believe his ability to identify investment opportunities was an innate quality that had been honed over time, that his vast fortune—nearing ten figures now—had been built on merit. But a little voice inside his head

said don't look back you can never look back

argued that many of his financial decisions had been nothing more than guesses. Sure, Qualcomm had for a while been everyone's favorite telecom pick, but few investors had been perceptive enough to divest before the company's stock was shot down like an enemy jet. David had also purchased plenty of Amazon and Apple and took chances on some long-forgotten dot-coms, but what had possessed him to inexplicably plow his fortune into low-risk securities just before the stock market became a sinkhole in 2000?

"Let's go to bed," he said to Meredith. "Thanks for offering to listen but I don't have anything to say right now."

In the sheets Meredith curled behind him, and the fiery warmth of her skin pressed against his, typically a guarantee of arousal, repulsed him instead. He could not think of a physical sensation less desirable than another human's touch.

"If you don't want to talk," she said in a soft voice, "why not think of all the good things you remember about him?"

David couldn't remember a single good thing about his father. He could only recall the pointless rules and structure the man lived by, the exacting principles he enforced, and the eventual betrayal of said principles.

"Try to imagine the ways he shaped you," Meredith whispered. "Good or bad, we all eventually resemble our parents."

That made David think of the time he had betrayed his best friend. When he had, for no good reason, kissed Jonathan Crane's girlfriend. He could see that day clearly, could picture himself riding a bicycle in slow motion, pedaling down Shady Lane toward some unknown destination.

Except when he finally saw her silhouette in the front yard, pulling weeds with her mom, David was forced to admit he had sought her out on purpose.

Alicia approached him across the lawn, wearing a light blue T-shirt that didn't quite reach her pink shorts. Her skin was brown and shiny with sweat, and he could see her bellybutton. She was wearing sunglasses and pink jelly shoes. Soundtrack music played in the background.

I can see your brown skin shining in the sun, you got your hair combed back and your sunglasses on, baby . . .

Meredith was still whispering to him, soothing him, but her voice was becoming lost in the dissonant sounds of his past. Now David saw the house on Driftwood, first during their afternoon rampage and later the night of the fire. Todd's control over them had been considerable. At times he had seemed more adult than child. Then Joe Henreid had appeared, his eyes floating like orbs in the smoke, and they had fled. They had left him for dead.

I never will forget those nights, I wonder if it was a dream . . .

He knew it wasn't a dream, he knew what had happened was real. And the consequences of his actions then had extracted a price from him now, twenty-five years later. Maybe he had fallen out of love with his father, maybe he was glad the old man had been put out of his misery, but even so his murder would require a response. At the very least it would compel David to visit his hometown and clean up whatever mess Fred Clark had left behind. But there was also the chance that his father's death was only the first event in a much larger unfolding of truth, that David's return to Wichita Falls would force him to confront that which he had fled to forget.

If he understood what made him different than everyone else, could David finally get busy living his life? Because now, despite every advantage he enjoyed, despite all his worldly possessions, something was holding him back. Something unresolved.

Was this a new beginning rushing toward him, or the end?

11

Everything had been wrong since the moment Jonathan Crane opened his eyes this morning.

He'd come starkly awake a few minutes before six from a terrible nightmare, and as he lay there waiting for his alarm to go off, sweating in the sheets, Jonathan tried to remember what had been wrong in his dream. There had been a lake, large and calm and completely empty of human concerns. Near this lake stood a neighborhood of deserted houses where Jonathan had been searching for someone who wasn't there. And while he saw all this, a song had been playing in the background, music he had been hearing in his dreams for years, though he could not remember which song it was.

On the way to school, driving down Southwest Parkway, Jonathan looked around and realized he'd seen this street in his dream. Just before the light at Kemp he spotted the entrance to a neighborhood that he also recognized from the night before. He'd searched that neighborhood for someone, though he wasn't sure who, and beyond that, barely a mile away, was the northern shore of Lake Wichita.

Empty lake, empty streets, the sun goes down alone. I'm driving by your house, but I know you're not home . . .

The tune in question was Don Henley's "The Boys of Summer." He had dreamed, basically, the song lyrics themselves. The reason he knew this was, many years ago, Jonathan and his friends had been part of a club that took its name from the song. That was the year they'd all met Todd Willis, the year Jonathan had fallen in love with Alicia Ulbrecht, a summer that had been consumed by fires and betrayal and the disappearance of an eleven-year-old kid named Joe Henreid.

Today, Jonathan was thirty-eight years old and taught eighth grade social studies at McNiel, a junior high school at the southwest corner of town. In 1979 McNiel had earned the dubious distinction of becoming the first structure hit by the terrible tornado that had changed the city (and his own life) forever. The school had been obliterated by the storm, and eventually rebuilt, but none of Jonathan's students seemed to know that or care. As they neared the end of their formal education's eighth year, he'd hoped to impart upon them a curiosity for history, but so far he'd found little success. They were fourteen years old, after all. George W. Bush was the only president they'd ever really known, and even the terror attacks of September 11th were historical. Any year that began with a "1" was positively ancient.

Relating history to them personally didn't help, either. When Jonathan told his students how his own father had died during the tornado, how the old man had been torn from their house and dropped near a road three miles away, they seemed bemused he'd ever known a father at all. As if they believed Jonathan had arrived on Earth as a full-grown adult, a man with no prior history and no purpose other than to deprive them of adolescent freedom.

All day he thought about the dream. Everything was masked by a film of wrongness, a dread he couldn't shake. By sixth period, the last of the day, Jonathan was mentally spent and eager to enjoy a few drinks and dinner. Typically he would devote the balance of his evening to progress on his newest novel (this one was called *The End of the World*) but he doubted there would be energy left tonight for that.

"In the textbook," he said to the class, "you'll find a quote about history commonly attributed to the philosopher George Santayana. Can anyone tell me what it is?"

Sixth period students were both the most energetic and least engaged of the day, agitating with the knowledge of their impending freedom. Of the twenty-seven pairs of eyes before him, only half were even looking in Jonathan's direction. The rest were staring down at the textbook or at someone else in class or out the window. At this point in the day, less than ten minutes from the final bell, Jonathan could hardly blame them.

"Is there any chance someone here read yesterday's assigned chapter? Even one person?"

A forest of hands reached into the air.

"Then surely one of you can remember the quote. Or perhaps source it from the textbook?"

"I know it," said Brooklyn Keeley. Far and away the most dedicated student in sixth period, she answered roughly half the questions Jonathan posed to the class.

"Brooklyn. Of course. Let's hear it."

"'Those who cannot remember the past are condemned to repeat it,'" she said with girlish authority.

"That's great. And can you tell us what you think Santayana meant by that?"

"He meant," said a voice from the back of the room, a male voice belonging to Blake Cannon, "if you fail history you don't get to play football anymore!"

Blake was a big-boned tailback already being drooled over by the high school football coaches. He was popular among the students and most everything he said in class generated laughter, including this.

"George Santayana wasn't much of a sportsman," Jonathan said. "But thank you for the contribution, Blake."

"Totally!"

As the laughter continued, another hand went up. This one belonged to Jonathan's newest student, Thomas Phillips. Thomas had come to McNiel a few weeks ago, which was curious timing considering how little of the school year remained. He was also vaguely familiar looking. Jonathan had made a few attempts to engage Thomas in conversation, hoping to understand what had brought him to McNiel so suddenly, but the kid was as sharp as he was quiet.

"Yes, Thomas?"

"The quote means, if you don't understand why certain things in the past happened, you're likely to make similar mistakes in the future."

"Excellent," Jonathan said. "It's nice to know at least one of you completed and understood the assigned reading."

"Thank you. But I don't think I agree with the quote."

"No? What makes you say that?"

"Well, everyone has to take history to get a degree in college, right? So why do the same mistakes keep happening over and over? We had this whole Iraq war that seems just like Vietnam. Some of the generals in the Army probably even *fought* in Vietnam, but we started another dumb war anyway. It doesn't seem to matter how much history people learn because they do stupid stuff even when they know it's a bad idea."

"That's very insightful," Jonathan replied. "Have your parents taught you about Vietnam? I know it's not included in our curriculum here at McNiel."

"It doesn't matter," Thomas explained. "Stupid stuff happens right here in Wichita Falls, too. You know the restaurant that was torched last night? Apparently the same place burned down like twenty-five years ago, and both times the fires were set on purpose. It's like the world is on some kind of loop. You see what I mean?"

Jonathan didn't see at all what Thomas meant. He couldn't see anything, because the disquiet he'd felt all day, the sense of dread that had lurked out of sight, now filled his entire field of vision.

"What restaurant?" he asked, though he had a feeling he already knew.

"Lone Star Barbecue," said Thomas. "It was all over the news this morning. Some guy named Bobby Steele did it. He used to be a high school football star and now he's dead."

Jonathan wondered if someone had turned up the heat. The classroom seemed thirty degrees warmer than it had just moments ago. When he looked at the clock, he saw there were less than three minutes to go until the final bell. But he wasn't sure he could hold it together for another three seconds, let alone minutes. How could Bobby be gone just like that? And why burn down the restaurant? Again?

"Mr. Crane," Thomas said. "The news said this guy was thirty-nine years old. Isn't that about the same age as you?"

"Pretty close, yeah."

Now there were two minutes to the final bell.

"So did you know him? Did you guys grow up together?"

Jonathan didn't see any reason why he should lie to the kid (and the entire class, let's not forget), but he lied, anyway. And was sure every student could see right through him.

"I sort of knew him. Everyone did. Like you said, he was the star quarterback when we were in high school."

Jonathan saw fire rising, a swirling vortex. He smelled smoke. The five of them gathered in a circle while Todd explained to them about the end of the world.

"You guys weren't friends before that?" asked Thomas. "My mom told me once about this kid who woke up from a long coma—"

"It was a long time ago, son. I'm not sure."

One minute till the final bell. All twenty-seven pairs of eyes were looking at him now. The classroom was so silent that Jonathan thought he could hear the clock ticking off each one of the remaining seconds.

"Isn't he the one who burned down the restaurant back then? Todd Willis?"

"I'm not sure what you're talking about, Thomas."

Even though no one spoke again after that, the sound of the final bell was so distant that Jonathan almost missed it.

"You can go," he announced, his voice small and uncertain. "Have a good afternoon."

Most of his colleagues at McNiel waged war with their students, but Jonathan had always been proud of his ability to maneuver past the raging hormones and budding rebellion to gain their trust. As sixth period filed out the door, however, he could sense new distance and discomfort that he didn't care for at all. And how the hell had Thomas known anything about Jonathan's relationship with Bobby? Or the first restaurant fire, which predated his birth by twelve years?

As adults, Bobby and Jonathan had drifted away from each other, perhaps because they'd never had much in common, or maybe because they were both baffled by the ongoing relationship between their remaining parents. Carolyn Crane and Kenny Steele had lived together, off and on, for almost twenty-five years, which meant their two sons had grown up in an unconventional fraternal arrangement. Not actual brothers, not really friends, they awkwardly occupied space together until high school graduation and then saw a little less of each other until their contact ended for good two years ago. Now that Bobby was dead (if he really was dead), Jonathan wasn't sure how he was supposed to feel.

The timing of it all was even more confounding. He'd learned the news about Bobby only a few minutes ago, but this morning's strange dream had occurred hours before that. And it was impossible not to see a connection between the two events. Maybe he had overheard the news about Bobby in some kind of unconscious way, maybe while watching television last night, but Jonathan was pretty sure he wouldn't have missed any kind of news like that. And being the pragmatic person he was, a man who regarded the fantastic with a high degree of skepticism, how was he supposed to accept a dream that seemed to anticipate what Bobby had done?

When he arrived home, Jonathan stopped first at the mailbox and discovered a large, familiar envelope folded into it. The delivery address had been written in his own handwriting, the postage also paid by him. On a day that was already raining shit, it was no surprise to find more bad news: Another literary agent had rejected his manuscript.

In the kitchen, before he found the bottle of Jameson, Jonathan read a letter included in the envelope:

Dear Mr. Crane:

I appreciate the opportunity to review sample chapters of your novel, THE END OF THE WORLD, but after careful consideration, I feel this project would be difficult to place in today's painfully discriminating fiction market. I'm sorry I won't be able to work with you further.

Later in the letter, the agent shared a few personal thoughts about Jonathan's work, comments like *Normal people with dull lives thrust into extraordinary circumstances—your story brings nothing new to this unimaginative and weary plot device,* and *Perhaps you have interpreted the adage "Write what you know" too literally.* On a typical day this sort of rejection might have rattled him, since *The End of the World* was his third (and best) novel, and it was being ignored by New York just as the other two had been. But today there was finally a more pressing issue at hand.

He poured a few ounces of Jameson over ice and went into his office. While he waited for his computer to come to life, Jonathan tried to recall fond images of Bobby and him together, but somehow the only memories he could recall were awful ones from the summer when Todd had joined their club. Like the five of them together at the fort, or inside the house on Driftwood, or standing outside the same house late at night while it was consumed by flames. Where they had left Joe Henreid to die.

In the Google search field he typed Bobby Steele and Lone Star Barbecue, and the first result, from Channel 6, confirmed what Thomas had told him in class and revealed news even more horrifying: Bobby had been killed by a responding police officer after allegedly murdering the owner of the restaurant, Fred Clark. The fire Bobby set had destroyed the restaurant and burned the dead bodies beyond recognition.

"Oh, God," Jonathan murmured. "Bobby, why?"

He sucked down the rest of the Jameson and went to make another, bigger drink. Until now he had clung to the possibility that Thomas was incorrect or had fabricated his story completely, but it was obvious the events were even worse than Jonathan had feared. It seemed impossible that Bobby would have murdered David's dad, but who could say what the guy had been thinking? Something terrible had happened at the restaurant when they were kids, something that had been eating at the fringes of Jonathan's consciousness for years, and maybe he wasn't alone.

His head was beginning to swim a little now. He took the Jameson back into his office and sat down in front of his computer. Instead of *The End of the World*, which he couldn't bear looking at this evening, Jonathan opened a new file and begin to type.

> The five of them stood in a rough circle between three barbecue pits. It was a little after two o'clock in the morning, and the city was asleep.
>
> Todd smiled dreamily, his eyes far away, as if he were enjoying a movie only he could see.
>
> "Tell me again," Adam complained. "Why do you want to burn down your own dad's restaurant?"

Why, exactly, *had* they burned it down? David had been angry with his father, but that wasn't a good enough reason to torch the man's business. No, the real reason was related to Todd's secret, which he had shared with them just before the first match was lit. Jonathan couldn't remember the secret, not consciously, but he felt sure he would understand what was wrong with the world if he could just—

There was a siren then, or rather a ringing, that he realized was the doorbell. It was rare for visitors to stop by and rarer still for someone to do so unannounced, so he was immediately curious about who it might be. He was also drunker than he had realized.

Jonathan opened his front door to find two men standing on the porch, men in matching dark sports coats, men he didn't recognize. The one who spoke looked athletic, an inch or two taller than Jonathan, a little over six feet. His hair was dark and cut short. The other fellow was older, mostly bald and thicker around the middle.

"Jonathan Crane?"

"Yes?"

Now the fellow held up a badge, something Jonathan had never seen happen outside of the movies and television, and for a strange moment he felt there must be a camera crew lurking just out of sight. It didn't seem realistic at all that two policemen had suddenly appeared on his porch.

"I'm Detective Frank Daniels. This is my partner, Detective Jerry Gholson. Would you mind if we asked you a few questions?"

"Um, sure . . . I mean, no. I wouldn't mind. Please come in."

He moved aside and the detectives stepped into his home. The light was on in the kitchen, and his visitors naturally headed in that direction. The bottle of Jameson was out where anyone could see it.

"Having a drink after work?" the older fellow, Gholson, asked.

"Yeah."

"Stressful job?" he asked with a smirk. "Teaching kids?"

"Not usually. But I just found out an hour ago what Bobby did. I guess that's why you're here? To ask me about him?"

Daniels motioned toward the bottle of Jameson. "How many of those have you had, if you don't mind me asking?"

"Two," Jonathan said, though considering the size of his second pour this answer wasn't necessarily accurate.

"You feel comfortable talking to us under the influence of alcohol?"

"Yes, of course."

"It shouldn't take long," Daniels said. "We do have a few questions about Bob Steele."

Jonathan had nothing to hide from them, at least nothing about the events of the present day, but still his heart was beating so hard in his chest that he wondered if the detectives could hear it.

"We're sorry to come here under these circumstances," Daniels said. "I'm sure it must be pretty tough for you, Bob's death and all. I guess you two were pretty close."

"We were friends as kids."

"Just friends?" Gholson asked. "Didn't you live under the same roof for a while?"

Jonathan nodded. His ears buzzed.

"I was about to say we spent a lot of time together because of our parents. My mom and his dad dated off and on for many years."

"Your mom still dates Kenny Steele," Gholson said. "Isn't that right?"

"As far as I understand."

Jonathan could feel his perception wandering, could feel the Jameson doing the job that had been asked of it, and he wished he'd hadn't poured such a stiff second drink.

"I don't really talk to her much anymore," he added.

"You don't have a good relationship with her?" Daniels asked. He took out a notepad and wrote something.

"My mother and I never really got along. I wish it were different, but I don't think there's much to be done about it now."

"When was the last time you spoke to Bob?" Gholson asked.

Their communication as adults had been sporadic and finally ended for good when Jonathan wondered aloud if Bobby's dad had turned his mom into an alcoholic.

"A couple of years ago."

"Well," Daniels said, "the next logical question to ask is if you have any idea why your friend would want to assault Fred Clark and burn down his restaurant."

This question was burdened with significance so overwhelming that Jonathan almost laughed.

Instead, he said, "I only just heard about it, but I sure can't think of any reason why he would do something like that."

"So that's it?" Daniels said. "There's nothing at all you can tell us? Anything you can think of would probably help, no matter how small it seems to you."

Jonathan had the feeling these detectives knew more than they were letting on. It also occurred to him that, five minutes before, he had stupidly typed on his computer the details of a crime he had committed with Bobby and the others many years ago. The evidence would be impossible to hide if these detectives wandered into his office, which was the next room over.

"So you're just going to stand there and lie to us?" Gholson asked.

Jonathan stepped involuntarily backward.

"What?"

"You'll have to excuse my partner," Daniels explained. "All he does anymore is sit around and tell boring stories from his glory days. And lately he's been going on and on about these cases of arson he worked back in the eighties. Apparently there was some kid named Joe who burned down a house and then disappeared. A week after that, some *other* kid from the same neighborhood burned down a restaurant. And now yesterday this fellow, Bob Steele, burns down the exact same restaurant and this time murders its owner. Since all you kids were friends, Gholson has the crazy idea everything is connected somehow."

Jonathan understood any police department would keep records of past cases. He knew these records were stored in computer databases, and maybe by now even the old case files had been archived electronically. But that he was standing in front of the same detective who investigated crimes Jonathan had helped commit twenty-five years ago— this was difficult to believe. Yet here Gholson stood with his partner, Daniels, asking about what happened at Lone Star Barbecue and how it might be connected to Jonathan's past. It didn't matter that he had never been officially implicated in those childhood crimes. Gholson obviously believed Jonathan knew something or else he wouldn't have come here tonight.

Back then Todd had taken the blame for burning down the restaurant, which was no small crime. But Joe Henreid was a missing child who had never been found. Could Bobby's behavior last night have reopened interest in that missing person case? Why the hell had he written that shit on his computer?

"Really?" Jonathan finally said. "You think there's a connection?"

"So you remember the cases I'm talking about?" Daniels asked.

"Of course I do. I knew Todd Willis. I vaguely knew Joe. Of course I remember them."

"The way it went down," Daniels said, "at least as far as we understand it, is this: Joe Henreid burned down the empty house, which was in Tanglewood, where all of you lived. Afterward, he ran away from home and is presumed to have been abducted. A week or so later Lone Star Barbecue was burned down, and though all five of you were close friends, including David Clark, whose father owned the restaurant,

Todd Willis admitted to setting the fire alone. Does that sound right to you?"

"That's how I remember it," Jonathan lied.

"Have you spoken to Todd since?"

"No. He moved away from Wichita that summer and I never heard from him again."

"No idea where we might find him?"

Jonathan shook his head. "No, sir."

Gholson stepped forward, halving the distance between himself and Jonathan, his breath juicy with tobacco.

"Mr. Crane, let me tell you something. I may not know exactly what happened that summer, but I know the official story is total bullshit. I don't believe for a second that an eleven-year-old kid torched a house on his own. And if I'm correct, who might have had helped him do it? Maybe some other kids who lived over on the next street? Especially since, a week later, one of them burned down a restaurant where his buddy worked? Do you see what I mean? I don't believe Oswald acted alone and I don't think Joe Henreid did, either."

Jonathan's brain buzzed angrily, like the busy signal of a land line telephone.

"What do you want me to say?" he finally croaked.

"Tell me what really happened that summer. You know something. I can see it in your face."

Jonathan opened his mouth and said nothing.

"You tell us something, and we'll tell you something," Gholson said. "We'll tell you what Bob said right before he was shot."

Jonathan blinked. Now he understood why the detectives were pressing him so hard about events that had transpired twenty-five years ago. Whatever Bobby had said, it was complicating their investigation . . . and if they were willing to share it with him, maybe they didn't consider him a suspect. Maybe he could admit knowledge of the childhood fires without implying his own participation. Even if they found what he had written on the computer, surely the statute of limitations on that crime had run out long ago.

And he really wanted to hear what Bobby had said. Had he remembered what Jonathan could not?

"You know how Todd Willis was in that weird walking coma?" he finally said to Gholson.

"Of course I do. All the parents in your neighborhood used that against him when the restaurant burned down."

"At first we thought what happened to Todd was pretty cool, so we invited him into our club. But then Joe set that house on fire and Todd became obsessed. He thought we had been upstaged by some little kid. And since David was always complaining about his dad, how he was a shitty boss, Todd got the idea to burn down the restaurant. I mean, it was insured, so he saw it as more of a statement. A rebellious thing. When none of us would play along, he did it himself."

In this situation, Jonathan found lying came quite easily, as if he were building a scene in a novel.

"So you knew he was going to burn down the restaurant?" Gholson asked. "Back then the rest of you claimed no knowledge at all."

"Our parents forced us to say that."

"Because they thought their reputations in this town mattered more than my investigation."

"Look, we were children, and Todd was disturbed. He was always saying weird things, doing weird things. It's not our fault he—"

"You could have told someone before he did it. That's if what you're saying is true, which I wouldn't bet my pension on."

If this was all they had to work with, Jonathan thought, Gholson and Daniels were never going to understand Bobby's motive for visiting Lone Star Barbecue. For that matter, neither would he.

"You say this is all ancient history," Gholson continued. "But when the same restaurant is intentionally destroyed in this manner not once but twice, I don't care how many years separate the two crimes— there is probably some kind of connection between them. When you consider the incidents this week involving Alicia Ulbrecht and Adam Altman— friends of yours, both of them—maybe you can see why we're asking you some tough questions, Mr. Crane."

Jonathan had not heard Alicia's name spoken aloud since high school, and it was surreal to hear it now, especially in this context. She was the first girl he had ever loved, and Jonathan had wondered about her many times over the years. He had never made any attempt to look her up, however, in part because he assumed she had moved away long ago.

"Alicia Ulbrecht?"

"So you're telling me you don't know about that?"

"No," Jonathan said. "I don't."

"I guess you don't watch the news around here. Three nights ago, Alicia Ulbrecht's house was burned down. The night after that, a new construction project in Tanglewood went up in flames, a house being built by Adam Altman. Then we have Bobby's visit to Fred Clark's restaurant last night. All three of these victims are connected to you, or at least they were back when you were kids."

"So what you're implying is I'm a suspect in these crimes."

"I didn't say that," Gholson said in an amused voice. "Frank, did you hear me say that?"

Detective Daniels shook his head. "No, I didn't."

"This is ridiculous. I didn't know about any of this until tonight. I haven't spoken to Alicia or Adam in like twenty-five years."

"We wouldn't expect you to come right out and admit the crime," Daniels said. "But you should probably consult with an attorney."

"You've got to be joking. Why?"

"This morning someone sent an email to our sergeant," Gholson said. "We think it was a reference to these crimes."

"Whoever it was," Daniels added, "was smart enough to use Gmail in a way that hides his IP address."

"Why would that concern me?"

"The email wasn't a useful tip or anything like that," said Gholson. "It was some kind of clue. A cryptic message. The title of the email was 'THE CITY WILL BURN.' Written in all caps for maximum effect."

"We think the content of the email might be song lyrics," said Daniels. "We're not exactly sure."

A memory occurred to Jonathan then: Todd with his keyboard, playing music for them.

"Are you going to tell me what was in the message?" Jonathan asked them.

Gholson cleared his throat, as if he were standing in front of a television camera. He recited the lyrics robotically.

"'I'm gonna get you back, I'm gonna show you what I'm made of.'"

The memory was clear now, bright and clear. Jonathan wondered how he had ever forgotten Todd playing this music for them. Even this morning, when he had awoken from the strange dream, the significance of the song and Todd's playing of it had not occurred to him.

"That ring any bells with you?" asked Gholson.

Jonathan realized his hands were shaking, and he was tempted to pick up his drink and down the entire thing, detectives or no detectives.

Instead he said, "I'm not sure. It does sound familiar."

Gholson looked at him gravely. "Maybe I can refresh your memory. What was the name of the club you invited Todd to join?"

He pretended to think about it, if for no other reason than to buy himself time. Here Gholson thought he had discovered some explosive truth and Jonathan was struggling to understand a memory that was basically impossible.

"Our club was called The Boys of Summer."

Gholson smiled triumphantly. "So you can see why we have interest in your childhood exploits. Three of your friends have been involved in some kind of arson incident since Monday, and in the last one, two people died. You could make the argument that Bob Steele set all three fires, but he probably can't send email from the afterlife. Which means someone with information about these crimes remains at large. And considering this newest clue, lyrics from a song called "The Boys of Summer," you can understand why we want to know everything we can about your club."

"Yes, I can understand," Jonathan said. "But I wasn't the only person in the club. I haven't set any fires this week. And I sure as hell didn't help kill someone."

Gholson and Daniels just stared at him.

"So what did Bobby say before he was shot?" Jonathan asked.

Daniels looked down at his notes.

"He said Todd Willis told him this was the end."

Jonathan thought he might pass out. His mind was swirling out of control. Something was wrong, really wrong, and the lyrics Gholson had quoted earlier were the answer to a question he wasn't sure how to ask.

He wished the detectives would leave. He wished they would leave so he could finish his drink and make five or six more of them.

"I know this has something to do with that summer," Gholson said. "If you're innocent, as you claim, why not just tell me what's going on?"

"Because I don't know what's going on."

"You sure?"

"You think I'm lying?"

"I think," Gholson said, leaning close to Jonathan again, "that you've been lying since we got here."

Daniels grabbed his partner's arm. "All right, Jerry. I think we have what we need. Thanks for your time, Mr. Crane."

"No problem."

"Think real hard about what happened back then," Gholson added. "And the next time I come by, maybe you'll have more to say."

ZONE FORECAST PRODUCT
NATIONAL WEATHER SERVICE NORMAN OK
TXZ086-022200-
WICHITA-
INCLUDING THE CITIES OF ... WICHITA FALLS
947 AM CDT THU JUNE 2 1983

.TODAY ... SUNNY. HIGH AROUND 102. WINDS SW 10-15 MPH AND GUSTY.
.TONIGHT ... MOSTLY CLEAR. LOW NEAR 80. SOUTH WIND 5-10 MPH.
.FRIDAY ... SUNNY. HIGH AROUND 105. SOUTH WINDS AROUND 10 MPH.
.FRIDAY NIGHT ... CLEAR. LOW IN THE LOW 80S. SOUTH WINDS AROUND 10 MPH.
.SATURDAY ... SUNNY. HIGH 107.
.SUNDAY ... SUNNY. HIGH NEAR 110.

12

Until two days ago there had been an antenna mounted to the top of his black plastic jambox. The jambox was a dual-deck model with two rows of red LEDs that flickered metronomically when you played a cassette. He enjoyed recording from the radio, and he liked to play those songs back in fits and starts as he learned to pick out their melodies on his Casio keyboard. He possessed no background in music except for a few lessons handed down by his Grandpa Willis. He did not play in the school band. But he could imitate songs he heard on the radio, and he would have been doing that now if he hadn't accidentally snapped off the antenna two days ago. You couldn't pick up many stations without the antenna. In fact, the only station clear enough to hear played country music, which wasn't music at all, which was more of an oxymoron when you really thought about it.

Todd Willis had been awake for almost six weeks now, awake in the sense that he was apparently living in the real world again. The problem was, when he had been asleep, he had dreamed things that seemed real when he was dreaming them. Like for a while he had believed himself to be a kid named Thomas. For several summer weeks, or so it seemed, he had spent his days with Jeff and Greg Stillson, two brothers who played oddly futuristic video games and swam in their backyard pool and always smelled like chorine. The Stillsons were kind to him, and they didn't seem to mind that he never spoke aloud. They didn't even care when he beat the crap out of them at their own video games. And then one day, with no fanfare or explanation, Jeff and Greg had disappeared and Todd retreated again into the white and empty void where there was no sound or color or smell or taste. In this void the only sensation was fear that vibrated at him from everywhere. A while later he would dream something else, like he was the very first human to test a new teleportation machine, or a famous scientist, or a man whose whole life was really a movie someone was watching. Sometimes, instead of visual dreams, he heard music, amazing songs that would have been famous had anyone else known about them. But no matter what he dreamed, no matter what he heard, eventually he was forced back into the endless white void. It was a realm where isolation consumed you from the inside, where you could not ignore the pointlessness of all life in the universe, and Todd feared it like nothing else.

It was no wonder, then, even though he had been awake for some time now, that Todd suspected he might still be asleep. How could he know for sure these six weeks weren't just another dream, that eventually his parents wouldn't disappear, along with this new neighborhood where they lived? Honestly he didn't care all that much. Todd would accept any reality in place of infinite white nothingness.

His doctor was an older man, very thin and athletic-looking for his age. His name was Robbins. He wore shiny and spotless pointed shoes and looked at Todd like he was some kind of science project. Dr. Robbins had been treating him for more than four years, and upon Todd's (miraculous) awakening, had explained his condition in simple terms.

"Your brain became locked into a slow wave sleep-like pattern that would normally last only a few hours. This happened because you experienced a very serious head injury when you were hit with debris from the tornado, and your brain needed special help to heal. Unfortunately this healing process took much longer than we expected."

Todd could not remember the tornado, nor anything about the four years since it had ravaged the town, and this gap made the world seem very strange. For instance, one of his last memories was a conversation with his friend, Matt, about the upcoming sequel to *Star Wars*, which Matt had heard was being filmed in Europe. They had spoken breathlessly about what might happen in such a movie, since Luke had already destroyed the Death Star, but then the tornado happened. While Todd was asleep the second movie had come and gone and now there was a third *Star Wars* movie in theaters. Darth Vader had turned out to be

Luke's father, Princess Leia was his sister, and the whole world seemed to have lost its mind.

The changes to his physical form were even stranger. His body had swollen with muscle, sprouted pubic hair overnight, and everything in the world was nine inches lower than where he expected it to be. To top it all off, whenever he spoke, it sounded as if there was a frog in his throat. But in this case Dr. Robbins could not be sure if it was a symptom of puberty or because he had so rarely exercised his ability to speak over the past four years.

His doctor was unsure about many things. For one, he didn't know why Todd had remained asleep for so long—it seemed people rarely suffered a condition like his for more than a few weeks, let alone months. The official title of his diagnosis was "catatonic schizophrenia," though his mother didn't care for the second word, because she said it implied he was crazy. The doctor also wasn't sure what sort of long term consequences Todd might face as a result of his injury and sleep, and could not rule out a relapse into the catatonic state. Which was just another way of explaining how the white void was still out there waiting for him.

The other thing his doctor did not understand was the reality of his dreams. Dr. Robbins accepted that Todd had experienced dreams, but didn't believe these "episodes" had anything to do with the world around him. When he tried to explain how he had seen things in his dreams that he could not have known, that no one could have known, the old man smiled in a condescending way that made Todd want to punch him.

There was great concern over his education. Lately his parents had been talking with a counselor from the school district to decide what grade level would be most appropriate. His dad refused to send him back to the fourth, but his mom was afraid Todd would be so far behind students closer to his age that he would hate going to school and fail every class. She seemed to think any kind of school would ruin his whole life and as such wanted him to learn at home. But Todd's four-year sleep had filled him with a loneliness so intense he could not imagine another day with only his mom and dad as company.

Today was the first time he'd been given approval to venture out the front door on his own. Until now his time outdoors had mainly been spent in the back yard throwing the football with his dad or having dinner with both parents on the back porch. The way his mom looked at him in these moments made him feel like an insect being examined under a microscope, and whenever she whispered something to his dad, Todd wanted to yell, "I'm right here, Mom! I know you're talking about me!" Finally, yesterday evening, his parents had taken him for a walk through the new neighborhood—over to Shady Lane, around to Craigmont, and back to their house again. His dad explained this two-street loop was as far as he was allowed to venture and called the area his *perimeter*. He emphasized it that way, like with italics, in case Todd didn't know what the word meant. As if Todd were still nine years old.

This morning his mother had come into his room, her voice all fake and singsong, imploring him to "Rise and shine, sleepyhead," explaining how today was the first day of the rest of his life. She couldn't wait for him to venture outdoors and informed him about two boys she thought might live over on Shady Lane. But Todd wasn't stupid. He could hear the anxiety in her voice, which only served to magnify his own fear.

The thing was, he shouldn't have been afraid. Just yesterday Todd had seen what it looked like out front: houses and trees and streets, just like any other neighborhood in town. But this morning, when he first approached the door, Todd couldn't bring himself to open it. And if it felt terrible and pathetic to fear going outdoors on his own, his mother watching from the living room made it that much worse. It was awful to be unable to perform a basic human task, but it was far worse for someone to witness such a failure. There was a particular word for that feeling, one he'd learned while asleep: *impotent*. A terrible word for a terrible feeling.

After the failed attempt he retreated to his room, and a few minutes later his mother appeared in the doorway to announce she was headed to Safeway for some groceries.

"You want me to stay inside until you get back?"

"Not at all," she replied. "I hope you have a great time. Remember those boys I told you about. And please don't do anything crazy. The doctor says your head is fine, but I don't want you to hurt yourself again."

She hugged him and left, which had been ten or fifteen minutes ago, and now he was still sitting here with his Casio and his non-working radio. He spun the tuning knob back and forth, more and more slowly, until finally he was able to extract the fuzzy beat of "Billie Jean." But there was too much static, terrible canyons of static, like he was picking up a radio station from Mars. He switched off the radio.

Sat there in silence.

Finally he stood up again and walked out of his room. The front door was only moments away, and soon he was in front of it, his hand on the heavy brass knob. All he had to do was turn the stupid thing. Turn and pull. But he couldn't.

He was afraid when he opened the door he would find nothing but white on the other side, that he was still asleep, and this whole episode of waking up was just another dream.

The doorknob felt warm and alive in his hand, as if it might recoil from his touch. But it didn't. He turned it nanometers at a time. The knob squeaked slightly and the latch released with a soft click.

Todd closed his eyes, pulled the door open, and felt heat wash over him.

The neighborhood was still there.

He stepped furtively onto the front porch and pulled the door shut behind him. The sky was clear and nearly white with heat. Across the street stood a sprawling house, white with a gray roof, and all around him Todd heard the buzz of cicadas hidden in trees. Air conditioners droned, struggled in the humidity.

Todd stood there, still waiting for the dream to end, because it seemed so unlikely that he really was awake.

And yet the world continued to exist. A red Honda Accord approached the corner and turned left. Todd thought about waving to the driver but didn't.

With nothing else in the world to do, he set off in the direction of Shady Lane, wondering if he might run into the boys his mother had seen. He wasn't really expecting to see anyone, and wasn't sure what he would do if he did. He ambled down the street, past large brick homes, past expansive, green-brown lawns, and had the feeling he had seen this place before. Not just yesterday but sometime before that, more than once, like maybe he had walked through this neighborhood hundreds of times. Or more.

Eventually Todd reached Shady Lane, expecting nothing, but in fact he did hear voices yelling as he passed a brown, two-story house. The voices sounded like boys. They appeared to be coming from the back yard. Todd stood there, listening, until the yells gradually quieted and then stopped. He wanted to investigate, even introduce himself, but you couldn't just walk into someone's back yard, could you?

Then the gate opened, and a wet, muscular kid in red swimming trunks emerged with a large beach towel slung over his shoulder.

"I thought I saw someone through the fence," the kid said, walking over. "New around here?"

"Yeah. Moved in a few weeks ago."

"I'm Bobby."

"I'm Todd."

"Jonathan has a pool. You want to come in for a swim?"

Sweat was running down Todd's neck and had soaked both sides of his shirt. The sun was beating on him like a hammer. He would have killed to cool off in the water, but his trunks were back at home, and he didn't relish the idea of going back to get them. If his mom had already returned from the store, she would probably think he had lost his nerve. He didn't want her to think he was a coward.

"My trunks aren't unpacked yet," he lied, "but I could hang out with you guys if you don't mind."

"That's cool," Bobby said. "Come on back."

Todd followed at a reasonable distance as this well-built Bobby trudged with purpose into the backyard. The pool was a kidney-shaped hole in a kidney-shaped slab of concrete. The water shimmered. A much scrawnier kid floated on an inflatable raft, his eyes closed, the sun glinting off his hairless chest like fire. Somewhere out of sight a radio was playing "Every Breath You Take."

Bobby smiled and shed his towel, bounding toward the pool in three leaping steps. He grabbed his knees as he flew through the air, tucked them against his chest, and hit the water in a great, liquid explosion. The scrawny kid screamed as if shot. He scrambled for the concrete edge of the pool.

"Bobby!" he yelled. "Dammit! I hate you!"

"No, you don't," Bobby laughed, wading through the water. "I'm your favorite person in the whole world. Admit it."

"Whatever!"

Bobby grabbed him. "Tell me I'm awesome or I'll dunk you again."

"No!"

Still laughing, Bobby pulled the scrawny kid from the edge of the pool and shoved his head under water.

"This is too easy," Bobby said. "Todd, meet Jonathan. Jonathan, this is Todd."

Jonathan's arms flailed out of the water and clawed in vain for Bobby's face.

"You're a lot stronger than he is, I guess," Todd suggested.

"Them's the breaks."

Not sure what else to do, Todd stood there and watched Bobby hold his friend underwater for what seemed like eternity. If this is all they were going to do, this David and Goliath bullshit, Todd wasn't interested. This was the same crap that went on in every city in America.

But just when Todd decided to leave, Bobby relented. Jonathan shot out of the water like a torpedo, coughing and choking.

"Sounds like my Aunt Jesse," Bobby laughed. "She's got cancer or emphysema or whatever. At Christmas she hacked the whole fucking time we were trying to open presents."

Todd acknowledged this and then pointed at Jonathan, whose face seemed to be darkening. "I don't think he's getting any air."

Jonathan's face was indeed turning purple, and he wasn't choking anymore, either. Instead he was trying to suck in little bursts of air that didn't seem like breaths at all. His mouth made a sound like water trying to drain down a pipe that had no room for it.

"Oh, shit," Bobby said. He turned Jonathan around and pounded on his back. "Breathe, man. Breathe!"

Jonathan's eyes seemed to be propped open. They were wide and glassy. He didn't breathe.

"Goddamn it, Johnny," Bobby yelled and pounded some more. "Breathe already."

"Maybe you should try the Heimlich maneuver," Todd said.

"Huh? The what?"

"The Heimlich maneuver. I don't know if it will work with water, but you wrap your arms around him and push up below his rib cage like this." Todd simulated the procedure on himself, but Bobby didn't seem convinced.

"Just try it. Try something."

Bobby nodded, and a couple of lucky thrusts later, water urped out of Jonathan's mouth. In its place he sucked in a lungful of air, then another and another. He surged through the water toward Bobby.

"You idiot. I hate you!"

Bobby stepped backward and held Jonathan at arm's length. "Stop it. You're killing me, tough guy."

Jonathan's arms flailed wildly, unconvincingly. "You are such an idiot! You think because you're strong that no one can hurt you?"

"At the very least I know *you* can't."

Jonathan's attack subsided and finally stopped. He looked up at Todd and then back at Bobby.

"Don't ever do that again, Bobby. What if I had drowned?"

"What if, what if, what if. Get a sense of humor already."

"Everything is such a big joke to you. One of these days you'll do something really stupid and it won't seem so funny then."

"Whatever, tough guy. This is Todd. He just moved in down the street."

Jonathan's smile seemed forced as he turned to Todd. "I'm Jonathan. Nice to meet you."

"You, too."

"Where'd you move here from?"

"We used to live over by Weeks Park."

"Oh, I thought he meant from out of town," Jonathan said. "Why'd you move to Tanglewood?"

Todd shrugged, pretending there was no particular reason. "My parents liked the area. I guess this is the place to live these days."

"Best neighborhood in Wichita Falls," Bobby bragged. "So what do you like to do? You play sports?"

"Not in a while. I like football and basketball, though."

"You any good?"

"I don't know."

"If you don't know," Bobby said, "then you're not any good. My dad always says, 'No one will believe your greatness until you do.'"

"Bobby's the quarterback for the junior high varsity team," Jonathan added. "The Old High coaches are already scouting him."

As starved as he was for interaction with other kids, Todd was already tired of these two. Jonathan pretended to have no patience for Bobby's brainless antics but also seemed to idolize the guy. Bobby himself appeared to be a simple jock cliché. The whole scene couldn't have been more predictable, except for one important detail—Todd's ability to assess the situation. He felt oddly in control here, like he'd brought a gun to a knife fight. His parents worried he might still have the mind of a nine-year-old, but inside Todd felt more like nineteen. And from that standpoint, the only interesting thing about talking to these kids was to have a little fun with them.

He looked at Bobby. "The high school coaches are already after you, eh? You must be a superstar."

Bobby grinned stupidly. It seemed like he was about to say something and then stopped himself.

"So what else do you like to do?" Jonathan asked. "Were there a lot of kids in your old neighborhood?"

"There were a few. These two brothers had a pool, so I hung out at their house most of the time. Sort of like you guys."

"Did you have a club?"

"Was I in one? No."

"We have one," Jonathan said proudly. "It's called 'The Dragons.' We have four members. Bobby is the president."

"I could have guessed."

"What does that mean?" Bobby asked.

"Just an observation."

"An observation of what?"

"I just can't see you allowing anyone else to be president of your club."

Bobby looked at Jonathan and then back at Todd. "We took a vote. I won. I don't know what you're trying to say, buddy, but I think your mouth is about to get you into trouble."

"Come on, Bobby," Jonathan interjected. "This isn't how you make friends."

"I don't think this guy *wants* to be friends," Bobby growled. "He sounds like he wants to start some shit."

"I'm not the one who held my own friend under water until he choked," Todd said.

"I was horsing around. Jonathan is my buddy."

"Fine."

"You're new around here, man," Bobby continued. He waded to Todd's side of the pool and climbed out. "You don't know how we do things, so I don't think you ought to judge us."

"Maybe I should leave, then, since the autocracy around here doesn't like to be questioned."

Bobby stepped forward until only a few feet separated the two of them. "Maybe you better, smart ass."

From a self-preservation point of view, it made sense for Todd to concede defeat and leave, or apologize and stay. Because if he fought this punk he would lose. Bobby was three inches taller and maybe thirty pounds heavier than him. He was likely a better fighter. But Todd also knew he would see Bobby again—either during the summer or afterward in school—and there was no way he could show his face in public if everyone knew he had backed down from this meathead. People would believe he was either a coward or that he was marginalized because of his head injury, and both of those things were patently false.

To Bobby he said, "Or maybe I'll just stand here and see what you do about it."

Surprise lit the kid's eyes. Surprise and amusement. "What I *do* about it?"

"Yeah," Todd said. "I don't like being pushed around."

Bobby chuckled. "You've got balls, buddy. I'll give you that."

"Yeah."

"You can shove them up your ass."

Bobby pushed him in the chest, and Todd stepped backward. He was helpless to stop himself. The pool was behind him but he didn't go in.

"Fuck you, jock," Todd shot back. He planted his hands on Bobby's chest, but shoving him was like trying to shove an oak tree.

Bobby laughed. "You pussy."

"Whatever, cocksucker."

Now Bobby's eyes widened, the lids opening like blinds. "That's it," he said, grabbing Todd by the chest, ready to toss him into the pool.

"Bobby, come on!" Jonathan pleaded.

Todd was going in, of course. There was no stopping it. But as he was slung in the direction of the water, Todd grabbed Bobby's arms, just enough to share momentum with him, so that together they crossed the threshold between dry land and pool. The two of them hit the water like a wild bull thrown overboard. Appendages flew through the air, wet, meaty smacks as fists collided with chests and arms and faces. And in the briefly infinite moment of it, Todd felt a certain kind of energy as he realized that it didn't matter if he bled, if his nose got smashed, if he lost a tooth. He had already been hurt in a way no neighborhood bully could ever reasonably manage, and these injuries had nearly killed him. But he hadn't died. He had lived. And now that he was here, back in the real world, what was a little pain in exchange for his self-respect, for standing here like a man and delivering blows to this brainless idiot? He realized any fear of fighting this fellow wasn't borne from pain but the *idea* of pain, and any pain short of a life-threatening injury would go away. Nothing this kid could do would last forever, nothing except steal Todd's self-respect.

He waded in closer, where Bobby made direct contact with his jaw, and the flaring pain almost made Todd reconsider. But then he landed a right cross of his own. Bobby stepped back. Todd could see in the kid's eyes that he wasn't used to getting hit.

Behind them Jonathan was yelling something, Todd couldn't tell what, especially not after Bobby smacked him in the ear hard enough to make it ring. His hands went to his head, the world began to gray, and fear seized Todd as he imagined the white void coming for him again. If he went back there again he didn't think he would escape a second time.

But he didn't go back. He remained in the pool. And when Bobby leaned in to hit him again, Todd turned and threw all his weight into his right arm, connecting directly with Bobby's nose. There was a cracking sound, like popping knuckles, and Bobby backed away. His hands cupped his nose as if he were afraid it would fall off. Blood dribbled between his fingers. It traced a crooked path down his wet arm and dropped into the pool, little red explosions in the pristine water.

"Holy shit," Bobby said.

Jonathan waded up, splashing like a toddler. His voice was small, awestruck. "Are you all right? Bobby, are you okay?"

"Holy shit this hurts," Bobby answered.

"Is it broken?"

"Maybe." And then to Todd, "Thanks a lot, buddy."

"Thanks for making me deaf. I think my ear fell off."

Bobby sprayed blood into the pool. Red bubbles formed between his lips and popped. His eyes were narrow, as if he were scowling. Or smiling.

"Do you mind looking for it, Jonathan?" Todd said. "My ear? I don't want it to get sucked into the filter."

Now Bobby dropped his hands and laughed out loud. Todd joined him, in spite of his ringing ear. Jonathan looked bewildered, as if the two boys in his pool were not laughing but baying like hyenas. He shook his head and began to laugh himself.

13

Todd was trying to understand how these two guys had ever become friends.

"So you guys aren't brothers, but you live together here?"

"I wouldn't say I *live* here," Bobby said.

"But that's your football."

"Yeah."

"And those are your Atari cartridges?"

"Well, some of them are mine, I guess, but Jonathan's mom paid for them—"

"His mom died," Jonathan said. "My dad died. And my mom and his dad . . . after the tornado they . . . they sort of got together."

The three of them were inside now, in a dark and messy game room, the blinds drawn. They were sitting at a round card table and a television stood a few feet away. Jonathan didn't bother to store his Atari in any kind of organized way. It just sat on the floor, wires snaking into shadows behind the TV, and game cartridges were everywhere. So was the Dungeons and Dragons paraphernalia, the oddly-shaped dice and adventure modules and hardcover reference manuals. Todd remembered the game vaguely, populated by fighters and wizards and monsters like bugbears. He never understood why anything would be called a bugbear.

"His mom got a big insurance settlement," Bobby said. "She wanted to build a new house out here in Tanglewood, and my dad works in construction."

"So they fell in love?"

"Pretty much," Jonathan said.

The three of them had come in after the fight, and it was just like you saw on TV, just like you read about in books, where a kid stands up to the bully and becomes friends with him. Todd's ear still hurt like hell, and Bobby's nose was red and swollen, but they were sitting there talking as if none of it had happened. He had the strange feeling they weren't actual boys at all but rather actors in an after-school television special.

"My dad was picked up by the tornado and dropped a few miles away near a highway," Jonathan said. "His mom died in our back yard."

"She ended up in a tree," Bobby added. "She was stuck with . . . you know those big scissors. Pruning shears."

Even though it had happened four years ago, Todd heard their voices wavering as Bobby and Jonathan recalled the tornado. He wished he could call upon memories of the storm to help describe his own experience. It seemed unfair that the tornado had extracted such a cost from him and yet he had no recollection of the freight train sound or the black sky or whole neighborhoods being flattened. But the story he *did* have was his and his alone.

"If you lived over by Weeks Park," Jonathan said, "your house must've gotten hit. That's not that far from where I used to live, and our place was blown away."

"Our house was torn in half," Todd admitted. "We rebuilt it, but later my mom decided we should sell it and move to Tanglewood. She said we needed a fresh start."

"Four years after the tornado?" Bobby asked. "That doesn't sound very fresh."

"Wait a minute," Jonathan said, and Todd saw recognition flicker in his eyes. "You're that kid who woke up, aren't you?"

Todd nodded. "The one and only."

"Holy crap. You were like in a coma or something, right?"

"Sort of. It's called being catatonic. In a coma you're laid up in bed, and over time your body shrivels up. My brain was asleep but my body walked around and did stuff."

"Like what?" Bobby asked. "Look through your mom's underwear?"

Jonathan blew out an exasperated sigh.

"It's fine," Todd said. "I know it sounds weird. I got hit in the head with a piece of debris and it scrambled my brain or something. I was in the hospital for several months and, like, a clinic after that. But eventually I went home. You can't stay in a hospital for four years when you're basically just sleepwalking."

"Wow," Jonathan said. "Sleepwalking for years."

"But what did you *do*?" Bobby asked. "I mean like every day, what did you do? Just sit there?"

"I ate three meals. My mom read to me. I watched TV even though I don't remember it. And there were lots of exercises to keep my muscles from shriveling up."

Bobby seemed skeptical. "You sure you don't remember anything?"

"I dreamed a lot, but I don't remember ever being awake. It's hard to describe. I didn't really know where I was . . . or *who* I was."

"That's far out," Jonathan said. "It reminds me of this Stephen King book I just read called *The Dead Zone*. The dude in that was in a car accident and went into a coma for like five years or something. When he woke up he could see the future."

"Can you see the future?" asked Bobby.

"Hell yes, I can. I guessed all your boxing moves and that's how I smashed your nose."

Bobby didn't respond to this right away, and from the confused look on his face, it seemed the kid had taken the joke literally.

"I'm messing with you, man. I can't see the future. If I could, I would pretend to get sick anytime my mom got the dumb idea to make tuna casserole."

"Gross," Jonathan said. "What's in that?"

"Macaroni, mayonnaise, mushrooms."

"Oh, gag."

"Corn, tuna. Melted cheese!"

"It sounds like actual barf," Jonathan added. "Like in a pan instead of the toilet."

Seemingly out of the blue, Bobby said, "So can you see the future or not?"

"Dude, he was kidding. What's wrong with you?"

"I just want to make sure is all. A lot of weird shit happened in that tornado. Sleepwalking for four years takes the cake."

"I can't see the future. At least not that I know of."

"Well, let us know if that changes. We could make some money on the Super Bowl."

Todd chuckled.

"Or you could tell this turkey what would happen if he finally got up the nerve to call up his wannabe girlfriend. Unless he already did."

"You know I didn't," Jonathan admitted.

"He's got a crush on this girl, Alicia. Who happens to know this, and who happens to like Jonathan, too. Believe it or not."

"You don't *know* that."

"Everybody knows, dude. And every day you don't ask her, the more you look like a wuss."

"He's right," Todd said. "Not asking is more embarrassing than being turned down. It takes balls to ask. Girls like that."

Bobby was about to say something else when a woman's voice interrupted him.

"Jon-a-THAN!"

Her voice, heavy and ragged, bawled down the hallway.

"That your mom?" Todd asked.

"Yeah," Jonathan said. He struggled out of his chair and slumped toward the door.

"JON-a-*THAN!*"

"I'm *coming,* Mom."

When Jonathan was gone, Bobby said, "His mom is a demon. I don't know what the hell my dad sees in her."

"Maybe he likes her because she's feisty."

"Feisty? You should hear her. All she does is bitch. At everything. Listen, I bet if we—"

But preface wasn't necessary, because just then they heard the ragged voice again.

"What is *this?*"

Jonathan's voice followed, low and indecipherable.

"New kid?" his mother said. "I don't give a *shit.* I asked you what this was."

The low voice again.

"I *know* it's a shirt, you Dodo. You think I don't know it's a shirt?"

Todd said, "Is she like this all the time?"

"Every day, man. Every single day."

"It's *inside out,* Jon-a-THAN. How many times do I have to tell you not to put your clothes in the hamper *inside out?*"

Jonathan said something else.

"No, it *does not,* you Dodo! Stop acting like a stupid Dodo bird!"

"She calls him names?" Todd asked.

"Every day, man."

14

At age fourteen, if David Clark had learned anything from his father's values, it was that a man's nature was measured by his character. Only character didn't necessarily mean integrity, or moral fiber, but rather the hours of hard work a man had put in, the number of pleasures he had denied himself. Character was earned by these actions, measured in quantifiable units, and cumulative over time.

His dad said typical dad things, like *Kids your age don't even know what real work is* and *Money doesn't grow on trees* and *It's time you learned the value of a dollar.* But what his old man didn't seem to understand was that David already knew the value and importance of money. His lucrative cinnamon toothpick business could transform a two-dollar investment into twenty bucks in his pocket. He could buy a pack of bubble gum at Walgreen's for a quarter and sell individual pieces at school for the same amount. The way to make money was to offer a product people couldn't get anywhere else, and then charge them a little extra than what you paid for it. It wasn't rocket science. But until someone else figured it out, David was a virtual monopoly when it came to selling snacks in school, and to him the income seemed limitless.

But as proud as he was of his business acumen, David knew these schemes would have enraged his father. They exemplified the worst of all sins: unwarranted income. Faggot musicians and athletes from the ghetto and trust fund babies were among the great criminals of the world. They flew around in private jets and married gorgeous models and skied in Aspen without having done an honest day's work in their lives, and his father hated all of them.

So to demonstrate he was capable of hard labor, that he truly understood its value, David asked for a summer job at Lone Star Barbecue, his father's restaurant. He was still too young to legally work, but volunteered to do any job his father wanted.

This was how David found himself in the pit room clutching a four-foot wooden pole with a tool on the end of it that looked like a giant ice scraper. The head cook, who called himself "The Turk" (but whose real name was apparently Tommy Guinn), was explaining how to clean the barbecue pits. The Turk was a little less than six feet tall, sported a basketball of a gut, and could have been twenty-five or forty-five. His stringy hair was dishwater gray and he was missing at least a third of his teeth.

"Okay, so before you can scrape the grease out of the pit, you gotta loosen it. The way you do that is set the pit on fire."

"Set it on fire?"

"Right. Let me show you."

The pit room was technically outdoors, a lean-to built against the restaurant's western wall, a fenced-in area of thirty-by-thirty feet with a sloping roof made of corrugated steel. The barbecue pits themselves were iron cylinders, six feet in diameter and ten feet tall. There were three of them. They may have originally been sections of oil pipeline, The Turk wasn't sure. Carved into each cylinder were three doors, arranged verti- cally. Through the top two you could reach the circular grates, the shelves on which the briskets cooked. You loaded firewood through the bottom door. Briskets expressed thick grease as they cooked, grease that dripped onto the fire and also coated the inside of the pit. This grease was a potent source of fuel, and if you didn't scrape it out once a week, flare-ups would catch the grates on fire. Briskets could burn. Money could be lost.

"So what you do is, is you set a controlled fire. Like this."

All three doors of the pit were open. The Turk stoked the fire and they watched together as long tongues of flame began to climb up the cylinder's inside wall. As the flames lengthened, as they grew taller, they formed a sort of spiral shape. David noted with wonder that it looked like a fire tornado. The Turk closed the bottom door.

"It's going pretty well now, the fire, so we can also close this middle door, too, and just leave the top one open. If you left 'em all open, in a few minutes you'd have fire shooting out of all three."

David looked and saw flames, deeply orange, flickering in shadows near the top of the pit. The whole interior was on fire, and it was unnerv- ing how much it looked like a tornado in there. David himself had not seen the tornado, but that didn't mean he couldn't sense how it had changed Wichita Falls forever. How it had changed something in him.

"Okay, so now you take your straight hoe there, and you use it to hold the door halfway open."

"What do you mean?"

"You want to get it nice and hot in there, so you have to let it burn for a while. If you shut all the doors the fire would suffocate."

David held the top door partly open as The Turk had instructed. He didn't want anyone to suffocate on his account.

"You can *feel* it," he said. "The fire. Pushing on the door."

"Yeah. Almost like it has hands. Like someone is in there, trying to get out."

For an instant David imagined there *was* someone inside trying to get out. Like an innocent kid left for dead, buried alive, suffocating.

The sensation was so strong that he was forced to stop himself from reopening all the doors to let the poor kid out, even though cognitively he knew there could be no one inside the pit.

"Okay, you can go ahead and push the door shut with your . . . yeah, like that. So now we wait a few minutes for the fire to go out, and then you get in and scrub the walls with your straight hoe there. You clean the grates with this wire brush."

"You want me to get in?"

"Well, not completely. But you climb up on this scaffold and lean in and scrape away all the grease you can. Then you shovel it out of the bottom and dump it into those barrels over there. When you think you're done, come inside and let me know. I'll decide if it's good enough."

"You're leaving me by myself?"

"You said you were fine. It's too hot to stand out here and watch."

The Turk disappeared into the restaurant, and David looked warily at the pit. He could not understand why his dad was obsessed with this kind of work when there were so many easier ways to make money. It was insane. His dad was insane. And yet David's desire to please the man was no less for knowing this. He put on a pair of black work gloves, grasped the handle of the top door, and went to work.

Fifteen minutes later, he was black. In the damp strands of his hair. In the potential space under his fingernails. His blue T-shirt and jeans were blue no longer. His shoes . . . Jesus Christ, they were ruined.

The pit was an oven. Sweat poured out of him as he scraped its insides, as black grease disintegrated like mica shavings and stuck to his arms, his face, to every square inch of his body. The gunk was in his eyelashes, and he couldn't wipe it away. It got into his mouth, onto his tongue. It was in his ears.

David leaned against the scaffold and wiped his black arm on his black forehead. But he didn't rest long, because he didn't want to leave any doubt about his performance. He scraped and scraped and scraped some more. Thought about Alicia Ulbrecht for no particular reason. She had been in his Texas History class last semester, and he'd developed a crush on her after they talked a few times. But he'd never summoned the nerve to ask for her phone number, and now it turned out Jonathan was in love with her.

The Turk returned sometime later. David didn't know if it was minutes or hours.

"Damn, Dave. You about done?"

"Almost. Just trying to be thorough."

"Let me take a look."

David stepped down from the scaffold and for a moment thought he heard an approaching train. He imagined there was a kid on that train, the one who had almost burned up inside the pit because they left him there to die.

"You okay, man?"

David looked up. The Turk was staring at him with his head cocked, like a curious dog might.

"I'm fine."

"Did you get too hot?"

"I've been inside a barbecue pit. Who wouldn't get too hot?"

"You sure you're okay? Maybe we should go inside and let you cool off."

"I'm fine," David said. "Just don't say anything to my dad, all right? I don't want him thinking I'm some kind of wimp."

"All right. If you say so."

"So did I do a good job?"

The Turk kept looking at him for another moment and then peered into the pit.

"Looks great, Dave. Did you take any breaks or just work all the way through?"

"All the way through. I didn't want the grease to get cold. You think my dad will like it?"

"He usually doesn't look at stuff like this. He's got the whole restaurant to run."

"Right, right. Well, if he asks, will you tell him it was good?"

"No problem," said The Turk. "You sure you feel okay?"

"I'm great. So what do I do now? What's my next job?"

Six hours later David was on the way home, sitting in the passenger seat of his dad's pickup truck. His shirt was damp, stuck to his abdomen, and the grease on his arms had faded to a ghostly grey. He smelled of stagnant water and body odor and imagined with delight what it would feel like to stand in the shower beneath a curtain of hot water. For a while his dad drove without speaking, without even turning in David's direction, his eyes watching the road but obviously seeing something much farther away.

Outside the window, the dark city passed by.

"Tough day today?" his father finally asked.

"It was all right."

His dad was still staring forward, looking at something that wasn't the road.

"Tired?"

"A little. Cleaning that pit was tough."

"You said you'd do any job I could find."

"I know," David said. "So can I do it again next week?"

"I'm counting on it. I'm down a cook now that Rodney's gone, so dishwashers are having to pull double duty. I can let you work three nights a week if you want. That's sixty bucks a week."

Maybe manual labor wasn't such a bad gig after all. Sixty bucks a week was actual money. The kind of money that made selling snacks at school sort of pointless.

"What's a fourteen-year-old kid like you gonna do with sixty bucks a week?"

"I don't—"

"You're going to save half of it," his father interrupted. "That's what you're going to do. I'm not rich. You aren't getting a free ride to college. You put away half the money you make between now and the time you're eighteen, and I'll match everything you save. Deal?"

David mourned all the potential purchases he had just made with $240 a month. But he couldn't exactly say "no" to his father.

"Deal."

They drove in silence, through the red and white darkness of Wichita Falls, and by the time they made it home David had reached an important conclusion: He hated this town. Probably his father wanted him to take over the restaurant someday, but after this evening there was no chance that would ever happen. David was going to create a different life for himself, figure out how to have fun and see cool places and meet interesting people.

He thought maybe, when he was older, it would be cool to live in California.

15

Adam Altman was sitting on the floor of the living room, in front of the television, trying to beat his high score on Pac-Man. With a redesigned maze, washed-out colors, and blinking ghosts, the Atari version was a poor impersonation of the arcade game, but it was easy to look past these shortcomings because at home he could sit in front of the television and play for hours without having to pump in quarters. By now he had worked out most of a pattern that would allow him to consume maze after maze of pellets without ever being killed by a ghost. Given another hour or two he would likely have the pattern solved, and that meant he could dominate any challenger the next time they were all over at Jonathan's house.

But he didn't have another hour or two to play, because it was almost 8:30 and his dad, Jimmy, would be home any minute. The usual time for his dad to arrive was more like 5:30, but lately he'd been working late. Every night his dad talked at length about oil, how each time the price of it dropped the family lost money. He had no kind words to say about the people who ran OPEC ("those money-hungry sand niggers") and said only slightly less derogatory things about America's own government. Ronald Reagan drew particular ire, a President who, according to his dad, was trying to ruin the oil industry by artificially lowering prices. But this confused Adam, partly because he knew nothing of the family's finances, but mostly because he remembered how happy his dad had been the night President Reagan was elected. There had been cheers and beers and derogatory statements about the "liberal peanut farmer," so it seemed silly that his dad's opinions had changed so dramatically.

But however upset Jimmy Altman was about the suffering oil business, Corrine, Adam's mom, was even angrier. Not about the oil business itself but at her husband's response to it. Every time Jimmy walked in late from work, Corrine was waiting to pounce. She would sit in the kitchen with her black St. James Bible, flipping pages and occasionally underlining passages, and when his dad walked in the front door, his mom would pretend not to notice. Eventually Jimmy would walk into the kitchen, and Corrine would look up at him as if he had interrupted her judicious Bible reading, when in reality she probably hadn't even seen the verses she was pretending to read. Jimmy would crack some kind of joke, hoping to make her smile.

"So how does it end, my love?" he might ask, gesturing at the Bible. "Same as always?"

It made Adam smile to think of the Bible as a book with a beginning and an end, like any old book you might read. The Bible was much more than a story . . . it was a book about the world itself.

His mom wouldn't find this as humorous, however.

"Don't you joke about God's Word, Jim. Especially when you're three hours late. Again."

His dad might open the refrigerator while he composed a reply, delivering it as he cracked open a Miller Lite.

"I believe the Bible says you should honor me as you honor thy Lord, and there's nothing honorable about your tone of voice right now."

At this Corrine would likely shoot him a withering look. "Oh, that's great. Keep making fun. Like that's going to help the situation."

"There's no situation, Corrine."

"And if you're going to quote the Bible, I suggest you consider the seventh commandment."

This would finally capture his dad's full attention. He would shut the refrigerator with such authority that Adam would hear glass bottles crashing against each other . . . in fact one might fall to its death on a lower shelf and shatter into jagged pieces.

"You think I'm cheating on you?"

The pitch of Jimmy's voice might cause Corrine to reconsider, and during that slight pause his dad would surely inject his query again.

"You think I'm *cheating* on you?"

"You never used to stay late before you moved into that office building downtown! I know you must see a lot of foxy women in tight business suits when you're riding the elevator in the morning. Or getting coffee. Or whatever. You never used to work late before!"

"I never worked late because money was rolling in, that's why! You know this! I tell you every night how—"

"That's right! You don't ever come home for lunch anymore, and you stay late, and then when you do come home, you only think and talk about work! When are you going to put your family first again like you used to?"

Here his dad would, predictably, lose his cool.

"I am putting my family first! I'm trying to keep us from going bankrupt! You see all the houses going up for sale, people losing everything, and the reason you get to stay home and read Bible verses all day is because you still have a home to live in! Jesus Christ!"

A gasp here from Adam's mom, also predictable.

"Jimmy Richard Altman! Do *not* take the Lord's name in vain! Our only child is in the next room!"

"Our only child," Jimmy might repeat in a mocking voice. "Our only child. You had to throw that in there, didn't you? Because it's all my fault Christi is gone. It's always my fault. Everything around here is my fault, even though I'm the only one doing anything to save us from ruin."

"Money is not the only important thing in a marriage!"

"It's the only thing keeping you off the street, Corrine! You and our *only* child."

"And anyway, you're exaggerating. We've made so much money the past few years there's no way we're going broke. You're just using that as an excuse because you don't want to come home. You hate your life."

Adam would not be able to watch this confrontation take place, because instinct told him not to venture anywhere near an open battlefield (alternatively known in this case as the kitchen). But by now he was fairly sure his dad would be standing directly over his seated mother, whose neck would be craning to look up at him, and both she and Adam (and possibly Jimmy himself) would wonder if this was the time he would finally lose his cool and hit her.

"And what if I do hate my life? Don't you think this might be part of the reason why? You never lay off, Corrine. You never have a nice thing to say. Ever."

"That's a lie," his mother might say. "I support you the way a wife should. The way the Lord expects me to. And—"

Here his mother might pause for a short interval and then say the next unsurprising thing.

"No wonder you're so touchy tonight. You've been drinking. I can smell it on you."

"I *am* drinking, Corrine. Right this second. Or do you not see this beer in my hand?"

"You think your little tricks can fool me? It's coming out of your pores, Jim. You smell like whiskey."

Silence would ensue while his dad considered a response.

"If I'm going to stay at the office this late I deserve a glass of whiskey."

"How many glasses was it? Three? Five?"

"Get off my case, Corrine. I'm warning you."

"You mean you're threatening me. Again. God expects more from us, Jim. We sinned in His eyes and He has punished us. If we don't honor Him, He will punish us again."

"How can He punish us worse than taking Christi?" Jimmy would likely say. His voice would lose some of its intensity and all of its volume. "It's unthinkable God would take more from us. I don't want to believe in a God who would do that. I won't."

Corrine might respond with a much softer tone.

"Maybe you're having a crisis of faith. Pastor Phelps warned us this might happen. Maybe you don't want to come home because it reminds you too much of Christi and our failure to protect her from evil."

"No," his father would surely answer. "It's been four years. She's been dead four years. She was taken from us for some reason neither of us understand—"

"I understand perfectly. We didn't protect our son from impurity."

She might whisper the next part, but not low enough for Adam to miss it, because by then curiosity would have overcome fear and he would be standing near the entrance to the kitchen.

"He sinned against the Lord and even though we threw ourselves at God's mercy and changed our ways and became right with Him, there was still punishment. There was a lesson to learn. We gave our life to

His only Son, but then we faltered. We did not live righteously, and He served judgment upon us."

"Corrine."

"Come sit with me, Jim. We must pray. You shouldn't feel the need to work late and drink whiskey when you could be at home playing with your son, sharing an evening with your wife. We must set a good example for Adam. We're his only chance at a good life. At a righteous life. We both know he has a weakness for lewd impulses. We can't allow him to fall victim to the dark path."

At this point in the argument, Adam, as he always did, would shiver at the mention of this unnamed sin he was said to have committed. But he could not remember exactly what he was said to have done. He could only picture a girl in her nightgown, the bellowing voice of his dad and the shrieking cries of his mom.

"Fine," his father might say. "I'll pray with you if we can move past this and maybe have some dinner. I'm starving."

"Adam and I have already eaten. There's a plate for you in the oven. Put it in the microwave and then come join me at the table."

Along with the sounds of reheating his meal, Adam would probably hear the crack of another beer being opened. Or maybe two cracks depending on how quickly his mom's anger cooled.

Then his dad would sit next to her at the table, and soon afterward Adam would hear the murmurs of their prayers. He would go back to his game of Pac-Man and hopefully solve the pattern before his 9:00 bedtime.

Except it was already 8:45 and his dad was nowhere to be—

Then he heard it, for real this time. The sound of a car pulling into the front circular driveway. A few moments later the door burst open, and there was his dad. Adam couldn't help but smile.

"Hi, buddy. Where's your mom?"

"In the kitchen, I think."

His father briefly tousled his hair with one hand as he walked by, headed for the kitchen. He left a sour smell in his wake, the way he always did when he drank alcohol. Adam looked at him and then back at the television. He started a new game and began the process of mindlessly consuming pellets while he waited for the last bit of the pattern to emerge. His father's voice was loud in the quiet house, full of good humor.

"So how does it end, my love? Same as always?"

16

One of Alicia Ulbrecht's favorite things in the whole world was to look at the stars with her dad, partly because she liked to learn new things about the world, but mainly because she loved listening to his voice, so patient and intelligent and instructive. Its mellifluous sound induced literal tingles on her head and neck and back, especially late at night when he often spoke in a quiet voice, barely more than a whisper. Tonight they were out to see planets like Jupiter and Saturn and Neptune, but Andromeda wouldn't rise till much later, and her dad said they might not make it home until like four o'clock in the morning.

Typically it thrilled Alicia to know her friends were home asleep while she was out with her dad, looking through his big telescope and sometimes binoculars at the dark sky. On these nights she felt almost grown up. But tonight her heart wasn't into it and it didn't take long for her dad to recognize this.

"Something on your mind, Pumpkin?"

"Yeah," she said. "But I don't know how to tell you about it."

"Are you okay? Is it an emergency?"

"No, nothing like that. It's just . . . you know I spent the night with Brandi on Saturday, right?"

"The little girl who wears too much makeup."

"I know she's not your favorite, but she's really fun and a lot more outgoing than I am."

"So what happened?"

"It was pretty fun overall. We made these giant chocolate chip pancakes and watched MTV until, like, midnight. But when we went to bed, I couldn't sleep. It was hot and Brandi was right next to me and I was pretty uncomfortable."

"It's hard to sleep in a place that's not your own bed," her dad pointed out.

"So, anyway, I got up to use the bathroom and I heard her parents talking. Their room was down the hall. They were talking about me. And you."

"Oh, yeah? What did they say?"

"That they felt sorry for me because my dad was more interested in chasing storms like a crazy person instead of taking care of his daughter."

"Excuse me?"

"And they think it's terrible we don't go to church. Like it's not fair to me."

"Not fair, huh?"

"They invited me to service the next morning. I figured it would be interesting to see what it was like, so I went. I hope you're not mad at me."

"Why would I be mad?"

"'Cause we don't go. You and Mom probably don't like it or think it's stupid."

"I don't think it's stupid, Alicia. Some people go to church and some don't."

"It seems like most people do."

"Around here that may be true," her dad agreed. "Do you feel left out because we don't go?"

"I guess. It makes me different than everyone else and I think sometimes people look at me funny. A lot of my friends know you almost died in the tornado, and I guess most of them think you're kind of, um, weird."

As soon as the words were out of her mouth, Alicia wished she could have them back. She hadn't meant to imply that *she* found him weird. He was anything but weird to her. She loved him desperately.

"When you get older, Pumpkin, you're probably going to enjoy being different than other people. But I remember being in junior high, and that's not the best time to stand out in a crowd. I'm sorry for that."

"So how come you and Mom don't believe in God when most people do?"

Her dad smiled at this. "That's not the easiest question to answer. It's not that your mom and I don't believe in God. There could be a god, sure. We just don't believe much of what the Bible has to say. Or any of the religions people made up."

"But how do you know they're made up? Aren't you afraid, if you die, you won't go to Heaven?"

"The thing with the Bible is that we know what people understood about the world at the time it was written. And they didn't know very much, Pumpkin. People will tell you God helped write the Bible, but if He did, you would think He would have known how old the universe is, and how the Earth is not the center of it, and how the night sky isn't some black curtain where He painted pretty white dots."

Alicia had never imagined her dad would know so much about the Bible. He had never mentioned the book to her before. Like ever.

"Okay," she said, "but if the Bible isn't real, if God isn't real, then what happens when we die? Doesn't that make you afraid?"

"What makes me afraid is the idea of leaving you and your mom alone. I'm extremely careful now when I chase storms. That day in 1979 I was very stupid. I felt guilty for a long time about that, and I'm sure Brandi's parents think I'm a big dummy for doing what I do. But we chasers don't follow storms just for the adrenaline rush. When I see tornadoes, I call them into local towns or TV stations so people know to take shelter. Tornado chasing and spotting helps keep people safe."

She was feeling better now, and maybe a little angry at Brandi's parents for talking about her dad like he was some kind of jerky idiot. But questions remained.

"I just don't understand where everything came from, then. It seems like someone had to have made it."

"Yeah, whoever made it, where did he come from?"

"Maybe God just *is*," she suggested.

"Maybe so. But the difference between Brandi's parents and me is I'm willing to accept that as a possibility. Whereas most religious people are very certain about the things they believe. And that can be dangerous, because if you're very certain about something, you don't leave open the chance to learn new ideas. Do you still believe in Santa Claus?"

"Of course not!"

"Well, people used to believe the Sun revolved around the Earth. When Galileo tried to tell them differently, the Church found him guilty of contradicting the Bible. And he discovered many amazing things, including the moons of Jupiter we saw a few minutes ago. Imagine being so excited to discover new stuff and then being told you were wrong by people who didn't know what they were talking about."

"That would suck."

"Yes," her father said, laughing. "It would suck. You know what else would suck?"

"What?"

"Some people think the whole world might not even be real. Like it might be some kind of game and we are just characters in the game."

"What? How would that even work?"

"Well, if you were a player in a video game, everything inside the game would look like the whole world to you. Maybe it's like that for us, too, but way bigger and more complex."

"That sounds impossible."

"Maybe it is. But if you were in the game, and everything looked real to you, how would you know? Maybe on the outside of this world, the actual world looks completely different. Maybe the sky is purple and space is white and all the stars are black."

"You've got to be kidding," Alicia said, and rolled her eyes.

"I'm not! You should ask that friend of yours, the one who writes stories, if he ever heard of Philip K. Dick. He writes stories about fake worlds and I bet your friend would be impressed that you know of him."

Her dad was talking about Jonathan, a boy she had spoken to a few weeks before school let out for the summer. Alicia had never met someone who enjoyed reading as much as her, let alone a boy who actually wrote his own stories. So a few days later, when their P. E. class had drawn names to select partners for the year-end assembly project, and she had selected from the red wicker basket a piece of paper on which the words Jonathan Crane were scrawled, Alicia saw the coincidence as a clear message from the universe.

"I would, but now that school is over I've got no way to talk to him."

"Does he have your phone number?"

"He asked me for it before the school year ended, but he hasn't called."

"I bet you he's probably nervous," her dad said. "For a boy his age, calling a girl on the phone can feel like the scariest thing in the world."

"Why is that?"

"Because you don't know if she really wants to talk to you."

"Then why in the heck would I give him my phone number?"

"Sometimes a thing that seems really obvious to one person isn't very obvious to the next. Especially when your self-confidence is shaky."

"Oh."

"Give him time," her dad said. "I bet he'll come around."

17

The phone was in the kitchen, mounted to the wall in the space between the cabinets and the countertop. It was almond-colored, and you could dial numbers on the handset, and the cord was a mile long. But it still wasn't long enough. If Jonathan called Alicia from here, he would never be able to have a conversation without his mother knowing about it. Her room was directly around the corner from the kitchen. He could hear the rhythmic ticking of her rocking chair as she sat there doing nothing.

Jonathan missed his father in many ways. He missed running through the yard, catching footballs. He missed proudly showing off his straight A's report card every six weeks. He missed playing chess with him, missed watching Roger Staubach and the rest of the Dallas Cowboys on television, missed lying in bed while his dad told him a new story every night. He missed him for all these reasons, the right reasons, the stuff that sometimes still made him cry when he was lying in bed, trying to fall asleep. But he also missed his dad because now the checks and balances of the Crane democracy were gone. In their place, an unmerciful dictator had seized control of the household.

His mother had turned into a predator since the tornado. She sat in her rocking chair all morning, all afternoon, coiling her legs, ready to pounce the moment Jonathan walked in the door from school. And she would yell at him about anything. One day she might think he was home late from school and another day she would decide he was home too early . . . even though the bus dropped him off at pretty much the same time every day. If he went to get a drink of water she would yell at him for being too loud and if she didn't see him for a few hours she would yell at him for being too quiet. She would call his name from across the house, like a pterodactyl, and whenever she did this his arms broke out in gooseflesh.

Which is why he loved school, loved those gorgeous hours of freedom. It was a miracle when female teachers complimented him on his well-written papers and studious extra credit. He also loved bedtime, when he was finally allowed to close the door against his mother and dreamily recharge his batteries before the next day's battles. And, despite the ignorance and vulgarity and beer drinking, he actually grew to appreciate Kenny Steele.

This wasn't easy to admit, since there was no way the man could ever replace Jonathan's father. And yet after the storm, before the government trailers arrived, Kenny had been the only one to offer them shelter. Sure, the old house smelled funny, and the two boys were forced to sleep in the same bed together, and Jonathan knew his father was never coming back. But having a real place to stay, not being stuck in some weird trailer, was part of the reason Jonathan managed to survive the pain of his father's death. Nine months later they moved into the new house in Tanglewood, which was huge and smelled of new wood and fresh paint, and his mother always left him alone when Kenny came to visit.

At the moment Jonathan had stretched the phone cord as far away from her room as he could manage. Kenny and Bobby weren't here tonight. Presently Jonathan was weighing the chances of his mother overhearing this phone conversation against the likelihood of Alicia Ulbrecht saying "yes" through the telephone handset, a calculation that strained the limits of his seventh-grade math skills. Even so, the fear of his mother was leading Alicia's agreement by a two-to-one margin.

So he just sat there and stared at the phone.

And stared.

And stared some more.

He couldn't bring himself to pick up the phone because the question he wanted to ask was emotionally significant but logistically absurd.

Will you go with me?

The natural response to such a question was to ask, *Go where?* But the question wasn't meant literally. It was the invitation to a relationship, like the junior high version of asking someone to marry you.

Jonathan imagined how such a phone call might transpire. He could call and ask how Alicia's summer was going, like had she read any good books or had she gone to see the movie *War Games* yet? He could admit that he'd finally taken her advice and tried his first Stephen King novel, *The Dead Zone*, and it was the best book he'd ever read in his life. He could talk about anything, for hours he could, but he could not picture himself believably uttering the phrase, *Hey Alicia, will you go with me?*

A couple of minutes went by and finally he let go of the plastic button on the handset. Then pressed it down again. Stared at it for a while. Imagined the musical sound of Alicia's voice through the little speaker, the sunny pitch of her vowels, her crisp consonants, her bright laughter.

Jonathan allowed himself to be distracted by other thoughts, like the new story he wanted to write about *Pitfall*. *Pitfall* was a video game where this dude ran from screen to screen trying to find bags of gold and silver, and the other night Jonathan had wondered how the little pixel guy would feel if he one day realized he was living inside the television. Imagine if he would, just once, stop paying attention to things inside the game and instead look at the screen. Would he see a giant kid looking back at him? Would he care?

He let go of the hook button again. Tried to stretch the cord a little farther, see if he could make it into the hallway. The handset buttons glowed green. He could hear the dial tone. He waited too long to enter a number, and the phone buzzed angrily at him.

Now he tapped the hook button once more and this time dialed. Alicia's number had been committed to memory long ago. 5-5-5-1-2-0—

Jonathan punched down the hook button and this time held it firmly. He couldn't call her. Even if he could fool himself into asking the absurd question, there was a nonzero chance she would say no. He could take the math that far at least.

But he couldn't stand here forever, because his mother would eventually march around the corner and see him talking to no one. Her bulldog curiosity would compel her to attack him with questions until she worked out what he was doing, and then she would ridicule the idea that a girl might actually like him, might want to hold his hand or (God forbid) kiss him. If that happened Jonathan would be crushed for life.

The dial tone again. 5-5-5-1-2-0 . . .

Eight. He couldn't press the number eight.

The hook button beneath his thumb again.

The dial tone again.

He tried to fortify his confidence by recalling Todd's assertion that being turned down was like a badge of honor. And, you know, there was something strange about that kid. He was really smart when, after being asleep for four years, he should have been sort of stupid. And—

And he was stalling. At this rate he would never get Alicia on the phone. Surely he would rather be turned down instead of never asking at all?

He hastily punched in the numbers again. 5-5-5-1-2-0 . . . 8.

It was ringing. The phone was ringing.

Once.

Twice.

"Hello?"

It was a woman. Not Alicia. Jonathan had never considered someone else might pick up the phone. What a moron! He had no strategy for this!

"Hello?" she said again.

"Um . . . is Alicia there?"

"No, I'm sorry. May I take a message?"

"I . . . uh . . . will she be back soon?"

"She's out with her father. I think they'll be pretty late. Can I get your name and ask her to call you back tomorrow?"

Tomorrow? Jonathan wanted to scream. I have the nerve now! RIGHT NOW!

"Uh . . . okay, I'm Jonathan. I know Alicia from school? Can you tell her I called?"

"No problem," the woman said.

"Okay, thanks."

"Hey, Jonathan?"

"Yes, ma'am?"

"Does she have your number?"

"Oh. Good point. I don't think so." He recited his phone number. The woman thanked him and said goodbye.

Jonathan hung up the phone. Made a beeline for his bedroom. Closed the door, turned on his radio, and crawled into bed, giddy with the knowledge that Alicia would soon know he had called, that she would likely call him back the next day . . . and of course knowing *that* made him fear for his life. But even the fear was a good thing, really. It was a fear borne from action, from progress, from having stepped into a place from which there was no looking back. He fell into sleep, and dreamed the two of them were on a couch, sitting close together, so close he could smell her, so close he could feel her, and then they leaned together and kissed. In the dream Alicia was an adult but he recognized her anyway. She was so kind and sweet, she held his hand and pressed her warm lips to his mouth, then pressed them to his ear, her voice lighter than air, whispering softly, how he was a handsome young man, how he was such a good writer, whispering over and over and over that she loved him.

18

Adam didn't care very much for Todd.

In the span of a week, the guy had wormed his way into their group, first with an endorsement from Bobby and Jonathan, and later winning over David with his wry observations and witty sense of humor. But Adam disliked showoffs. He deplored people who wouldn't conform to social norms. When you were the new person in a group, you were obligated to take a backseat during conversation and debate, you were supposed to sit back and watch the group dynamic and keep your stupid mouth shut.

Then there was the notion of Todd's medical condition. You could call it catatonic schizophrenia or walking coma or whatever you felt like, but in the end the idea boiled down to the kid having sleepwalked for four years. He couldn't believe anyone would take the idea seriously, especially Jonathan and David, who were skeptical about everything. Instead, the two of them were fascinated with Todd, and only Bobby seemed unconvinced about the coma. Adam didn't relish the idea of solidarity with Bobby. It was difficult enough to stay right with Jesus without inviting a connection to the biggest sinner in the entire group.

Presently the five of them were at Jonathan's house, hanging out in the game room on a Saturday afternoon. Todd was on the sofa attempting to reproduce a vaguely familiar melody on his Casio keyboard. Bobby was in front of the television trying to beat his high score on Kaboom!, swearing at the Atari every time he missed one of the falling bombs. Jonathan and David were at the card table hoping to organize a Dungeons and Dragons adventure, rolling dice to build new characters for everyone, and they were cheating as usual.

"What's this guy's name again?" David said. He tossed the six-sided die three times and recorded the total. "Glorfindel Cremlock? He's rolled a six for strength—"

"He can't have a six," Jonathan shot back.

David kept rolling the die and recorded another total.

"Intelligence is nine. Looking like another dumb thief."

"David, come on. I need a Magic-User."

"Wisdom is seven."

"David!"

"All right, all right. So what do you want him to have?"

"We used to make eleven the minimum for any character trait."

"Isn't that cheating?" Todd asked, looking up from his keyboard.

Adam rolled his eyes. As much as he despised Dungeons & Dragons (all the black magic seemed too much like Satan's work) he hated even more that Todd had just stuck his nose in the middle of it.

"It's not cheating," Jonathan explained. "We just tilt the tables in our favor a little bit. Because otherwise it's not that fun."

"But it isn't real if all your characters are Superman," Todd countered, and then set the keyboard aside to address the room. "Actually, none of this is real. Bobby's pretending to catch bombs on the Atari, and you guys are pretending to be warriors in a fantasy world, and I'm here writing songs on an artificial piano. Do you realize these are all counterfeit versions of real things? Shouldn't we be outside doing something of our own creation?"

"We do real stuff," Bobby said. "We play football, we swim. Sometimes we hike up the river and camp."

"But since I've been hanging out with you guys, we mostly sit in this game room. One of these days we're all going to wish we'd had more fun as kids."

Adam couldn't believe Todd had the nerve to call them out like this. He should have been grateful just to *be* here. Who cared if he fought Bobby to a draw?

"Everything is different when you grow up," Todd explained. "It doesn't matter if you sell used cars or become a teacher or if you turn out to be a millionaire and move to California. This is the only time in our lives we'll be smart enough to do cool stuff but not have any responsibilities."

"That's, like, really profound and all," David said, "but it's too hot to play football right now. It's 110 or something out there."

"Too hot? We're thirteen years old."

"Since you're such the go-getter," asked Bobby, "what do you suggest we do?"

"I don't know. But there must be something we can do for excitement."

"You mean something we can do to get in trouble," Adam said. Even if the world of Dungeons & Dragons was rife with black magic, at least it wasn't real.

"The point would be to stay *out* of trouble," Todd said. "Do something that *could* get us in trouble, but not. Think of a roller coaster—it *feels* like you're going to die, but you don't."

Adam didn't say anything else. He'd always been the outcast in this group, the friend least likely to be invited for a sleepover or a pool party or to play football. Since none of them ever talked about Jesus, and since they all knew Adam's parents were devoutly religious, he assumed the other guys resented him for his Christianity. For his occupying of the moral high ground in every situation. But he wondered how they might feel about him if they knew the secret darkness that lay within his heart, if they knew he was the committer of ancient sins. Had any of them ever looked down at their baby sister and seen her head caved in, seen a blood-soaked brick where her face was supposed to be? What would they think of Adam if they knew of his immense guilt, of the desire he sometimes felt to inflict pain—on himself, on anyone—for having failed his baby sister?

"I know something we could do," Jonathan said.

"Oh, yeah?" Todd replied. "Let's hear it."

"You know that little dead end street after you turn right on Ridgemont, when you're heading toward Turtle Creek?"

"Driftwood," David said.

"Right. Well, there's this house there, it was built a while back and no one ever moved in."

"Yeah," David said. "My dad said the couple got divorced while the house was still being built."

"Well," Jonathan said, "I was at the fort a few days ago, looking for a different trail out of the woods, and I came out near the backyard of that house. And, I don't know, I just went up to the house for some reason and started checking the windows."

"Checking them?" Adam asked.

"Yeah. Bobby's dad told me that construction workers will sometimes leave a window unlocked in case they forget their keys. So I wanted to see if I could get inside the house."

"You broke in?" Adam asked.

"No, the first window I tried was unlocked. I just opened it and went in."

"Is there electricity?" Bobby asked. "Is the water on?"

"I think so."

"Well, let's go!"

"Why?" Adam asked.

"Why not? It's better than sitting around here."

19

Ten minutes later the five of them were standing in an empty den, looking around with a sort of awe. They'd all been inside houses that were *being* built—Adam particularly enjoyed the earliest stages, when the projects were still just flat concrete slabs—but until now only Jonathan had stepped foot inside an empty house that was completely finished.

"It feels like we're trespassing," Bobby said.

"That's because we *are*," Adam pointed out.

But no one seemed to care. At David's suggestion, they had brought along a cassette player for music, some Cokes in a small ice chest, and the D&D gear in case they got bored. Todd carried his keyboard as well.

"There's power," Bobby said. He flipped a light switch, and a chandelier flickered on in the formal dining room. "See?"

"Yeah," David said. "You can tell the A/C has been running because otherwise it would be an oven in here."

"I bet we can make it even cooler," Jonathan said. He put down the cassette player and walked down a short hall, where a thermostat was mounted to the wall. "What would you guys like? Seventy-five degrees? Seventy?"

"Turn it down to sixty," Bobby said. "Make it nice and cold."

"Electricity costs money," Adam said. "They have the thermostat turned up for a reason."

"Fuck 'em. They shouldn't leave their house unlocked."

There were three bedrooms and a study. The walls were white, except for one in the den that was paneled with artificial wood laminate. There were two bathrooms. Linoleum on the kitchen floor, and a bar between the kitchen and den.

"This is great," David said. "This could be our clubhouse when it's too hot to hang out in the fort."

Todd had taken his position against a wall in the den and switched on his Casio. "What do you guys do in the fort?"

"We meet there," Jonathan said. He pushed some buttons on the cassette player, but no music came out. Adam wondered what he was doing. Recording them, maybe?

"What do you meet about?"

"Well, if we're going to have a vote, or—"

"We don't do anything with the club," Bobby interrupted. "David had already built the fort, so we just called ourselves The Dragons and made it our headquarters."

"We keep our secret stuff there," David pointed out. "We've got some porno magazines and a couple of packs of cigarettes."

"And three beers," Bobby said. "I got 'em out of my dad's cooler last week, when his friends came over to watch the Rangers."

"See there," Todd said. "I knew you guys had a mean streak in you. Jonathan, you should totally bring Alicia here and make out with her."

"I would if I were you," David said. "That girl is so hot."

"I have to ask her to go with me first."

"You better," David suggested. "If you don't, someone else will."

Jonathan shook his head but didn't say anything.

"Why do you keep porn magazines in the fort?" Todd asked. "Why don't you take them home where you can make use of them?"

No one volunteered an answer for that.

"Come on. Surely the four of you don't just huddle around those magazines and talk about how big the tits are."

Everyone remained silent.

"It's beat-off material," Todd continued. "That's what they make it for."

Adam had known from the moment he laid eyes on Todd that the kid was trouble. He wanted to say something to that effect—or simply leave—but again he was reminded of being the outcast, the one who mattered least. Adam knew his relationship with Jesus was far more important than being friends with these boys. He knew this and still he couldn't let go of his pressing desire to belong. It seemed like the more Todd wormed his way into the group, the further Adam was pushed to the side. He couldn't stand it.

"I don't do that," Bobby mumbled.

"Me, either," Adam agreed.

"Yeah and both you guys are full of shit."

"I am not," Adam said.

Bobby would neither confirm nor deny.

"I beat off every day," Todd said. "At least a couple of times. Sometimes when I wake up, and always when I go to bed. I only wish I had nudie magazines to look at."

"I do it, too," Jonathan abruptly said.

"Yeah," David added. "Me, too."

"You don't have to be ashamed about it. It's fun. Every kid our age does it. At least those who know about it."

"All right," Bobby grunted. "I do it, too." He looked around, daring anyone to laugh at him. "Fuck, I never thought I'd admit that."

Todd looked at Adam. "What about you?"

"I already told you. Not me."

"So what do you do when you look at the magazines?" Todd asked him. "Just read the articles?"

"I really don't like looking at them, to be honest."

"That's a lie," said Bobby.

David shot a look at him. "Bobby, don't—"

"What?" Adam asked. But he was afraid he already knew.

"He's seen you at the fort by yourself," Bobby said, thumbing at David.

"So what if I—"

"More than once."

Adam stood up. He could feel the blood in his face, knew his cheeks were beet red. They really did hate him. All of them.

"Screw you guys. I'm going home."

"Sit down, Cartman," Todd said.

"What?"

Todd stood up and intercepted him. "Come on, man. It's not a big deal to admit it, all right? You don't have to be embarrassed."

"That's because I don't *do* it!"

"Everyone else admitted it. It's no biggie."

For just a moment, a brief and fleeting moment, Adam considered telling the truth. Yes, he'd gone to the fort many times to look at the magazines—it was fascinating to see the women up close with their legs wide open—but something told him this whole conversation wasn't what it seemed. Why was Jonathan recording them? Were they hoping to get him on tape so they could blackmail him?

"I don't know what you want me to say. I couldn't pray with a clean conscience if I did that."

He knew this was probably the end for him. With everyone on one side of the truth and him on the other, Adam didn't see how he could continue to be part of the club. He wondered what he would do now. Where would he find new friends? There were no other boys in Tanglewood his age. He would be all alone.

But then Todd smiled and put his hand on Adam's shoulder.

"All right, man. I didn't realize it was a religious thing. That's cool."

Adam felt like snapping Todd's arm in half. He could maybe use the broken pieces to gouge out his eyes. He smiled.

Finally Todd turned away and sat back down against the wall. Adam glanced around to see if anyone was smirking at him, judging him, but no one seemed to care. He might have relaxed, except he was already imagining the prayer of apology he would offer to Jesus tonight. Sometimes he could be such a hateful and imperfect boy.

"Who wants a Coke?" David asked. His question seemed to break the tension, and suddenly every one of them was thirsty.

While David went into the ice chest to grab sodas, Todd sat back down and resumed tinkering with his keyboard.

"You're pretty good with that thing," Jonathan said, gesturing at the Casio. "You know how to play any real songs?"

Todd hit a couple of the buttons above the piano keys and then tapped out a few notes. Adam realized it was the chorus to "Down Under."

"Dude," Bobby said. "That's pretty good. What else do you know?"

Now he switched the instrument again and played the opening bass line to "Billie Jean."

"I can play the other part, too," Todd said, switching the instrument and keying the string chords that came next. "But it's difficult to play them at the same time. I wish I had a four-track recorder. With that and a drum machine, I could record real songs."

"How do you know how to do that?" David asked. "Did you take piano lessons or something?"

Todd shook his head. "My Grandpa showed me some stuff, chords and whatever. But basically I just started messing with it after I woke up. My parents noticed, when I was asleep, that I seemed to respond to music more than anything else. Especially MTV. Apparently I would sit for hours watching and listening, and my mom said sometimes I would hum or sing along with the music."

"Sing?" Jonathan asked, sounding skeptical.

"She said it was like whispering. And kind of robotic, like someone sounds when they're talking in their sleep."

"That's creepy," Bobby said. "It's like you were possessed or something."

Jonathan still looked skeptical.

"Anyway, my parents got me this keyboard as a gift when I woke up. They thought it might help me, you know, rehab or whatever. The doctor said I needed to exercise my brain, and that music would be a great way to do that. I figured out pretty quickly I could record songs off the radio and learn to play along with them. It doesn't take that long. I figure them out pretty fast."

"Have you tried writing songs of your own?" Jonathan asked.

"Well . . . " Todd answered, and then trailed off.

"Hey," Bobby said. "Don't tell me you're embarrassed, Mister Badass."

"Let's hear it," Adam agreed. He couldn't imagine Todd being uncomfortable about anything, but he was interested to see it.

"All right," Todd said. "I've got two. The first one doesn't have many words, though. It's called 'In the Name of Love.'"

He selected an instrument and then looked up at them. "I don't know how to sing, so don't laugh, all right?"

No one said anything, thereby reserving the right to laugh at whatever they wanted.

"It's only a chorus."

"Just play it," Bobby said.

So he did. It was a six note melody, followed by the lyric "in the name of love." Then the same six notes and the same lyric. Then the same six notes a third time, except the lyrics changed to "I can't get enough." It was repetitive, but Adam liked the melody. It had a familiar quality to it, almost as if he'd heard it somewhere before.

"That's all right," Bobby said.

"Yeah," David said. "Not bad."

"But maybe it could use some other lyrics," Jonathan suggested.

"It's just the chorus," Todd explained. "And I'm trying to think of some lyrics to sing over that melody."

"What else do you have?" Adam asked.

"Well, I came up with this other song last week. It's about a dream I had a lot when I was catatonic. About this girl, like the hottest girl you've ever seen. I think she lived on the beach in California, or at least I wished she did. Every time I dreamed about her, she was walking down the sidewalk of her house, toward me, wearing a light-blue half shirt and pink shorts. She had a perfect tan and her bellybutton was just, like, you couldn't not look at it. She always had sunglasses on but they were pushed back on her head, and she wore those—what do you call them?—jelly shoes. Pink jelly shoes. They made her seem so feminine."

Here was something that interested Adam, this description, because he had seen girls like her, had (God help him) lusted after them. She was the kind of girl any guy might dream about. Todd had drawn their full attention now.

"So this song is about her?" David finally asked.

"I wrote it for her."

"Play it," Adam urged him.

Todd tinkered with the buttons on his keyboard again. "All right," he said. "Here goes."

This time he began playing a slow melody with his left hand, and then accompanied it with a faster one with his right. There was an intro, and then Todd began to sing:

Nobody on the road
Nobody on the beach
I feel it in the air
The summer's out of reach
Empty lake, empty streets
The sun goes down alone
I'm driving by your house
Though I know you're not home

But I can see you
Your brown skin shining in the sun
You got your hair combed back and your sunglasses on, baby
And I can tell you my love for you will still be strong
After the boys of summer have gone.

"And then it goes on to the next verse," Todd said. "But I don't have any more than that yet."

Adam couldn't believe it. The song was fantastic. It was just like something you'd hear on the radio.

"Holy shit," Jonathan said. "That was really good."

"It's fucking awesome," Bobby added. "That's what it is. How do you know how to do that?"

Todd smiled and even blushed a little. Adam wondered if maybe the guy was powered by human blood after all.

"I don't know how I do it. The songs just come to me, almost like I've heard them before. For this one I thought of the melody first, like it would play in my head when I dreamed about her. And the way she looked made me think of those words, or some of them at least, and the rest just sort of came to me."

"She must have been a fox," Bobby said. "In your dream, I mean."

"She was. Every time I go to bed at night I hope I see her again."

"What was it like?" David asked him. "Like, for real? I don't know how to say this, but we've all been talking about it since we met you. It seems like you ought to be, I dunno, stupid or maybe immature. You missed four years of your childhood, but instead of being younger you seem way older than us."

Todd didn't answer right away. He looked at David for a very long time, for what felt like forever. Adam watched both of them and wondered if there would be a fight.

"I've thought about the same thing, David. A lot. And I don't know what the answer is, because you're right—it doesn't make any sense. What I can tell you is that I dreamed some pretty weird things when I was asleep."

"Like what?" Jonathan asked.

"Sometimes I saw still pictures instead of movies the way dreams usually are. Sometimes there was nice music, like when I saw the girl. And sometimes the music was scary and loud, not the sort of thing you hear on the radio. Once I dreamed I was in a city in Europe, and in that one I could actually feel the cobblestones under my feet. I could hear the warbling trains. One time I saw a cloud hovering over New York City. I saw cars I didn't recognize, cars with rounded shapes that looked like they were out of some futuristic movie. I saw a burning house. A football stadium. A school. And the more I think about it, the more I remember hearing that song I just sang for you guys, repeating itself, and even now I can recall more lyrics, some other guy's voice, not mine, singing *I saw a Deadhead sticker on a Cadillac, a little voice inside my head said don't look back you can never look back . . .* "

Todd's hands went to his temples, as if he were trying to rub away a headache. He closed his eyes and drew in a deep breath.

"Things went wrong when that tornado hit," Todd said. "It's like it started something in motion, and I swear I can hear it somewhere, the inner workings of a machine that will eventually end the world."

"They were just dreams," David said. "You're a kid. We're all kids. We don't have to worry about stuff like that."

"But we do!" Todd shot back. "You think you've got all this time, but you don't. Maybe it seems great now, because Wichita Falls has been rebuilt, but it's not going to last. The recovery is an illusion. On the surface everything seems great, but underneath it's all getting worse. Things are gonna just keep on getting worse."

"I don't agree," David said. "We have our whole lives ahead of us."

"Maybe you're right. I mean, out of all of us you seem the most like someone who would actually, you know, be successful. You said the other day how people will do anything if you just ask them. You're a natural salesman at school. You could probably turn your dad's business into a chain of barbecue restaurants, but it'll never happen because all he cares about is forcing people to 'work hard.' And by work hard he means suffer. It's like he willingly bets against his own interests."

"My dad's a good man. He built his business from the ground up."

"But it's almost like he doesn't *want* it to be more successful. Like he believes he doesn't deserve it for some reason. And he makes his own son do the worst jobs in the whole restaurant."

"I know what you're saying," David said. "But he's still a good man. He's my dad."

"What about you, Jonathan?" Todd asked. "Are you ever going to call Alicia? Are you going to let your whole life go by while you wonder if she really likes you?"

"Actually I did call, and her mom answered. She said she would pass along my message. But Alicia never called me back."

"How do you know she got the message?"

"I don't think her mother would forget about it."

"But she could have," Todd said. "You're honestly going to give up that easily?"

"I think maybe she just doesn't like me that way."

Todd put aside his keyboard and leaned forward. "Come on, man. You honestly think she wouldn't at least return your phone call? Does she strike you as that kind of person?"

Jonathan shook his head, but Adam didn't think he would call her again. Some guys were afraid of girls, and nothing Todd said could change that.

"You guys are smart dudes," Todd said. "Each one of us is. But if we sit here and do all the same shit every other kid does, we'll grow up to be like everyone else. Is that what you really want? To be nobody, like any old sheep in the herd?

"Or do you want to be different? Do something special? If you want that, the time to start is now. We won't have this summer forever. And if we waste it, we'll grow up and get jobs and we'll look back on this time and wonder what we did with it. Did we do something when we had the chance? Or did we sit around playing video games all day?"

For a moment they all sat there, absorbing what Todd had said.

Then Bobby spoke up. "I like that song of yours. I think you should be in our club. Does anyone disagree?"

Adam knew it was a foregone conclusion. Everyone but him was fascinated with Todd and the things he had just said. It made him think of Matthew 7:15: *Beware of false prophets, which come to you in sheep's clothing, but inwardly they are ravening wolves.* Todd was pretending to tell them how wonderful they were, how they could change the world, but really he was planting the seeds of their downfall. Once he was welcomed into the club, it would only be a matter of time before everything ended poorly.

"I appreciate that," Todd said. "Thanks for having me. I think the five of us can do something really special."

"I agree," David said.

"And you know what else?" Jonathan asked them all.

"What?" Bobby said.

"I think we should rename the club. I think we ought to name our-selves after that song."

And here it was, already starting. Todd was going to change everything.

"Let's call ourselves The Boys of Summer."

A beat of silence passed and Adam hoped someone might disagree.

"I love it," Bobby said. "What does everyone think?"

"I like it, too," said David.

"Works for me," Adam lied, and when he glanced around the room again, he saw Todd was looking right at him. They made eye contact and held it for a second, and then another, and Adam began to feel vulner-able, like Todd could see right through his fake smile and into his dark heart.

20

Later that afternoon, as a strong south wind moved the trees to dance and their leaves to sing, Joe Henreid entered this story doomed from the first word because of a desire to hang out with Bobby Steele and his friends.

He'd seen the boys many times in the woods behind his house, sometimes down by the river, sometimes at the fort that stood just out-side the barbed-wire fence. More than once he'd seen them playacting a live version of Dungeons and Dragons with wooden swords and shields and battle axes, which was surely the coolest thing in the world. But at eleven years old, two grades behind in school, he was invisible to them

Even if Joe could've found the nerve to approach the boys, at the moment it didn't matter because he wasn't allowed to leave his room. He was grounded for having made a "C" in Social Studies two times in a row, and he wouldn't breathe fresh air for another four more weeks. His parents were morons.

Joe's room faced the backyard, and if you looked a little further, the woods. From here he could just make out the rectangular shape of the fort. Bobby and his friends kept the main door locked, but Joe had watched them enough to know that a few of the fence planks on this side of the fort were loose and used as a secret door. You could push your fingers under these boards, pull them up and out, and the nails at the top became hinges. Sort of like opening the door of a DeLorean.

Joe wasn't sure why he was so obsessed with the contents of the fort. It's not like the boys used it all that much, especially during the brutally hot summer. But you didn't lock a room unless you kept something in there you didn't want people to see, which made people (like Joe) only want to see it more. And the strangest thing of all was that Bobby and his friends visited the fort way more often individually than they did as a group.

It sucked being on the outside of things. And since none of the boys would ever dream of allowing him into their stupid club, the only way he would ever learn their secrets was to sneak over there, grounded or not, and have a look for himself. For weeks he had waited patiently for his chance, and today, finally, his dad was playing golf and his mom had left him home alone while she went shopping with one of her friends.

So he put on a pair of Nike tennis shoes and opened his door. He padded down his hallway, crossed through the living room, and slipped out the sliding glass door. Across the green Bermuda of his backyard, over the chain link fence, and into the woods. Once he reached the trees the fort was only thirty or forty yards further.

But standing in front of it, he paused. It was one thing to sit on his bed and *imagine* sneaking into the fort, but actually doing so was something else altogether. So rather than just barge in, he leaned forward and pressed his ear against the wood exterior. Heard nothing. But still, what if he snuck inside and the guys showed up later? He'd be trapped inside and caught like a thief.

In the end Joe's curiosity was stronger than his fear. He dug his fingers into the dirt below the loose fence planks, pulled, and the hidden door worked as expected. He ducked under the open boards and scrambled inside.

What he found was profoundly disappointing: a dark and nearly empty space lit only by ribbons of sunlight that peeked through the gaps between fence planks. There were a couple of wooden swords and a shield propped against the far wall, a tattered magazine called *Rolling Stone* rolled up in one corner, and a square of discarded plywood lying at a casual angle in the middle of the dirt floor. Had he really risked more trouble with his mom, risked discovery by Bobby and his friends, for this? Why did they bother to come here if there was nothing to do?

Hold on. When he looked at the plywood again, he thought maybe its place on the floor looked a little *too* accidental. Carefully, Joe reached down and picked up the wooden square, where he found a hole in the ground underneath. A plastic trash bag was stuffed into the hole. He pulled the bag open and reached inside, and what he pulled out was his answer to the mystery of the fort.

It wasn't the pack of Winston Ultra Lights 100s. It wasn't the can of Silver Creek snuff, or the three cans of Miller Lite. No, the real attraction, Joe felt sure, was the nudie magazines. There were at least ten of them. *Hustler* and *Oui* and *Cheri* and *Penthouse*. A couple of *Playboy*s. Where had they all come from?

A few months ago Joe had seen a magazine like this at a friend's house. The friend, Nigel, had found it in his father's nightstand. Nigel was only ten, and together they flipped through the glossy pages with a sort of disgusted awe . . . at least at first. After a little while, to Joe's surprise, he began to see the women differently. His own private parts seemed more interesting than normal, the way they felt in math class when he got a good look at Shannon Streemer's butt. Before the fifth grade he had never looked twice at a girl's butt, but lately he couldn't stop looking at them.

Joe dropped the trash bag back into the hole and sat down. There were naked women on almost every page of the magazine, and plenty of naked men with them. A lot of the pictures looked like people pretending to do it. Joe wondered briefly if his own mom and dad made those faces and wore strange underwear when they did it, but the idea of his parents doing anything of the sort was flat-out sickening.

He found the cover girl toward the middle of the magazine. In one picture she was standing with her back to the camera, head turned over her shoulder, and Joe couldn't stop staring at her butt. What was so special about two cheeks of skin connected to her legs? He couldn't say. But they made him want to do it with her, if only he knew how to actually do it. The version he learned in health class made no more sense to him than his dad's strange explanation one evening after baseball practice.

At some point Joe became aware that his private parts felt super and excellent and he decided he should take one of these magazines home. He imagined all the time he could pass, grounded to his room, looking at a magazine like this. The rest he began to stuff back into the trash bag, and he was about halfway done when he thought he heard something outside the fort. He froze where he was and listened carefully.

Someone was coming. All at once he could hear voices and footsteps, and to Joe it seemed like all the blood in his body was collecting in his legs and feet. What the heck was he going to do now? How had he let this happen? There was nowhere to go!

"Look," someone said. "That tape is not in the fort. And if it is, it'll be melted, and it will never play right again."

"It might."

"What will it hurt to look?"

"I'm just saying—"

Joe heard fingers scraping on dirt as one of them reached under the loose fence planks. He was distraught. There was still nowhere to go. He looked down and saw the copy of *Oui* in his hand. He dropped it on top of the bag and tried to push the whole works back into the hole, but a rectangle of light opened and fell directly upon him. Blinding him.

"What the—"

"Check this out," someone said. "We got a spy in here."

"Who is that?"

"It's that kid who lives around the corner. Think his name is Joe. Is that right? Your name Joe?"

His eyes were beginning to adjust to the light. He could see the silhouettes of three boys outside. One of them crawled into the fort with him. It was Bobby. David followed.

"He asked if your name is Joe," Bobby said.

"Yeah, it is."

"Well, Joe, what are you doing in our fort?"

Joe opened his mouth and nothing came out. The truth was impossible.

Now Jonathan, Adam, and some other kid scrambled into the fort. Joe vaguely recognized the new kid but couldn't place him. David walked over to the hole in the ground and pointed at the plastic bag. The copy of *Oui* was only partially tucked into it, and the plywood wasn't covering anything.

"He was looking at our porn," David said. "See?"

"How did you know we had porn in here?" Bobby asked him. "Did someone tell you? Have you been spying on us?"

"No, I didn't know. I just—"

"You just what?"

They were going to beat him up. Bobby would throw the first punch, and they would all join in, and he would be bruised and bloody when he left here. His mom would know he had left the house against orders. His dad would ground him for the rest of his life. This was all going to end very badly.

"I didn't know. I just wanted to see what it looked like in here. I just—"

"You just what?" the new kid said.

"I just want to be part of your club," Joe answered. He was dangerously close to tears. "That's all. I see you guys playing all the time and I just want to be part of it."

For a few seconds no one said anything, like the calm before a storm.

Then Bobby told him, "We don't need any new members. And we don't need little kids invading our private space, either. I ought to smack you in the face for sneaking in here."

"How did you get in, anyway?" Jonathan asked.

"The loose fence planks. I can see the fort from my bedroom window."

"You've been spying on us?" Adam asked.

"No, not spying. I've been grounded to my room for eight weeks in a row and all I do is look out the window."

"Eight weeks," David said. "Why?"

"Bad grades."

Bobby was looking at him with narrow eyes and balled-up fists, and Joe kept wondering when he was going to smack him in the face. But then the new kid stepped forward and smiled.

"I don't see what's wrong with having a new member. I mean, five people, is that really a club?"

No one answered.

"But we can't just take you on, Joe. If you want to be part of our club you'll have to earn it."

Bobby looked at the new kid, then exchanged glances with David, as if they were sharing a secret. But Joe didn't mind. As long as he left the fort with his face intact, he could care less about his dignity.

"Okay," he said. "What do you want me to do?"

"Well, we could initiate you, but that's boring. Every club does that. How about this: Instead of *us* doing something to *you*, why don't *you* do something for *us*? Think of something out of the ordinary, something that shows us how much you want to be a member of the club. And if we think it's worthy, maybe we'll let you in."

Joe had no idea what the kid was talking about. Do something for them? Like what? Did it matter as long as they let him go?

"Should I come to you when I figure out what I want to do?"

"No," the new kid said. "Don't ask us. Just do it. Then we'll decide."

"Okay," Joe said. "I guess I better get back home before my mom comes back from shopping. Since I'm still grounded and all."

"I guess you better," Bobby said. "Better run home to mommy."

Joe waited another moment and then started toward the hidden door. Bobby loomed large as he walked past him, and the new kid grinned in a way that made Joe uncomfortable. Again he had the feeling he'd seen the guy somewhere before. But they let him pass, and Jonathan even held the door open for him as he crawled out. Someone laughed as the fence planks dropped shut behind him, and though he wanted to run back to his house, back to his room, Joe forced himself to walk. He knew they were making fun of him. Still, the new kid had made him an offer, and Joe planned to take him up on it. Maybe they weren't serious, but that didn't mean Joe couldn't do something anyway, something big, something that would convince them all he deserved to be part of their club.

21

It was evening, three minutes until eight o'clock. The kitchen phone beckoned, silently urging him to call Alicia again.

Jonathan had been stalling since dinner. Whenever Bobby and his dad stayed at their own house, his mom usually declined to cook an actual meal, and tonight was no exception. Instead she had warmed up two Swanson pot pies, which they shared at the kitchen table in near perfect silence. His mom stared out the window until she was finished eating and badgered him only once.

"What have you been doing in your room all afternoon?"

"Reading," Jonathan said.

"You spend half your life reading. You might try living in the real world sometime, because you aren't going to find a job living in someone else's fantasy like that."

Fantasy. Funny she would call it that, because lately that's what Jonathan's own world had felt like. Sure, everything had been weird since the tornado, with his own dad gone and the introduction of Bobby and Kenny into their lives. But Todd's arrival had only intensified the strangeness.

Some things were weird for obvious reasons, like how your new friend had been on television three times because of his strange medical condition, yet he hung out with you every day like he'd never received any special attention at all. Or how he seemed more intelligent and wise about the world than everyone else his age, even though he had lost almost a third of his life to the strange medical condition.

But in other ways the strangeness was difficult to describe. When Todd was around (which was all the time now) the dynamic of their group was different, as if the five of them had somehow vaulted past junior high and landed in high school or maybe college. Even stranger was the feeling that time was somehow irrelevant when Todd was around. Like they would get to talking or playing D&D or Atari or whatever, and Jonathan didn't even notice how much time had passed. Five hours might seem like five minutes. Or the reverse. In the presence of Todd, Jonathan got the feeling they were somewhere else entirely, where clocks might not even tick. Which was a very strange thing to think, yet he could not stop thinking it.

Finally, reluctantly, Jonathan crept back to the kitchen. He stood near the corner where the phone was, listening, but there was no sign of the rocking chair. Without knowing the exact location of his mother, there was no point in making the call. He absolutely would not permit her to stage one of her surprise attacks, not while he was making the most important phone call of his life, which meant he had no choice but to retreat and consider his options.

But then he heard a drawer open in the bathroom, heard the metal and plastic sound of her hand searching for a brush or lipstick or a nail file. When his mother wasn't in the rocking chair, she sat under the bright lights of her vanity and stared into the big mirror. Jonathan wasn't sure why she did that, why she applied makeup at night when she had no intention of going anywhere, but he did know that from the vanity you couldn't hear someone talking in the kitchen.

Jonathan approached the phone and instructed his hand to reach for it, but the hand refused him. It remained against his side as though it were perfectly within its rights to ignore direct orders.

What was the big deal? Why couldn't he—

Jonathan picked up the phone. Dialed all the numbers at once. Screw this stupid fear. *Fuck* it.

5-5-5-1-2-0-8.

The phone rang once, twice. A voice answered. The mother again.

"Hello?"

"Hi, is Alicia there?"

"Yes, she is. May I tell her who's calling?"

"It's Jonathan."

"Okay," she said, and then paused. "Jonathan, you said?"

"Yes, ma'am."

"Oh, no. Jonathan, I am so sorry. You called last week, didn't you? And I never gave Alicia the message. You poor boy. Let me get her at once."

Relief consumed him. The mom *had* forgotten about the message. Todd was right. Holy shit, he was right!

"Hello?"

"Hi, Alicia. It's Jonathan."

"Hi, Jonathan!" Her voice was as bright and shiny as he remembered. "My mom just said you called before and she didn't give me the message. I'm so sorry."

"Oh, don't worry about it." He felt like a hero, letting her off the hook like that.

"I'm surprised you didn't call back sooner. Was it anything important?"

"I was just calling to see what you were up to," he told her. "Have you been reading much?"

"Yeah," she said. "Right now I'm reading *Time Out of Joint* by this guy named Philip K. Dick. Have you ever heard of him?"

"I haven't," Jonathan said. "But I did take your advice about Stephen King. They had *The Dead Zone* at the library, so I checked it out and read it in three days."

"See!" Alicia said, laughing. "I *told* you!"

"Yeah, you did."

He laughed along with her, and then sort of trailed off. Things had started out well, but now what?

"What else have you been doing since school?" he blurted.

"Oh, just hanging out with friends. You?"

"Pretty much the same. Actually, we met this kid, you may know him, he's the guy who was catatonic for four years after the tornado?"

"Yes, I heard about him! He lives around here now, right? What's he like?"

"He's not like what you would expect. He's really cool, actually."

Jonathan talked for a while about Todd, about their club, even a little about his writing. Alicia told him how she'd gone stargazing with her dad and had seen Jupiter and Saturn and some of their moons. But it was obvious to Jonathan a cloud was hanging over their conversation, a cloud of expectation, and the closer he came to the big question the more he feared it. What if he opened himself to her and she cut him in half with machine gun fire?

No. He could do this. She was just a girl. A very kind girl, which is what had drawn him to her in the first place. She was on the phone with him, willingly, going on about Europa and Io and Ganymede, and all she expected out of him was a little confidence. All she wanted was to say "Yes." If he could just form the question, if he could just ask her, say it out loud . . . but again there was the nonzero chance she would turn him down. It was conceivable she was only tolerating this entire conversation, and—

And no. That was crap. Either he was the kind of person who could summon the nerve to ask for what he wanted, or he wasn't.

"Hey, Alicia," he said, when she ran out of Jovian moons to name. "I actually wanted to ask you something."

"Oh," she said. "What's that?"

And here it was. No turning back now. All he had to do was spit the goddamn words out of his mouth.

"I was wondering if . . . if maybe you wanted to go with me."

The pause was less than a second, but it could have been an eternity.

"Sure!" she said, and there it was.

"Really?"

"Of *course* I will. You were worried I might say 'no,' huh?"

"You bet I was worried."

"Well, stop worrying! I'm so glad you asked me. Ever since we worked on the assembly project, I just really felt like I wanted to get to know you better."

"Yeah," Jonathan admitted. "Same here. When we talked before I never wanted to stop. It seems like we could talk for hours."

"Oh, we definitely could. I like smart guys. I like *you.*"

The relief was so great it was like someone had turned off gravity. Not only was the weight of asking her gone, but so, it seemed, was his own weight. Jonathan felt as if he could float around the room on a cloud, the cloud that just moments before had been casting a shadow over him.

Their conversation gradually wound to a close, and Jonathan assured her he would call again tomorrow. He was so excited and filled with joy that he forgot where he was.

"Bye, Alicia," he said.

"Goodbye, Jonathan. Sleep well, all right?"

"Okay. You, too."

"Okay, bye."

"Bye."

He hung up the phone, and it was all he could do not to scream *Hallelujah!* at the top of his lungs. All he could do not to erupt into somersaults and cartwheels and jumping jacks right there in the kitchen. Tonight he felt like he could sit down and write an entire short story in one sitting, maybe a whole novel, a teenage love story about—

He heard a creaking sound then, what he recognized instantly as his mother's rocking chair.

"Jonathan?" his mom called. Her voice was uncharacteristically calm. "Can you come in here for a minute?"

It was grave, the error he had made, but somehow in his giddiness Jonathan wondered if his mom might be happy for him, wondered if she would even be proud of him. At dinner she had challenged him to live in the real world, and what could be more real than finding the courage to ask someone like Alicia to be your girlfriend?

He turned the corner, stepped out of the kitchen and into his mother's bedroom. Her hair had been recently brushed, her makeup was fresh, but she was wearing a red flannel nightgown and sitting in the wooden rocking chair.

"Who were you talking to on the phone just now?" she asked in that same voice, the calm one that was nothing like her usual reptilian hiss.

"This girl I know from school."

"What were you talking about?"

Jonathan had never fought in a war, but he knew what a minefield was, and talking to his mother was like trying to cross one.

"Oh, different stuff. Books we've read. She was telling me about her dad's telescope."

"What else did you talk about?"

"I told her about that kid, Todd. I told her about my other friends, what we've been doing since school let out."

His mother smiled, but her lips pulled thin when she did it, and in her expression Jonathan could read nothing but bitterness.

"What else?"

The discussion wasn't a minefield anymore. His mother had abandoned any pretense of stealth and was simply lobbing grenades at him in plain sight.

"I asked her to go with me."

"Go where?"

"It's not . . . it's not a specific place. I—"

"Jonathan, you aren't making sense."

"But it's not, I mean you don't underst—"

"What the hell are you talking about?"

"I was asking her to be my girlfriend."

"Ah," she said. "Now it comes out."

"I was trying to tell you."

"You were *trying*," his mother hissed, "to *hide* it from me. 'We were talking about *school*! We were talking about *telescopes*! We were talking about that kid, Todd!'"

"We were talking about those things."

"You're only thirteen years old, Jonathan. What do you suppose you're going to do with a girlfriend?"

"I don't know," he answered. And it was true. He couldn't invite her to come over, not with his mother here, and Tanglewood was so far from the rest of town that there was nothing to do within bike-riding range. No movie theaters, no shopping malls, nothing they could get to without an adult chaperone. And still his mom sat there, waiting for an answer.

"We'll just hang out, I guess."

"No, you *won't*," she hissed. "You're only thirteen years old. You think you can have a girlfriend and go on dates and kiss girls without my permission?"

Jonathan didn't see how any of those things were her business, but he didn't say that. What could he say to her without his dad to run interference?

"There you go again, you Dodo bird! You are *forbidden* to go on a date until you are sixteen years old. Do you understand? Sixteen. And then you'll be driven *to* and *from* the dates by me. No Dodo son of mine is going to get a girl pregnant while he's still in junior high."

"But Mom—"

"You're not to call her. You're not to see her. And if I catch you slinking around behind my back, there will be hell to pay. You can bet on that."

What was the point of arguing? Right or wrong, who could stop her?

"Do you understand me?" she asked.

"Yes."

"Are you sure?"

"Yes, ma'am."

"Fine."

Jonathan stood there defeated.

"You can go now," his mom said. "Go to your room and live in your fantasy world until it's time for bed."

22

The song played at a thunderous volume, and images flickered one after the other, black and white film clips of a child playing the drums, a couple on a beach, a pretty girl painting her toenails. The song was "The Boys of Summer," Todd's song, only the lush recording of real guitars and percussion produced a sound impossible to create on his own keyboard. And the voice was not his. It belonged to a man Todd had never seen, who was singing the lyrics as if he had written them himself. Who was the kid? Who was the girl? Who were any of them, and what were they doing in his head?

Todd knew something was coming. Something bad was going to happen.

And then he saw it, a tornado in the distance, black and orange and churning into the ground. Though it was miles away, the storm somehow stretched the width of the entire horizon, and it sounded like a distant but powerful train. As it widened and became louder, Todd realized the storm was not going to pass harmlessly by the way most tornadoes did. No, this one was headed right for him, growing so huge and so near, so *loud*, that it was too late to run away. It was going to get him.

Again.

He was dreaming.

The thing was, though the tornado was the defining event of his life, Todd could remember almost nothing about it. The only thing he could recall about April 10, 1979 was the failing progress report he had received for Social Studies, and how he had been halfway through forging his mother's signature on it when the world had gone crazy. Of his two parents, his mother's script was less precise and thus easier to imitate. He had done it three other times already with great success. Todd often wondered what had become of that progress report, since his parents had never mentioned it. Had it been lost in the storm, or had its importance been lost when Todd was so gravely injured? He would have liked to ask, but if his parents had no knowledge of his propensity for forgery, there was no reason to bring it to their attention now.

And none of this mattered because the tornado was still bearing down upon him. As it approached its structure became more detailed. Now he saw long, spiraling tentacles orbiting the tornado as if the entire thing was some kind of gigantic, whirling octopus. The sound of it became less like a freight train and more like a lion's growl. He saw it demolish the junior high school and tear the press box off the football stadium. He saw it reach Southwest Parkway, where it ripped a bank from its foundation, leaving only the vault behind. And he saw it tear through The Plex, an amusement park where you could ride go karts and play putt-putt and video games all day long.

Except there was no place on Southwest Parkway called The Plex.

It was only a dream. Dreams were usually weird and often ridiculous. Yet Todd could not shake the feeling he was seeing a real business being destroyed, some complex where he had watched Adam and his daughter play miniature golf, where Bradie had spoken the truth her father was too afraid to admit.

He saw the tornado lower itself further, squatting upon the ground, widening, until it had engulfed the entire city, until it was a swirling monster the size of Texas. Across the landscape it plowed, destroying discriminately, into cities across the state and beyond, somehow always leveling the worst damage upon trailer parks and other low-income neighborhoods. Todd watched the disaster unfold with awe and disgust, unable to comprehend such willful destruction, but he was even more baffled by victims unable or unwilling to get out of the way of it. If someone didn't stop this murder machine, it would destroy the entire country. And yet it seemed to go on for years, thirty years or more, which to Todd seemed like forever.

Underneath it all, with spooky, chamber-like reflections, the song continued to play. Certain lyrics called more attention to themselves than others, including these lines that might have repeated thousands, even millions of times:

I saw a Deadhead sticker on a Cadillac
A little voice inside my head said
"Don't look back, you can never look back."

By now the tornado covered his entire field of vision, and Todd felt himself being sprayed, even soaked by the blood of its victims, the millions of defenseless victims. It was all over him, sticky and warm and smelling of copper.

He screamed.

He screamed anger and sorrow at a population who had been given plenty of information and ample warning and still chose to turn a blind eye to the approaching destruction.

He at once hated and pitied them.

He screamed again, louder this time, and thrust his fists into the air.

"Todd!"

His fists operated as if by their own command. He swung and connected with something hard.

"Ow!" a woman screamed.

"Okay, that's enough," a man replied.

Hands grasped his arms, and Todd felt himself being sucked upward by the tornado, shaken back and forth, and gradually he swam up and out of sleep.

"Todd, wake up! Todd!"

He opened his eyes and saw his father's face only inches from his own.

"Todd," his father said, calmer now. "Are you awake?"

Moments ticked this way and that as Todd shook free of the grogginess and collected himself.

"Yeah, Dad. I'm awake."

"You hit your mother."

Todd turned his head and saw his mother sitting on the floor against the far wall, hand cradling her jaw.

"Shit. I'm sorry, mom."

"Todd!" his dad said. "Language!"

"Crap. Sorry."

"What were you dreaming about?" his father asked. "Was it a nightmare?"

"It was the tornado. It was killing everything."

"You remember the tornado? I thought you said that was all blank."

"It wasn't *the* tornado, not the real one. It didn't look like the pictures you showed me, anyway."

"He needs to see the doctor, Pete. Like tomorrow."

"He's fine, Cassandra. He just had a nightmare."

"He looks fine," his mom said. "But it's still so new."

"It's been two months."

"He was asleep for more than four years! Just because he's found a few friends and seems okay, that doesn't mean he *is* okay, Pete! He was asleep for four years!"

"Todd," his dad said. "Do you feel okay?"

"Yeah. I just had a bad dream."

"I think we should treat him like a normal thirteen-year-old instead of a medical patient. He can't go through life worrying all the time. If he feels fine, I'm inclined to believe he is."

"He is not qualified to diagnose himself," his mother insisted. "I'm making an appointment tomorrow. I don't care what the two of you think."

She stood up, glared at his father, and walked out of the room.

"It's all right, buddy. She's just upset. We thought you might never come back to us, and your mother is worried you could leave again, this time for good."

Todd rubbed crystals of sleep out of his eyes.

"Are you worried about that?"

"Sure. Of course I worry about it. But I think you're going to pull through, and I'm going to focus on that until something changes."

Todd smiled and hugged his dad.

"You going to be okay, son? Think you can fall back asleep?"

"Yeah, Dad. I think so."

"Not going to think about that dream?"

"I'll try not to. But I do have a question."

"Oh, yeah? What's that?"

"What do you think it would mean if you saw a Deadhead sticker on a Cadillac?"

PART FOUR
May 29–30, 2008

ZONE FORECAST PRODUCT
NATIONAL WEATHER SERVICE NORMAN OK
TXZ086-301000-
WICHITA-
INCLUDING THE CITIES OF ... WICHITA FALLS
839 PM CDT THU MAY 29 2008

.TONIGHT ... CLEAR. LOW NEAR 75. WINDS S 10-15 MPH.
.FRIDAY ... MOSTLY SUNNY. INCREASING TEMPS WITH A
HIGH AROUND 102. SOUTH WIND 15-25 MPH.
.FRIDAY NIGHT ... PARTLY CLOUDY. LOW IN THE LOW
80S. SOUTH WINDS AROUND 10 MPH.
.SATURDAY ... SUNNY. HIGH AROUND 104. SOUTH WINDS
15-30 MPH.
.SUNDAY ... SUNNY AND WINDY. HIGH NEAR 108. STRONG
SOUTHWESTERLY WINDS.
.MONDAY ... TURNING CLOUDY AND SHARPLY COOLER WITH
A CHANCE OF THUNDERSTORMS. HIGH IN THE UPPER 80S.

23

After the detectives left, Jonathan stood in his kitchen for a while contemplating the bottle of Jameson and also what exactly he expected from the world.

Last night's dream, already a mystery, now seemed supercharged with meaning. Dissonant music playing against a surreal, slow-motion backdrop of his hometown—this was the sort of scene you expected to find at the beginning of a Hollywood thriller to set the mood for outlandish or extraordinary events to come. And today had indeed produced some remarkable developments, first the news of Bobby's death at the restaurant, and then a visit from detectives who asked difficult-to-answer questions and who seemed to believe (rightfully so) that Jonathan possessed relevant information he was not willing to share. But what had shaken him so badly, what had left him staring stupidly at the bottle of Jameson with no clear idea of what to do next, was neither of these tangible events. It was a memory that had come to him while speaking to the detectives, a crystal clear recollection of Todd playing music on his little keyboard, a song that had sounded impressive when first performed and now seemed impossible.

Still moderately buzzed, Jonathan poured himself a smallish drink and went back to his computer. Into Google he typed The Boys of Summer. The second result was the Wikipedia entry for the original Don Henley hit, and a quick perusal of the text revealed the song was no remake of some older version. On another site he learned Henley had written the lyrics after hearing a track composed by guitarist Mike Campbell, and from what Jonathan could tell this had happened sometime in 1984. Since the song was released in October of that year, the timing made sense.

What made no sense at all was Todd playing the same song for them the previous year.

If someone else had told such a story to Jonathan, his immediate and only reaction would be the teller of the tale had remembered it wrong. Either the timing of the events was inaccurate or some other song had been played. Another possible explanation for Todd knowing the song in 1983 was that his parents were friends with Don Henley himself, and during some prior social occasion the song had been discussed or performed. But Jonathan had just read about the song's genesis in 1984, and anyway, what was the likelihood Todd's parents were friends with a famous musician and not one person in town knew about it? Not very, but for Jonathan it was the only explanation he would have been willing to accept from anyone other than himself.

Why he had not realized any of this until today, Jonathan could not say. The memory of Todd's performance would have been much stronger in 1984, when Don Henley's single was released, than it was now. Yet none of them had said a word about the song when it showed up on the radio, a glaring omission that somehow seemed more implausible than the music itself.

Jonathan sipped on his drink and considered his options. One possible next step was to contact the others and ask if they remembered Todd's music, if anything about it seemed strange to them. But who could he call? Bobby was gone. Adam had distanced himself from them after that summer and found new friends at church. David had moved to California years ago, and Todd's family had left Wichita Falls shortly after Lone Star burned down. When Jonathan explained to Gholson how the events of that summer were ancient history, he hadn't been exaggerating. Before today, he couldn't remember having thought about his friends from junior high in years. In *decades*.

Well, that wasn't entirely true. From time to time he had wondered about Alicia. Was she married? Had she moved away? Was she still as beautiful as he remembered? These questions remained unanswered for years because there didn't seem to be any point in reexamining an old, painful wound. But now Alicia's house lay in ruins, Jonathan had just been interviewed by the police, and there seemed to be something very strange going on that connected them in a way he didn't yet understand. As if someone had generously handed him the perfect excuse to reach out to her.

The difficulty, assuming he could get Alicia on the phone, was what he might say. He wouldn't lead with the impossible song from the past, that was for sure.

To solve the first problem, Jonathan used Google to find the only two phone numbers in town listed under the Ulbrecht surname: one for Alicia and one for a Sean and Sarah. He assumed the latter number belonged to her parents, because the listed address was Shady Lane in Tanglewood, and that's just where they had lived when he first met Alicia. It also seemed likely, with her house destroyed, Alicia would stay with her parents until she found another place to live. So if she didn't answer her own number, he would try the second one.

The next problem was summoning the nerve to actually place the call.

Even after all this time it was frustrating to remember how Alicia had betrayed him for David, how difficult it had been to ignore her the following school year. In high school, avoiding her had been somewhat easier, since the halls were longer and the classrooms more numerous, and you could go a whole day, even a whole week, without seeing another particular person. By then she was a teenage starlet, and he was a taller and pimplier version of his scrawny junior high self. At football games they sat in different sections of the stadium bleachers. At school dances they stood in different areas of the dark gymnasium. He could still picture Alicia leaning against her boyfriend at half court, disco lights playing against her sweater and jeans, while Jonathan and his dorky friends loitered near one of the free throw lines. The football boyfriend had been huge—not just tall, but stout, adult-like, with thick wrists and a wide jaw and coarse facial hair. Jonathan's own beard hadn't matured until he was twenty-three, but this football guy had been shaving seriously at age sixteen. How could you compete for a girl's attention when you looked thirteen and some other guy looked thirty?

Jonathan took a sip of his drink and picked up his cell phone. He could call her from anywhere in the house if he wanted, could take the phone outside and walk halfway up the street. But with no Mom or Bobby or anyone to overhear his conversation, that sort of thing wasn't necessary anymore.

He punched in the digits to Alicia's home number and heard the familiar fast busy signal. *You've dialed a number that is disconnected or no longer in service.* So now he was left with the second number, and it seemed almost comical how he had arrived at this place again, calling Alicia's parents, hoping to speak to their daughter. This was the sort of scene he might place in a novel to demonstrate how history had a tendency to repeat, how life often circled back on itself.

He dialed slowly. 5-5-5-1-2-0 . . . 8.

The phone rang once, twice. A voice answered. The voice of an older woman.

"Hello?"

"Hi, is Alicia there?"

"Why, yes. As a matter of fact, she is. May I tell her who's calling?"

"It's Jonathan Crane. An old friend."

"Oh. Well, that's great. Jonathan Crane. I think I may know your mother. Is her name Carolyn?"

"It is."

"Well, okay. Let me get Alicia for you."

Mrs. Ulbrecht put her hand over the mouthpiece. Jonathan heard muffled voices and what he thought might have been laughter. Then the audio became clear again and someone else was on the line.

"Hello?"

Hearing this voice was like traveling back in time, like the intervening twenty-five years had been deleted, like he had spoken to Alicia only yesterday. Only this time his mother wasn't sitting around the corner, waiting to fuck up everything.

"Alicia? It's Jonathan Crane."

"Jonathan, oh, my God! I thought my mom had lost her mind. How in the hell *are* you?"

"I'm okay. I'm sorry to call out of the blue like this, but I just heard about your house and I wondered if you were all right."

"I'm okay, I guess. It's pretty surreal to come home and find your house in flames. It looked like something in a movie, just an inferno. I lost almost everything."

"I'm so sorry."

"Well, it could have been worse. It was only stuff. Nobody got hurt. The weird thing is these other fires that have happened since. Did you hear about Bobby Steele?"

"I did," Jonathan said. "It's part of the reason I'm calling you."

"Are you okay? I know you guys were close."

"We used to be, but in the past few years we fell out of contact."

"Well, I'm sorry, anyway. All these fires are very strange. Have you talked to anyone else?"

"Like who?"

"Like David Clark? Since Bobby killed his dad?"

She used his last name, Jonathan noted, as if to clarify which David she meant.

"So far I haven't spoken to anyone but you."

"I can't believe we're talking after all these years," Alicia said. "You must be married, have kids, the whole nine yards."

"I was married. We were divorced last year."

"Oh, I'm sorry."

"No kids, so it could have been worse. What about you?"

"Never married. No kids. Old maid."

"Hey, these days lots of women are—"

"Not in Wichita Falls, they aren't," Alicia said. "Around here I might as well be fifty."

"Did you ever think of moving somewhere else?"

"Yeah, I'd love to. But my mom . . . she . . . "

"Is she all right?"

"She's okay. It's just . . . do you really want to do this on the phone?"

"Uh—"

"What I mean to say," Alicia continued, "is do you want to meet for a drink somewhere?"

"Oh," Jonathan said. "Sure. Do you have work tomorrow?"

"Yeah, but it'll be fine. Is Toby's okay with you?"

"Toby's sounds perfect."

"Great. Give me a minute to get ready and I'll meet you over there."

24

The last time Jonathan had spoken to Alicia, before tonight, was during their one and only phone conversation twenty-five years prior. His mother had commanded him to never call her again, never to see her, and Jonathan had stupidly put up no fight. The incident injured him so thoroughly that he had failed to ask out another girl until he was nineteen, and even in adulthood he'd found it impossibly difficult to approach women. For a while Jonathan had blamed his mother for his struggles with the opposite sex, but eventually he'd come to understand the problem was really his own. Thirteen years old or not, he should have stuck up for himself, should have told his sadistic mother to stay the hell out of his business. When he hadn't, David had used the opportunity to move in on Alicia, and Jonathan had spent years trying to rebuild his confidence.

By now all this should have been ancient history, but as he stepped out of his car and approached the bar, Jonathan could hear Alicia describing Jupiter's moons, could viscerally remember the elation he felt when she agreed to be his girl . . . the click of his heels on concrete could have even been the rhythmic ticking of his mother's rocking chair. His recollection seemed like a digital recording of the event instead of human, chemical memories that were decades old, and Jonathan wondered how Alicia remembered that time, if she would be curious about why he had never called her again. But it seemed just as likely she had forgotten their phone call completely.

When he opened the door and stepped into Toby's, it was ten minutes before nine o'clock. The bar was mostly full, today being Thursday, but Jonathan was fortunate enough to grab a booth against the wall. He ordered a drink and faced the door, anticipating the moment when Alicia would walk through it. How different would she look? Would he recognize her? His heart thudded with anticipation.

Then the door did open, and a woman in a light blue blouse walked into the bar. If this was Alicia, she was taller than he expected, her hair darker than he remembered, and his legs tingled as he stood up to wave her over. By any standard she was an attractive woman, but her smile seemed strained somehow, the lines around her eyes deeper than he might have expected. It was easy to forget she was nearly forty years old, the same as he was.

"Alicia?" he said, and the receptive look in her eyes eased his uncertainty. "Wow. You look great."

She reached for him and they hugged. He thought how foreign this was, how familiar.

Alicia stepped back and considered him. "Jonathan," she said. "You're so much . . . bigger than I remember."

"They call that fat."

"You're not fat," she said, and laughed. "Your body has just matured. You were so skinny as a kid."

They sat down and the waitress appeared with his drink. Alicia ordered a beer.

"This is so weird," she said. "Just seeing you here. Have you lived in Wichita since high school? Or did you leave for college?"

"I stayed here. Went to Midwestern, got an Education degree. I teach over at McNiel Junior High now. I figured a job with easy hours and three months off in the summer would make it easier to write. I thought I would be publishing bestsellers by the time I was twenty-five."

The waitress appeared with her beer, and Jonathan charged it to his tab.

"Thanks," Alicia said, and together they toasted this unexpected encounter. "So you're still writing? How's that going?"

"It's tough. You need a literary agent to sell your work, and I haven't found one yet who will give me the time of day. I keep thinking I'm close, but agents are so selective. I guess they have to be."

"It must be nearly impossible. I mean, of all the people who *want* to publish books, and the few who actually get to . . . So what do you write? Short stories? Novels?"

"Both, but mostly novels now. Well, I've written three. They suck."

Alicia laughed again. "I'm sure they don't suck. You let people read them?"

"Sure. I mean, if they want to, of course they can read them."

"Can I read one?"

Jonathan smiled in spite of himself. He couldn't believe he was sitting here having this conversation. The whole situation seemed almost too perfect to be real.

"Well, yeah. Sure you can. So what have you been doing all this time? If you've been in town, I don't know how we've never seen each other in all these years."

She told him about Texas A&M, about her doomed relationship with a business major, Kyle. She told him about Brandon, her last boyfriend, who had worked at the particle accelerator in Olney. Brandon moved away after it was destroyed and didn't ask her to come with him.

"He was from Philadelphia. He hated Wichita. Called it the asshole of Texas."

"Sounds like a real jerk," Jonathan said.

"I know, but I loved him a lot. And sometimes I think he was right about this place. Did you ever notice how nothing ever changes? How the city doesn't grow? I swear it's like all the clocks stopped ticking sometime in the 80s."

The waitress came around again, and he was about to order another round when Alicia beat him to the punch.

"Hi," she said, and Jonathan noticed Alicia's eyes had a certain glint in them, as if she were keeping a secret that only she knew. "Could you bring us two more drinks and two shots of tequila, please? No salt on mine."

Jonathan blinked. "Or mine."

The waitress left, and Alicia turned back to him, her eyes still glinting, her smile wide and bright.

"We should shift into a higher gear, don't you think?"

"I like your style."

"I feel like I need a buzz to talk about this," she said, "because I don't know why anyone would want to burn down my house. I assume Bobby Steele had to have been involved somehow. It can't be a coincidence what he did to the restaurant only two nights after my house was burned down. And for David's dad to die? It's just so brutal."

Jonathan didn't know what the detectives had shared with Alicia, but from the sound of it, maybe not much. Once she learned about the cryptic email, that there was still at least one suspect at large, would she believe the suspect was him? Would honesty ruin his chance to get to know her again?

"It's not a coincidence."

Her eyes grew wide as he said this, and Alicia was about to respond when their drinks arrived. Jonathan picked up his shot glass and waited for her to follow.

"To old friends," he said.

"And new beginnings," Alicia added. She knocked back her tequila and switched to the lime in a single, fluid motion. During his entire marriage Jonathan had never seen Karen take a shot of liquor, nor drink anything with such finesse.

"So you were saying?" Alicia asked. "You don't think it's a coincidence?"

"I know it isn't."

"You look like you know something you're not telling me."

"Well, for one thing, there have been three fires in the past three days, not two."

"You mean that construction project in Tanglewood?"

"So you know about that?" Jonathan asked.

"It's two blocks from my parents' house. But why does it have anything to do with this?"

"Because the builder is Adam Altman."

"Adam Altman? Why does that name sound familiar?"

"He was one of my friends back in junior high. He was in that club we had."

Alicia's eyes slowly widened and Jonathan could see her working it out.

"So wait," she said. "Bobby burned down the restaurant, he killed David's dad in the process, and someone also burned down a house Adam was building. Which means three of your friends were in some way involved."

"That's right."

"Does that mean all this has to do with you?"

"Not exactly," he said. "I suppose it could. But there was a police officer at the restaurant, and he heard what Bobby said right before the building went up in flames."

"What was it?"

"That according to Todd, that was how his life had to end."

"Who's Todd?"

Jonathan was surprised she didn't instantly remember this.

"You know that kid who went into a coma after the tornado? Todd Willis? The one who—"

"Of course! That's the guy who . . . holy shit, Jonathan. He burned down the same restaurant when we were little. I remember because David—"

Alicia's hand went to her mouth and she stopped herself. Jonathan felt a little stab of jealousy at how she remembered enough about that summer to protect his feelings.

"I wonder how much the police know about this," she finally said. "Something premeditated is going on, and I'm caught in the middle of it. I was friends with you guys, too. Could it be Todd? Whatever happened to him, anyway?"

Jonathan took a long sip of his drink and decided to plow forward. Why even bother with all this if he couldn't be honest with her?

"Alicia, Todd didn't burn down the restaurant by himself. We all did it. All five of us in the club."

"What?"

"Yes, we—"

"I knew it. I knew David was lying to me. He was so weird after that happened."

"Yeah, well the reason I know all this is because a couple of detectives stopped by my house tonight. They interrogated me like they thought *I* was involved. And then, at the end, they told me about an anonymous email someone sent them."

"Detectives came to see you?"

"The subject of this email was 'The City Will Burn' and the text was some kind of clue."

"Clue? What clue?"

"Lyrics from a Don Henley song. Which said, 'I'm gonna get you back. I'm gonna show you what I'm made of.'"

Alicia's blank look made it clear the lyrics meant nothing to her.

"So David never told you the name of our club?"

"No. Should he have?"

"The name of our club was the name of that song. 'The Boys of Summer.'"

"And someone is making reference to it now, all these years later? Sending cryptic emails to the police? This is like something out of a movie."

Jonathan nodded, and Alicia drew circles on the table with her beer bottle.

"What did you say happened to Todd again?" she asked.

"All I know is he moved away after the restaurant burned down."

"I imagine he was pretty pissed," Alicia suggested, "if you guys all set fire to the restaurant but only he got busted for it. Why did you do that?"

"Why did we burn it down or why did we let him take the blame for it?"

"Both."

"It's a long story. Todd was very strange. He wasn't like the rest of us. And that wasn't the first fire we set."

"No?"

"We also burned down the house on Driftwood. Like the week before."

"Oh, yeah. I remember that. But I thought the kid who disappeared set that fire."

Jonathan shook his head.

"Then what happened to him? Everyone said he ran away so he wouldn't get in trouble."

"I don't know what happened to Joe," Jonathan said, which was technically true. Any other details, no matter how guilty they might make him feel, were only speculation.

Alicia reclined in her chair and crossed her arms over her chest. She was farther away from him now, Jonathan noticed, than at any time since she'd arrived at the restaurant.

"So everyone thought Joe burned down the house, and then he disappeared—like forever—and none of you said anything."

"We were thirteen, Alicia. It was obviously stupid and selfish."

"But you could have helped the police. If they knew he didn't burn down the house, that might have changed their investigation."

This was true. Nothing Jonathan said now could change the decisions they had made then.

"Why the hell did you burn the house down in the first place?" Alicia said. "You're talking about someone's life, for God's sake."

"This particular house was empty. No one had ever lived in it. We hung out there a few times, and one day we snuck some alcohol in with us and got really drunk. Things got way out of hand and we messed up the place pretty badly."

"Messed it up like how?"

"Just a lot of physical damage. Stuff we couldn't repair. Todd explained about forensics, how we'd never be able to erase the traces of our presence there. He told us fire was the only way to cover our tracks. We were desperate. It was a really stupid thing to do."

"This isn't easy to hear," Alicia said. "But I appreciate your honesty. It makes more sense now why David acted the way he did back then."

"What do you mean?"

"After his dad's restaurant burned down, David was withdrawn. Unhappy. Based on what you're telling me now, maybe he felt guilty for what happened. But he pretended like the fire was great, that his father somehow deserved it. And he kept telling me he knew a secret. He said he knew something no one else did and it was going to make him rich."

"I guess he was right," Jonathan said. "Since he's like a billionaire and all."

"I know. It's pretty creepy. And the weird thing is, I had completely forgotten he told me that until you called."

"Did David say what the secret was?"

"No. But his eyes, Jonathan. He looked crazy. When he told me all this, he looked like he belonged at that mental hospital out by the lake."

Jonathan remembered feeling the same way. But he could not recall what had happened at the restaurant, besides the fire, that had induced such feelings. For a moment he considered telling Alicia about Todd's impossible music, but he wasn't quite ready yet. He still wasn't sure how he felt about the idea himself.

"I don't know what's going on," he said to her, "but my arson days are over. You don't have to believe it, but I'm as baffled as you are about what's happening."

Alicia drank the rest of her beer and said, "Who else could it be, then, besides Todd?"

"I don't know. Maybe he convinced Bobby to burn up the restaurant for some reason and Fred Clark got in the way."

"I feel so bad for David," Alicia said. "Are you going to talk to him about this?"

"I would if I had a phone number for him. But maybe he'll come back here to take care of his dad. If he does we could sit down and talk to him about it. Ask what he thinks is going on."

"People just don't go around setting fires like this. I think it's pretty obvious whatever is happening now is related to what happened before, back when you guys knew Todd. I think I'd be worried if I were you. You could be next."

"I hadn't thought of that," Jonathan said, and it was true. Was his house on fire right now, while he was here with Alicia? "I guess I better keep my eyes open."

"It really seems like some kind of revenge on Todd's part."

"Okay, but why come back now? Why wait so long?"

"Maybe it doesn't seem like that long ago to him," Alicia said. "Maybe it seems like it was just yesterday."

25

It was nearly ten o'clock by the time Gholson wandered over to say good-night to his partner. Daniels, recently divorced, was prowling around Match.com again. Over the past few months he'd been fucking some twenty-five-year-old bartender who relocated from Olney, Eve or Eva or something like that. Lots of people had moved to Wichita after the super collider accident, but the economy around here couldn't handle it.

The physics machine had been hailed as a savior for the area, but after it shut down the downward spiral only intensified. Dying slowly before, the city was in real trouble now.

"What do you think?" Gholson said. "About Crane?"

"I think he's a schoolteacher. I think regardless of what you believe happened twenty-five years ago, he didn't send that second email."

Gholson looked back at his own desk. The email Daniels was referring to had arrived while they were away interrogating Crane. In fact, based on the time stamp, the message had arrived *while they were at Crane's house.* Talk about an alibi. There was no way Crane could have sent the message, not while they were standing there talking to him. A further complicating factor was the email had been sent directly to Gholson this time, which meant the author had somehow learned of his assignment to this case. There was a printout of the message on Daniels' desk, which Gholson picked up and read for the seven hundredth time.

remember how I made you crazy? remember how I made you scream?

FUCK YOU Gholson. You'll never catch ME.

"Look at this bitch," Daniels said. He clicked a link, and a badly-lit digital photograph on his screen became larger. The girl in the picture was a brunette and had obviously spent too much of her young life simmering under UV lamps. Her cocktail dress was hiked up and you could see a black thong underneath. "Lives in Dallas. I gotta get over there more often."

Daniels didn't have his head in the game since the divorce.

"So this perp calls me out," Gholson said. "Calls *us* out, basically, and you don't see any course of action. Our only suspect has an alibi for this email and you're content to find some ass online."

"You're going to put a car on Crane, right? If it turns out he's part of this, you've got him, right?"

"I've got a patrol in his neighborhood, but I think maybe I'm going to watch him myself."

Now Daniels looked up. "Look, Jerry, I'd be pissed, too. If someone called me out like that, of course I would. But you've got to keep some distance here."

"Okay, but—"

"I don't think Crane is telling us everything he knows. You're right about that. But unless you can establish a connection between him and Todd Willis—until you can even prove Willis has come back to Wichita—this theory of yours has no legs. We can't put Crane anywhere near the houses or the restaurant. The only evidence we have for Willis' presence in town is a one-sentence accusation from a man with a gun pointed at him. That's not enough. That's nothing. No offense."

"I just can't believe it's a coincidence that Fred Clark's restaurant was torched back then, and these kids were involved somehow, and now Bob Steele burned down the same restaurant last night. We've got a murder victim, Frank. We've got three structures destroyed in three days. This is the biggest case we've worked in months and we have no leads other than the members of that club."

"The rich guy in California is part of it, too, you're saying."

"Why not?"

"Fred Clark is David's father. Why would he want his own father dead?"

"They haven't been on speaking terms for years," Gholson said. "Maybe there was a fresh disagreement we don't know about."

"Phone records don't support that. And what would they argue over, Jerry?"

Gholson couldn't answer that, so he didn't.

"What's the latest on the background check on Willis?" Daniels asked. "Anything come back from the Bureau?"

"No trace of the guy. Obviously, he doesn't want to be found."

"Or can't be found. We know he likes dope. Maybe he OD'd or found some other trouble that got the better of him."

"Maybe. But then what the hell is going on here?"

"Look," Daniels said. "All I'm saying is maintain perspective. It's what you're always telling me. Don't get personal with the case. It's good advice. You should keep it in mind."

26

An hour or so later Gholson was sitting in semi-darkness with his wife, wondering if maybe the only point of life was for it to turn out differently than you expected.

How else to describe his tenure with the WFPD? He'd hit the streets as a patrolman at age twenty-three, with no degree and no law enforcement experience, yet after only four years he had become one of the youngest officers on the force to ever make detective. Now, after beginning his career with such promise, the kid who had been called a "shooting star" by his lieutenant was still doing the same work at the same rank more than twenty-five years later. Only he was no longer a kid. Daniels was also no kid, though he was forever pretending otherwise, and recently he'd introduced Gholson to a Web site called LinkedIn. On LinkedIn you put up a description of your work history and accomplishments, sort of like an online resume, and then you waited for a private company to snatch you up and make you their head of security. If you believed Daniels, this sort of thing happened all the time. But when Gholson had considered what personal and career information he might put on such a site, he realized his job history would consume all of three lines of text, which was just one more depressing reality in a life full of them.

You might wonder if Gholson's career had suffered because of his insistence upon a healthy work/life balance, that he had foregone rapid advancement to enjoy rich and fulfilling family living. And in fact he'd been married for over thirty years and was the father of a strong-headed young man named Lance, who had run off to Oklahoma and was studying to become a chiropractor. But Lance was angry at Gholson for a variety of reasons and rarely called or visited. In the past few years he'd come back to Wichita for only one occasion, his mother's birthday, and the only way Gholson knew that was because of an elderly nurse named Phil who fashioned himself as a therapist of sorts for the families of his patients.

Gholson's wife, Sally, was one of those patients, and had been going on five years now. Once a tall, lithe blonde who could nail baseline jumpers with her eyes closed, Sally had seemed unattainable to Gholson the first moment he saw her bouncing a worn leather basketball on a rectangle of blacktop in Archer City. She stood an inch taller than him, and passed insults around as easily as she passed the ball. But in a conversation afterward, over barbecue ribs and cans of Schlitz, it had been clear there was something between them, an electric sort of connection that still made Gholson smile when he thought about it.

"I thought you might be interested in this new case I'm working on," Gholson said to her now as she lay motionless in bed. "It's a new case related to an old case. Or maybe the same case. You would probably like to hear about it, in any case."

His wife didn't acknowledge the joke. She was awake, her eyes were open, but those things were irrelevant because three years ago she had finally stopped talking altogether. This period of silence had followed a gradual decline over the course of twenty-six years, after she had suffered a minor head injury during the tornado in 1979. Nowadays, Gholson paid weekly visits to her at the hospital—North Texas State Hospital—which over the years had borne other names, such as Wichita Falls State Hospital and the more ominous Northwest Texas Insane Asylum.

"For some reason I never made the connection, how that Willis kid stopped talking after the tornado. It was a long time ago, sure, but it's just like what's happened to you. In fact when I went back and looked at the case file, even the clinical diagnosis was the same. That's pretty strange if you ask me."

A sconce burned on the other side of the hospital room. It was the only light he'd turned on, and half of Sally's face was darkened by shadows. Visitors' hours were over, of course, but as a law enforcement officer he could come here anytime, and had long ago worked out an agreement with the nursing staff.

"For you it happened a lot slower, I guess, but in the end I can't help but wonder if you both went to the same place. Wherever that is."

Sally moved a little in the bed. It wasn't unusual for her to stir at the sound of his voice, but tonight he was hoping for something different.

The doctor's name here at the state hospital was Young. He claimed schizophrenic catatonia was still common in some parts of the world but almost unheard of in industrialized nations. Gholson wondered how that could be true when two unrelated people in a town like Wichita

Falls had been diagnosed with it, but he hadn't thought to ask this before because he'd forgotten about Todd's illness. Young explained that certain drugs were usually able to bring catatonic patients back to reality, but since Sally's mental health had deteriorated over such a long period of time, it was possible no type of therapy would reach her. And so far Young had been correct in that assessment.

"Sally," Gholson said. "I know I didn't believe a lot of the things you told me. I know you were angry at me for that. But the reason we fought so much is you could never understand my side of it. I'm a man who needs to see something to believe it, especially when it's something so *difficult* to believe. When you tell someone you can see things that haven't happened yet, it helps if you can prove it."

Her sickness had begun with dreams a few weeks after the tornado, terrible bouts of nighttime terror that turned Sally into an insomniac. The first time it happened, Gholson woke up and thought his wife was dying, so painful and shrill were her screams. It took half an hour to calm her down, and when she was finally able to speak, Sally still couldn't put into words what she had experienced. *I've never seen a place so empty* was all he could get her to say.

Later she would claim her dreams were mainly about the tornado in '79, how she was afraid another giant storm would come and take them both. But Gholson suspected she was hiding something, because Sally sometimes spoke during her dreams, and she never said anything about a tornado. She did, however, mention people's names he'd never heard of, she talked a lot about windows, and on more than one occasion she seemed to be speaking to someone named Thomas. Gholson couldn't help but wonder if she was cheating on him, and one day he almost confronted her about it, but how could you accuse someone of infidelity because of what they said in their sleep?

A few weeks later Sally announced she was pregnant, and the good news seemed to clear whatever had darkened her internal skies. She told Gholson the dreams had probably been caused by hormones, and her doctor concurred. Over the next seven months her nightmares were almost non-existent, and it seemed the psychological trauma had passed.

But it had not passed.

"Sally," he said, "I think maybe I believe you now."

His wife stirred again. Her legs jerked a little under the covers. But that was all.

The evidence bag sat in his lap. He picked it up and removed the item inside. It was a spiral-bound notebook. A notebook with all sorts of things scrawled in it, drawn in it.

Song lyrics were written in it.

"Honey, this journal . . . it belonged to a kid I arrested in 1983. I took it from his home that year to use as evidence during trial. I told you about this case a long time ago, how Sgt. Curtis basically ignored it, and the kid walked? Well, tonight I went to our evidence archive and managed to find this journal again. We've had the thing for twenty-five years."

Gholson reached forward and put his hand around her wrist. He hoped she might turn toward him and smile. He always hoped that, but it never happened. Three years ago his wife had finally reached the end of a long descent into mental illness, and though he could sit in this room and speak to her, she was lost. She had retreated into a world where things were not the same as the way Gholson understood them, and he missed her deeply.

"Something is really wrong here," he said to her. "I don't know what it is yet, but I've got a feeling it's related to what happened to you. And if I can figure all this out, maybe we can get you some help. I sure miss you a lot."

Sally stirred. Didn't say anything.

27

The insulated cabin of David's Gulf Stream was whisper quiet, and the interior looked more like a small hotel room than the human sardine can familiar to most air passengers. Kimberly, the flight attendant, was discreet and (at David's request) rarely emerged to check on them.

Across the aisle, Meredith lay sleeping on the sofa, her hair a blonde waterfall spilling toward the floor. David sat with his seatback in the full, upright position. He was working on his second Mountain Dew, struggling to hold sleep at arm's length, because if he napped during the day he could not fall asleep at night. And sleep was difficult for David under even the best circumstances. There had been so many occasions recently where he lay awake for five or six hours, sweating into the sheets, that two months ago he'd installed an HVAC system that could chill the ambient air temperature in his master bedroom to fifty-one degrees. So far, however, the cold weather hadn't made it easier to sleep. Its only measurable effect had been on Meredith, who was now forced to sleep under an electric blanket whenever she stayed over.

Hidden in the console next to him was a mini flat screen monitor. He flipped it out and pushed buttons until a GPS map popped up. The plane was currently 51,000 feet above the southernmost tip of Nevada, cruising at an implausible ground speed of 613 miles per hour. More button pushing changed the channel on the flat screen until he reached the view of the underbelly camera. There was Lake Mead, narrowing into the Colorado River as the plane raced eastward. He looked out the window for a wider view and saw brown earth stretching into infinity.

From this high up the world looked more like a map than reality. He couldn't imagine the blasted landscape below as a place where real humans lived, and he wondered if, far above, someone else was looking at David and his $75 million plane from a similar perspective.

Even now it was difficult to reconcile how money of such magnitude gave him license to do whatever he wanted. Fair or not, David could find a way to arrange almost anything. Buy it. Watch it. Play it. Hear it. Almost anything.

But money couldn't stop you from wondering if your life wasn't really your own.

Imagine a world in which you looked at a stock ticker and believed you could see information that should not be there. How the first time you saw the Yahoo! search page, in 1995, it seemed familiar to you somehow. Imagine yourself unsurprised by iPods and iPhones, how between 1998 and 2008 you earned just shy of $290 million by investing in the corporation that manufactured such products. These things could be no coincidence.

If David were honest with himself, he would concede that in the past few months he had become afraid of sleep. When he put his head on the pillow and closed his eyes, he heard footsteps, slow and inexorable. He couldn't shake the feeling they were following him somewhere, that he was marching toward an unknown destination where something terrible was going to happen. And when he did finally fall asleep his dreams were often bizarre, like how he once found himself inexplicably trapped beneath a mountain of manila folders, so many he could not claw his way out of them. In another dream he had fled at inconceivable speeds down metallic-looking hallways from enormous, fuzzy balls of lightning. And several times he had watched as a giant tornado with great spiraling tentacles snatched him out of the sky, the image and sound of it so real, so lifelike, that upon wakening he could not shake the feeling that he hadn't really been asleep at all.

Certainly he had not been sleeping in 1983 when he listened to the tinny notes of a monophonic Casio keyboard and Todd's warbling, off-key voice. He could remember the moment clearly, or so he believed.

Todd's eyes had seemed like black holes, curving infinitely upon themselves. The lyrics, he claimed, were his own.

Nobody on the road
Nobody on the beach
I feel it in the air
The summer's out of reach
Empty lake, empty streets
The sun goes down alone
I'm driving by your house
Though I know you're not home

"What are you thinking about?" Meredith asked him.

David looked over and saw her sitting up on the sofa. He hadn't even noticed she was awake.

"Nothing. Just the past, I guess."

"Missing your dad?"

Ever since the news had come from Texas, Meredith had been waiting to rescue David from grief. She didn't accept the indifference he felt toward his past and specifically his father. The longer David held off the inevitable tearful breakdown, the more Meredith agitated, unsure of her place in his life or on this trip.

"No," he said. "There's just going to be a lot of work to do. And I might see some friends I haven't spoken to in a long time. People who knew Bobby."

"You think someone might know why he killed your father?"

"I wouldn't count on it," David said. "But it's been so long since I've talked to anyone from my past that it might be nice to verify I have one."

"What do you mean?"

"I mean, when you live your whole adult life in a place different than where you grew up, your childhood feels like maybe it didn't happen. Like it's all fake."

"Um," Meredith said. "Okay. So the plan is talk to the police first and then look up your old friends?"

"I suppose. I don't know how long this is all going to take. I'll have to find my dad's attorney and figure out if there's a will, how to execute his financial and legal situation. I'll need to arrange a burial or cremation, depending on if he had any requests or preference for that."

"So you don't know *any* of this? You guys didn't speak every once in a while?"

"I told you already I hadn't spoken to the man in close to twenty years."

"Yeah, but I thought you meant you, like, *barely* talked. Not that you literally didn't speak at all."

"Why would you think anything other than exactly what I told you?"

"Because, David, you don't like talking about your past. It's hard to know how you feel about any of it."

"I prefer not to think about it."

"But he was your father. Aren't you upset you didn't get to say goodbye to him?"

When David had begun to make real money, when he first moved to California, he had often fantasized about an eventual confrontation with his father. He imagined a heated exchange where he would point out how *wrong* his father had been about *everything*. The old man believed the only honest way to make a buck in the world was to earn it through sacrifice and suffering. He believed simple, hard-working folk from small towns were the backbone upon which the entire free-market economy of the United States rested. In order to prove the old man wrong, David's plan had been to earn a better living than his father without ever having to hold an actual job. When that goal was achieved with almost no effort at all, David redefined his barometer of success and decided he should wait until he had earned a full million dollars. But in 1989 he met a man named Beny Alagem, who wanted to exploit the growing market for personal computers, and David invested a few hundred thousand dollars in the company called Packard Bell. Alagem and his buddies at California State Polytechnic cultivated relationships with Sears and Wal-Mart and within a few years became the biggest seller of PCs in the United States. By the time he was 27, David had already earned $86 million from this investment, and his father was a lifetime away. It seemed pointless to explain real wealth to a man who still believed barbecuing meat was a noble way to earn a living, who personally manned the register so he could chat with each guest. That his father referred to his customers as "guests," that he believed a smile on every face was vital to his business, made David want to scream. In the first few years of sales, for instance, Packard Bell's return rate had reached 17%, and customer dissatisfaction was so high it became nearly impossible to take the company public. David had earned millions anyway.

"We looked at the world through completely different eyes," he explained to Meredith. "He hated my life and I hated his. After my mother died we had nothing to talk about, so no, I'm not disappointed I didn't get to say goodbye to him. If he had died slowly, like wasted away with cancer, it would have put us in the awkward position of pretending either of us cared. Honestly, this way is better."

"That's awful," Meredith said. "That's no way to think of your father."

"You don't know shit about my father."

Meredith looked away, clearly hurt, and he knew he was treading on thin ice with her. Which was sort of the point, wasn't it? To find ice thin enough to fall through?

But when she looked back at him, she had composed herself. Clearly her reserves of patience were far greater than his own.

"I can understand if you don't want to talk about your father. What about your friends, then? After we see the police, who will you call?"

"When I was younger we had this club. The guy who killed my dad was the president of this club."

"Oh, God. So you think the attack was personal?"

He could see why it might look that way to someone on the outside, but David was fairly certain Bobby's problem had not been with his father. Probably the old man had simply been in the wrong place at the wrong time.

"I have no idea if it's personal or not. I'll guess we'll see what the detective says."

"And the other guys in your club?"

"Yeah, it will be helpful if I can find any of them. The other kids were Adam and Jonathan and Todd. Jonathan was probably my best friend, but we had a falling out after I put the moves on his girlfriend."

"Why'd you do that?"

"I didn't do it on purpose. She and I got to talking one day and we kissed."

"High drama on the Texas prairie," Meredith said. "So does Jonathan still live around here? Will you call him?"

"I suppose I'll at least look him up. Adam was hard to know, and Todd moved away before I did, so I doubt he'll be around."

"Well, I hope you find some closure on this trip, David. I get the feeling you have a lot of unresolved issues from your past. You've always been hard to know, but lately you've been even more distant. You haven't been acting like yourself. And I mean before your dad was killed."

David wondered if the time frame she was referring to coincided with the purchase of the engagement ring. She was probably sensing his indecision toward her, and it was impressive how supportive she was being even after he had spoken to her so harshly. Either she was afraid of killing the golden goose or she really did care about him. The problem was he couldn't tell the difference.

"I get the feeling," Meredith added, "that you knew something bad was going to happen before it actually did."

28

An hour and a half later they were on the ground in Wichita Falls. David rented a silver BMW SUV and called the detective, who was available to meet right away. As they drove into town, he could feel the city sucking the life right out of him. The oppressive heat, the flat topography, the familiar landmarks and poorly-maintained expressway—these were things David had left behind for a reason.

They drove over a bridge and Meredith pointed across the river.

"Is that the 'Wichita Falls?'"

"Sort of."

"Why does it look like that? Why is it beside the river?"

David smiled wryly. "The old falls weren't much to speak of, and the river absorbed them a long time ago. So in the 80s we 'Put the Falls Back in Wichita Falls.'"

"I see."

"Willard Scott came with the *Today* show."

"And you told me this place was the middle of nowhere."

David smiled and kept driving. According to his GPS receiver, the police station was less than five minutes away. As they approached, he called information to ask for Jonathan Crane's phone number. When there was no listing, he called Erik, a friend of his who worked for the NSA, and asked him for help.

"I've got a cell number here for a Jonathan M. Crane in Wichita Falls, Texas," said Erik almost immediately. "Schoolteacher. That sound like him?"

"Maybe," David said. "Let's have the number."

Meredith seemed amused by this. "So you just call your buddy and get someone's cell phone number in three seconds?"

"Erik is good like that."

"Must be nice to have whatever you want at the snap of your fingers."

"That's what I pay him for," David growled.

They drove for a bit longer and Meredith didn't say anything else. Her silence grew pregnant with meaning.

"David, what are we doing?" she finally blurted.

"The police station is just up here on the right."

"No, what are we *doing*? Are we going anywhere, or are we just passing the time?"

One of life's great contradictions was how worthless it felt to discuss your relationship with a woman, and how the one thing that could silence her was something you couldn't bring yourself to do. The longer she went on, the more he wanted to flush her $740,000 engagement ring down the toilet.

"I know you don't like talking about it," Meredith said, "but we have to sometime. And all you ever do is change the subject."

"I enjoy being with you," he answered. "I think you enjoy being with me. Why do we have to be going anywhere?"

"Because I can't wait on you forever. I want to have children someday."

"I've told you I'm open to marriage. Why do you have to push so hard?"

"Push so hard? If I even bring up Christmas plans you freak out. You're thirty-nine years old, David. You can't live like this forever."

"I have an expiration date. Is that what you're saying?"

"Of course not. But you've said before you want to have kids. Do you want to start when you're fifty? Do you want to be nearly seventy when they graduate from high school?"

A few months ago, to free himself from a conversation similar to this one, David had suggested he would consider having children someday. Now he wished he could reach into the past and punch himself in his own fat mouth.

"I'm going to be thirty-one in a month," Meredith added. "It's not so great when women try to have kids after thirty-five."

"I understand," he said. "I know you can't wait on me forever. I think we should sit down and have a serious talk."

"What is there to talk about? Do you want to be with me? Or do you want to let me go and look for someone else?"

"I want to be with you."

"Is it a prenup thing? Are you worried about money?"

"Of course not."

"I don't want us to have a prenup," Meredith said. "But I will if it'll make things easier for you."

"We don't need a prenup."

She smiled a little. Her eyes glistened with tears. "I appreciate that."

"Sure," he said. Though if they were ever married he would definitely insist on a prenup.

In California, municipal buildings were erected tall and with personality, but this police station was a squat tan and white rectangle adjacent to the freeway. The parking lot was literally under the overpass.

"So far," Meredith said, "I am very impressed with Texas. Flat and hot and angry. No wonder everyone here carries a gun."

They climbed a few steps and went inside the station, where they were greeted by a hurricane of cold air and a fat woman behind a desk. The woman was wearing the largest police uniform David had ever seen. On her neck was a mole or a skin tag the size of a marble.

"We're here to see Detective Gholson."

"So you're David Clark," the woman answered. "Freddie's boy. Damn shame what happened to your daddy."

"It's terrible, for sure."

Tinted windows cast the reception area in shadowy, industrial light, and the sound of the highway outside was a deep and constant rumble. David was struggling to accept the reality of his presence again in Wichita Falls.

"You come back to rebuild Lone Star? Lord knows someone needs to. Best barbecue in town."

"Not sure what will happen to the restaurant at this point."

"Well, I'm sorry for your loss. Can't believe what got into Bobby Steele. Everybody loved that kid when he played quarterback at Old High."

The receptionist finally placed a phone call to Gholson, and Meredith fidgeted while they waited for the detective to arrive.

"You some kinda movie star?" the woman asked her, staring.

"No, I run a bridal boutique."

"You're pretty enough to be in movies. Around here, though, a girl your size would blow away in the wind."

"Thank you. I guess."

"I don't know what you folks eat out in California, but maybe you ought to try some barbecue while you're in town. Before you waste away to nothing."

David was about to interject when a door opened at the far end of the reception area, and a stocky man in suspenders appeared.

"Mr. Clark? I'm Detective Gholson. Could you follow me, please?"

David smiled coldly at the receptionist and took Meredith's hand. They strode together toward the open door.

"What the hell was her problem?" Meredith whispered.

"Mainly where we live. Around here, California means communist."

Gholson introduced himself to both of them and led them down a short hall. The detective's office housed two messy desks and a couple of computers. David was struck by how empty the police station seemed to be. At the moment he didn't see anyone else around, even though today was Friday and presumably a business day even for law enforcement. It didn't seem like a real police station at all.

"Did you have any trouble finding us?" Gholson asked.

"No," David said. "Straight down the freeway from the airport."

"Well, I'm sure you folks are probably tired from your trip and would like to get on with your day. I'll keep this brief. Your dad's body is down at Bethania Hospital. Even though we know it's him, as the victim of a crime we are required to make an official identification. For that we'll need dental records. As I mentioned on the phone, the circumstances of death left very little in the way of soft tissue. I'm sorry to say."

David remembered, when he cleaned the barbecue pits at his father's restaurant, how the heat was so intense it felt like his skin was cooking. To imagine the actual burning of flesh, his own father's face consumed by flames. . . .

"Have you obtained the records you need?" he asked the detective.

"Not yet. We can check with every dentist in town, but if you happen to know which one he used, it will make the process go a lot faster."

"I don't really know," David admitted. "I might be able to find out by looking through his financial records."

"That would be helpful. When could you do that?"

"I think we'll head to his house after we're done here."

"That would be great. Because we'd like to release the body to you as soon as possible so you can arrange for disposition. The hospital can recommend a mortuary if your family doesn't already have a preference."

Meredith took his hand and squeezed, as if she thought he might want some emotional support. David ignored it.

"Do you have any more information on the fire?" he asked the detective. "Have you figured out what Bobby was doing at the restaurant in the first place?"

"Our investigation is ongoing, but at this point we don't believe Bob Steele's actions were an isolated incident. There were two cases of arson in town before what happened at your father's restaurant, and closer examination has led us to believe all three fires may be related."

"Why is that?"

"They all seem to be connected to childhood friends of yours, Mr. Clark."

"You mean Bobby set them all?"

"We aren't sure. But the victims of the first two fires were Alicia Ulbrecht and Adam Altman. I believe you knew both of these individuals when you were in school here, is that correct?"

David turned to Meredith. "Alicia is the girl I told you about, the one who was Jonathan's girlfriend. And Adam Altman was in our club."

"That's awfully concerning," Meredith said. "Would this Bobby guy have some bone to pick with you and your friends?"

Before he could answer, Gholson said, "Mr. Clark, what was the name of this club you mentioned?"

David had always understood his visit to Wichita Falls would involve more than just taking care of his father's dead body. He knew there were questions to be asked and answered, and it was possible he might not like what he learned. But however he chose to confront the doubts about himself and his past, they were ultimately philosophical concerns. David had no interest in addressing them with some detective he'd only just met. But he also couldn't refuse to answer direct questions, and since he hadn't yet spoken to Jonathan or anyone else, it made no sense to lie. He'd been stupid to visit Gholson first.

"I believe we called ourselves The Boys of Summer."

"That's the same thing Jonathan Crane told us. The reason I ask is because someone has been sending emails to this station that make reference to a song by the same name, and this has us pretty confused."

"I'm sorry?" David said. "You say someone has sent you emails about a song called 'The Boys of Summer?'"

"Correct."

David pretended to be unimpressed by this revelation. But the truth was he had been thinking a lot about the song in question since he learned of his father's death, because the news from Wichita Falls had dislodged a memory he had long since forgotten: Todd playing "The Boys of Summer" in front of the entire club one afternoon. What made this memory significant was Todd's claim that he had written the song himself. Back then, in 1983, there had been no reason to doubt such a statement. But a year later, when the song appeared on the radio, it should have been obvious to David and all of them that something was amiss. What explanation could there be for Todd having known about a famous song a year before it was released? And why had no one realized it then?

David had a feeling the answers to these questions were like keys that might unlock a much larger mystery.

"When did you receive the most recent email?" he asked Gholson.

"Last night about eight o'clock."

"*After* Bobby and my father died in the fire," David pointed out.

"Yes," Gholson said. "Also, an officer arrived at the restaurant just before Steele torched the place. What he said to that officer leads us to believe Bob wasn't working alone."

"Can you tell me what he said?"

"He said, according to Todd, his life was supposed to end in that way."

Gholson was looking at him intently, obviously hoping for some kind of reaction. And though David declined to give him the satisfaction, he was nevertheless shaken deeply by this news. Bobby's reference to Todd suggested he had been suffering from the same sort of anxiety that had plagued David over the past several weeks, a sense that something was very wrong with the world and had been ever since Todd Willis had come into their lives. He had always known he would someday be made to answer for the sins of his past, and if Bobby had mentioned Todd directly, David suspected a moment of reckoning was near. A storm was coming and they were all directly in its path.

"Todd?" he finally asked the detective, as if he were confused.

"You must know who he was talking about."

"I assume he meant Todd Willis. The kid who—"

"Yeah, yeah," Gholson said. "The one who woke up from the coma. That's the same thing your buddy, Jonathan, said. As soon as I mentioned Todd, he couldn't wait to tell me how strange the kid had been and how it was his idea that made you boys burn down the restaurant."

"We didn't burn down the restaurant," David said automatically. "Todd did that on his own."

"You're sure about that?"

David couldn't know what Jonathan had told the detective, but it didn't seem possible he would have admitted to any crimes, no matter how long ago they had occurred. Any deviation from the story they had constructed back then might open a new inquiry into the fate of Joe Henreid, which was something none of them could afford.

"I don't appreciate your tone," David said. "I'm here to bury my father, and you act like I'm under some kind of suspicion."

"No, no," said Gholson. "Not at all. But whoever is sending these emails, Mr. Clark, is threatening to burn down my town. I'm obligated to follow any lead, no matter how old or how irrelevant it might seem."

David felt Meredith's hand on his own, there again to comfort him. He jumped a little because he had forgotten she was sitting next to him.

"My primary task here in Wichita Falls is to get my father's affairs in order," David said. "But I'm happy to help you in any way I can."

"I appreciate that. The first thing you can do, as I said before, is find the name of your daddy's dentist. Beyond that, I'll be in touch."

David stood with Meredith and they shook hands with the detective.

"I'm sorry again for your loss," Gholson said. "Fred Clark was a pillar of our community and he will be missed. I sure hope you'll take Penny's advice and consider reopening Lone Star. Otherwise I'm gonna have to get my dinner from the Branding Iron."

David smiled, but honestly he could think of no better fate for his father's restaurant than to see it reduced to ashes.

"I'll be in touch," he said to Gholson.

But not before David first spoke to Jonathan Crane.

29

The constant inbound phone calls were torture. For eight hours every day between Monday morning and Friday afternoon, Alicia was tormented by the same inane questions about the same products over and over and over. But the true misery of her existence was adhering to a rigid schedule, having to wake at five o'clock every morning so she could be on the phone not a minute later than six-thirty. There was no escaping the routine, no room for a long shower or an extra cup of coffee or time to iron a stubborn blouse into submission.

This morning was especially tough because even though she drank only three beers and a shot last night, sleep had been a long time coming. She felt helpless occupying her old room at her parents' house, as if the pages of her life had flipped themselves backward, or like she was so non-functional as an adult that she couldn't afford her own place. And the news Jonathan had delivered last night made everything more confusing. Had her house really been burned down as some kind of revenge plot? And did that mean her parents were at risk, too?

Eventually she had fallen asleep, but only barely, so when morning came too soon she decided not to wash her hair. Put on a blouse and slacks that should have gone to the dry cleaner's a week ago. Made it to the office by 6:28, logged in to the phone at 6:30, and answered her first call at 6:31.

"Thanks for calling Deckard Digital, this is Alicia, how can I help you?"

"You can *help* me," an elderly male voice said, "by getting your *god-damned* program off my computer."

It was easy to abuse someone you couldn't see. Without fear of physical retribution, you could throw civility out the window and speak to a fellow human being with contempt that was unacceptable elsewhere in life.

"Of course," she said. "Which software product is it?"

"I've got the word processor and the music mixer and I want them both off! Do you have to know *what* they are to get them *off?*"

"Well, the uninstall procedure is different based on—"

"You companies are all alike. You trick us into buying poorly-designed programs and then make it impossible to delete them. I've had enough! You'll be hearing from my attorney!"

The line went dead. She wished she could reach through the phone and clamp her hands around his neck. Would he talk to his own daughter that way?

The phone beeped in her ear again. This was how it went. You didn't pick up a handset and place it against your ear. You didn't push a button to admit the phone calls into your headset. No, you were always on, always available to receive a call, and you sat there waiting like the victim of a firing squad, with your back turned to the callers, who picked up their telephones and fired into your head and you were helpless to stop it.

"Thank you for calling Deckard Digital, this is Alicia Ulbrecht, how can I help you?"

"Leesha *what?*"

"Alicia Ulbrecht."

"Hi there, Leesha Fullbright. For some reason your music mixer is saving files in my folder full of written documents and I don't like it. I'm an author and I don't want my music files mixed up with my stories. You need to fix this and fix it *now*."

And so it went. She took twenty-six calls before her break, during which she quickly sucked down two cups of coffee, and then brought a third back to her desk. By lunchtime she had answered forty-one calls. At this pace she might reach ninety by the time she left work at three-thirty.

On her way to the cafeteria she threaded her way through the cubicle maze, the network of gray fabric walls, and listened as other reps repeated the same answers and suggestions she employed throughout the day. She felt the strange sensation of being on a movie set, some dystopian corporate doomworld where she would be sentenced to toil away, on a recurring loop, forever. She walked past motivational posters that lazily paired dramatic landscape photos with captions like PATIENCE and LEADERSHIP and SERVICE. She saw hand-drawn images of mousetraps and cheese, grammatically incorrect flyers advertising departmental promotions, incitements like "Don't just answer the

phone. De-light callers with *WORLD CLASS CUSTOMER SERVICE!!!*
And don't forget to *SALE UPGRADES AND ADDONS!!!*" Because it
wasn't enough to simply provide customers with useful assistance. The
real goal was to think of innovative ways to sell additional products to
defenseless customers who called looking for technical support.

In the cafeteria there were ten or fifteen tables and a television.
Diners were sprinkled throughout the room except for six or seven who
were clustered in one corner playing bingo. Alicia bought a salad and
noticed the cafeteria was out of fat free dressing again. They were always
out of fat free dressing.

She found a place near the television and dug into the leafy rough-
age of her salad. She'd been threatening to go on a diet for a while, but
now it was time to get serious. Meeting Jonathan yesterday had been
a spotlight trained on the stagnant nature of her life. How many years
since she'd seen him? Twenty since high school graduation, twenty-five
years since they'd spoken last. And what was different about her life now
compared to then? She spent her days at work instead of school. Mother
and daughter had traded the role of caregiver. But beyond those two
things her life was pretty much the same as it had been when she was a
thirteen-year-old girl hoping to be noticed by a boy.

Since her relationship with Brandon ended, Alicia had been bid-
ing her time here in Wichita, waiting for her father to retire, assuming
she would eventually move to another city where there was culture and
more rewarding jobs and more interesting men. She had been waiting
for real life to begin while everyone else was raising children and making
the most of what they had. And all along Alicia had thought *she* was the
smart one.

Her cell phone rang, and she reached into her purse to retrieve it.
"This is Alicia."

"Hello," a voice said. "May I speak to Alicia Ulbrecht?"

Because her job involved so much time on the phone, Alicia could
not tolerate even the smallest mistake on calls of a business nature. Like
someone not listening to the greeting where she *already said her name.*

"This is Alicia," she said again.

"Hi, Ms. Ulbrecht. My name is Kat and I'm calling on behalf of
Allstate Insurance."

"Oh, right. I checked with you guys yesterday on the status of my claim."

"Yes, well I'm required to inform you that processing of your claim has been put on hold pending an arson investigation."

"What? Why?"

"A criminal investigation raises concerns about the nature of the damage to your property, and Allstate policy requires us to gather more information before approving or rejecting your claim."

"How can you reject it? I didn't burn down my own house."

"We make no accusations, Mrs. Ulbrecht. But, as I already stated, Allstate policy requires us to gather more—"

"When do you plan to gather this information? I've been paying premiums to you guys for like eight years. My house is gone and I've had to make arrangements to find a place to sleep, and now you're telling me you don't want to pay my claim?"

She was near tears and hated herself for it.

"Ms. Ulbrecht, I cannot make an assessment about the validity of your claim or the likelihood of it being approved or denied. But Allstate policy requires us to gather more information—"

"Will you stop repeating yourself?"

"Mrs. Ulbrecht. There is no reason to become belligerent with me. I am required to—"

"I'm required to tell you to go fuck yourself."

She pushed a button and ended the phone call. The bingo players glared at her with looks of disapproval.

The phone rang again, and this time Alicia planned to ask for the woman's boss. What right did they—?

Then she looked down and saw Jonathan Crane on the display.

"Hi, Jonathan."

"Hey, Alicia. What's up? Is everything okay?"

"Trying to have a little lunch, but Allstate just called and said they're not sure they're going to approve the claim on my house. I can't believe it."

"What? Why?"

"Because of the ongoing arson investigation."

"That's ridiculous. You weren't even there when it happened. How can they try to blame it on you?"

"I guess they don't know who to blame it on. What am I going to do if I lose my house and the equity because of all this shit? I've been paying on the damned thing for eight years."

"That's not going to happen," he said to her. "You didn't have anything to do with this. Insurance companies are evil. They'll deny a claim for anything, but once the cops make an arrest I'm sure everything will be fine."

"When do you think that's going to happen?"

"I don't know, but maybe there will be some movement soon. I just got off the phone with David. He's in town and just talked to the police, and he wants to meet with us this evening."

"He's here now?" Alicia asked, startled.

"Well, he has his own plane, I guess. The detective asked him to come to Wichita to handle his father's remains and all that, but when David got here the guy asked him a bunch of questions about the summer when we were kids. He tried to trick him into admitting we burned down the restaurant back then."

"So obviously the detective thinks you guys are involved somehow."

"Alicia, we're not. At least I'm not. But someone is sending emails that appear to make reference to our club and make it look like the past is repeating itself. So we all need to talk about this. David is coming by my house tonight, and I'd like you to join us."

Alicia wasn't sure what to say. She found it difficult to believe David Clark was going to be in town this evening. Did she want to see him? Was she prepared to? He was probably tanned and fit and looking like the millions of dollars he was worth. She hadn't been to the hair stylist in nearly six months. And she was still shaking over the call from Allstate.

"Alicia?"

"I think I can make it. What time?"

"Around seven. I can give you directions if you want."

"Just text me the address and I'll find it."

Jonathan waited a minute and then said, "Did you get any sleep last night?"

"Not a lot. I'm feeling kind of stressed, actually."

"I can only imagine. But we are going to figure this thing out. I promise."

"Or hopefully the police will. I don't think Allstate will put much credence in our opinions."

"That's true."

Alicia wasn't in the mood to talk, but she didn't want to be rude to him.

"Thanks for meeting me last night," he said. "You looked great, by the way."

"Thanks. I had a good time."

"And now tonight, seeing David. Imagine how strange that's going to be."

Alicia wondered if he was referring to what had happened when they were kids. How Jonathan had never called her back. How she ended up falling for David.

"I was surprised you didn't bring this up last night," she said.

"Bring up what?"

"What you're thinking about. David and you and me."

Now Jonathan didn't say anything. Silence hissed through the little speaker in her phone.

"I know it was a long time ago," she said, "and it doesn't matter now, but I don't know what you expected me to do. You never called me back."

"You're right. It doesn't matter now. We were children."

"We were childhood friends, we still live in the same town, and we haven't spoken since we were thirteen."

Alicia remembered the first time she saw him, in the P. E. classroom, seated in the first row of desks. She remembered his blond, floppy hair and the way he looked at everything (including her) with a kind of intense curiosity. Once she noticed him it was difficult to stop noticing him, and every time she glanced in his direction he was looking back at her. Finally, he spoke to her one day at lunch. Their conversation had been easy, their interests similar, and she had been smitten hard for the first time in her life. It was this overwhelming blush of emotion, of puppy love, whatever you wanted to call it, that she had never forgotten. Maybe pubescent hormones had triggered such an exaggerated reaction, but like the lingering emotions after an intense dream, Alicia was somehow affected now by the way she had felt for him then.

"It was my mom," he told her. "It seems so silly now, but she over-heard when I called you. When I asked you to be my girlfriend. She said I could never see you or talk to you. I'm sure David told you about her."

"He didn't."

"We had a horrible relationship. She pretty much hated me. I don't know why."

"That's . . . I'm sorry, Jonathan. Do you have a relationship with her now?"

"She and Kenny still live in the same house in Tanglewood. I haven't spoken to her in a couple of years. I guess she's an alcoholic."

"Kenny is Bobby's dad?"

"Right."

Alicia was quiet for a moment and then said, "Maybe you could have told me. At least I'd have known what was going on."

"It was so embarrassing to be treated that way. I couldn't imagine telling you or anyone. It took every ounce of courage I could summon to call you that night, and she was sitting around the corner, listen-ing. When I got off the phone she made fun of me for calling you. I should have stood up for myself, but she'd been terrorizing me for years. Whenever she yelled, I did whatever I could to make her stop. I had a lot of growing up to do, and I did it late. I'm a lot different than that now."

"But you still didn't talk to me even after school began."

"I was really embarrassed. I'm sorry. Like I said, we were just kids."

"We were just kids," Alicia agreed. "But those experiences stick with us. They shape the way we look at the world and how we feel, even now."

"Yeah. So why don't you show up a little early tonight? You and I could talk more, have some wine before they get here."

"Who's 'they'? Is David bringing someone?"

"His girlfriend, I think."

"Oh. Of course he is."

Silence crept into the phone. She didn't want to let it go on too long.

"All right," she said. "I'll come by like an hour before they do. We can have a little wine, relax before the big meeting. I want us to catch up for real this time."

30

Outside, on the back porch, Maxie barked. Once. Twice. Adam was helping Rachel put away groceries, and he waited for another bark. There was no stopping it, really. Once Maxie began yapping, she might not stop for an hour. Or more. And it didn't help to go out there and yell at her. It didn't help to feed her a treat. She just kept on yapping and yapping like she was on some kind of loop. Rachel hated it.

"How is the cleanup at your project coming?" she asked him. "Can Juan start framing again?"

"It's on hold until the police have gathered more evidence. I told you this yesterday."

"Sorry. I was just checking. This is a big deal, Adam, and you've hardly mentioned it."

Rachel was about to say something else when Maxie barked again.

"I wish that dog would be quiet," she said.

"Maybe we should give her away."

"But Bradie loves her. Kids love dogs."

"Bradie never plays with her," Adam pointed out. "She never even goes in the back yard."

"Of course Bradie plays with her."

Adam looked around the corner and saw his daughter sitting twelve inches from the living room television set. SpongeBob was on.

Yap! said Maxie.

Rachel dried her hands and marched into the breakfast room, where a set of French doors opened on the back porch. Adam could see Maxie from here, staring into space, yapping. He had never understood why the dog would do that, or what it was barking at, but right now he felt like following its lead. Imagine the cathartic release of staring into the sky and screaming until your lungs bled. Imagine the great weight unshouldered, the liberation from guilt, finally telling the world who you really were.

Rachel opened the door.

"Maxie. Shut up."

Maxie just stared at her.

"Okay, then," Rachel said, and shut the door.

Yap! said Maxie.

Rachel jerked the door open. She reached out and popped Maxie on the nose. "You shut up, you stupid dog!"

The dog yelped and scooted backward.

"That's enough! Do you hear me?"

Maxie just stared.

His wife went into the kitchen and grabbed a box of treats. She tore the box open as she reached the door and then threw it at the dog.

"Why don't you shut up? You must be stupid stupid stupid!"

Some of the treats, brown and yellow and orange, spilled onto the concrete patio. Maxie spotted the windfall and trundled over. She settled in and began to eat.

Rachel slammed the door. "That ought to keep you busy for a while."

"We really should give the dog away," Adam told her.

"We're not giving her away. Pets teach children how to build relationships."

Adam was debating whether he should press the issue with Maxie, or walk over and strangle his wife to death, when the phone rang. He picked up the cordless handset and looked at the Caller ID, which said CRANE, JONATHAN.

The phone rang again.

"Aren't you going to answer it?" Rachel asked him.

Had his wife not been standing there, Adam probably wouldn't have. But ignoring the phone now would prompt questions he didn't care to answer.

"Hello?"

"Hello, Adam? It's Jonathan Crane."

"Jonathan," he said, and drifted out of the kitchen. He walked past the living room, headed for his office. "How are you doing?"

"I'm all right. Have you heard about Bobby? About David's dad?"

"I have. Apparently Bobby burned down a house I'm building, too. Did you know that?"

"I did know that," Jonathan said. "Some detectives came by my house last night and interrogated me about it."

"Why you?"

"Because they suspect Bobby didn't act alone. They think he was working with someone who is still at large."

"Why would they think that? Have there been more fires?"

Jonathan told him about the emails, about the song lyrics.

"I don't understand what the lyrics have to do with anything," Adam said.

"At the restaurant, right before the fire, Bobby told a policeman it was his destiny to die that way, like Todd had made him do it or something. And now that someone is sending clues about the song, it makes it seem as if all three fires are connected. The detective knows what the name of our club was back in the day. Do you remember?"

"The Boys of Summer. Of course I remember. How does he know that?"

"He just does."

Adam was deeply troubled by this news. He sat down at his desk and stared at the dormant computer screen.

"So if Bobby mentioned Todd, why did the detectives interrogate you?"

"He believes all of us were involved in the original fires back when we were kids. He doesn't believe it was Todd and Joe Henreid. By that reasoning, the detective assumes I know something about what's going on now."

It had taken Adam years to forget about Joe Henreid and all of this. He had no interest in undoing so much effort.

"Is it possible," he asked Jonathan, "that Todd could be back to exact some kind of revenge?"

"I don't know, but I think we should talk about it."

"Isn't that what we're doing now? Talking about it?"

"I mean sit down and talk in person. David's in town to take care of his dad, and he's going to stop by my house tonight. I thought you might like to come by, also."

"I don't think so," Adam said. "Rachel and I have plans."

"She can come, too. David is bringing his girlfriend, and Alicia Ulbrecht is going to be there as well. You remember her?"

"I've got to get going. My daughter has an appointment."

"Adam, wait. Do you remember that keyboard Todd used to carry around?"

A sound startled him, and Adam jerked his head around. He was sure he had heard feedback, a guitar or maybe a walkie-talkie, as if someone else were trying to communicate with him.

"Say 'hi' to David for me. I'm really sorry I can't make it tonight."

"What about Joe Henreid? What if—"

Adam pushed a button and ended the phone call.

Memories were bubbling, threatening to surface, and he pushed them back under. Tried to bury them, suffocate them. He stared out the sunny window, watching trees blow in the wind, until Rachel appeared in the doorway.

"Who was on the phone?"

"Jonathan Crane. You remember him."

"I don't think so."

"I knew him in school. He's a junior high teacher now."

"Oh, yeah. Wants to be a writer."

Adam realized he wasn't looking at his wife. He glanced up and said, "That's him."

"So? What'd he want? Does he have a book coming out?"

"No, he called to talk about what happened at the restaurant."

"Oh. I thought you said you weren't very close friends with Bobby or David."

"I wasn't. But Jonathan was sort of Bobby's half-brother. So it's a bigger deal to him, I guess."

"Are you going to meet him?"

"Of course not. I have work to do."

Rachel didn't say anything for a moment, and then, "You know, about what happened at the restaurant . . . "

Adam wasn't looking at her again. With great effort he glanced up and said, "What about it?"

"Well, this is going to sound so stupid . . . I don't even know how to ask you."

You wouldn't think your heart rate could increase so quickly, not without some kind of physical exertion, and yet all at once his chest was being trampled by the thundering hooves of a cattle stampede.

"What is it?" he asked.

"Well, I couldn't help but overhear you talking on the phone."

"Yes, you could have. I walked out of the kitchen."

"Your voice carries further than you think, Adam. Anyway, I heard you mention lyrics and that song, 'The Boys of Summer.'"

"Yeah?"

"Well, you have that notebook you use for work. And I've flipped through it before, you know, to get an idea of your days."

"You look through my notes?"

"Not to snoop. I'm just curious about your work. You don't talk about it very much."

Adam glared at her. He wondered if Rachel suspected him of adultery. In fact he sometimes *did* think about cheating on her, about finding a loose woman to do the kind of naughty things Rachel wouldn't. But after Jesus had forgiven him for his childhood crimes, he had no room for more sin in his life.

"Anyway, I've seen those lyrics in your notebook. From that song."

"So? It's a good song."

Rachel chuckled. "I suppose it is. It just seems a little odd that . . . I mean everything you said on the phone, detectives and fires and lyrics and the name of that song . . . "

"It was the name of our club when we were kids. The Boys of Summer. It doesn't mean anything."

"Okay, but that's not how it sounded on the phone. And it just seems a little odd that you write out those song lyrics, like a lot, and now all this, and . . . Honey, you sounded so frightened on the phone just now."

Adam stood up. "You shouldn't have been eavesdropping on me."

"I know. I'm sorry. I just want to help if you're worried about something. Talk to me, Adam."

The uneven light accentuated the angles of her face, the prominence of her cheekbones. Rachel had always been a beautiful woman, and Adam could remember when just the sight of her made his heart thunder the way it thundered now. He stood mere inches from her, close enough to kiss.

"This is a stupid conversation," he said. "And I'm through with it."

31

A licia sat on Jonathan's leather couch, waiting for him to return with the wine. In less than an hour David would arrive with his girlfriend, but for now it was just the two of them.

A few feet away, Julia Roberts was trying in vain to purchase clothing on Rodeo Drive with a wad of Richard Gere's money. For some reason it occurred to Alicia how Julia Roberts would always and forever be doing that, taking her handful of hundred dollar bills and shoving it at Héctor Elizondo, the hotel manager; that time would always stand still for those characters even as their real-life counterparts succumbed to gravity and aging skin and withering bones. It also occurred to her that while an eternity of soft skin and functioning organs might be a blessing, being stuck in an eternal *Groundhog Day*-style loop would not . . . even a loop in which Richard Gere would forever be climbing up the fire escape to rescue his princess.

And then Jonathan was back, carrying a tray with the bottle of white wine, two glasses, and a plate of cheese and crackers.

"Wow," she said, smiling. "I didn't realize this was going to be so formal."

"This is what guys do when we're trying to impress you. Later it's beer and brats."

"That would have been fine this time."

He laughed and went to work on the bottle of wine. She picked up a cracker and munched on it.

"I like your house. It's not too dirty but it's not too clean, either."

"Not too clean? You're saying I'm a pig?"

Alicia laughed. "No! That's not what I meant."

"You haven't been here five minutes and already you're trying to change me."

"Will you stop? Your house is great. Although your movie theater living room could use a feminine touch."

"Chicks never want a TV in the living room."

"Whatever. Maybe a plant or two? A chair over there? You've got a couch and a wall of electronics."

"Tough crowd tonight. I'm not letting you anywhere near the kitchen."

Alicia laughed and punched him on the arm. Jonathan poured a glass of wine and handed it to her.

"So Karen lived here with you?"

"We bought the house together six years ago."

"Did she . . . I mean, what happened with you guys?"

"It's a long story. The simple answer is she thought I was selling myself short at work. That I could make more money if I put a little effort into it."

"How would you do that? Isn't school funding low already?"

"She thought I should aspire to be an administrator. Principal, superintendent, that sort of thing."

"And you didn't want that?"

Jonathan drank a little of his wine. "I didn't get into teaching to work my way up the ladder. I got into teaching to help kids. And to have a salary until I could publish novels and write full-time."

"So Karen didn't see the same potential in your writing as you?"

"I guess you could say she was more pragmatic than me. She thought of it more as a lottery. Spend a little time writing, you know, an hour or two on the weekend, after work, whatever . . . and maybe one day I'd land a big book contract and we could both quit our jobs. But the more time I spent on it, this pipe dream, was less time I was devoting to my 'real' career."

"Do you think you'll ever make money at it? Enough to give up your day job?"

"I used to think so. I'm no Stephen King, but I think I write pretty well. I don't know anyone in publishing, though, and it seems like that's the only way to make it."

"I don't blame you for sticking to your guns," Alicia said. "Who's going to make your dreams come true if you don't?"

Jonathan smiled broadly at this. "Exactly."

Still, Alicia could understand the challenge of being married to a struggling author.

"Did you ever wonder if Karen was jealous of your writing? Maybe her concern wasn't so much about focusing on your school career as you having just *one* career. If you wrote every night after work, it probably didn't leave a lot of time for her."

"Yeah, I thought of that. But honestly all our issues were just symptoms of a larger problem."

"Which was?"

"I didn't love her. We fell into a relationship mostly by accident, and staying in it was easier than breaking up and finding someone else. In retrospect the relationship doesn't feel like it really happened. Like it was just a placeholder until my real life began."

"So what about now?" she asked him. "Has your real life begun?"

He looked over at the television, then back at her. "Do you really want to watch *Pretty Woman*? I could put on some music."

"Music would be wonderful."

Jonathan leaned near her and pressed some buttons on a remote control. The dark melody that followed, unfamiliar to her, seemed to change the mood of their conversation. As Jonathan leaned back on the couch, he looked directly into her eyes as if he might want to kiss her.

"I don't even know what real life looks like," Alicia said. "I see friends and family all doing the 'normal' thing, buying bigger houses, driving their kids to church in SUVs, and when I look at them it makes me cringe. For some reason I get the feeling there's something out there extraordinary waiting for me. How arrogant is that?"

Jonathan was looking at her carefully, the way she remembered from their junior high days. She loved it now the way she had loved it then.

"I sound ridiculous," she said. "I know I do. I'm sorry."

"You don't sound ridiculous."

"I feel like a pretty strong woman, you know? I hate my job, but I work hard at it. I make decent money for a town like this, and I take care of my mom when my dad is away on business. I tell myself I don't need a relationship to be happy. If I meet someone, fine, and if I don't, well that's fine, too. The last thing I've ever wanted is to force it to happen. And still almost every day there's some woman at work who wants to set me up or wonders why I'm 'still single.' As if 'single' is an affliction I'm trying to cure. And the dumbest thing is you should hear how they complain, these women, about their husbands and their kids and how the world is going to hell because the government took prayer out of schools. Everyone seems so damned miserable and yet they judge me because I have the audacity to do what they wish they had."

"And what's that?"

"To hold out for, you know, the fairy tale."

Alicia looked at Jonathan and felt with a strange and sudden clarity they would have a future together, even though her ideal fairy tale partner looked somewhat different than this. Jonathan was ordinary-looking. He wasn't particularly confident or witty or any of the things she might notice in a man. But he was emotionally transparent and she loved the logical, almost scientific way he looked at the world. Also, the interest he still showed in her after so many years made her feel more attractive than she had in some time.

Alicia finished her wine, and Jonathan poured more for both of them. It was six-thirty, half an hour before David and his girlfriend were scheduled to arrive. Was she looking for something in Jonathan because David was bringing a woman along? Surely not. Hopefully not.

"This whole thing is surreal," Jonathan said. "The fires, the detectives, seeing you grown up. I haven't thought about any of this in forever and now, suddenly, it's like it all happened yesterday. Remember in junior high when I called you on the phone? I swear I can still hear you telling me about the frozen oceans on Europa."

"Jonathan, I'm trying to . . . This is complicated, I know. Being childhood friends and all, and now the two of us here as adults, having wine together, and—"

He leaned forward and pressed his mouth against hers. She could taste the ripe flavor of cheese on his tongue, could smell the wine on his breath. He ran a finger down her chin, then backed away and touched the same finger against her lips.

"Who's going to make my dreams happen if I don't?" he said. "Right?"

She squeezed his hand and then touched him on the forearm. It was ridiculous, being here with him, kissing him. On Monday she had gone to Chili's with that Stuart fool, absurdly sure she would never meet a decent man in Wichita, and had come home to find her house in flames. At that moment her emotional spirit could not have been more wounded, at least not until this afternoon when she heard the news from

Allstate. Now she was sitting on the couch of her first crush, feeling as if she were somehow a kid again. Or like she was a character in one of Jonathan's novels.

He leaned into her, taking his time, and she decided it was okay, for now, whatever he was trying to do. They kissed for a while. She warmed to him. Tingled.

32

A few minutes before seven, Jonathan poured himself the rest of the wine while Alicia went into the bathroom to freshen up. His heart was beating faster than it should have been. His head was swimming a little from the wine. It had been years since he'd kissed a woman other than Karen, and it felt as weird as it did wonderful.

Any minute now David would arrive with his girlfriend, and Jonathan was growing more nervous by the moment. For one, if he was ever going to discuss his thoughts about Todd and the impossible music, tonight was the time. The problem was Alicia seemed like a pretty level-headed girl, and Jonathan didn't want to come off looking to her like he was a gullible fool. Especially not in front of David.

Jonathan heard the popping sound of gravel outside, a car stopping in front of his house. He looked through the blinds and saw a silver BMW SUV.

"Alicia," he called. "They're here."

A moment later the doorbell rang. Jonathan approached the door and opened it. David was tanned, fit, dressed in a golf shirt and slacks. The large watch on his wrist looked like it was made of solid platinum. Meredith's blonde hair was shoulder-length, her arms lithe and bronzed.

"David," he said. "Wow, it's been a long time. You guys come in."

David shook Jonathan's hand and hugged him, and then he introduced Meredith, who handed over a bottle of white wine.

"Very nice to meet you, Meredith. Thanks for the wine. Alicia's inside if you guys want to follow me."

He took them through the living room and into the kitchen.

"Alicia," David said, and stepped forward to hug her. "It's been for-ever. You look great."

"You, too," Alicia replied. "California obviously suits you."

David smiled. He put his arm around Meredith and said, "Alicia, this is Meredith."

The two women shook hands and smiled at each other.

"I've heard a lot about you both," Meredith said. "Thanks for allow-ing me to be here. I sort of feel like I don't belong."

"Nonsense," Jonathan said. "We could use some outside perspective."

She smiled at this.

To David, Jonathan said, "Man, I'm so sorry about what happened to your dad, that you had to come out here under these circumstances. You must be devastated."

"Thank you. It's a terrible thing for sure. But he and I didn't see eye-to-eye on a lot of things and had fallen out of touch. I hadn't spoken to him in years, to be honest."

"Oh, David," Alicia said. "That's terrible. You must be overwhelmed right now."

Meredith grunted agreement.

"I could think of better ways to spend my time," David said. "But the bright side of all this is I finally get to see you guys again."

This seemed like a good time for Jonathan to pour wine and hand glasses to each of them.

David said, "On the way to the police station today, Meredith was telling me how impressed she was with Wichita Falls. What did you say? Flat and hot and angry?"

"Oh, I was just joking around."

"It's all right," Alicia said. "I'd move away in a heartbeat if I could."

"What's keeping you here?" David asked.

"My mother. She has MS and my dad is on the road a lot."

Jonathan couldn't help but imagine, if he were worth millions, how easy it would be to turn Alicia's dreams into reality. If he were a rich and famous author, he could simply hire a full-time nurse for her mother and whisk Alicia away to New York. They could find a super cool apart-ment downtown and do hip things like eat hot dogs on the street and have sex every night to jazz music on vinyl. Or whatever hip and artsy people in New York liked to do. Honestly, they could do similar things in downtown Wichita Falls, except they would probably need to bring their own hot dogs and jazz records.

"I'm sorry about your mother," David said.

"Thank you. It's been tough on both my parents, but they've handled it as well as they could, I think."

Jonathan didn't like the way Alicia was looking at David.

"So, Meredith," he said. "You were telling us how much you wanted to live here in Wichita."

She laughed. "Well, I'm sure it sounds shitty coming from an outsider, but something about this place doesn't seem quite right. The people we've met, I don't know, they seem to just be going through the motions. Like they've got nothing to live for, like the city is doomed or something."

"I don't know if we're doomed," he said to Meredith. "But there definitely is some insecurity about being so remote and forgotten. Everyone thinks Wichita Falls is in Kansas."

Meredith nodded at this, but when no one said anything else, Jonathan decided a change of scenery was in order.

"You guys want to go sit down? If we're going to chat for a while we might as well get comfortable."

Soon the four of them were in the living room: Jonathan and Alicia together on the couch, David and Meredith on the adjacent love seat.

"I can't believe it's been so long," David said, looking directly at Alicia. "Our twenty-year reunion is next fall. You going?"

"I doubt it," Alicia said. "I went to the ten-year and the only interesting thing was to see how fat everyone was. I noticed you didn't bother to show."

Jonathan hadn't attended the reunion, either, but Alicia neglected to mention that.

"Was your old boyfriend there?" David asked. "The linebacker?"

"He weighed probably three hundred pounds. Works for Terminix or something."

"He kills termites?"

"And spiders and scorpions, I presume."

Both David and Meredith chuckled. Alicia took a long drink of her wine, and Jonathan realized his was gone already.

"So what do you guys do?" David asked.

"I work in tech support for a software company," Alicia said. "All the people who can't figure out their computers, they call me."

"I'm one of those," Meredith said. "I run a bridal boutique, and I swear half the time I try to launch my inventory program it crashes the computer."

Everyone laughed at this.

"And you, Jonathan?" Meredith asked.

"I teach Social Studies to junior high students."

"Oh, that's a great way to give back," David said.

"He also writes books," Alicia pointed out.

"Really?" Meredith said. "What kind of books do you write?"

I write books like this, Jonathan felt like saying.

Instead, he told her, "Speculative fiction. Stories with strange things going on, like *The Twilight Zone*."

"Anything published?"

"Not yet."

Jonathan wondered how much longer he should wait before broaching the topic that had brought them together in the first place. He couldn't put it off forever, but he was in no hurry to bring up Todd and his music.

David, however, seemed to anticipate his thoughts.

"I want to catch up with you guys," he said, "but we also need to figure out what the heck is going on in this town. I want to know what happened to my dad. I want that detective to stop acting like I had anything to do with it."

"Why would he believe that?" Alicia asked. "You don't even live around here."

David looked at Jonathan, "What exactly did you tell the detective?"

"I told him our original story. The only thing I changed was that we knew in advance Todd was going to burn down your dad's restaurant."

"That's good," David said. "Consistency is good. The problem is Gholson doesn't believe it. And if he ever finds proof, the next question he'll ask is what happened to Joe Henreid."

"I thought you didn't know what happened to Joe," Alicia said.

"We don't," David replied. "But I don't want some local yokel detective using this business to reopen a missing person case and drag my name through the mud. Do you?"

"No," Jonathan said. They were both declining to reveal crucial information about Joe, which wasn't really fair to Alicia (or Meredith), but this didn't seem like the best time to address the topic. And really they didn't know what had happened to Joe. They only suspected.

"So where's Adam?" David asked. "I thought we were all going to be here."

"Said he had other plans."

"We should project a united front. We have no idea what Adam has said to Gholson. He needs to be here."

"He was pretty adamant," Jonathan explained.

"Which makes me think he's nervous. I never really trusted that guy, if you want to know the truth."

"Look," Alicia said. "What happened twenty-five years ago might be interesting to you guys, but my insurance company is withholding payment until the arson investigation is complete. I need to know what's going on *today*. And besides, if someone is still out there, they might keep doing this. They could try to burn down Jonathan's house, or Adam's, or who knows what."

"But why?" Meredith asked. "That's what I don't understand. If this Todd guy is back in Wichita Falls, is it for some kind of revenge? How in the world did he convince your friend, Bobby, to burn down the restaurant? And kill David's father in the process? I mean that is some serious shit. What is he trying to accomplish or communicate by doing all this?"

No one had an answer. They all just sat there. And where he had watched David control the conversation earlier, Jonathan decided now was his chance to steer them in the direction he had intended from the beginning.

"Detective Gholson has every reason to suspect us," he said, "because the lyrics in these emails are obviously connected in some way to the name of our club. But if he's done any research, he must be confused about what the connection is. He must know by now we named our club The Boys of Summer more than a year before the song actually came out."

Jonathan looked at David for recognition. He found nothing.

"Why does that matter?" Meredith asked. "Just because you didn't name your club after the actual song doesn't mean the emails aren't meant as some kind of clue."

"The thing is," Jonathan said, "we *did* name our club after that song."

He could see Alicia and Meredith calculating the ways this could be true. And once they arrived at the same impossible conclusion, they would question it as he had. There was no reason for either one of them to believe something so ridiculous, but David had been there in 1983. The two of them had seen and heard the same things. If their memories matched, did that mean it might be true after all?

Finally, David breathed out a sigh of what seemed like relief.

"Most of the time Todd used his keyboard to play music he heard on the radio. But sometimes he wrote his own songs, and Jonathan's correct: One of them inspired the name of our club."

"'The Boys of Summer,'" Alicia said.

"You're saying it's actually the same song?" Meredith asked. "You're saying Todd played it before you ever heard it on the radio?"

"Yes," Jonathan blurted.

"Okay, but who knows when the song was actually recorded?" Meredith asked. "Maybe the popular version is a remake."

"I looked it up," Jonathan told her. "Don Henley wrote the song with a guitarist who played with Tom Petty. In 1984."

"There must be some kind of explanation. Maybe it was another song he played, and you guys remember it wrong. There are a lot of options more likely than a time warp, right?"

"I know how it sounds," Jonathan said. "But if there's a better explanation, I can't figure out what it is."

33

Alicia understood a writer might want to find drama in everyday situations, but when you blamed the supernatural for faulty childhood memories, you were in the territory of alien abductions and Elvis sightings. She would have expected Jonathan to realize this about himself, considering his logical nature, but judging by the earnest look on his face he seemed to have already accepted his incredible conclusion as fact.

When she was a little girl, psychic abilities like telepathy and second sight had seemed frighteningly possible, but her father's regular and patient lessons about science helped her look at the world through more pragmatic eyes. Alicia still wanted to believe in the impossible, in something beyond the physical world, but by now she understood that extraordinary claims could only be supported by extraordinary proof.

"I think Meredith is right," she said to Jonathan. "There must be some kind of other explanation. Either you guys remember it wrong or he heard the song somewhere."

"I don't see what difference it makes, anyway," Meredith said. "Why are the fires and the song necessarily related?"

"Whoever is sending emails to the detective must believe they're related," David pointed out.

"Or at least they want you to think that."

"Both of us remember Todd playing this song when he shouldn't have known about it," Jonathan said. "Even if there were no fires and no emails, isn't that pretty significant?"

"It's significant you guys believe it," Meredith said. "But couldn't Todd have known about the song in a more believable way?"

"How?" asked Jonathan. "Wouldn't someone have known if his family was friends with a famous singer?"

"Probably," Meredith said. "So maybe Todd wrote the song and he or his family sold it to Don Henley."

"Honestly," Alicia said. "What would you guys think if the situation were reversed? Would you believe something like this if we didn't have proof?"

Jonathan opened his mouth, presumably to argue the point, but then said nothing.

"I think it's a whole lot more likely you guys have remembered it wrong," Meredith added.

"You know what?" Jonathan said. "I might be able to help with this."

He stood up and headed toward the kitchen.

"Where are you going?" Alicia asked him.

"Be right back."

As Alicia watched him go, she wondered if maybe Jonathan wasn't as logical as she first believed. What could she realistically know about him so far, other than he was funny and a pretty good kisser? Also, since Alicia could still taste that kiss on her lips, why did she keep stealing glances at David and his hot, young girlfriend?

"Jonathan seems nervous," Meredith said. "He sucked down those first two glasses of wine pretty fast."

"I can understand why," David said. "I only remembered about the song on the flight over, and the more I thought about it, the more I felt like I was nuts."

"You didn't mention it to me," Meredith said.

"I thought maybe I was dreaming it up. If Jonathan hadn't said something I don't think I would have, either."

She looked at him skeptically, or so it seemed to Alicia.

"So right now," Meredith said, "the biggest problem is the emails. There haven't been any more attacks since Bobby's visit to the restaurant, right?"

"Correct," Alicia said. "But the emails have kept the case open, which doesn't help me at all."

"Surely your insurance company will have to pay at some point," Meredith said. "How can they deny the claim if there's no reason to believe you set the fire yourself?"

"The emails are not the only issue here," David said. "Why are you so confident Jonathan and I are full of shit about the song?"

"Because what you guys are asking us to believe isn't possible."

It was amusing to watch them bicker. Alicia didn't have to be proud of this for it to be true.

Soon after, Jonathan reappeared carrying a worn cardboard box that must have come from his attic. Alicia could see the dust from across the room.

"This box is pretty much all I have left from those years," Jonathan said.

From the corner of her eye, Alicia saw Meredith glance at her, as if the two of them were a team now, as if they had found solidarity defending the material world from supernatural intrusion. But Alicia wasn't interested in sharing common ground with David's girlfriend.

"There are a bunch of record albums and cassettes in here. I used to record songs off the radio, just like Todd."

"It was the 80s," David said.

Jonathan sat down and pulled a pile of books out of the box, pushed aside a row of record albums, and rummaged in further. He retrieved a couple of cassettes with black shells and white labels. A few scraps of paper also fluttered out of the box, what looked like notebook paper someone had intentionally ripped to shreds.

"But now I'm wondering if these . . . ." He held one of them up, and then stood again. "Let's see what they are."

Jonathan popped the cassette into the stereo above his television. He hit a button and then another, and a song began to play. It was muffled and distorted and there was too much bass.

"What music is that?" David asked.

"Don't pretend you don't know," Jonathan said, smiling.

"It's Midnight Star," Alicia said. "And you guys are both Freak-A-Zoids for expecting us to believe this."

Jonathan stopped the tape and began playing it again. This time it was something that sounded like Kenny Loggins. He ejected the cassette and turned it over. The other side was a recording of The Rick Dees Weekly Top Forty.

David pointed at the other cassettes on the carpet. "I think I know what you're looking for. What about those?"

Jonathan ejected the cassette and picked up another one. One of the scraps of shredded paper was stuck to it, and Alicia saw a momentary look of confusion on Jonathan's face as he removed it. As if there were meaning associated with the paper, something he had just now remembered.

Then he tossed the scrap aside, pushed the cassette into the stereo, and pressed a button.

This time there was more than just music. There was also the muffled sound of someone talking.

"Lot of tape hiss," David noted.

Jonathan turned up the volume and hit a button on the tape deck. The hiss disappeared, and Alicia could hear a quiet melody, as if someone were in fact playing an electronic keyboard. There was also a voice on the tape. A boy's voice. The loudness of Jonathan's stereo, the amplification of these ancient sounds, generated for Alicia a profound sensation of disembodiment, as if she had opened a window to the past and was poking her head through.

"Who won at football?" the boy asked. A bit of silence followed. Then, "Bobby's team, right?"

"Fucking bullshit," another voice said. A boy with a deeper voice.

"Let it go, dude," a third voice said. "You lost. Get over it."

Alicia looked from Jonathan to David. David was smiling.

"That's me," he said.

"You've got one hell of a southern accent," Meredith remarked.

Alicia looked back at Jonathan. "Rewind it. We're missing stuff."

"Sorry," said Meredith.

As Jonathan rewound, Meredith asked, "Are you saying you have it on tape? This kid, Todd, singing the Don Henley song?"

"Maybe. These tapes are from that summer."

"Come on."

Jonathan looked at David and said, "Do you remember the football game?"

"Of course. We destroyed them. This is also the day we wrecked the house. I can't believe you have this."

"Me, either," Meredith deadpanned.

Alicia didn't expect the recording to deliver what Jonathan and David seemed to be hoping for, not at all, but now that the tape was playing she found it fascinating anyway. After all, she had known these boys in that time, and hearing their young voices signaled other memories from that summer to come forward: Jelly shoes, the smell of swimming pool chlorine, dancing with her friend Brandi to Michael Jackson and the Culture Club. But where memories were often exaggerated or left wanting for detail, the tape represented a version of the past that could be reproduced with exacting precision. The tape was reality, or the closest thing to it.

But would anyone ever want their memories served up so perfectly? The most vivid image she could recall from that time was drawing a white slip of paper from a red wicker basket and discovering Jonathan's name written on it. When she made eye contact with him, the way he grinned back at her, it was something that still made her smile after all these years. But if Alicia were able to access a video file of that scene, watch their encounter rendered in the merciless authenticity of pixels, how would reality compare to the moment she so fondly remembered?

"Who else is talking?" she asked.

"The first voice was Adam," Jonathan said. "He was asking about the game because he didn't play in it. Then Bobby, then David. You'll probably hear Todd and me as well."

He pushed a button on the tape deck, and they picked up the conversation again.

"Let it go, dude," young David said. "You lost. Get over it."

"What?" Bobby said. "What did you say to me?"

"You heard me. Stop whining like a little baby."

"If you don't watch it, you're gonna be the one whining like a baby."

"Whatever, Bobby," David answered. "You're not our boss, all right? You're—"

Alicia listened as the confrontation on the tape intensified, until threats were replaced by the sound of punches and grunts and swearing. Despite the yawning valley of years that had elapsed since the tape was recorded, she nonetheless was impressed with David for standing up to Bobby Steele, a brute of a kid who first became a football hero and later a cold-blooded killer. Alicia glanced over and noticed David watching her. She looked away and hoped she wasn't blushing.

On the tape, the fight didn't last long. A period of silence followed, and then Bobby said, in a small voice, "Holy shit."

They all listened for what would come next, but the tape stopped.

"That's it?" Meredith asked.

"It's the end of this side of the tape," Jonathan said. "Let me turn it over and see what's on the other side.

He did, and they listened for a while. But all they heard was silence.

"Put it back on the first side again," David said. "Rewind it all the way. We started near the end."

Jonathan turned the cassette over and rewound the tape until it stopped, then played it from the beginning. Alicia glanced at David again, but this time his attention was focused on the stereo and he was holding hands with Meredith.

The first thing on the tape this time was a loud shuffling sound. Then a boy said, "We don't do anything with the club. David had already built the fort, so we just called ourselves The Dragons and made it our headquarters."

"Is that Bobby again?" Alicia asked.

Jonathan nodded. "This must be another day. Sometime before we burned down the house."

"We keep our secret stuff there," David's younger self said. "We've got some porno magazines and a couple of packs of cigarettes."

"Porn?" Meredith asked, smiling. "In junior high?"

"See there," someone on the tape said. "I knew you guys had a mean streak in you."

"Is that Todd?" Alicia asked.

"It is," Jonathan said.

On the tape, Todd said, "Jonathan, you should totally bring Alicia here and make out with her."

"I would if I were you," young David said. "That girl is so hot."

Alicia smiled. She couldn't help herself. Even when they all looked at her, and she felt herself blushing, the smile didn't go away.

"I guess you were quite an item back in the day," Meredith said.

"She was," David agreed. "All the guys in school were after her."

"Oh, whatever," Alicia said. "I was not an item."

"You should rewind the tape," Meredith said. "We're missing stuff."

Jonathan rewound a bit and they listened again as the conversation evolved from porn magazines to masturbation. It was impossibly cute to hear how innocent the boys had been.

"Wait a minute," Meredith said.

"What now?" David asked.

Meredith turned to Jonathan. "Would you rewind the tape a bit? I must have heard that wrong."

Jonathan restarted the tape, and they listened to the last few seconds of it again.

"He's seen you at the fort by yourself," young Bobby said.

Adam said, "So what if I—"

"More than once," Bobby added.

David looked at Meredith, as if ready to explain something, but she put her finger up to stop him.

On the tape, Adam said, "Screw you guys. I'm going home."

And Todd said, "Sit down, Cartman."

"There," Meredith interrupted. "What the hell is that?"

"What is what?" David asked.

"Cartman is the fat kid from 'South Park.' Tell me he didn't just say that."

They all looked at each other.

"I've never seen 'South Park,'" David said.

"It's a cartoon on Comedy Central," Meredith told him. "It was really popular a few years ago. And that's one of Cartman's signature phrases. 'Screw you guys, I'm going home.'"

Even if Alicia didn't want much to do with Meredith, she nevertheless had been happy to enjoy another voice of reason in the room. Now her unlikely ally appeared to be wavering.

"It doesn't necessarily mean anything," she said. "Anybody might say something like that."

"Sure," Meredith answered. She took a drink of her wine and put her hand on David's thigh. "But how many Cartmans do you know?"

A few years back "South Park" had been one of Alicia's favorite television shows. She'd never even heard the name Cartman before then. Not once.

"Still," she said. "That's not . . . I mean, who would consider that certain proof?"

Meredith shrugged. "I don't want to believe it, either. So how do we explain it?"

On the tape, Jonathan's younger self said, "You're pretty good with that thing. You know how to play any real songs?"

A few seconds of silence went by, and then Todd played a melody on the keyboard.

"This is the kid who was asleep for four years?" Meredith asked. "He woke up and could just play the keyboard that well?"

"It sounds impossible," David told her, "but it was national news at the time."

On the tape, young Jonathan said, "Have you tried writing songs of your own?"

"Well . . ."

"Hey," Bobby said. "Don't tell me you're embarrassed, Mister Badass."

"Let's hear it," Adam said.

Alicia realized she was leaning forward, as if doing so would make it easier to hear what would come next. And though her rational mind flatly rejected the idea of Todd's impossible music, another part of her felt something like destiny, as if this tape had been recorded for the sole purpose of them listening to it now.

"All right," Todd said on the tape. "I've got two. The first one doesn't have many words, though. It's called 'In the Name of Love.'"

A simple melody followed, one Alicia recognized immediately, so her natural response was to feign ignorance. This was ridiculous. It was farcical.

Jonathan and David looked at each other. Their eyes were wide, their brows raised.

"I know that song," Meredith said. "It's from the 80s, right?"

"It sounds like 'Pour Some Sugar on Me,'" Alicia said. "But those aren't exactly the right lyrics, are they?"

"Maybe not," David acknowledged. "But do you think he's playing some other song?"

"No," Meredith answered. "There's no question it's the same song. The music is exactly the same."

The question floated in the air around them, waiting to be summoned, and Alicia could restrain herself no longer.

"What year did that song come out?"

"*Hysteria* was one of my favorite albums," David said. "It came out the year I got my driver's license and I played it in my car nonstop. That was 1987."

Alicia could not imagine how their conversation would proceed from this point. She knew what she heard could not be true, and yet who could argue with an actual recording? The only way to reconcile this conflict was to consider the tape a forgery.

On the tape Todd was tapping out another melody. Alicia recognized it, they all did, and then the kid began to sing.

Nobody on the road
Nobody on the beach
I feel it in the air
The summer's out of reach
Empty lake, empty streets
The sun goes down alone
I'm driving by your house
Though I know you're not home

But I can see you
Your brown skin shining in the sun
You got your hair combed back and your sunglasses on, baby
And I can tell you my love for you will still be strong
After the boys of summer have gone.

"And then it goes on to the next verse," Todd said. "But I don't have any more than that yet."

The only person or persons who could have executed a fraud like this were Jonathan and David. Jonathan for access to his personal belongings, and David because he possessed the financial means to achieve a quality result.

But the obvious question for which Alicia had no answer was: Why?

"Holy shit," young Jonathan said. "That was really good."

34

When David had remembered this event on the plane, Todd performing "The Boys of Summer" for them, it had been possible he was remembering it wrong. Even when Gholson had informed him of the mysterious emails that seemed to reference their childhood club, David could still pretend the whole situation was an unlikely coincidence. But now that Jonathan had produced the tape, there were no more doubts about the reality of the song.

Todd Willis had been connected in some way to a time that hadn't yet occurred.

Once you accepted the reality of the music, some questions naturally followed: How did it physically happen? And why? The first thing anyone might point to was Todd's head injury, because wasn't it always like that in movies, where some dude gets into a car accident, slips into a coma for five years, and comes out on the other side in possession of extraordinary mental gifts?

But David had not sustained any head injury. He'd never broken a bone or even pulled a muscle. And yet it seemed obvious that his proclivity for extraordinary financial decisions was either similar or identical to Todd's ability to hear music from another time. There was no other way to interpret the situation. The main difference between them was David had turned his ability into a financial empire, and Todd had disappeared into oblivion.

Meredith said, "Is there any chance the tape was recorded after the time you guys think it was?"

"It doesn't matter," Alicia said. "The tape could have been edited. With a computer and the right software, a person could fake something like this." She looked at Jonathan. "Right?"

Alicia seemed like an intelligent woman, and she'd kept her body in fantastic shape. If Meredith and Jonathan weren't around, David might have fucked her. But good body or not, it was irritating for her to accuse them of intentionally editing the tape. As if he didn't have better things to do with his time.

"You just saw me pull the cassettes from the bottom of a dusty box I took from the attic. I probably hadn't looked at them in ten or fifteen years."

"But I don't know that," Alicia said. "Neither does anyone else. How can we know for sure it's real?"

"Alicia," David said. "Why would we go to that kind of trouble to fool you? For what purpose?"

"I'm not saying you have," she answered. "It could be true, what you guys are saying. All I'm saying is that this tape isn't necessarily proof.

And anyway, whether the music is real or not, we still aren't any closer to understanding what's going on."

Jonathan started to say something, but Alicia continued.

"I mean, let's be clear. David's dad is dead. Bobby is dead. Someone is still out there sending emails to the cops, my insurance settlement is on hold, and—"

A crash interrupted her. An explosion of glass. A thud on the carpet. They all looked in the direction of the front door.

"What was that?" Alicia said.

Jonathan jumped up and ran for the door. David followed him. There was another crash and then a third.

"Holy shit!" Jonathan yelled. "My office is on fire!"

The windows in the entryway were intact, but as David rounded a corner, he saw flickering yellow light in an adjacent room. He realized what had happened just as Jonathan emerged and reached for the front door.

"My computer!" he yelled. "Oh, shit!"

For a moment David couldn't understand where Jonathan was going, but when he looked out the front door, he saw. There was a water hose out front.

Jonathan was already on his way back inside.

"Grab the hose, will you? Make sure it doesn't get stuck on something!"

David stepped past Jonathan and reached for the hose, which indeed had already caught on the flowerbed edging. He freed it and fed more line to Jonathan.

"My computer!" he heard Jonathan yell. "My books!"

David was about to run back inside to help when he saw, through the front windows, more flickering light.

There were at least two other rooms on fire, and the acrid smell left no doubt about what had happened: Someone had thrown burning bottles of gasoline through the windows. Someone was trying to destroy Jonathan's house.

He ran back toward the front door and into the house. Jonathan was in his office, still spraying the fire with water, but he didn't seem to be having much luck.

"I don't think you're supposed to do that," David said. "If it's gaso-line, I don't think water will work."

From the direction of the living room, Alicia came running.

"Jonathan! The whole house is on fire! We have to get out of here!"

"But I can't! I'll lose everything!"

"Jonathan!" Alicia cried. "Fire is coming down the hallway. I just called 9-1-1. We have to get outside!"

Meredith appeared and David pushed her toward the front door. He grabbed Alicia and pointed her in the same direction.

Jonathan didn't seem to realize the water was having no effect on the fire. If anything, the flames were spreading. David put his hand on Jonathan's shoulder.

"Come on, man. Come on. We've got to get out of here."

"I can't. I already lost my computer. Everything I've ever written is on that goddamned laptop."

"The fire department will be here soon," David said. "You can't do anything at this point except get yourself hurt. Come on."

Jonathan finally seemed to realize the futility of his efforts and shut off the water.

"Fuck!" he yelled.

David took Jonathan by the shoulders and pushed him toward the front door. As they walked outside, tires screeched on the street in front of them. A man jumped out of a blue Ford sedan and sprinted up the sidewalk. David realized it was Detective Gholson.

"What the hell happened?"

"My house is on fire!"

David looked and saw flames flickering in three windows. Black smoke poured out of them.

"I leave my post for five minutes," Gholson said, "go take a piss and grab another cup of coffee, and now this? It's just like the movies. Like the fucking Keystone Cops. I can't believe it."

Up and down the street, David saw homeowners standing on their lighted porches, looking toward Jonathan's house. Meredith and Alicia stood beside him, shaking. Alicia in particular looked horrified.

"This is bad," she said. Her voice was quiet and uncertain. "I don't understand why this is happening to us."

David didn't understand it, either, but he was determined to find out.

"So you were watching my house?" Jonathan asked.

Gholson nodded. "I told you—"

"Did you see who did it?"

"No, I—"

"Do you still think it's me? Do you think I would burn down my own house? Aren't you going to do something?"

"I already called it in," Gholson said. "Fire trucks will be here shortly."

"But what about the person who did it? He was here. He stood in front of my house and threw bottles of gasoline through my windows."

"I know," Gholson said. "I'm sorry. But—"

"But you left for doughnuts. And meanwhile, the person who was watching you watch me used your laziness to set my house on fire."

Alicia approached Jonathan and put her hand on his shoulder.

"Jonathan," she said. "I know you're upset. Believe me, I get it. But it's not his fault."

"Then whose is it?"

"Look," Gholson said. "You people are the victims, not the criminals. I realize this."

"What gave you that idea?" Jonathan quipped.

"But you know something more than what you're telling me. I can see it in your eyes. I can't help you if you don't tell me what's going on."

David could hear sirens approaching. It was almost dark and Jonathan's house still burned and black smoke reached toward the sky. The scene unsurprisingly reminded David of the night they burned down the house on Driftwood.

"I don't know what's going on," Jonathan said. "But when I figure out who did this, he and I are going to have a little chat."

35

Adam's bedroom was dark and crowded with three-dimensional shadows—the locomotive bulk of the dresser, the rectangular chest of drawers, the skeleton framework of their stereo rack. The only sounds were atmospheric, like conditioned air moving through the house and his wife's rhythmic breathing. The pillow-top mattress was a little too soft, the sateen sheets too slippery, the fitted sheet wasn't fitted enough and thus a rippled mess beneath him, and Adam lay there damning the conspiracy of it all. Because you couldn't will yourself to sleep. The more you concentrated on relaxing, the more remarkable and surreal it seemed that a person could move from a state of consciousness to unconsciousness. It was impossible to register the exact moment when you crossed that threshold, but that didn't stop Adam from examining every moment on the way to the threshold, and this action, by its very nature, pushed the threshold farther away. Chasing sleep was a nightmare hallway that stretched longer the faster you ran.

Adam had refused to meet with Jonathan and David tonight, and now he wondered if he'd made the correct decision. Because they would have discussed the fires, especially who might be setting them. Maybe they believed Todd had returned to exact some kind of vengeance. Maybe they suspected Adam. Jonathan had asked weird questions on the phone, questions Adam had not wanted to hear, let alone answer. Jonathan had even asked about Joe Henreid.

He imagined he was standing in front of one of his new home sites where a foundation had just been poured. The concrete was a flat, rectangular shape with other, smaller rectangles jutting out in functional locations. Surrounding the slab was a plain of red dirt dotted here and there with mounds of soil that had been pushed aside. And then wind was suddenly pushing against him, blasting him with dirt, pounding him with debris. His sister lay motionless at his feet. Adam guessed he was dreaming when he noticed he was pushing a construction wheelbarrow that moments before had not been present. When he looked down he saw his dead sister lying in the carrier, her body folded at a weird angle, and he couldn't believe he was looking at her again after all these years. Because in real life she was buried in a cemetery. He knew this because as a nine-year-old he had stood beside her grave, gaping at the hole where they were going to put her. He could not believe this girl, who only days before had been running up and down the hallway in a Wonder Woman T-shirt and red rain boots, was about to be lowered into the ground where she would remain forever. He would not look directly into the hole because something was moving down there. He could hear the dry scraping of hands on soil, the raspy cough of dirt being choked up. He refused to look because what he saw would surely make him sit up in the bed and scream, and if that happened he would never get back to sleep again.

36

The next morning Adam snoozed the radio alarm twice before finally climbing out of bed. He stumbled into the bathroom around 6:45, leaned into the shower, and turned it on. Waited a minute for the water to warm up and then stepped inside.

Something was on his feet. Something the water was trying to pry away. Adam looked down, and for a moment he thought he was dying. For a moment he thought he was bleeding to death. But it wasn't blood streaming into the drain.

It was red dirt. Mud.

His feet were covered with it.

PART FIVE

June 14–18, 1983

ZONE FORECAST PRODUCT
NATIONAL WEATHER SERVICE NORMAN OK
TXZ086-142200-
WICHITA-
INCLUDING THE CITIES OF ... WICHITA FALLS
1114 AM CDT TUE JUN 14 1983

.TODAY ... SUNNY AND HOT. HIGH AROUND 107. WINDS SW
15-25 MPH AND GUSTY.
.TONIGHT ... CLEAR. LOW NEAR 80. SW WIND 10-15 MPH.
.WEDNESDAY ... SUNNY AND HOT. HIGH AROUND 109.
SOUTH WINDS 20-30 MPH.
.WEDNESDAY NIGHT ... CLEAR. LOW IN THE LOW 80S.
SOUTH WINDS AROUND 25 MPH.
.THURSDAY ... SUNNY AND HOT. HIGH NEAR 110.
.FRIDAY ... SUNNY AND VERY HOT. HIGH NEAR 112.

37

Jonathan was in his room with the door closed, a spiral notebook on the bed in front of him. He was listening to one of his father's favorite cassettes, *Bo Diddley*, which had somehow survived the tornado's wrath, and which lifted his mood whenever he played it. After a few minutes he picked up the pen and wrote a sentence, crossed it out, and wrote something else he sort of liked. This morning he had woken with a story idea ringing like a siren in his mind, where an injured writer (Paul) was held hostage by a terrible woman (Annie) who turned out to be his number one fan. He imagined Paul could not get out of bed, that for every physical need he depended on a woman who hated him as much as she loved him. For some reason this concept struck Jonathan as morbidly hilarious and he could not wait to see how the story would turn out.

Three days had passed already since he had been forbidden to contact Alicia. And if that had been the only barrier to cross—disobeying orders—Jonathan would already have ridden to her house by now. Unfortunately the bigger problem was admitting to Alicia that his mother was nuts, that if the two of them wanted to conduct a relationship it would have to be private. Maybe in a novel or movie it would seem romantic for two young lovers to fight for their feelings against insurmountable odds, but in the real world it was ridiculous and embarrassing that a 13-year-old kid couldn't have a junior high girlfriend. Like they were really going to have sex. He didn't even know how to have sex.

What hurt most of all was that his feelings for Alicia, desperate as they were, now had nowhere to go. Jonathan had long cultivated fantasies of them holding hands and talking about books and kissing each other on the lips. He'd been able to sustain such fantasies because it was possible, however unlikely, they might someday come true. But now that he'd blown his chance, now that he was unable to speak to her again, Jonathan could no longer delude himself. It hurt to think about her now. The pain was a physical thing, nearly unbearable.

The only thing that made him feel better was to shift his attention elsewhere, and this new story concept was perfect for that. At the moment he was writing an amusing scene where Annie was about to cut off one of Paul's feet as punishment for trying to escape. She was just about to swing the axe when his mother's voice interrupted him.

"Jonathan," she called from across the house. "Hey, Jonathan. Come here."

He found her in the kitchen, where she stood in front of the breakfast table. One of the chairs was pulled away from the table, and Jonathan wondered for a moment if she wanted him to sit.

"Yes?"

His mother smiled and said, "You and I have a lot of battles, don't we?"

Jonathan didn't know how to answer that. Battles, as far as he understood them, were fought among willing participants.

"Do you know why we have so many fights? Why I get on to you so much?"

He shook his head.

"Because of your lying. Ever since you were five years old, when you and Thomas spray-painted Mr. Donovan's house, you've been lying to me. You can't keep doing that, Jonathan. You just can't."

Blooms of dread opened in his stomach. His balls shrank against his body. His mother's entire case for this supposed chronic dishonesty rested on a misunderstood crime committed against a neighbor who had once lived across the street. Jonathan hadn't painted Mr. Donovan's house. He had simply watched his friend, Thomas, paint.

"I'm going to make it really easy for you this time," she said. "I've done my homework, everything is all figured out, and all you have to do is tell me what I already know. I'm giving you the perfect opportunity to get us back on the right track. I don't want to fight any more than you do. Really, I don't."

Jonathan might have found that funny if he hadn't been so nervous.

His mother said, "I already asked Bobby if he did it, and he said 'no.' We know Kenny didn't do it, either. *I* certainly didn't do it, so that leaves you, Jonathan. It just leaves you."

"What is it? What did I do?"

His mother pointed one of her sharp fingernails at the kitchen chair.

"There's a hole in the Naugahyde. A little tear. You see it there?"

Jonathan looked. He could indeed see a split in the seat of the chair, about a half-inch long, as if someone had gashed it with a knife.

"I didn't do that," he said automatically.

His mother just stood there, staring at him, and he half-expected laser beams to shoot out of her eyes like Superman.

"I'm telling the truth. I didn't cut this chair."

His mother's voice was calm, like the surface of a quiet pond, a pond in which a giant boy-eating monster lurked at the bottom.

"Jonathan, please. Please make this easy. I already know you did it. If you'll just admit it, I promise I won't get mad. I won't tell Kenny about it, either. You know how he gets when I ask him to punish you. Tell the truth. Just this once. Admit you did it, and we'll forget the whole thing. Okay?"

It was a dangerous dilemma. If she meant what she said, he might walk away from this skirmish unscathed. But could he really do it? Admit to something that wasn't his fault? Was it better to tell the truth and encourage his mother's ire, or lie to make her happy?

He thought about it a long time. He wavered back and forth for at least thirty seconds.

"Okay," he said. "I did it."

His mother beamed. "See there. That wasn't so hard, was it?"

"No." It had in fact been relatively painless.

She pushed the chair back to its place against the table. "So tell me, Jonathan. How did you do it?"

Shit. Here was something he hadn't considered. When you lied about doing it, you had to lie again to explain *how* you did it.

"I was, uh, tossing a steak knife up and trying to catch it by its handle. One time I missed, and it fell right down on the chair and cut it."

"When did it happen?"

"A couple of days ago."

His mother thought about this for a minute and then smiled again. "Well, thank you for owning up to it. You can go back to your room and read or do whatever you like. You've earned it."

Jonathan turned away from her, deliberately, as if the whole episode was a big joke. It made no sense to him, this new tactic of his mother's, and he could not believe she would let him walk away without extracting some kind of penalty. But she said nothing more, and soon he was alone in his room again, where the spiral notebook beckoned. He sat down at his desk and picked up the pen. It wobbled in his hand as he stared at the blank page. He wrote:

"I swear to God I'll be good, Annie! Please..."

The strange thing was how the words seemed to flow right out of mind and onto the page. Instead of picturing the scene itself, like the look on Annie's face and the bloody axe, in this case he was hearing specific words and phrases. Like "left leg just above the ankle" and "Indian warpaint." He'd never even thought of Indian war paint before.

"Almost over," she said.

38

By the next afternoon Jonathan had incorporated a new idea into the story, where Annie snoops through Paul's private things and discovers a new manuscript he's just finished. She reads this novel, hates it, and burns it in a charcoal grill while Paul helplessly watches. If this weren't awful enough, destroying thousands of hours of work, Annie then presents her own story idea and forces Paul to write it for her. Jonathan was beginning to realize that the way to build a good story was to figure out what a character would like and then give him something different or even the opposite thing. It was more interesting when people suffered, he noticed, than when everything worked out for them.

Now Jonathan was reading through the new version of his story, pretending it was a book on the library shelf, as if he were any old eighth grader looking for a good read. He wanted to distance himself from the words, imagine someone else had written them, to get an idea how good the work really was. But it was no use. Every line and every word was familiar to him. What he needed was for someone else to read it.

Bobby didn't own a single book and never read outside of school, so there was no sense in asking him. He would have loved for Alicia to read it, but for obvious reasons that was not currently an option. That left one of the other guys, probably David or maybe even Todd.

Jonathan was on his way outside, spiral notebook in hand, when he encountered Kenny Steele. Kenny was carrying a beer and a package of Doritos toward the back door.

"Hey, Mr. Steele."

"Jonathan, I keep telling you to call me 'Kenny.' This 'Mr. Steele' stuff is too slick for a guy like me."

"Okay," Jonathan replied. An adult's first name felt large and awkward in his mouth. "Kenny."

Kenny lifted his beer and nodded. "Much better. Whatcha got there?"

Jonathan looked down at the notebook as if he hadn't realized he was carrying it. He didn't know what to say.

"Cat got your tongue?"

"It's a, uh . . . it's a notebook. I've been writing in it. A short story."

Kenny looked at him as if a Martian were standing there instead of a thirteen-year-old boy. "You're writing a story? A made-up one?"

"Yes, sir."

Kenny offered his hand. "For real? Can I have a look?"

"Well, sure. I guess. I mean if you want to. It starts like eight pages in."

Jonathan watched as Kenny flipped through the notebook looking for the title page.

"'Misery', by Jonathan Crane," Kenny read aloud, and then burped. "Well, I'll be goddamned."

"You can take some time if you like. I don't—"

"I ain't much of a reader, but why don't you follow me outside and I'll take a look. I was just about to take a break by the pool."

Kenny turned and walked toward the back door. Jonathan followed. When he stepped outside he saw Bobby at the far end of the pool, resting against the concrete edge, breathing hard. Bobby enjoyed the butterfly stroke because of the way it built his shoulders, and he often spent hours in the pool swimming laps. So while it wasn't surprising to find him out here now, it was nonetheless terrible timing, because the last thing Jonathan wanted was to hear his story critiqued by Bobby's dad in front of Bobby himself. Only bad things could come from this. Like Jonathan taking shit from Bobby the rest of the summer.

His stomach churned with an uneasy combination of anxiety, curiosity, and pride as he watched Kenny read. It was frankly bizarre for another person to consume the words you had written, even if the whole idea was for other people to read them, and it was especially weird to watch it happen in real time like this. Once or twice he glanced over at Bobby and saw him looking in their direction. Jonathan wondered what he was thinking. Whatever was on his mind didn't seem to please him very much.

"I got just one piece of advice for you," Kenny said when he finally looked up. He had made it to the third page. "Don't quit writing."

"No?"

"Like I said, I ain't much of a reader. But if I'd been as smart when I was a kid as you are now, I sure as hell wouldn't be no framer."

"Well, I—"

"I'm not saying let that go to your head. What I'm saying is you got a skill just like my boy does. And just like he's gotta work his ass off to make the high school squad and impress those college scouts, you gotta work hard at this writing. My guess is not that many people get to be a professional writer. I sure don't know any, do you?"

Jonathan shook his head. He glanced at Bobby again, who looked angrier than ever.

"But I bet it's just like sports. I bet those who *do* make it, I bet they make a pretty good living at it. So don't ever quit. Keep at it until you get it done. Understand?"

"Thank you, Mr. Steele. That's really good advice. And thanks for taking a look. I really appreciate it."

Jonathan glanced toward the far end of the pool once more before going back inside. When he did, he saw Bobby push himself out of the pool and dry off without turning back to look at them. Was he angry about something? Did he think Jonathan was a nerd for wanting to write stories? It was impossible to know without asking, but who really cared, anyway? An adult had just looked at Jonathan's work and found it promising. Maybe he really did have a future as an author. And maybe, when he finished the story, he could visit Alicia after all and show her what he'd done. Maybe there was still a chance to make things right with her.

Maybe anything was possible if you worked at it hard enough.

39

An hour ago Bobby had been sitting in front of the television, playing Kaboom!, but finally he tossed aside his controller and gave up because there was no point. Jonathan had set a new high score several days ago, more than 15,000, and it was obvious Bobby was never going to catch him. He could see the bombs falling just fine but he couldn't make his hands obey commands reliably enough. And whenever he finally did get a good game going, whenever he felt even a little hopeful about his chances, something in his brain went haywire and he would inexplicably fuck up. Finally he gave up and went outside, and luckily Jonathan wasn't in the pool. It seemed like he couldn't get away from that kid lately. More and more his dad wanted to stay over here at night, which meant Bobby was forced to stay, too.

Maybe it wasn't so bad. At least in Tanglewood he could pretend he wasn't poor. In his own neighborhood it was all peeling paint and rotting wood and crumbling concrete driveways. The houses there were so small Bobby wondered if they might be shrinking, as if someone were working over the neighborhood with a giant eraser, making rooms and screened-in porches and second stories disappear.

Bobby didn't often consider ideas that weren't staring him in the face. He saw life primarily as a series of obstacles to overcome, and spent most of his time reacting to situations as they occurred. But there was one idea that sometimes did keep him awake at night, and that was the fear that his life was already decided for him. That no matter how hard he tried to reach his goals, there would always be a limit to what he could achieve because of the world he had been born into.

When he was younger, back when his mom was still alive, Bobby had paid close attention to his grades and sometimes even made A's. His report card was a source of pride, and every six weeks, as long as there were no C's on it, she would take him out for pizza and root beer. But now his mom was gone, and his dad had expended great effort to erase her influence. He pointed out that not many eighth-grade athletes were courted by high school coaches, especially not to become quarterback of the oldest high school in Wichita. He also asked if Bobby had ever heard of a junior high student being recruited by high school teachers because of his amazing grades? The obvious point being that, around here at least, athletics were more highly valued than academics.

But was it possible to be both a good athlete *and* a good student? If his dad hadn't lost his mind the day of the tornado, if his mom were still alive, would Bobby's life would be different now? Maybe so, but that's not what had happened. What happened was his stupid dad picked a fight over chess and two people died.

The most ridiculous thing was how spectacularly his dad's actions had backfired. The old man hadn't wanted his son to spend time with Jonathan, and now spending time with Jonathan was all Bobby ever did. Sometimes it seemed like the whole world was someone else's sick joke.

He could still feel his mother trembling next to him, the two of them cowering in Jonathan's pantry, after his father abandoned them. How she had trembled, how she had screamed at the terrible sound of the house collapsing around her . . .

Bobby stood up quickly and jumped into the pool. From time to time the reality of his life overwhelmed him, and when this happened the only way to make the pain go away was to punish his body. From one end of the pool to the other he swam, back and forth, his arms and shoulders and legs working in unison to propel his torso through the water. The butterfly stroke was the most difficult and therefore his favorite. He swam as hard as he could, and with each stroke he thought about his mother a little less. With each stroke the pain eased a little.

Finally he felt more like himself again and stopped to rest at the edge of the pool's deep end. He'd been there less than a minute when the back door opened and his dad appeared, followed closely by Jonathan. They gathered near one of the chaise lounges and his dad began to read something. Bobby was fairly sure it was that red notebook Jonathan sometimes carried around with him. His dad seemed engrossed by whatever he was reading, and Bobby couldn't fathom what it might be. Kenny Steele could barely sit still long enough to get a number out of the phonebook.

But then his dad stopped reading and issued advice to Jonathan. *Don't quit writing,* he said. *If I had been as smart as you when I was a kid, I sure as hell wouldn't be no framer.*

It seemed like the world was turning red somehow. As if everything he saw, everywhere he looked, there was blood. And a high pitched sound, like some kind of electrical feedback, began to make his head hurt.

Bobby looked over at Jonathan and for a moment their eyes met, but honestly he could barely see anything at this point. What his dad had just said to Jonathan was inconceivable. He put on his shirt and stepped into a pair of flip flops and walked out of the back yard, rubbing his eyes as if there was something in them. Then he marched to the end of the street, across Ridgemont, and through David's yard. Pretty soon he was in the trees, and finally the fort.

Now he could cry in peace.

Because let's get real, how the fuck could his dad encourage Jonathan to pursue his intelligence when the old man had explicitly commanded Bobby to do the opposite for years? Apparently his intellect was so worthless that it demanded no attention whatsoever, whereas Jonathan was suddenly an expert at writing, he was Stephen fucking *King*.

Bobby cried for a while, he couldn't say how long, but eventually the tears dried up and he wiped his face clean. He was about to head back home when someone knocked on the door.

"Who the hell is that?"

"It's Joe," a voice said. "I was wondering if I could come in for a minute?"

Through the gaps in the fence planks, Bobby could see the form of a kid.

"What do you want, Joe?"

"I, um. I thought of something I could do for you guys. To be in the club."

Under most circumstances Bobby would have opened the door and told the kid to fuck off. He knew like they all knew that Joe was too much of a baby to be a member of their club. Under most circumstances he would have scared the kid and been done with it.

Instead, for a reason he didn't understand, Bobby said, "What is it?"

"Well, do most of you guys mow your own yards?"

Bobby pushed open the loose fence planks and stepped out of the fort into the blinding afternoon sun.

"You want to mow our yards?"

"Yeah."

"Listen," Bobby said. "I'm going to do you a favor. I'm only going to do it once, and if you tell anyone I'll punch your face in. Got it?"

Joe nodded. He was probably thirty pounds lighter than Bobby, and maybe four inches shorter. But really he was big for his age.

Bobby said, "That kid, Todd, doesn't like to do things in any normal way. He didn't challenge you because he wants to get out of mowing his yard. He's more like a mad scientist. He likes to put people in uncomfortable situations to see what they do."

Joe just stared at him.

"He's just pushing your buttons, kid. If it were me, I woulda told you to beat it. But Todd isn't like that, all right?"

Now Joe nodded.

"Look, I'm telling you this for your own good. Don't take shit from people. As soon as you take shit from some dude, he knows he can boss you around forever. You gotta stand up for yourself every chance you get. Even someone like me who's twice as big as you, you gotta stand your ground. Because guess what? I don't really like to fight. Even if I can completely kick your ass, you might hit me once or twice out of blind luck. Plus it hurts my hands to punch you in the face. Why would I hurt myself if I don't have to?"

Joe seemed skeptical of this reasoning.

"Look. A guy like me isn't going to keep picking on someone who fights back. It's too much work. I got plenty of other people I can bother who don't cause me trouble. You get what I'm saying?"

"You're saying it's an act?"

"Call it whatever you want, kid. Just don't take shit from other people. Because once you start taking shit, you might not be able to stop. All right?"

"All right," Joe said. "So what should I do then? Just show up one day and say I'm in the club?"

"No, that ain't gonna work. Todd already set these ground rules for you. I say, if you want to go through with this, you gotta blow him out of the water. Don't offer to mow our yards, all right? Turn the tables on him and think of something really fucked up, or really crazy, or unpredictable. Something."

Joe started to smile, but appeared to catch himself. Instead he stuck out his hand and said, "Thanks, man."

Bobby looked at the hand like he'd never seen one before. He almost told the kid to get out of his sight. Instead he reached out and shook with him, but when Joe tried to pull away, Bobby held him tight.

"That's the only lesson you're ever going to get from me. And if you tell anyone, you'll be sorry. Clear?"

"Clear," Joe answered.

"Now get out of here."

40

By the following morning, Jonathan had written all the way to the climax, where Paul pretends to burn the book he wrote for Annie and then kills her with a typewriter. With his creativity in overdrive,

Jonathan felt more and more as if he were onto something special with this story. He was connected to the characters in a way that made them seem almost real, like Paul was a person who might stop by for a Coke and maybe throw the football with him. Annie and his mother, Jonathan felt sure, would become fast friends.

But before he could begin the final scene, his mother's voice startled him back into reality. She was yelling at him from across the house.

He found her in the kitchen again, standing in front of the wounded chair, and Jonathan understood the time had come to pay for his lies. His stomach settled into his groin.

"You know," she said, pointing again at the brown Naugahyde surface, "I was thinking about this chair last night. About how you said it got cut."

Jonathan could think of no conceivable response. Why would anyone sit around and ponder a damaged chair three days after the issue had presumably been closed?

"I was thinking you couldn't have done it the way you said. Our steak knives aren't that sharp, and the Naugahyde is pretty strong."

Jonathan had no idea if such a thing was possible or not. The story was a total fabrication.

"But that's how it happened. I already told you."

"I know you did, Jonathan. But it's just not possible. The knife wouldn't be heavy enough to puncture the Naugahyde or make a cut that long."

"Mom, I'm telling you—"

"Jonathan, stop. Please just stop. Do you really want to undo the goodwill you built the other day?"

"No, but—"

"Then just be honest. I promise you won't be in trouble. I won't say anything to Kenny about it. I just want you to be honest from now on."

Lying a second time was much easier than the first.

"Okay, well . . . I was playing with the knife, trying to see how hard you had to push to make the knife puncture the chair. I didn't mean to tear it. I thought it would just make a tiny hole."

"So you had to push pretty hard, then?"

"Yeah," Jonathan said. "Real hard. That Naugahyde is strong."

"Well, can you tell me something, then?"

"What?"

"Why'd you lie to me about it? Why didn't you tell me this the other day?"

"I don't know."

"If you don't know," his mother said, "who does?"

"I guess I didn't want you to know how it happened."

"But that doesn't make sense. I promised if you were honest, you wouldn't get in trouble."

No shit, he wanted to tell her. *It makes no sense because I invented it to get you off my case.*

But instead he said, "I guess I didn't want you to know I did it on purpose."

"Even though I gave you the perfect opportunity to finally be honest with me? Even though I promised everything would be okay if you just told the truth?"

The whole chair scenario was like a bad joke, like someone was intentionally messing with him. His mother seemed obsessed with the telling of truth and yet the last thing she welcomed was genuine honesty. What she really wanted, whether she knew it or not, was a story that fit her version of reality. In this reality the source of all problems in the household was Jonathan, her only child. Any event that did not support this controlling idea did not belong and was thus rejected. When Jonathan had "admitted" cutting the chair by accident, this initially had seemed like an acceptable answer. But further consideration had led his mother to believe only intentional fault could match her reality. And so he was forced to lie again, further incriminating himself, and God only knew what penalty he would face this time.

"It was pretty dumb of me," he said.

His mother smiled at this, that calm, monster smile, and sent him back to his room. Once he had settled himself, Jonathan went to work on the climax, where Paul throws the heavy typewriter at Annie's head and then shoves handfuls of burning paper into her mouth. But she was an imposing woman, strong in will and heart, and did not go away easily. Several times he stopped to rest his hand, which had cramped from gripping the pen so tightly. Hours sailed by unnoticed.

It was late afternoon when he reached the story's final lines. By then his right hand was so sore it would barely hold the pen. Something else Jonathan had just realized about storytelling was how neat you could make your artificial world, how in the hands of a grand designer the ending could be satisfying in a way that rarely happened in the real world. It seemed like most books and stories ended like this, with everything tied up perfectly, all questions answered, all desires fulfilled.

But wouldn't it be more interesting to end his story in an honest way, where maybe you never understood exactly why Annie behaved the way she did? What if the reason you would never understand her motivations was because you couldn't summon the nerve to simply ask?

And for whatever reason, the words this late in the day had stopped flowing as clearly as they had before. He forced out the story's final lines with pure will.

> The pain in Paul's leg was almost unbearable, but still he was able to push himself away from Annie's dead bulk. He could not believe she was gone forever. And though it was frightening to imagine her alive again, Paul wished the vile woman could come back to life for just another moment, long enough to ask her a final question.
> Why?

41

David was off work, cruising around Tanglewood on his Mongoose. Cicadas buzzed and the wind blew and the sun hammered him without mercy. He made frequent stops in the shade as he traced a route along the curvy streets, but the heat was cleansing somehow, as sweat beaded on his brow and stung his eyes. He pumped the pedals as if he were going somewhere important, as if he were making progress toward some lifetime goal. You couldn't just sit around and expect the world to come to you, after all. You had to get off your butt and *do* something.

And when he finally saw Alicia in the front yard, helping her mom pull weeds, David tried to tell himself that he hadn't sought her out on purpose, but that was a lie.

It was obvious Jonathan would never summon the balls to put the moves on Alicia, which meant eventually some other guy would, if some other guy hadn't already. At least this was what David told himself as Alicia stood up from the flowerbed, rubbed dirt out of her hands, and waved.

"Hey, Alicia," he said. She approached him across the lawn, wearing a light blue T-shirt that didn't quite reach her pink shorts. Her skin was brown and shiny with sweat, and her bellybutton was there where anyone could see it. A pair of sunglasses pinned her hair back. She was wearing pink jelly shoes. David blinked, and for a moment he imagined he wasn't even standing here, that he was in bed dreaming this, or maybe it was a scene in a movie someone was watching. Because wasn't this too familiar to be real? Didn't it feel exactly like that song Todd had written?

"Hey, David. What's up?"

"Just cruising around. Jonathan isn't home, and Todd's mom says he's not feeling well."

"If you're bored, you can help me pull weeds."

David opened his mouth to answer, but nothing came out.

"I'm just kidding. But why don't you come inside for lemonade? I was about to get some myself."

When David hesitated, she reached forward and tugged playfully on his handlebars.

"Come on. You look like you're about to have a sunstroke."

They stopped briefly and spoke to Alicia's mother, and then Alicia opened the Plexiglas storm door. Her hair was wavy, shoulder length, somewhere between blonde and brown.

In the kitchen she poured two tall glasses of yellow-green lemonade. The ice clinked and popped. Her shirt pulled tight as she held the pitcher, and David noticed her boobs were coming along nicely.

"What do you think of Todd?" she asked him. "It's so weird that he was asleep, like, forever."

"I don't know what to think. You would expect him to be all kinds of messed up, and I guess he is in a way. He definitely doesn't act like a normal kid."

"What does he act like?"

"Like a grownup. We all expected him to be kind of slow, you know? He basically missed four years of his life. But instead of being dumb it's like he was away at college all that time. On top of that I think he's some kind of musical genius. He writes songs that sound like they should be on the radio."

"Well, maybe he's super smart, but I still don't like him very much. He creeped me out the other day."

"He did? How?"

"I was on my bike, heading over to Simone's house, when I saw Todd standing in his front yard. He gestured and got me to stop."

"He did?"

"I'd seen him around, I think everyone has, especially since he's been on the news and all that."

David nodded.

"When I pull over he says, 'Hi Alicia, I'm Todd.' Like it was totally obvious we should know each other already. I guess someone must have told him about me. Maybe Jonathan."

David nodded knowingly, as if it were obvious why Jonathan might have done such a thing.

"He was smiling the whole time, but it wasn't a very nice smile. And he looked at me with these faraway eyes, like I was down the street instead of standing right in front of him.

"That's odd," David said. He tried not to let his own eyes fall to her T-shirt, or that strip of tanned skin above the waist of her shorts.

"Yeah, but here's the weirdest thing. He said I shouldn't give up on Jonathan. He said we would have a second chance after the fires."

"Fires? What is that supposed to mean?"

"I don't know. I asked him which fires he meant, but he said he wasn't allowed to tell me that.'"

David set his lemonade glass on the counter. "That's really weird."

"Yeah. I guess he must know Jonathan asked me to go with him."

It was amazing how quickly a balloon could deflate. How fast the pressure could bleed away. David was a balloon, a popped balloon.

"Jonathan asked you?"

"Yeah. He called me up one night and asked, but I haven't heard a word since. I thought we were going to be, you know, a couple."

"When was this?"

"Five days ago."

"You agreed to go with him and he hasn't called you for five days?"

Alicia drank the last of her lemonade. "Yeah. It's kind of embarrassing. Todd said to not give up on him, so Jonathan must have told him the whole thing. I don't get it."

"You haven't talked to him at *all*?"

"Nope."

"I know he likes you a lot," David admitted. "When you said 'yes,' I figured he would have been calling you left and right. He's been trying to get up the nerve forever."

"I wish he would call. But he won't. So here I am, pulling weeds with my mom."

She smiled, and David noticed for the first time her eyes were blue, the light blue of a summer sky.

"And here you are, drinking lemonade in my kitchen."

"Here I am, all right," he said.

"You were like a little corporation in school this year, huh? All your gum and cinnamon toothpicks."

David smiled proudly.

"Did you make a lot of money?"

"Enough," he admitted. "I'm working at my dad's restaurant this summer, too, but he's making me save half of it for college."

"Bummer. But that's pretty productive of you. You must be able to buy whatever you want."

"I guess. I'd like to move away from here someday. Live in Colorado or California or someplace in the mountains. Wichita is pretty boring."

"Tell me about it," Alicia said. "If there's a bright center of the universe, this is the city it's farthest from."

"You think you'll ever leave?"

"I think maybe I'll become a doctor. Houston is like this Mecca for hospitals."

"They have hospitals in California, too," David said impulsively.

"Oh really?" Alicia smiled and moved subtly closer to him. "Why would I want to live in California?"

"Because," he said, and honestly it was like there was a robot in his mouth, moving his jaw and tongue and lips without consent. "I'll be there, too. You can come over and I'll pour *you* lemonade."

Alicia's smile could have powered an FM radio station. One hundred thousand watts of delight. And though her mother had seen him walk in here, and though she might enter the house at any moment, David reached forward and took Alicia's hand anyway. He knew it was wrong, advancing on this girl who was the object of Jonathan's dreams, but the guy didn't own her. And now, standing in this kitchen not twelve inches from her tanned skin and wavy hair and blue eyes, could Jonathan blame David for reaching for Alicia when he had given away any chance to do so himself?

He pulled her closer, and her skin was so warm it could have been on fire. David had never kissed a girl before, but he'd seen it on TV many times, and he tried to replicate exactly what he remembered. Leaned forward. Tilted his head. Pressed his lips against hers, first lightly and then with more pressure. Her tongue, a wet and marbled muscle, slipped out of her mouth and tickled his lips. He laughed a little when she did it. So did Alicia. Eventually he pulled back from her, still holding her hand, smiling, and she smiled back, and the sun was a lake of fire on the breakfast room table, and somewhere nearby he could hear the hollow drone of a lawn mower, but it was muted by the sound of blood pulsing in his ears, by the electric beat of his overwhelmed heart.

42

"Y ou see this?" Kenny said. "You worked hard to build this, didn't you?"

It had been David's idea to build swords for use in live-action Dungeons & Dragons. When you mounted yard stakes as blades to wooden closet poles as handles, when you coated the assembled product with metallic paints, you found yourself with a realistic looking weapon. Jonathan had improved on the original idea by devoting much of a weekend to sanding and carving intricate patterns into the handle and hilt, and yesterday David had been so impressed with the finished product that he offered fifteen dollars for it. Jonathan turned him down because ten hours of work at minimum wage totaled more like thirty-five bucks. David had laughed at this counteroffer, but his desire for the sword was obvious, and Jonathan had a feeling he would eventually come up with the cash.

Now the sword lay across the step that separated the kitchen from the sunken dining room. His mom stood behind Kenny, her expression grim, and Jonathan wished she were dead.

"When your mom told me about the chair the other day, how you accidentally made that cut, I wasn't mad. Accidents happen, right?"

Jonathan just stood there. His mother had promised from the beginning not to say anything to Kenny.

"But now I find out you did it on purpose. For fun. Do you think money grows on trees? Do you think your mother's property is less important than yours?"

Jonathan stood there looking at Kenny, looking at the sword, and now he wished he could go back to the real truth. The actual truth. All he had to do was explain how his mother had coerced the confession out of him, how she forced him to lie.

The problem was Jonathan had told those lies like they were the truth and he couldn't take them back. No one would ever believe him. The new truth was the story he had made up to placate his mother, who was the actual liar here, who promised she wouldn't tell Kenny but had done so anyway.

"How long did it take you to build this?" Kenny asked.

"A whole weekend."

"So if I broke this, you would understand what it feels like for someone else to destroy your property, wouldn't you?"

"Yes, I would understand. But I think I understand already. Destroying stuff on purpose is wrong."

Kenny was quiet for a moment. He looked at Jonathan's mom.

"Maybe I don't want to break this thing after all."

The silence was complete. No one said anything. Jonathan was afraid even to move, as if the smallest distraction might shatter the man's fragile mercy.

"Go to your room," Kenny said. "Get that spiral notebook."

Comprehension was a willful thing. You could reject it if you wanted.

"That story you showed me. 'Misery.' Go get it."

Jonathan didn't move. His feet simply refused.

"Now."

On the way to his room Jonathan began to imagine his pleas, began to pray for some sort of reprieve, tried to think of a way he could sidestep this travesty. Could he somehow fool Kenny into destroying some other story? Probably not when Kenny knew the title and had read the first three pages.

Jonathan grabbed the notebook and flipped through it on the way back to the dining room, trying desperately to commit whole paragraphs to memory. This story was far more important to him than any sword. Encoded in the sentences and paragraphs of this piece of fiction was the very essence of Jonathan as a human being, even though the characters in the story went by different names and lived different experiences. To hand them over would be, with no exaggeration, like handing over a part of his soul.

"Hurry up," Kenny commanded from the dining room.

Jonathan rounded the corner and walked back to where Kenny and his mother were standing. He could not bring himself to make eye contact with either of them. He wondered what Todd would do in this situation: Beg for mercy or bare his teeth in defiance?

"Your kid showed me this story the other day," Kenny said, holding the notebook out for Jonathan's mother to see. "He's worked hard on this, and it's pretty good."

Jonathan saw his mother lean forward to look at the notebook.

"So that's what you've been doing in your room all the time," she said. "You never stop lying, do you?"

"I think your son has a future in this," Kenny continued. "But if we're going to teach him a lesson, we've got to hit him where it hurts."

Jonathan knew the choice to lie had been his. He could hear the sound of Todd's voice, the truth that couldn't be denied: All of this was Jonathan's fault.

And further, if Kenny destroyed a story that contained a scene about a fictional story being destroyed, did that mean Jonathan had somehow willed it to happen? Was it possible, in a way, to write your own destiny?

"I'm sorry," Kenny said. "But Jonathan, you gotta learn how to respect other people's things."

He ripped pages from the notebook. Bits of connective paper fell to the ground like snow.

And then the real tearing began.

43

David was at the restaurant, bored out of his mind. His dishes had been finished for twenty minutes, the restaurant had been closed for an hour, and he'd asked his dad twice if they could leave. But a big catering job tomorrow meant extra work for the kitchen manager, Julie, and they couldn't lock up the restaurant until she was finished.

Finally David could wait no longer. He trudged into the business office, ready to ask again, but this time his dad stopped him.

"Tell you what," Freddy Clark said, holding up a ring of keys. "Since you're stuck here with me, and since you've been doing such a good job lately, I'll make you a deal. You let me work on these ledgers, while we wait on Julie to finish, and I'll let you drive the delivery truck for a little while."

"By myself?" David asked, reaching for the keys. "You mean now?"

His dad jerked the keys away. "You remember the last time you drove, how we just circled through the neighborhood?"

"Yeah. Of course."

"Stay nearby. Do *not* go where there are any stoplights. You got it?"

"Sure, Dad. No problem."

"You remember how to start it?"

"Definitely."

The keys exchanged hands.

"Stay under the speed limit," his dad said as David bent around the corner, headed for the back door. "Use your signals! Come back in half an hour!"

Ten minutes later he was sitting in the dark and smelly cab of the delivery truck, his head resting against the plastic steering wheel.

Sitting there defeated.

He'd had problems starting the truck before. You inserted the key into the ignition. You pumped your foot against the gas a few times. Then you turned the key, and the engine was supposed to crank for a second or two until it roared to life. He'd seen his dad do it successfully a thousand times.

But now the stupid truck was mocking him. It almost started on the first try, but when it didn't he pumped the gas again, and turned the key again. The engine didn't start then, either. So he shoved his foot against the gas several more times, thinking the extra gas would help, but it didn't.

He couldn't imagine going back inside to admit defeat to his dad. He couldn't confess his inability to even *start* the truck, let alone drive it.

But in the end he was forced to do just that, go inside, because he also couldn't sit outside for thirty minutes and then lie about it. His dad would know. He always knew.

So David went back into the restaurant and closed the door behind him, carefully, because the hydraulic arm was broken. He ambled into the kitchen, then turned right and went out to the serving line where the register was. Grabbed a Reese's and stuffed both cups into his mouth. And if they were waiting on Julie to finish with the kitchen, where was she? Where was his dad? Why the hell couldn't they go home?

The serving line bent around a corner, and he followed it, imagining what it would be like to work alongside the girls who stood here in their tight jeans and T-shirts while they built plates of brisket and sausage. They were really sexy, the girls. Sometimes David imagined himself having sex with them, especially Terry, whose butt was perfect, like an upside down heart. Sometimes, especially at night, he could hardly stop thinking about having sex with Terry. He guessed that, being sexy, she would really like doing it and would want to do it all different ways, that she would be kind of, well, slutty. Slutty like the girls in the nudie magazines with their aggressive poses and their open mouths.

Strange how much more beautiful Alicia was than these barbecue girls, and yet somehow less sexy. He'd never imagined having sex with Alicia. He couldn't imagine it now.

David walked toward the break room door and heard his dad's voice as he was opening it.

"You like that, don't you, baby?"

Later he would tell himself that things could have been different, that he should have recognized what he heard in time to not open the door. But that wasn't what happened.

What happened was David pushed the door open and stepped into the break room. From there a person could look into the business office, which he naturally did.

His dad was bent over Julie, the serving girl, who was kneeling in the desk chair. His dad's penis was much larger than his own, longer and much thicker. He was thrusting into the woman, roughly, and from the look on her face David couldn't tell if she was loving or hating it. He backed away and bumped into the time clock, the one employees used to track their work hours each day, and his dad's head jerked toward him.

"David?"

The elder Clark's voice sounded unsteady, nothing like his normal commanding tone. He pulled away from Julie and reached for the office door. "David, get out of here. Go outside."

The door closed. David stood there in the break room.

The time clock ticked.

Why the hell was it called a time clock? What was any clock for except to tell time?

In the business office, behind the door, David heard clothes shuffling and Julie complaining and his dad answering harshly.

"David?"

"Yes, Dad?"

"Go outside, son. Get in the truck. I'll be there in a minute."

Later, sitting in the passenger seat, David saw Julie exit the restaurant and march toward her own car. She peeled away a moment later, and then, as if on cue, his dad appeared and climbed into the truck.

They sat there for a minute not looking at each other.

"David," his dad finally said, still not looking at him. "David, I—"

They sat there a while longer.

"I know it wasn't right, what you just saw. I mean, that's the kind of thing I should only be doing with your mother. I'm sure you know that."

David couldn't imagine his father doing anything remotely like that to his mother.

"It's wrong what I've done, son. But if you tell your mom, things are going to be a whole lot different. She isn't the same woman she used to be. In the old days she was so confident and energetic and now she just sits in her room all day. I'm afraid if she found out, and we got divorced, she might not fare too well."

"Like you care," David said.

They still weren't looking at each other.

"I do care, David. I do. And what I'm saying is, as wrong as I am in this, I still think she might be better off not knowing."

"Maybe. But you're definitely better off, right?"

More silence. David could hardly believe he was sitting here. Maybe it was a nightmare. Maybe any minute he would wake up and find himself in bed.

"You want to go to college?" his dad asked.

David wondered what that question had to do with anything.

"You want to keep having nice things? If your mom and I get divorced, sure, I'll pay child support, but you're not going to live like you do now. Nothing will be the same."

Was his dad threatening him? What would Todd do in this situation?

"Tell you what," his dad said. "I'm going to make you a deal. What'd you work, twenty hours this week? That's almost seventy dollars, right? Well, I'll keep putting my half into your college fund, and give you the other half . . . but you don't have to work here anymore. Thirty bucks a week, free and clear, no taxes, if you'll keep your mouth shut."

His father was looking at him now. David turned and met his eyes. Said nothing for five seconds, maybe ten. He hadn't cried since he was ten years old, the day of the tornado, but he was near tears now.

"Sure, Dad. For thirty bucks a week, I'll keep my mouth shut."

"Good, good. You've made the right decision."

His dad spent a few moments trying to start the truck and finally the engine caught. They backed out of the parking spot and started home.

"You know what, Dave? You're going to make something of yourself. I can tell. It's in your eyes."

The world blurred, and David looked out the window. When he blinked, tears leaked out of his eyes.

"You see things. The right way to go, the right choices to make. You see."

It was late. Dark outside. The world was shadows. Blurry shadows. That's all he could see.

Blurry shadows.

44

Todd had been in bed for a long time. Two or three days it seemed. He could remember getting up to use the bathroom, could remember eating a few bowls of soup prepared by his mother, and finally a short, tense visit from Dr. Robbins. The rest was mostly a blur of twisted sheets and hot pillows and drowning in the sweaty mess of his too-soft mattress.

According to the doctor he had not fallen into relapse. He responded well to stimuli and was aware of his surroundings. Dr. Robbins asked what Todd had been doing since he last saw him.

"Oh, mainly I hang out with friends. We go swimming and play video games and hike through the forest."

"Yes. I was pleased to hear of this when your mother called about the bad dream."

His mom was standing in the doorway, arms folded across her chest. The doctor smiled at her. She didn't smile back.

"So why aren't you with your friends now?"

"I haven't felt up to it the past couple of days. I feel sort of sick, like I've got a fever or something."

Dr. Robbins explained he was not suffering from a fever or any physical problem.

"Which is quite different than when you were sick before, Todd. Your neurological and physical responses were severely compromised when you first entered the catatonic state, but that is true no longer. If you're tired or feel under the weather, I suggest you go outside and get some sun. Play with your friends. Be active."

At this his mother interjected. "What about the chance for another head injury? Like should he be swimming? Playing football?"

"Mrs. Willis, your son's physical injuries healed long ago. His mental difficulties are not easy to explain, but now that he is back with us, interacting with the world again, the best way to keep him here is to let the world return the favor."

"It's been his choice to rest the past few days."

"Yes, but if he hadn't sustained a head injury, would you allow him to lie in bed all day?"

"No. But he did sustain a head injury."

Robbins was about to respond when his mother cut him off.

"Doctor, I'm scared. I'm worried I'm going to lose him again. Is that so wrong of me?"

"No, Mrs. Willis. Of course not. But a meek response is not always the answer to fear. You shouldn't always hit the brakes when an accident looms. Sometimes the accelerator offers the best opportunity for a positive outcome, and this is one of those times. You will hurt his chances to have a normal life if you shelter him. I don't think I can be more clear than that."

Later, after the doctor left, Todd's mom sat next to him on the bed and stroked his forehead.

"Do you feel like going outside today?"

"Not really."

"What about tomorrow?"

"Yeah, that sounds all right. I'll go find my friends tomorrow."

"I'm sure you'll have the best time. You seem to have really bonded with those boys."

His mother's intentions were good, and she only wanted the best for him. But since she was powerless to address the real problem, Todd found himself resenting her. She didn't understand the world was a farce, a sick joke. None of them did.

When he first awoke from his long sleep, Todd had felt empowered by his dreams and what he learned from them. He couldn't recall specific details, not then, but generally he understood the world was different than most people thought. Possessing this knowledge, he believed, made him special. It offered an edge over others, especially kids his age. If he had been evaluated by someone who could comprehend his newfound intellect, Todd believed he would have been considered a prodigy.

But over the next few weeks, as sounds and images coalesced in his mind, as their shapes revealed increasingly greater detail, Todd's feelings had changed. At night, in his dreams, he saw a wall of all-consuming fire. He heard music that wasn't his own and saw photographs of people he didn't know and experienced stories that could not be true and yet he somehow knew were true. In the photographs, he noticed the same few people again and again, a man and a woman about the same age as his parents and a little girl he assumed was their daughter. The locations of these pictures varied, like sometimes the family was inside their home, sometimes in the back yard, and other times they appeared to be on vacation in places like Boston or California or Switzerland. The girl aged over time, and in some of the more recent pictures there was a newborn baby.

The styles of music also varied, and the individual songs seemed to be without number. Todd knew if he could remember in the morning all the melodies and lyrics he heard in his nighttime dreams, if he could record them somehow, he would grow up to be the most famous songwriter of all time. And yet his knowledge of this music, these songs that were clearly not his own, rendered them meaningless. He understood they belonged to another place, or another time, and the only way he could make sense of this reality was to question his own.

Either he was still asleep or he was crazy or he lived in a world where nothing added up, and so everything seemed pointless to him.

The most difficult concept to understand was the story of this place, this city that had been promised greatness but instead would be wiped off the map one day in the future. The people here truly believed the lies they had been sold, that their choices mattered. But whoever was in charge didn't give a shit about them. Whoever was in charge was just using them the way the powerful had always used the weak.

Todd refused to be like the rest of them. He didn't want to be used. If there was any way to take control of his own destiny, it was to reject the very idea of this world, this story, this summer.

And if he wanted to save his friends, he would have to convince them to join him.

45

The descent was well under way when a football game sent the summer into a tailspin from which there was no recovery.

It was just after four o'clock in the afternoon. Their field was a recently mowed, flat rectangle of pasture. The sky was white, the air dry and hot and nearly tangible. Cicadas buzzed in trees that surrounded the pasture. Red and blue water jugs marked the four corners of the makeshift football field.

It was a summer afternoon in the dead zone of Wichita Falls.

It was the overexposed film of Todd's fevered dreamscape.

David and Jonathan lost the toss, and Bobby promptly ran their opening P-for-K (pass for kick) back for a touchdown. With the two strongest boys on one team, it was obvious a blowout was inevitable. But David whispered a suggestion to Jonathan, gestured toward the end zone, and then assumed the role of quarterback on offense. Fifteen minutes later, the two of them had put up forty-nine points to Todd and Bobby's fourteen.

Part of the reason the "better" team was losing was because Jonathan was a lot faster than he looked. He could get open nearly every play, and on defense he'd intercepted Bobby three times. But an even bigger problem was David's disturbing accuracy throwing the ball. He could hit Jonathan in stride on crossing routes, could time his throws so that when Jonathan turned to make a catch, the ball was already halfway there. And their deadliest weapon was the play David had dubbed "Home Run," where Jonathan simply ran straight ahead as fast as he could, and once he was behind the defender, the ball was delivered on target almost every time. Todd couldn't understand why they didn't run the play every down. It was virtually unstoppable.

At 70-21, Jonathan proposed they switch up the teams.

"Fuck that," was Bobby's reply. His face sparkled with perspiration, and his breath came in great hurricane bursts. "No fucking way. We'll come back, you just wait and see."

Todd had doubts about this but didn't voice them. The seeds of a plan had taken root in his mind, and he saw a way to maneuver them into a place where he could exert further control. Where he could help them understand what he had seen and knew to be true.

They played a few more minutes, and soon David had thrown his fifteenth touchdown pass, and the deficit was more than eighty points.

"This is fucking bullshit!" Bobby yelled as Jonathan celebrated halfheartedly in the end zone. "This isn't real football! Touch is for pussies!"

His statement wasn't directed at anyone in particular, but it was a challenge and demanded a response.

"I don't feel like playing tackle without pads," David said. "Especially on this lumpy field."

"You just don't want to lose," Bobby answered.

"Dude, it's 105-21."

"So? If I can't tackle Jonathan—"

"You can't tackle him anyway. He's running past you every time."

"Then why don't *you* run routes, Mister Hotshot? Let's see how you play after you take a couple of good licks. That's what football is about. Hard hits, intimidation."

"Why don't we go inside?" Todd suggested. "It's too hot to be playing right now. Let's go to the empty house and turn the air conditioning down to zero. Play D&D or something."

David and Jonathan looked at Bobby, who was still pissed, but who also seemed to realize the futility of football in the baking heat.

"Fine," he said. "This game is bullshit anyway. Fucking pussyball is what this is."

"We can swim if you guys want," Jonathan offered.

"No thanks," Todd said. The sky seemed whiter than before, the heat even more oppressive. He still didn't feel like himself and the unrelenting sun only made things worse. But the real reason he wanted to visit the house was to get them alone. "I think I'd like to get out of the sun for a while."

"Me too," David agreed. "Maybe we can swim this evening."

Twenty minutes later the four of them were sitting in the den of the abandoned house, sharing Oreos and Fig Newtons and pulling cans of Mountain Dew out of an ice chest. Adam couldn't join them right away but would come by soon, he promised.

"I don't feel like playing D&D," Jonathan said, leaning against the wall, eyes closed. "I just want to rest."

"Sounds like a good idea to me," David agreed.

Bobby just sat there, staring into space.

There was a different song playing in Todd's head, something he may or may not have heard on the radio this morning. Purple splotches of color floated in front of his eyes. He switched on his synthesizer and started playing with the keys, working out the melody.

"I like that song," David said.

"You play it pretty well," Jonathan added. "The Eurythmics, right?"

"'Sweet Dreams Are Made of These,'" Bobby observed.

"Of *this*," Jonathan corrected. "'Sweet Dreams Are Made of *This*.'"

"'This?' That doesn't rhyme."

"But it's what she says."

"Hey, Jonathan," Todd said, gesturing. "Hand me your tape player. I want to record this."

"These," Bobby chuckled humorlessly.

At some point the sliding glass door opened and Adam appeared.

"What are you guys doing?"

"Hanging out," Todd answered. "Feeling groovy."

Adam sat down, reached into the cooler, pulled out a Mountain Dew. "You guys look tired."

"Hot," David said.

"Who won at football?"

No one said anything.

"Bobby's team, right?"

"Fucking bullshit," Bobby answered.

"Let it go, dude," David said. "You lost. Get over it."

"What? What did you say to me?"

"You heard me. Stop whining like a little baby."

Awe silenced the room. A stunning challenge presented.

Bobby pushed himself up and walked to where David was sitting. He loomed over him, at least until David himself stood and met his friend eye to eye.

"If you don't watch it," Bobby said, "you're gonna be the one whining like a baby."

"Whatever, Bobby. You're not our boss, all right? You're—"

"I'm the president of this club."

"Yeah, because no one was willing to stand up to you. Well, I'm standing now. Enough is enough."

"Guys," Jonathan said, "you—"

"I've never had a bone to pick with you," Bobby said to David. "Why are you getting all high and mighty on me now?"

"You bully Jonathan all the time. You always want to decide what we do, and then today, when the football game wasn't going your way—"

"That was fucking pussyball. I'm the starting quarterback for the McNiel Mustangs. Old High is already—"

"I threw fifteen touchdown passes, Bobby!"

"In fucking pussyball!"

"You're just pissed because you're supposed to be the hotshot jock, and I'm a better quarterback than—"

And Todd could sense it coming, could almost see Bobby's arm jerk before it moved. He was beginning to understand that all of these things were destined to happen, and anyone who didn't know this was forever doomed to interpret the world the way a man looking through a keyhole might interpret a room. Whoever was in charge enjoyed watching this predictable fight play out in front of them, because these partisan battles distracted the common man from the real mockery going on in broad daylight.

So when Bobby's arm jerked and sent a fist toward David's face, Todd knew David would dodge the punch fluidly. When Bobby bull-rushed his opponent, Todd understood both of them would end up on the ground. And he could already predict how the rest would turn out: Bobby would climb on top of David, David would kick him in the groin, and Bobby would collapse sideways and pretend to be in agony. When David paused to catch his breath, Bobby's hand would reach out and fell him again. Bobby would stand and rear back to kick David in the head, but at the last moment he would think better of it and send his foot into the wall instead. At this point, predictably, Jonathan would begin to scold Bobby, who would grab Jonathan and pin him hard against the wall.

A head colliding with a wall should have been a loud, echoing boom, but instead the surface seemed to give way, sheetrock breaking like blocks of stale mozzarella, and before either of them could react to this, David was up again, reaching for Bobby. Soon all three boys were on the ground, or some combination of them were, and at one point Jonathan, pushed into the adjacent formal dining room by Bobby, arms flailing for balance, reached instinctively for the hanging chandelier, which pulled loose and crashed to the floor like a shattered window. The sound was sudden and irrevocable, and the only thing that could possibly follow it was silence, except for the tornadic breathing of three exhausted fighters.

Now there was a hole in the den wall roughly the size and shape of a football.

An elliptical galaxy of chandelier on the dining room floor.

"Holy shit," said Bobby.

"You're not kidding," said David.

Jonathan burst out laughing. They all did. All except Adam, Todd noted.

And then silence again, as breathing returned to normal, as emotion cooled on their skin like sweat. Increments of time spooled out like fishing line, seconds maybe, or minutes. In that span of time Todd saw their relationships strengthening, perspectives coalescing, the five of them becoming more than the sum of their parts.

"I put something extra in the ice chest," Bobby said later, "while the rest of you halflings stocked up on cookies."

"Alcohol?" David asked.

Bobby nodded. Subtly, like an adult.

"You didn't steal it from my mom's cabinet, did you?" Jonathan asked. "She—"

"Relax, John-Boy. I brought it with me. Hid it under your bed when my dad and I came over."

"Where'd you get it?" Todd heard himself ask.

"I've got friends in high school. They had someone buy it for me."

Bobby reached deep into the ice and pulled out a tall bottle filled with amber-colored liquid.

"This is spiced rum," he said. "We can mix it with our Mountain Dew."

"What's it taste like?" Jonathan asked.

"Sweet and spicy. Supposed to be a lot better than beer."

"We need glasses," Todd said.

Bobby smiled, reached into the cooler again, and retrieved a partial sleeve of blue Solo cups.

"So who's game?"

They gathered into a circle on the floor, even Adam, and Bobby poured until the five of them were served. The drink was greenish brown, like the color of an algae-covered pond in the summer, and smelled medicinal. An idea occurred to Todd, a familiar image, something he'd seen before, perhaps in one of his dreams. He held his drink toward the center of their circle.

"Cheers," he said.

The others just looked at him.

"We all hold them out," Todd instructed. "We all touch our cups and say 'Cheers.'"

The boys did so, awkwardly, and when Todd pulled the drink back to his mouth and sipped, so did everyone else.

"Wow," David said. "That's strong."

"I like it," Bobby countered.

Jonathan didn't venture an opinion, but his contorted face could not be mistaken for pleasure.

Adam just smiled. A dream robot. A motion picture extra.

Todd sipped again, more boldly this time. So did Bobby. So did Jonathan.

"Is this what you call a cocktail party?" David asked, drinking a full swallow.

46

Jonathan was finishing his second drink, but Todd, David, and Bobby were on their third. Adam felt like a loser because he'd consumed only half of his first. The rest of them were taking full swallows now, and still he nursed his like an infant, suffering under the glare of their contempt for him.

"Look at that hole in the wall," David said, smiling. "You tried to kick me in the head. You asshole."

"I pulled up at the last second," Bobby told him in an odd, apologetic voice. His slow enunciation was like those remedial kids who were not quite retarded. "I was pissed but I knew that was too much."

"If that was my head—"

"But dude, check out what happened."

Bobby stood up and attacked the wall like an NFL place kicker. His foot and ankle disappeared into it.

"Something's wrong with the sheetrock," Jonathan said. "It shouldn't break that easily."

"Maybe it got wet when the house was being built," Adam said.

Jonathan approached the wall, turned sideways, and kicked like a Kung Fu fighter. His leg buried so far into the sheetrock that Adam was sure it had emerged on the other side.

"Oh, shit," Jonathan squealed with delight. "I'm stuck."

David offered to help by tearing sheetrock away in chunks. And of course pried out more than was necessary to free Jonathan's leg. Bobby, still laughing, grabbed the chandelier and shoved it into the first hole he'd made.

"There," he said. "Much better."

Adam watched the senselessness of it all unfold before him, occasionally looking at Todd, whose eyes smiled endorsement. What they were doing was wrong. It was terrible. There would be consequences for this, he could already see it coming, the wrath of his parents, of the police. He was trying so hard to be a *good* boy, and things kept getting worse.

Somehow it was Todd's fault. Maybe he hadn't started the fight, maybe he hadn't brought the alcohol . . . hell, he hadn't even taken part in the vandalism of the house, but Adam still blamed Todd for everything. Would they even be here right now if he hadn't joined their club? No, they wouldn't. They'd be sitting at Jonathan's house playing Atari or D&D like normal kids.

But nothing could be done about it now. Todd had manipulated them into this place, and Adam was too exhausted to resist anymore. He was sick of feeling alone. He pulled the cup to his lips and drank several swallows at once, ignoring the burn in his throat, in his stomach. He swallowed until the drink was gone.

"Thissa fucking hilarious," Bobby slurred. "We could tear this place down."

Bobby backed up several steps, like a bull, and charged sideways at the wall. His shoulder and torso buried several inches into it. Great chunks of crumbling sheetrock fell to the floor as he jerked himself back into the den. They all watched him, they all laughed, and even Adam felt himself smile. It *was* kind of funny, the wall, even though doing this was wrong and terrible for the people who owned the house. To help himself forget about them, Adam reached for the bottle of rum and poured himself another drink.

"Thassa way, dude!" Bobby said. He came over and clapped Adam on the shoulder. "That's my man!"

"It's like I told the guy on ABC," Adam replied. "Danger is my business."

"Jeff Spicoli!" said Jonathan. "That's hysterical!"

Adam tilted the cup and drank more, swallow after swallow, and someone began chanting "Drink, drink, drink." This one didn't taste as strong as the first. He consumed the entire cup and topped it off with a tectonic burp.

"Hey, bud," he cried. "Let's party!"

They cheered for him and poured him another drink, so that he might catch up. But Adam could already feel the world drifting away, could sense his hold on reality slipping. The damage they had inflicted upon the house began to seem less dire. The concept of consequence, of personal cost, felt less important than earlier, than it ever had, and Adam wondered why he worried so much, why he couldn't just let it all go, the guilt over his sister's death, the screaming of Evelyn's mother, the screaming of his own mother.

Bobby wasn't finished with the house. His energy was hyperkinetic, its hold on him almost like possession. At some point he disappeared, and at some other, later point he reappeared with a wooden sword and battle axe from the fort, and gradually the den changed appearance, until you could see through a row of two-by-fours and into a small, adjacent bedroom. In that room was a window that faced the street, but no one really cared. The street was short, a dead end, and this was the last house on it. No one outside would know what was going on in here. Adam kept telling himself this. No one would know.

Okay, so Jesus would know, but He preached forgiveness above all else, and even through the haze Adam could see a point in the future when he would be terribly, terribly sorry for what he had done. But as long as they didn't get caught, it would be okay. It was imperative they not leave behind any evidence.

No evidence and no one would know.

47

They were sitting in the master bedroom now because the walls in the den were gone. Late afternoon sunshine lit the room in citrus hues, and everyone but Bobby had vomited in the adjacent bathroom.

"We fucked up," Todd told them.

Murmurs of general agreement took the place of coherent speech.

"We have to keep this to ourselves," he added.

This was undeniable truth, self-evident, and required no concurrence whatsoever.

"Our fingerprints are all over this house. Our hair, our skin. We'll never get it all out."

Now they looked up, all of them.

"We can't lift," Adam said, and then stopped. "Leave, I mean. We can't leave that kind of evidence. We've got to clean it up. We can't get caught."

"No shit, Sherlock," Bobby said.

"We can't clean it up," Todd informed them. "Police have forensics."

David nodded. "He's right. I saw something on '60 Minutes' once, about how the police proved this paperboy murdered some old lady when they found a microscopic fiber from his shirt in her hair."

"No way," Adam said.

"Wherever you go," Todd explained, "you leave a trail of particles behind. There's really only one way to get rid of it all."

"How's that?" asked Jonathan.

The answer was obvious, it had been there all along, hidden like clues within the fevered dreams.

"Burn it to the ground."

48

Mild rejection sharpened to outright refusal as the bedroom darkened, as afternoon became evening. The alcohol loosened its grip on them, the fog lifted, and the true nature of their dilemma became clear. The evolution of their reasoning, Todd thought, was fascinating to hear.

"I don't know what came over me," Bobby wondered aloud.

"We were drunk," Jonathan said.

"I knocked a hole in the wall before we drank. Same with the chandelier you pulled down."

"You shoved me into the chandelier. I didn't mean to pull it down."

"I didn't mean to kick a hole in the wall."

"It doesn't matter who meant to do what," Todd said. "We're here in this house, and when someone sees what we've done, they'll call the cops. And those guys will come in with their fingerprint kits and forensic tools and start asking questions. It won't take long for them to find us. Unless we get rid of the evidence."

"We can't burn the house down," Jonathan said. "We can't. That's ridiculous."

"The owners have insurance," Todd told him.

"It's still wrong. Totally destroying someone else's . . . "

But Jonathan trailed off, muted by the reality of what they had done. The enormity of it.

"What do you think will happen if someone finds out we did this?" Todd asked them.

"Probably they'd kick me off the football team," Bobby said. "I can forget about college."

"My dad would go crazy," David added. "My mom would never forgive me."

"*Your* mom?" Jonathan said. "What do you think mine would do?"

Everyone mumbled agreement.

"We can't get caught," Adam pleaded. "We can't."

"Then we have to get rid of the evidence," Todd told them.

"Okay, but what if they figure out who burned the house down?" David asked. "Aren't we going to be in a lot more trouble for that?"

"Sure," Todd answered. "It's a risk-reward decision. We can leave the house as is, virtually assuring we'll get caught, or we can cover our tracks with a fire, which will make it very difficult for someone to pin it on us. But if they do—"

"If they do, we're screwed," Jonathan said.

"We're fucked either way," Bobby pointed out. "I mean, will it really be that much worse if we get caught for burning it down? We're going to look like teenage criminals for tearing up the sheetrock, ripping down the chandelier. Hell, I even pissed on the wall in that other bedroom. At this point we're going to look crazy no matter what we do."

Todd nodded. "So do you think—?"

"I think we should burn it down," Bobby said.

The others looked at him. They looked away.

"But I'm just one vote," Bobby added. "I'm not trying to sway anyone else. You guys can say whatever you—"

"I don't want to get caught," Adam said. "I vote to burn it down, too."

Todd knew then what they would do, because Bobby's nudge toward a democratic decision meant one more vote could make it happen. But in the end it didn't matter.

"Fuck it," David said. "They've got insurance. It's not going to hurt anyone."

"Yeah," Jonathan agreed. "If it's not going to hurt anyone."

They all looked at Todd then, and he knew it wasn't his vote they were seeking, but direction. They wanted someone to tell them what to do next. He had led these boys where he wanted, exactly as planned, and it had been easier than expected.

The next step was to see them through to the actual deed.

From there, who knew?

49

That hammering sound in the room, the one he was afraid they would hear—it wasn't a drum. It wasn't the percussion of helicopter blades beating the air.

It was the sound of Joe Henreid's heart.

There had been a frightening moment an hour or so ago when Bobby exploded out of the house and bounded toward the fort. At that point Joe had still been on the back porch, peering in through the sliding glass door. He was certain, absolutely, that Bobby had seen him as he jerked open the door and took off across the yard. But when he didn't turn around—in fact he never even slowed down—Joe concluded Bobby had somehow missed him. Later, after the five of them had moved from the den into one of the bedrooms, Joe had snuck into the house and installed himself in the closet of an adjacent room. He listened as their energy gradually bled away, as their bizarre behavior subsided. For a while he wondered, honestly, whether something had happened to the boys, if perhaps they had gone crazy. There seemed to be no explanation for the way they had destroyed the interior of this empty house. But as their words drifted down the hallway, repentant, Joe realized they had been drinking. He didn't know much about alcohol, except that when his parents drank it they sometimes got into the hot tub with their clothes off, and they always played music too loudly. Alcohol seemed to make people act differently than they otherwise would, but Joe would never have guessed it could make five normal kids turn into monsters.

Several times he had considered walking into the other room and announcing his presence. His plan was to catch them in the midst of their guilt and use it to blackmail them. But there were multiple problems with this scenario: 1) being a tattle-tale wasn't cool, 2) even if they admitted him, they would always hate him, 3) if he told on them there would be no more club.

As he listened to their discussion, however, as he realized how desperate they were, a new plan occurred to him. The idea of burning this house down was ludicrous. He would never have imagined a bunch of kids from Tanglewood doing such a thing. But since they were planning to do it anyway, Joe decided he would join them. He would *help* them burn down the house. When they saw how dedicated he was, how selfless he was, the five boys would have no choice but admit him.

He listened for the details. They planned to come back later with cans of gasoline. So Joe would be ready with his own can.

There would be no sleep for him tonight.

50

Ever since the last sleepover, when Alicia overheard an unfortunate conversation about her father, her feelings toward Brandi had cooled. She wondered, naturally, if Brandi was judgmental like her parents were, if she maybe said cruel things about Alicia when Alicia wasn't around.

But that line of reasoning meant Alicia was really the one guilty of judgment, so she tried to put the memory out of her mind when Brandi called her on the phone. It was nearly 10 o'clock and past her bedtime.

"I can't believe this!" Brandi squealed. "First you're in love with Jonathan and now you're kissing David Clark! What a slut!"

"Brandi."

"You know I'm kidding. So are you guys going together now?"

"He asked me. We talked about Jonathan and I told him what happened, and after that he asked me. So I said 'yes.'"

More squealing from Brandi.

"I still don't know what happened to Jonathan," Alicia said. "I don't know why he never called me back. I really like him."

"I never understood what you saw in Jonathan."

"You wouldn't," Alicia said. "He's interesting and different. Nothing like the dumb guys you drool over."

Brandi didn't appear to hear. "I mean, he's better-looking than David, but David has so much more confidence."

"But when Jonathan and I talk to each other, it's like we're best friends. Not like you and I are best friends, but everything he says is, like, something I was just thinking. He knows about planets and stuff and he actually *writes his own stories*. How many guys do you know who write stories?"

"Maybe you and Jonathan just weren't meant to end up together," Brandi said, as if she had put the phone down the whole time Alicia was talking. As if she hadn't heard anything.

"I think you'll be much happier with David," Brandi continued. "The reason I like going with jocks is how confident they are. They just come right up and take what they want. Last week Brock and me were kissing over by the school, and he put his hand between my legs."

"Brandi!"

"It was just on the outside of my jeans. It wasn't nasty or anything. I sort of liked it."

"How did it feel? When he put his hand there?"

"I don't know. Nothing much. What excited me was that it was *Brock* doing it, Brock Harris. Star running back. It made me want to kiss him harder. I even thought about giving him a blow job."

"Oh, gag."

"You're not going to be very popular with the guys if that's your opinion."

"Brandi, how many girls do you know in our grade who have given a blow job?"

"Well, none, but—"

"Then don't form an opinion about giving blow jobs until you know what it's like."

Alicia heard something behind her. She turned around, slowly, and there was her father, knocking lightly on her door, which was standing ajar by an inch or two.

"But *all* the high school girls—"

Alicia held the phone away from her ear.

"Hey, Dad." Her voice wavered with fear, but she pretended like everything was completely normal. "What's up?"

"Time for bed."

"Oh, okay. Let me just hang up with Brandi."

"Do it quickly," he said. "You should have been in bed half an hour ago."

Alicia was mortified. What would her dad think of her? She would *never* do anything like that. At least not yet. But when she was older . . . what would it be like? To be in bed with a man, to lie right next to him. . . .

" . . . you there? *Talk* to me, Alicia!"

"I'm here. That was my dad. I think he heard me."

"Heard what?"

"We were talking about *blow jobs*," Alicia reminded her.

"Oops."

"Yeah, oops is right. Anyway, I gotta go. It's past my bedtime."

"All right, then. Picture David naked until you fall asleep and see if you can have some sweet dreams about him."

Alicia chuckled and hung up the phone. A few minutes later she was lying in the dark, eyes closed, thinking graphic thoughts. Brandi wasn't a tactful person, she usually said the wrong thing at the wrong time, but her ideas were typically on the money. Alicia was insanely curious what it would be like to be caressed and kissed, to feel a boy on top of her, to feel him inside her. Giving herself to someone so openly, so intimately, was a concept she didn't yet understand. But when the time came, who would it be? Was it already decided?

Sleep approached her, covered her like a warm blanket. Alicia smiled as she drifted away, and she dreamed scandalous dreams of a faraway hotel, meeting a boy there, being kissed by him all over her body.

51

Humid darkness. Clear, moonlit sky. A soundtrack of crickets. Coyotes in the woods patrolled their side of the barbed-wire border, stopping sometimes to consider the geometric human settlements, the hovering rectangles of light. Raccoons ignored the boundary between wilderness and civilization and raided outdoor trash cans for an easy dinner. House cats searched the neighborhood for mice and rabbits and unsuspecting birds, but kept their distance from the raccoons. Alien-looking opossums kept their distance from everything.

Including five boys, trudging through the trees, carrying steel and plastic cans of gasoline. Todd was in the lead, directing their every move, feeling like the king he was.

They wore gloves this time, rubber gloves that would later be hidden in the woods, in a deep hole that would be refilled and ignored for three months. Eventually they would dig up the gloves and burn them. Any clothing fibers or strands of hair that fell into the grass would be washed away by the fire department, they felt sure. Accelerant would be used in the den, in the master bedroom, and any other room where they may have left traces of evidence. But it would be used sparingly, and come from three different gas cans, so that no one father would be missing an appreciable amount of fuel.

Through the trees they jogged, approaching the house, and then through the sliding glass door. The first fire would be set at the opposite end of the house—in the master bedroom—and from there they would work backward, to the dining room and the sliding glass door again. Working backward would reduce the chance of getting burned, and also keep gasoline off their shoes, which could leave a trail for someone to find later.

Adam pointed a flashlight while David, Jonathan, and Bobby stepped into the room with their cans of gasoline.

"If anyone wants out," Todd said to them, "if anyone thinks we shouldn't do this, now is the time to speak up."

They all looked at each other, but no one said anything. Todd knew they were frightened, as he was frightened, but since they had come this far he knew they could come a little further.

"All right, then. David and Jonathan, pour gasoline around the perimeter of the room, working backward as you go. Bobby, you start in the middle and pour a line backward toward the door."

Once the work was done, the five of them retreated into the hallway. Adam was carrying six knotted handkerchiefs, and Todd reached for one.

"When I throw this, we have to move fast. We have no idea how quickly the fire will spread. Go to the next room, soak it with gas, throw in a handkerchief, and then do the next room, then the den, and then we're out. In less than two minutes. All right?"

Everyone nodded.

The loose end of the knotted handkerchief was lit. A tongue of yellow flame twisted the cotton fabric, devouring it, turning it black.

"It's better to burn out," Todd said, "than fade away."

He tossed the handkerchief into the room with a flick of his wrist. As it tumbled toward the ground, Todd wondered briefly if his idea would even work. Maybe he would miss the gasoline on the carpet altogether, or maybe he would succeed in burning a hole in the carpet and nothing more. But then the very air seemed to ignite, before the handkerchief even bothered to land on the floor. Heat rushed into the hallway, and flames turned nighttime to day.

"Holy shit!" said Bobby and David simultaneously.

"Come on!" Adam yelled. "Let's go!"

They replicated their work in the next room, then the next, and in less than a minute they had gathered in the den. Fire roared from the hallway. Heat baked the air, air that gagged them with the heavy smell of burning gasoline and drywall and carpet. Jonathan and Bobby retreated to the back porch. David was on his way out. Todd was readying the last of his handkerchiefs, and Adam was standing against the bar between the kitchen and den, directing the flashlight.

That's when Todd saw the eyes. Someone else was in the house with them.

"Who is that?" he asked.

The flashlight beam wobbled. Todd turned and saw Adam looking at this unknown boy, his eyes wide and terrified. The other boys had also stopped. Were also looking.

Flames crackled, devouring the house. Todd could feel heat drifting toward them from the other rooms. There wasn't much time.

The figure moved forward. Said something Todd couldn't hear.

"What are you doing here?" Adam replied.

It was only then that Todd realized this was the kid from before, the one who wanted to join their club. He must have been watching them the whole time. Since they arrived at the house, or since this afternoon, or maybe he'd been spying on them since the day they caught him in the fort.

"We have to get out of here!" Adam yelled. "Come on, Todd! Let's go!"

Todd stood there, indecisive. He didn't understand why Joe hadn't fled the house already. Was he frightened? In shock? Todd knew he should grab the kid and drag him to safety, but he was confused and didn't know what to do. He was suddenly afraid this little kid would ruin everything.

But one way or another they had to get him out of here. He was about to tell Adam to grab him when the kid turned and ran. Away from them. Toward the front of the house. Toward the fire.

"Where are you going?" Todd yelled. "Come back!"

The kid disappeared into a hallway dark with smoke and glowing with fire.

Disbelief washed over Todd.

"Throw the last handkerchief!" Adam hissed. "We have to get the hell out of here!"

Todd turned back toward the others. All four of them were staring at the place where the kid had disappeared.

Time seemed to stop, if it had ever been flowing in the first place.

Todd backed out of the den and threw the last handkerchief. From the porch the flames were so bright it appeared someone had turned on all the lights in the house. All the windows were lit yellow. He shut the sliding glass door and beckoned them to run. Which they did, through the woods, between two houses, eventually emerging on the street.

"That fucking thing is going up like a rocket," Todd said. "It'll light up this neighborhood like the sun in a few minutes."

266 THE BOYS OF SUMMER

The others looked at him, paralyzed by a hyperkinetic rush of fear and excitement and uncertainty.

Then David said, "That kid, Joe. What the hell was he doing in there?"

"We just left him," Jonathan moaned. "What if he's burning up in there?"

"He's not," Todd told them. "He ran away from us. He must have gone out the front door."

"Are you sure?" David asked.

"He had to have," Todd said, but they could all hear the doubt in his voice.

"We should go back," Jonathan said. "What if he's still in there? We can't just leave him in there."

"We can't do anything about it now," Todd countered. "If he didn't make it out the front door, not even a fireman could save him."

"We can't just leave him!" Jonathan said.

"Todd's right," David said. "Maybe we should have tried harder to help him, but he ran away on his own. There's nothing we can do about it now."

Bobby just stood there, silent, as if he were working through a difficult math problem.

"We have to get out of here," Adam told them. "We can't stand here in the street like this. Someone's going to look out their window and see us."

"What are we going to do?" Jonathan wailed.

"We're going home," David told him. "It's all we *can* do."

52

Adam ran hard, counting steps as he pounded the asphalt road. Probably he should have been walking, since running would make him look guilty, but he couldn't help himself. He ran from the fire, he ran from those glowing eyes, he ran from himself.

Occasionally he stopped and looked back in the direction of the house. He thought he could see a glow above the silhouette of roofs and treetops, but maybe that was just his eyes playing tricks on him. Finally he made it home and crept through the back door, to his bedroom, where he stripped down to his underwear and crawled into bed and shivered in the sheets.

A desperate part of him hoped Joe was dead. Because if he had made it out alive, there was no chance in the world he would keep his mouth shut about the house. Tomorrow Joe would tell his parents, and his parents would call the police, and pretty soon the phone at Adam's own house would ring. Then it would all be over.

Who was he kidding? It had always been over.

It had been over the moment Evelyn had lifted up her dress and let Adam see what he shouldn't have seen. The terrible thing was it hadn't been *Adam* who asked to play peek-a-boo. Evelyn had asked *him*.

He crawled out of bed and knelt before the Lord, and was about to begin praying when he heard the warning sound of sirens. It was the fire trucks, of course, on their way to the burning house. But to Adam the sound was not warning but a message. A message from God. His mom's voice had screamed when she found him with Evelyn. The tornado sirens screamed when Christi was killed. And now the fire trucks were screaming to him, the voice of God reminding Adam that he was not welcome in Heaven, that there was no special plan for him. And since his parents would surely renounce him for good when they learned about the house fire, Adam realized he was alone.

Except for his friends, he was completely alone in the world.

53

David's house was closest to the fire. Sirens grew louder by the second as the fire trucks approached. His heart thumped in his chest as he lay there in darkness, waiting for the sound of his dad's footsteps in the hallway, for the hall light to switch on. And still the sirens grew louder.

It seemed like forever as he stared into the darkness. David was near tears. How could they have left that kid behind? For some reason he had been paralyzed—they all had—and no one had done a sensible thing like grab Joe and drag him out of the house. They just let him run away. Why had the kid done that? What had he been thinking? What was he doing there, anyway?

David wanted to cry, but he couldn't allow it to happen. He couldn't betray himself when his dad finally woke up.

Eventually he heard the transmission whine of the fire trucks, at first far away and eventually outside his window. The thump of a hand on the wall, the flick of a light switch. David rolled out of bed and stumbled into the hallway to meet his dad.

"What is it?" he called groggily.

"Looks like a fire truck," said his dad, who was wearing a pair of flannel pajama bottoms and no shirt. "Get dressed and we'll go see what's up."

David pulled on a pair of corduroy walking shorts and an Op T-shirt and listened to the murmur of bedroom conversation between his mom and dad. He wondered how many of the other guys were doing the same thing, waiting on their parents to wake up, to get dressed and look outside. He realized his hands were shaking. If Joe had gone out of the front door safely, as Todd suggested, the kid was surely going to tell on them. Maybe it was a bad idea to go back over there. Wasn't that how criminals were always caught? By returning to the scene of the crime?

But then his father emerged from his bedroom and said, "Let's go."

It was a quick walk around the corner. Over the tops of the intervening houses David could make out a smoky, yellow glow, but he could not yet see the flames directly. He could hear them, though, and it was a deep, creaking sound, almost a growl. Beneath that were the groans and snaps of burning wood. He hurried along to keep up with his father, and noticed plenty of other people were awake as well. Lights in windows. Robed silhouettes in doorways. A few onlookers were also walking toward the spectacle of the house. David and his father turned the corner, onto the street, and here was the inferno, blazing orange.

Flames were shooting out of a gaping hole in the roof. Storm clouds of smoke rose above the flames. Windows glowed. The heat was scorching, as hot as the pit room when briskets were cooking, even though they were seventy or eighty yards away.

Firemen were yelling and maneuvering and shooting geysers of water at the house. The flames themselves didn't seem to notice.

"Holy shit," his dad said. "That's one hell of a fire."

David wanted to throw up. He couldn't believe they had left that kid behind. Was he here now? Would he point out David in the crowd? Or was he burning alive inside the house?

A man in a robe and jeans burst out of an adjacent home and began yelling something at the firemen. One of the firemen yelled something back and then pointed a hose at the roof of the man's house, soaking it. David was pretty sure the man was Joe Henreid's father.

More people gathered near the corner. None of them said much, but David could hear sighs, could see mouths open in wonder. He turned and saw Jonathan and Bobby standing together with Mrs. Crane and Mr. Steele. They were near the edge of the crowd, maybe thirty or forty feet away. He looked at his partners in crime with absolutely no expression, and they did the same to him.

Finally David saw Todd approaching, following a man who was obviously his father. The father seemed upset, strident even, in his purposeful advance and desperate face. Todd, by contrast, could have been waiting in line at McDonald's. He followed his dad until they reached the front row of the crowd, until Mr. Willis and David's own father were standing side by side.

"Hell of a thing," Freddy Clark said.

"Terrible," answered Mr. Willis.

David shot a look at Todd, who smiled and looked back at the fire.

"Fred Clark," his dad said, offering his hand.

"Pete Willis," said Todd's dad, and the two men shook.

A crash inside the house sent a wave of exclamation through the crowd. Sparks shot out of the hole in the roof like fireworks. A teenage girl squealed.

"People!" one of the firemen yelled. He raised his arms above his head. "Can I please get you all to step back? This is a dangerous situation! Please step back and let us do our jobs!"

The crowd shuffled backward, its many legs moving out of sync.

"What does he think?" Mr. Willis said. "We're going to get burned all the way over here?"

"It's a liability thing," answered David's dad. "If a window were to blow, or something inside exploded and a bystander got hit, the fire department might get sued for neglect. Big money in these negligence suits."

"Yeah?"

"I've been sued four times in ten years."

"Really. What do you do?"

"I own Lone Star Barbecue over on Broad Street."

Everyone stood there and watched someone's property being destroyed as if it were happening on television. And as the fire roared— still ignoring the streams of water pointed at it—as the crowd murmured, as glowing smoke surged into the sky, David noted with dismay that all this commotion had been caused, in part, by him. The thought was a distinct one, as if Todd were speaking in his head.

We did this. The five of us.

David looked over at Todd, who was watching him again. Who nodded to him, as if he knew exactly what David was thinking.

We could do it again if we wanted.

They could, and they did.

ZONE FORECAST PRODUCT
NATIONAL WEATHER SERVICE NORMAN OK
TXZ086-311000-
WICHITA-
INCLUDING THE CITIES OF ... WICHITA FALLS
1041 PM CDT FRI MAY 30 2008

.TONIGHT ... CLEAR. LOW NEAR 80. WINDS S 5-10 MPH.
.SATURDAY ... MOSTLY SUNNY. HIGH AROUND 105. SOUTH
WIND 15-30 MPH.
.SATURDAY NIGHT ... CLEAR. LOW IN THE LOW 80S.
SOUTH WINDS AROUND 20 MPH.
.SUNDAY ... SUNNY. HIGH AROUND 107. SOUTH WINDS
25-35 MPH WITH HIGHER GUSTS.
.MONDAY ... TURNING CLOUDY AND SHARPLY COOLER WITH
A CHANCE OF THUNDERSTORMS. HIGH IN THE UPPER 80S.
.TUESDAY ... MOSTLY SUNNY AND UNSEASONABLY COOL.
HIGH IN THE MID 70S.

After the fire trucks arrived, Jonathan was able to contain his emotions while the four of them spoke to Gholson, but only because Alicia was correct: The detective was not at fault and could not have prevented the fire unless he ordered nonstop, twenty-four-hour surveillance on Jonathan's house. Would that have made sense because of a couple of cryptic emails? And if the police were going to watch his house, why not Adam Altman's? Or Alicia's parents'? Or his own mother's house? Who knew what logic the arsonist was using to pick his targets?

The Molotov cocktails had been thrown through three windows into rooms that were connected by a long hallway, and once the individual fires had merged, they swelled into an inferno. Fortunately, his garage was detached from the house proper and Jonathan had been able to relocate his car to the street.

Everything else was bad news, however, and by the time the firemen had trained jets of water on the structure, the fate of his house was already decided. Honestly, Jonathan didn't care much about the house and most of its contents, but the files on his laptop were irreplaceable. And though he'd been smart enough to save some of his work on a flash drive, he had been stupid enough to store the drive in the same room as the computer. Which meant the only salvageable projects left from an entire lifetime of writing—almost twenty years of work—would be those he had emailed to someone, as well as the few printed excerpts of *The End of the World* that still languished in literary agent slush piles. Imagine the cruel irony, he told himself, if one of those agents ever wanted to see the full manuscript. If that happened Jonathan would probably laugh himself into the nuthouse.

He regretted now the enthusiasm he had felt toward Todd Willis and the memory of his incredible music. Jonathan had seen these events as a way to reconnect with Alicia, as a possible peek into something incredible about the world, but he had not expected to pay so dearly for the opportunity.

And there was something else bothering him, a memory, long submerged, that had been shaken loose when he looked into the box for those cassettes. Fragments of that memory had been floating to the surface of his consciousness just before their evening was interrupted by fire, fragments related to the scraps of paper that fell from the box where he found the old cassettes.

Those torn bits of paper were all that was left of a short story he had written during the summer of 1983. Kenny Steele had ripped up the pages of this story as punishment for a crime Jonathan had confessed to but had not committed. He had long ago forgotten the concept of this lost project, but it seemed important for him to remember it now, as if the memory might help him understand exactly what was happening to them.

The scraps were gone, however, along with everything else he had ever written. And once the fire had been brought under control, Gholson escorted the four of them away from the burning house. He stopped in front of a home where no lights were on and no neighbors were within earshot.

"Obviously, we will interview your neighbors. We'll also begin regular patrols in this area, as well as any other neighborhood that could contain a possible target. If someone saw who did this, if I can get a description, we'll go from there. In the meantime, I would appreciate any information you folks want to share. As I said, I do not consider you suspects at this point, but if it becomes obvious you are withholding information that could save lives or property, you could be arrested for obstruction. Mr. Clark, when do you plan to fly back to California?"

"I'm not sure at this point," David said. "Not for a couple of days at least."

"Please notify me before your departure in case I have any further questions for you. And get me the information we discussed as soon as possible."

David nodded.

"Doesn't it seem likely," Jonathan said, "that the other person involved is Todd Willis? If none of us victims are suspects, who else does that leave?"

Gholson pulled a Diet Coke bottle from his back pocket. The soda inside appeared to have coagulated or hardened in some way, but then he opened the cap and spit tobacco juice into it.

"I'm inclined to agree with you," Gholson told them. "Except I've been doing some research on that kid, and what I found isn't promising. He was in and out of trouble after his family moved away from Wichita Falls. He lived in Odessa and Corpus Christi but never graduated high school. The next time he popped up was in Austin where he was busted for possession a few times—mushrooms, LSD—but no actual convictions. He was in a band and lived in a city run by liberals, so it's no wonder the kid got away with it. But up until then he was at least paying taxes, rent, he had a couple of credit cards . . . all the usual things you expect to see from a person going from one day to the next. Then all at once his record just ends. No more busts, no more paying taxes, no nothing. He never applied for a passport. Just poof! Gone. Which tells me he either dropped off the grid and doesn't want to be found, or he's not around anymore."

Jonathan and David exchanged glances. Alicia and Meredith listened silently.

"So if it's Willis," Gholson said, "He has materialized from nowhere."

"Couldn't Todd have assumed someone else's identity?" David asked. "Gotten himself another Social Security number, that kind of thing?"

"Someone with your resources could probably arrange that, but I'm not sure Todd could. Besides, why would he? He wasn't ever in any kind of official trouble."

"There are a lot of ways to be in trouble besides with the law, Detective."

Gholson spit into his bottle again. The little flecks of tobacco stuck between his teeth looked like fleas.

"That's true. But right now, what happened to Todd Willis doesn't really matter to me unless he turns out to be a suspect. And we'll catch the guy, whoever he is. If we don't, the Rangers will probably come in and have a look. The State of Texas won't put up with some idiot trying to burn down the city one house at a time."

"Have you spoken to Adam Altman yet?" Jonathan asked. "We invited him to come here tonight and he declined. Not that it makes him guilty, but he sounded kind of odd on the phone."

"Mr. Altman is a victim just like you folks. I spoke to him briefly about the loss he suffered."

"But you haven't asked him the same questions as us?" David asked.

"I can't comment on that part of the investigation."

"I imagine he would be concerned," Jonathan said. "His wife and daughter could be in danger."

"We will have patrols in his neighborhood," Gholson replied. "We are putting a stop to this shit now."

As they stood there looking at each other, Jonathan noticed another official approaching.

"That's the arson investigator," Gholson said. "He may have a few questions for you folks. After that I would suggest you convene this reunion meeting somewhere else. There won't be anything you can do here after the fire is put out. It will be considered a crime scene and you'll need to give our teams time to examine the property. I'm very sorry for your loss, Mr. Crane. Call me when you feel like contributing to the investigation."

55

David listened to the arson investigator only where necessary to provide appropriate responses. The rest of his attention was directed inward as he considered Todd Willis and his ability to hear music that had not yet been recorded. If Todd was in Wichita Falls now, if he was striking back at his childhood friends because of some perceived (or real) injustice, David wanted to find him and talk to him. He wanted to understand what Todd knew and how he knew it. Maybe the two of them could work together somehow. What great achievements could be accomplished with not just hints about the future but some kind of clear picture?

What confused David was this: If Todd had known about these songs (and conceivably others), why had he not capitalized upon his gift? Why had he not chosen to record this music himself? Was there some limitation to what he could hear or see? Had his ability vanished long ago?

It galled David to even ask himself such questions, because he was and always had been a pragmatic man. He did not believe in God or ghosts or anything that defied reality as described by science. If no one else had remembered Todd's music the way he did, David would believe he had hallucinated these memories. But it was implausible to suggest that Jonathan shared a similar hallucination, or that he had faked the tape recording. Thus, the next step was not to ask how this could be happening, but how he could benefit from it.

When the arson investigator was gone, David said, "I don't care what Gholson thinks. Disappeared isn't the same as dead. I bet you the only thing he did was run Todd through some kind of criminal database. We could look for Todd's family ourselves. His parents must be alive. Maybe if we find them we can find Todd."

"Find him and do what?" Meredith asked.

"Figure out if he's the one doing this. Turn him into the cops. Something."

"I'm more concerned about where you're going to stay tonight," Alicia said to Jonathan. "I would offer my parents' house but they're out of beds. We could make you a pallet on the floor."

"Thank you. But I could use some time to myself tonight. I'll probably get a hotel room."

"What about our hotel?" Meredith asked David. "Could you call and get him a room?"

"Yeah, sure," David said. "But it's early still. Since I need to get some information for Gholson, why don't we all head over to my dad's house? On the way, I'll call a friend of mine and ask him to start looking into Todd for us. Maybe we can get some information and do a little digging ourselves."

David could have handled all this on his own, without the assistance of Jonathan or Alicia, but right now he didn't feel like being alone with Meredith. She'd already annoyed him with her skepticism of Todd and his music, and when the others were gone she might start in on him again about getting married. His dad had been a lover of scotch and would surely have plenty on hand. David was confident a few drinks would fortify his defenses against Meredith.

"Come on," he said to them. "Let's go have a drink and figure this guy out."

56

Jonathan and Alicia agreed to follow them. Meredith agitated in the front seat and David knew she wouldn't stay quiet for long.

"Jesus Christ. I can't believe this. Someone burned his fucking house down."

"Someone did," David agreed.

"And we were *in* the house!"

"We got out, didn't we?"

"Yes," she whined. "But I thought we came out here to take care of your dad. Not this!"

"You need to calm down. We're safe now."

"But what if the guy follows us? What if he tries to burn down your dad's house while we're there?"

"That's not going to happen."

"How can you be sure?"

"I'm sure. And anyway, if something *did* happen we'd walk out of the house like we just did."

Meredith didn't say anything for a moment and David hoped she had run out of energy. But he was wrong.

"So," she said. "How did it feel to see her again? Your childhood sweetheart?"

"She's not my childhood sweetheart. We kissed a couple of times before the eighth grade. I barely knew her."

"But you somehow remembered her boyfriend, Mr. Terminix."

"Meredith—"

"I guess all the guys would know since everyone in school was after her."

"Look, you can see Jonathan is trying to be close to her again. I was just playing along to be polite."

"You were looking at her the whole time we were there."

"I was not. She's old. She's got nothing on you."

This shut her up for a moment, and David used the opening to call Erik again. He barked instructions and shared everything he knew about Todd. Erik promised to call him in the morning with an update.

After he hung up, the two of them rode in silence for a while. The drive to Tanglewood was mercifully short, and when Meredith realized they were going to stop soon, she resumed her argument in a harried, repentant voice.

"I'm sorry. It's just hard being here. I feel like an outsider."

"They were nice enough to you, weren't they?"

"I mean I don't know what my place is. I don't believe what you guys were saying about this Todd dude, and I can't believe *you* do, either. You're not acting like yourself at all. You're acting like, I don't know, some kind of superstitious hick."

"What about that Cartman business?" he asked her.

"Jonathan probably faked the tape."

"Are you serious?"

"Come on, David. You're the most confident and literal man I know. For the longest time you wouldn't even tell me you loved me because you said love wasn't real. That it was just brain chemicals."

Actually, his position on this hadn't changed. Every thought and feeling a human being ever experienced could be reduced to physical properties in the brain, which meant love was no more special, chemically, than any of the rest. But Meredith couldn't handle this and threatened to leave him, so eventually he surrendered.

"And now you expect me to believe your childhood friend could sing songs from the future. Can't you understand why I'm worried?"

"Yes. I do understand. But since you know I'm a skeptic, I would hope you could trust me. It's not like I believe it because I saw something on TV. It happened right in front of me. Jonathan remembers the exact same thing."

They reached the house and David pulled into the driveway. He had long ago lost his key, but his dad always kept a spare above the door. If it wasn't there now they'd have to break in.

"Honey," Meredith said. His right hand was on the gear shift and she covered it with her own. "Jonathan is an author. He writes weird stories like this. I think he made all this up and has convinced you it's real."

David spit laughter at her.

"You're nuts. It's not easy to fake something like that, and anyway I remembered it on the plane before we ever got here."

"I know that's what you think. But what *I* think is that you're freaked out about your dad, whether you realize it or not. When your parents die, you grieve their passing, but you're also confronted with your own mortality. I had a friend—a smart, level-headed friend—who saw her mother's ghost at the funeral home where they picked out her casket. In the end she realized it hadn't happened, but it took weeks for her to come to terms with it. And maybe this thing with Todd is like that. Once you believe someone can see the future, maybe anything is possible. Maybe you're hoping he's still out there somewhere, doing all right."

David imagined what she would say if he told her about his own gift, how he'd built his fortune making investments with barely more than intuition. The thought made him smile.

"Laugh all you want," Meredith said. She pointed at his father's house. "But you haven't been here for almost twenty years. I hope you're ready for what you find."

"I'm ready," he said, thinking about the Johnnie Walker he would soon be drinking. "Let's go in there and get this over with."

Alicia and Jonathan had parked on the street and soon joined them on the driveway. David led the four of them to the back porch, where he expected to find the key, and sure enough it was perched on the stone outcropping above the door. He had never understood why his dad would leave himself so vulnerable. As thorough and protective as the old man had been, why didn't he realize any common thief would think to look there?

They walked through a small entryway and into the living room. The house was dark and the thermostat was turned way down.

"Jesus," Meredith said. "It's like an ice box in here. No wonder you run the air so cold at your house."

David grunted. He hated when she tried to relate him to his father.

His hands felt along the wall and found a light switch. He flipped it on and was not surprised to see the living room had been completely remodeled. The shag carpet had been replaced with hardwood, and the old faux wood paneling had disappeared. Mounted on the wall nearest him was a large flat-screen TV. The old fabric sofa and chair were gone and expensive-looking leather furniture had taken their place.

"Your dad had decent taste," Meredith said. "Being here alone."

In a recessed area of the room stood a wet bar. David stepped behind it and set up four glasses.

"Would anyone like a drink?"

They all nodded. David opened the cabinet underneath and reached inside for a bottle.

"So what does Gholson need?" Jonathan asked. "What does he want you to find?"

"Dental records," David answered. He found one liquor bottle and retrieved it from the cabinet. "He needs to know which dentist my dad used so they can request records to make a formal identification of his body."

"Oh, God," Alicia said. "I'm so sorry, David. He was burned that badly?"

"Apparently so. I haven't seen the body yet."

"I can't imagine what the hell Bobby was thinking," Jonathan said. "That's just awful."

The bottle of scotch wasn't Johnnie Walker. It was Cutty Sark. An old man's drink. He poured two fingers for each of them and three for himself.

"His office is this way," David said, and led them in that direction. "I assume he kept personal files in there. I need to look for checking account records, invoices, something like that, and then I need to find his will. Figure out if he wanted to be buried or cremated."

When he reached the office and switched on the light, the first thing David noticed were golf clubs standing in one corner. He'd never known his dad to play golf. Sitting beside the clubs were a couple of computer cases. Their shells were cream-colored and he recognized them even before he could make out the brand logo. They were old Packard Bell machines.

"David," Meredith said. She was looking at something else, but David was still trying to understand how his father had known about his involvement with Packard Bell. "Oh, my God, look at this."

He glanced up and saw Meredith looking at a corkboard mounted above his father's working computer, a recent-model iMac. Pinned to the board were newspaper clippings, magazine articles, and even printed versions of Internet stories. David recognized some of them immediately, like his short profile in *Business Insider* or last year's two-page spread in *C Magazine*. Others were more difficult to identify, but each one of them was obviously an article written about him or that mentioned him.

The board was almost completely covered. There had to be twelve, maybe fifteen clippings.

He could feel Meredith looking at him, and in that moment David hated her. He wished she had never come to Texas. He wished none of them were here. If he were alone, maybe he could make more sense of all this. Packard Bell machines, the Apple computer, these clippings—his father had obviously been following his career for years. Since basically the beginning. And David had run off to California because the old man could not stand the sight of him. To prove his father was an idiot, he had built his fortune without lifting a finger. Every time he fucked some model or wannabe actress, every time he went up into the stratosphere in his luxury jet, he spat in the face of his father's Middle American values and hypocritical morality. The old man expected honesty from elected officials, humility from famous athletes and celebrities, he basically expected the world he saw on TV to live with honor . . . even though Fred Clark himself was far from an honorable man. Had it been honorable for him to fuck some girl at the restaurant? Had it been fair to ask David to hide the truth from his mom? Why the hell had his dad followed his career like this when he'd been the one to chase David away in the first place?

He had approached the board and realized Meredith was standing behind him now. She put her hand on his shoulder.

"David, are you all right?"

"I'm fine."

"But this, I mean, he *loved* you. He missed you. He—"

"Hey," he said, and turned to face all three of them. "I guess maybe I have some things to do here. Beyond the dental records and whatever. Maybe we ought to get together again tomorrow."

"Of course," Alicia said.

"Yeah," said Jonathan. "Sure, man."

"I called my friend and he's looking into Todd. He's going to call me in the morning with an update. If he's found something, we'll pursue it. Sound good?"

"Looking forward to it," Jonathan said. "I want to find that fucker and ask him a few questions."

"We'll find him," David promised. "And I'm sorry I asked you guys to come all the way out here. But we have a busy day tomorrow and I suppose it's better if we get some rest tonight. Jonathan, I'll call the hotel and get you a room. We're staying at the Radisson by the river."

When they were gone, David poured himself another three fingers. Meredith followed him around like a child.

"Honey, don't you want to talk about this?"

"What is there to talk about?"

"I don't know, maybe the longstanding grudge you carried for a father who missed you terribly?"

"If he missed me so bad, he could have called. I've had the same cell number since I was twenty."

"And maybe he wished you would call *him*."

"To talk about what? The weather? Politics? My dad was a smart man who could not see beyond what FOX News told him to believe. He held everyone but himself in contempt. Everyone but him was living in the wrong way, either a hedonistic lifestyle or sucking off the government teat. My whole life is set up as a correction against my dad's, so I don't give a shit what he put on some board in his office. If he spent five minutes in Carmel, if he ever saw my house, he wouldn't have waited on Bobby to come after him. He would have just killed himself and been done with it."

"No," Meredith said. "He wouldn't."

"You. Do not know shit. About my father."

"Yes, I do, David. And the reason I know him is because you just described yourself. Maybe you have different economic views, but you judge people and situations in exactly the same way. And all this hard work you never did, so you could get back at him, it's all bullshit. You work your ass off. You're on the phone all the time. You can't even put the goddamned thing away at the golf course, not even when we're at someplace gorgeous like Cypress or Pebble. Most people would kill to play those courses even once and you don't take the time to enjoy them. Just because you don't scrub barbecue pits anymore or sit in a cubicle eight hours a day, that doesn't mean you don't work. You're driven to succeed by the same ambition he was, and he obviously loved you for it. He saw what he helped you become and lived vicariously through your success. You're a millionaire many times over because of your dad. You should remember him for that instead of your stupid grudge."

David had never struck a woman but he was tempted to now. Meredith had no idea what she was talking about. He was rich because of a strange ability that allowed him to see what no one else could. Well, at least one other person could, and David was determined to find out what Todd knew and why. His father and his stupid mural could go to hell.

He poured himself more scotch and glared at Meredith.

"Tomorrow we're going to find Todd Willis. You're welcome to be a part of it. But I don't want to hear any more of this shit about my dad. Don't tell me I'm like him. I'm nothing like him. Now, let's go back to the hotel and get some sleep. I don't want to spend another minute tonight in this house."

Meredith looked at him a long time before answering.

"Fine," she finally said. "But I'm driving."

57

Jonathan sat in the passenger seat of Alicia's car, looking out the window at the dark and smoldering ruins of his house. He was thinking about how David hadn't spoken to his father in years. Only now it turned out Fred Clark must have viewed their relationship differently than David, had maybe even wished for a reconciliation. How else to interpret that board of article clippings except as a father who deeply missed his son?

"You can stay over if you want," Alicia said. "I know it's not the most comfortable thing, but I'd be happy to make you a pallet. If you don't want to be alone in the hotel room."

"Thanks, but I'll be fine. I need some time to think."

"I'm sorry about your house, Jonathan."

"Thanks. It's so overwhelming right now it doesn't even seem real. It's like my whole life is gone."

"I know. And later you'll be angry that it was intentional. Whoever is doing this probably thinks he's making some kind of point or getting revenge or whatever, but these are our lives he's toying with. Maybe it's all just stuff, but what about the pictures and letters and other sentimental things? I can't replace those. It might not change anything, but I want the police to find this guy. I want there to be consequences."

"I lost most of my writing," Jonathan said. It should have hurt worse to say this, but in a way it felt cathartic to unburden himself from so much failure. "Years of work."

"I'm sorry. That's terrible."

"It is terrible. But a part of me thinks, what was I going to do with it all? Nobody wanted those stories, so maybe I'm better off not having them to fret over."

"When you sell your first novel, though, you might have enjoyed looking back at the steps that got you there."

"Maybe so," Jonathan said. "And I want the guy to pay. But imagine how David must be feeling now that he knows his father missed him."

"I know. If one of them had just picked up the phone, their whole relationship might have been different. And now they'll never get the chance."

Maybe, as he considered David and his father, Jonathan was really thinking about his mother, how their own relationship had fallen apart over the years. He thought again of the scraps of paper he had found, the memory of Kenny and his mother tearing his precious ideas to shreds. Was the universe telling him it was time to go see her?

Even from inside the car he could smell what was left of his house, the damp and smoky hulk of it, and in that moment he was struck by how much had happened over the past couple of days, how much their lives had already changed. And he was certain there was plenty of story left.

Impulsively, Jonathan leaned over and kissed Alicia. She seemed surprised at first but then put her hand around his neck and held him there.

"I've got another chance," he whispered to her. "And this time I'm going to make the most of it."

58

All night David had trouble sleeping. No matter how far down he turned the thermostat, it wasn't cold enough to stop him from sweating into the sheets. He felt like he was dreaming even when he was awake, and several times he confused the hum of the air conditioning unit with the sound of a jet engine. As if he were on his plane, flying back to California, instead of failing to sleep in this squalid hotel room that was somehow the most expensive property in town.

And if he listened closely, David could hear footsteps. Like someone was following him, watching him. But that was no surprise because someone had always been watching him. He'd first come to realize this that day in the forest, when hail had rained down like mortar shells, and though he tended to ignore the reality of it during the day, he could not deny the footsteps he so often heard at night. Whoever was watching him was crafty about it, lurking in shadows and around corners and at the far edge of his peripheral vision, resisting direct observation. But in the haze of half sleep, David understood his entire adult life had been fiction, a way to avoid the truth: Something was fundamentally wrong with the world.

In the bleakest hours of a sleepless night, David was often overcome with the terrible sensation that his life was being consumed as entertainment. Perhaps, at this very moment, someone was sitting in a chair or on a sofa or on an airplane reading about him in a novel.

Hey, reader! he wanted to scream. *I'm alive! In this novel world I experience doubts and heartache and euphoria, the same as you. And like every American I strive so hard to be happy!*

But to a person reading about him, David realized, he was nothing more than a reflection, a glimmer of reality. Time moved forward only when someone turned the pages of his life, and when the book was closed he ceased to exist.

For a moment he swam awake. The alarm clock read 3:14. His head hurt, his mouth was dry like sandpaper, and he was lying on an unfamiliar bed, twisted among alien sheets. The air conditioner droned nasally.

David had been dreaming about something awful but couldn't remember what it was. He did recall the previous night, however: the fire at Jonathan's house, the recordings of Todd's music, his father's strange and infuriating fixation on his career. He also realized they had not spoken much about Joe Henreid. David hadn't given Meredith the full story and it seemed like Jonathan hadn't revealed much to Alicia, either. And for good reason. Even though the kid appeared to have made it out of the burning house alive—his gasoline-smelling clothes had been found later, unburned—he had nonetheless disappeared. And since Joe was the only one besides the five of them who knew how the fire had started, no rational, informed adult could believe the kid had gone away on his own. Clearly, someone had taken it upon himself to silence the little brat. And what did silence mean in this case other than death?

He snapped awake again. His cell phone was ringing. Now it was 6:17.

"David Clark," he said into the phone.

"I found the mother in Corpus Christi," said his friend, Erik. "The parents are divorced. I'm still working on the father."

"Great," David said. He climbed out of bed and walked to the desk. Grabbed his organizer and a pen. "That's fantastic. Let me have the address."

When he was off the phone, he noticed Meredith was awake. She looked confused.

"Good morning, Mr. Busy."

"Hi there, gorgeous. That was Erik. He found Todd's mother in Corpus Christi."

"Where is that?"

"South of Houston on the coast. Beach town."

"So what's next? Do you have a phone number?"

"Oh, we're not calling her. We're going to see her. Today."

"David, why? You've barely spent any time at your dad's place. There's a lot of work to do."

"That can wait."

"But the detective specifically asked you—"

"It's Saturday, Meredith. What's he going to do with the name of a dentist on a Saturday?"

"What will it get you to talk to Todd's mother on a Saturday? What's she going to tell you? How her little boy was born with a caul over his face and could sometimes tell you what song was coming next on the radio?"

"You think this is funny?"

"I think you're not acting like yourself, David. I tried telling you this last night and you wouldn't listen. How are you feeling, by the way, after all that scotch?"

"I feel fine," he lied.

"You seriously must be the least happy billionaire in the world. You have everything a person could ever want and it's still not enough. Why can't you sit back and enjoy the things you've earned? Why does it always have to be more, more, more?"

"People who want to make it in this world would never think to ask that question."

"Make it? You already made it! You will never spend all the money you have, and you don't even have children to give it to when you're gone."

David couldn't tell her the real problem, which was that he hadn't won anything at all, not really. Not on merit. Not with this intuition he didn't properly understand.

"I'm getting in the shower. I want to be in the air as soon as we can manage. I'll call Jonathan and the four of us will take a little trip. It can't be more than a thirty-minute flight."

He walked past Meredith toward the bathroom. She didn't answer.

59

When he stepped out of the bathroom again, Meredith was sitting on the bed, watching television. David smiled broadly, because that's the kind of guy he was. A smiler. Meredith was probably angry with him for walking out on their conversation, so he would accept responsibility and then ask her to get ready for the flight to Corpus Christi. She wouldn't like it, but she would do it.

But then Meredith stood up, and behind her sat a suitcase, packed and ready for transport.

"I'm leaving," she announced.

"Meredith, I'm sorry I walked out in the middle of our conversation. I was frustrated, and you're right, I'm feeling a little shitty after last night."

"I'm feeling shitty for flying out here with you. You don't want or need me here."

"That's not true. I asked you to come because I wanted you here."

"You asked me because you didn't have any choice. You were afraid I'd be hurt if you didn't invite me, and you'll do anything to avoid talking about our relationship. You'll do anything to keep me happy except the one thing that would truly make me happy."

"Meredith—"

"Don't 'Meredith' me. Not only do you not want me here, but you were looking at *her* all night. Your childhood sweetheart."

"I told you she's not my childhood sweetheart."

"Whatever, David. I saw you looking at her. And anyway, it doesn't really matter, because childhood sweetheart or not, I don't want to be with someone who doesn't need me."

"I want to be with you. Look, don't leave, all right? Come with me to Corpus Christi."

"You *want* me in your life?" Meredith asked. "Or you *need* me?"

The answer to her question was the reason he could not present the engagement ring. But instead of telling the truth, David feigned ignorance. He understood his behavior made no logical sense and still he could not stop himself.

"What's the difference?" he said.

"It makes every bit of difference!"

"That's just semantics, Meredith. Want, need, whatever. I said I wanted you to stay, and I meant it."

Meredith picked up her suitcase. She approached David and set it down again.

"There is a big difference between 'want' and 'need.' If you want me in your life, it's a temporary thing. You could easily stop wanting me. But if you need me, if you don't want to live another day without me, that's something else altogether. That's love, David. Not convenience or passing the time or a fling—if you need me, you're in love with me. If you can do without me, you're not."

David stood there and didn't say anything. It was true he didn't need her. He could do without her just as he had for his entire life before they met.

"I'm sorry you lost your father," Meredith said. "But this is not the way to deal with it. Not by suddenly pretending to believe in the supernatural, and not by playing rich guy detective. I love you, David, and you're one of the smartest people I've ever met, but in some ways you're a kid. A big kid with a box full of toys. Pick one up, play with it, pick another up, play with that, and ten minutes later sit there and cry because you're bored with everything. You should be taking some time to remember your father. You should be going through his things, looking for clues about how he felt about you. If nothing else, his passing ought to give you closure, help you move on with your life. You could build a family of your own, maybe even a son or daughter you could spoil. But the way you're going now, it seems like you'll never need anyone but yourself."

In that moment he almost blurted the truth to her. It would be such a relief for someone else to know what he knew, that the world was an unfair place where a fortunate few were blessed with gifts that tilted the tables of life in their favor. But the awful reality, in the end, was that he didn't want to save their relationship. He was relieved she was going back to California. The most difficult thing in any breakup was opening a dialogue like this one, and now Meredith had done the heavy lifting. All he had to do was keep his mouth shut and it would be over soon.

"To be honest," she said, "I'm not even that hurt. Because I know it's not me. I'm sure you have a good reason why you think I'm not the one.

But see, there's always going to be something. Until you—or should I say 'unless'—*unless* you realize there is more to life than moving on to the next big thing, there will always be something wrong with whoever you're with."

She reached for her bag again. David, incredibly, felt the urge to put his hands on her. To stop her. How could he be so eager for her to leave and yet feel compelled to ask her to stay?

"Goodbye, David. Whatever you're looking for out here, I really hope you don't find it. You shouldn't have everything you want. You need a hole that someone else can help fill."

"Meredith, let me—"

"I'll get myself home, David. On a regular ol' plane. And I'll be just fine."

She opened the door and left. David just stood there.

60

Adam worked often on Saturdays. Not necessarily because his projects were running behind, but more to get out of the house. Because the site in Tanglewood was still under arson investigation, he had driven instead to his only other ongoing project: a large stucco home in Canyon Trails. His task here was to inspect the plumbing work, because on Adam's previous project, another custom home two blocks away, the new owners had already called to complain about leaky pipes and pressure problems. This seemed to confirm his suspicion that Bob Barnhardt, his best plumber, was working drunk again. Adam did not like to be drunk and had never understood why someone would want to spend most of their waking hours feeling that way. It seemed unproductive to be in such a disorganized state, so out of touch with yourself.

But right now, if someone had handed him a bottle of whiskey, Adam would have gladly poured himself a shot or four. He hadn't slept well. He was twitchy. This morning in the shower his feet had been covered with dirt.

Adam hadn't really believed it at first. Instead he'd imagined he was still in bed, dreaming the scene. Because dirt on his feet was simply not possible. Dirt on his feet meant he had either sleepwalked or blacked out and left his house in the middle of the night.

Then it occurred to him, if he really had gone outside, there would be dirt elsewhere. Adam shut off the water and rushed to the bed, where sure enough he found more dirt on the floor. And in the sheets. Luckily, Rachel was with Bradie in the kitchen, and Adam had been able to whisk the bedding into the wash and replace them with spares. When he wiped the floor, evidence of his nighttime excursion had been erased, and he was safe again. For the moment.

Still, people did not suddenly black out or sleepwalk for no reason. And if he could not account for his whereabouts during the night, he could not know exactly what he had done while he was out. There could be more evidence than just the dirt on his feet.

When he had finished his notes on the plumbing, Adam walked across the red dirt of the home site to his pickup. That's when he noticed a man approaching from the street. The guy was dressed in a worn chambray shirt, jeans, and black boots. On his head he wore a grease-stained cap branded with the logo of Thomas Petroleum.

"Adam Altman?" the man said.

"What can I do for you?"

The guy was old, in his sixties, maybe. His skin was permanently tanned, creased deeply, as if it had been twenty or thirty years since he'd been indoors.

"My name is Kenny Steele. You may not know it, but I did some work for you a couple a years ago. I occasionally fill in on Juan Romero's framing crew."

Adam looked the guy over again. Kenny Steele? That made him—

"I'm Bobby's dad. You and me may have met a time or two when you were a kid."

"Yes," Adam said. He walked closer to his truck, as if that would excuse him from this situation, but Steele followed.

"I'm sorry to bother you, Mr. Altman. I feel awful having to come here, but in this case I don't really have a choice. It's about my boy."

Adam kept trying to elude his past, but it kept chasing at him, nipping at his heels.

"I know he done wrong," Steele said, "and I ain't asking for much. I was just hoping you might talk to Jonathan Crane for me."

"I don't really know Jonathan anymore."

"I figured so. He won't even talk to his own mama these days. But I got his number right here. I was hoping he might be able to help us out with the burial. Bobby didn't have insurance, and as it stands now I'm gonna come up short. Carolyn don't have much money left, neither."

Steele was holding a yellow scrap of paper. His shaking fingers appeared to have been carved from wood. Dirt was a permanent stain under the nails.

"Please. I ain't asking much. If you could just call Jonathan. He won't pick up the phone if he sees the call come from us. I'm hoping he'll find a bit of mercy in his heart and help us out."

Adam was horrified to see Steele on the verge of tears. He grabbed the scrap of paper.

"Sure. I'll call him."

"Thank you much," Steele said. "I appreciate it, I really do. There ain't much worse in this world than having to bury your only child. There just ain't much worse."

Adam wanted to shout something to him, something like *There are things much worse than that! So don't whine to me about your stupid burial!*

Instead he said, "I'm sorry for your loss. I'll call Jonathan today."

"Thank you again, sir."

Adam stared at his feet. He couldn't call Jonathan without being asked about the fires again, about the music Todd played, about what had happened to Joe Henreid. If he was forced to talk about that shit again, Adam might lose his fucking mind.

If he wasn't already losing his mind.

61

Jonathan had never ridden on a private plane before, had never even seen one in person, so he was unprepared for David's Gulf Stream.

From the outside it looked more like a regional commercial jet, and Jonathan would have guessed the plane could seat fifty passengers, maybe a hundred. But then they boarded, and Jonathan found a space maximized for luxury, not economy. The maximum capacity was sixteen passengers, David said, though he'd never flown with more than eight. There was a couch, adjustable leather chairs, and a kitchen. A couple of bathrooms. Private quarters for the flight attendant, a smiling, sparkling blonde named Kimberly.

Moments later they climbed into the air, turned south, and Jonathan realized the cabin was quieter than his bedroom when the air conditioner was running.

"Too bad Alicia couldn't join us," David said. "Since she's so skeptical, maybe she would benefit from hearing what Todd's mom has to say."

"She seems pretty dedicated to her own mother," Jonathan replied. "They'd made plans already today and she didn't want to break them."

"I see."

"Sorry about Meredith," Jonathan said. "Relationships are tough, man."

"Thanks, but I don't want to dwell on it. We should figure out what we're going to say to Mrs. Willis. We'll be on the ground in half an hour."

"I'm just hoping she'll be home."

"You think we should have called first?" David asked.

"No. Calling would give her a chance to prepare for us. I want to see the look in her eyes when we start asking questions. How she reacts will tell us a lot, I think."

"Okay, so we ring the bell and she answers. You think she'll let us in?"

"Even if she does, then what?"

"Ask how her son could see the future?"

Jonathan smiled. Chuckled a bit.

"We're going to sound ridiculous," David pointed out. "There's no good way to address it."

"There isn't. But how else are we meant to interpret that tape?"

"Meredith thinks you're trying to turn real life into one of your books."

"Like I'm faking all this somehow? Even though you remember the song, too?"

"That's what I told her," David said. "But she thinks you've convinced me of something that didn't actually happen."

"Honestly, I would be saying the same thing if I were her. I still can barely believe it even after we listened to the tape. And we haven't talked about Joe Henreid yet."

Even as kids they had never discussed what happened to Joe. News of his disappearance had reached each of them independently, and when it became clear the police suspected the kid of burning down the house on Driftwood, their collective relief had been so great the subject had been dropped forever.

"I don't think there's any point thinking about Joe," David said. "I mean, unless you killed him."

"No, I didn't kill him. Did you kill him?"

"Of course not."

"But someone had to have," Jonathan said. "Don't you think?"

"Yeah. I think someone did. But we can't do anything about it now. It's in the past and that's where we ought to leave it."

"You took the time to come all the way out here," Jonathan said. "Don't you want to understand what happened so you can put all this behind you?"

"Of course I want to understand. What do you think we're doing on this plane?"

"Trying to find Todd."

"Exactly," David said. "I'm a whole lot more interested in Todd than Joe Henreid. Joe was just in the wrong place at the wrong time."

"And Todd? What was he?"

David was quiet for a moment. A couple of times he seemed ready to say something important, perhaps reveal something personal, but finally just shook his head.

"Hopefully we'll know soon."

They landed at Corpus Christi International Airport just after one p.m., and by one-thirty they were in a rental car, heading into the city. David drove while Jonathan keyed the address of Cassandra Willis into his iPhone. From the plane the city had looked beautiful, hugging the curved shoreline of a large bay that opened behind the coastal barrier islands. But on the ground, Jonathan thought Corpus looked like any other Middle American city, sprawling and suburban, dotted here and there with skinny palm trees.

In a few minutes they had reached their destination. The house was small and L-shaped. There were a couple of brick planters on either side of a cobblestone sidewalk, and a clear storm door was mounted in front of the solid-wood front door. They reached the porch and David rang the bell.

As they waited for someone to answer, Jonathan began to feel ridiculous. He'd just flown five hundred miles to interrogate a woman he'd last seen as a kid, and the questions he wanted answered were absurd. He found himself hoping David's investigator friend was wrong, that maybe Mrs. Willis didn't live here anymore. If she was so easy to find, why had Detective Gholson not called Mrs. Willis himself?

Jonathan was about to mention this to David when they heard a sound behind the door. It opened, and a small woman with short, steely-colored hair stood there looking at them from behind the clear storm door.

"Can I help you?"

"Mrs. Willis?" David said.

"Yes?"

"My name is David Clark. This is my friend, Jonathan Crane. We knew your son, Todd, when you lived in Wichita Falls."

Mrs. Willis didn't say anything right away, but recognition was obvious in the slackening of her facial features, in her eyes looking briefly at the ground.

Then she said, "I remember you boys. You made it easy on my son when he woke up. You were his friends."

Jonathan nodded and so did David.

"Then you betrayed him."

"Mrs. Willis," David said, "I know you must not have a high opinion of us. All I can say is we were children at the time, we were very confused, and both Jonathan and I would like to apologize for what happened. We are sincerely sorry."

"Deeply sorry," Jonathan added.

"So you admit it?" Mrs. Willis asked. She held the front door mostly open but continued to stand behind the storm door. "You admit you helped Todd burn down that restaurant?"

"We helped him," David said. "It was Todd's idea, but we agreed and were directly involved."

"Well," Mrs. Willis said. "I suppose it's old news by now, anyway."

She stood there looking at them, as if unsure what to say next.

"But you're not here just to apologize to me, are you?"

"No," David said. "We'd like to ask you some questions about Todd. If you have time, that is."

"Time is all I have, Mr. Clark. I suppose I can spare some of it for you."

Mrs. Willis pushed open the storm door and admitted them into her house. There was a small entryway, a dining room to the left, and family room straight ahead. She gestured to a large sectional sofa.

"Please have a seat. Would you like anything to drink?"

Neither of them did.

Mrs. Willis sat in a recliner opposite them and said to David, "It was your father's restaurant, wasn't it?"

"Yes, ma'am."

"Does he know you were involved?"

"No, I never told him what really happened. Unfortunately he's no longer with us."

Mrs. Willis considered this. "I'm very sorry."

"The reason we're here," Jonathan said, "is there have been some cases of arson in Wichita Falls over the past few days. At least one of them was a fire set by our friend, Bobby Steele, who also knew your son. He burned down the same restaurant again, killing David's father in the process. And Bobby himself was also killed."

"Oh, my word," said Mrs. Willis. "That's awful. I'm terribly sorry for your loss, Mr. Clark."

"Thank you," David said. He appeared, surprisingly, to be moved by this exchange.

"The reason we're here," Jonathan continued, "is because these arson incidents did not stop when Bobby was killed. And each fire has affected a small group of friends who were connected to the restaurant fire when we were kids. With Bobby gone, it seems he might have had an accomplice who is still at large, and who feels some animosity toward us. Since that person isn't David or me, that leaves either Adam Altman or your son. At this point we don't think the police consider Adam a suspect, because he suffered a loss as well."

Mrs. Willis looked away from them, and for a while all Jonathan could hear was the wind outside and the ticking of a clock.

"I figured my son was dead," Mrs. Willis finally said.

"Why did you think that?" David asked.

"He came to see me a couple of years ago. He'd been living in Austin since he dropped out of high school. He played in different bands over the years, and always told me he was going to make it big someday. He'd say, 'You wait and see, Mom. One of these days everyone in the world will sing my songs.' But when he showed up here the last time he was in terrible shape. It was the drugs. He used them even back in high school, I know he did, but when he came to see me I could tell his body was just about to give out. He was so frail, and his skin, it was so yellow and hard it looked like someone had tried to . . . "

Mrs. Willis trailed off and looked at the ceiling. Tears trickled out of her eyes and she absently wiped them away.

"I invited him to stay with me, but he said he had to go. He was twitchy and impatient and I felt so sorry for him. I tried to touch him and he nearly jumped out of his skin. He was always a haunted young man, but this was worse. He was terrified."

"I'm sorry," David said. "It must have been horrible for you. Did he say why he couldn't stay with you?"

Mrs. Willis reached for a box of tissues on the table beside her chair. She seemed unsure about confiding in them.

"I'm a terrible mother."

"I'm sure you're a wonderful mother," Jonathan told her. "Whatever the reason is that he didn't stay, I'm sure it was nothing to do with you."

"Well, Todd never married. But playing in a band as long as he did—in a college town, no less—I hate to say it, but I'm sure he had plenty of girls willing to give him a free ticket. As it turns out, one day some girl from Wichita saw him play and approached him after a show.

"She was a few years behind him in school, but I guess she recognized him. From all the news coverage when Todd was a kid, you know. And later that night they did what young people are prone to do when they're lonely and have been drinking all night."

Jonathan smiled, hoping to encourage Mrs. Willis, hoping he wouldn't offend her instead.

"As far as Todd told me, he spoke to the girl once or twice afterward but didn't see her again for a long time. Actually, he said they texted. I guess that's what passes for love letters and courting these days. Typing on your phone.

"Anyway, I guess this woman called him one day and delivered unexpected news: Todd had fathered a son. The child was about ten years old at the time, and the woman finally decided she should give Todd the chance to see him. That's why he came to visit me. To talk about what he should do."

Jonathan took in a hitch of breath. "Where does this woman live now?"

"In Wichita, of course. Todd said she flunked out of the university and moved back there. I believe she works as a nurse."

Jonathan exchanged glances with David.

"Mrs. Willis," he said, "how long ago did Todd visit? Exactly?"

She thought for a moment and then said. "I guess it's actually been about three years. I know because I turned sixty the month before he showed up."

"Do you have any contact with the child?" David asked her. "Since he's your grandson?"

"I would have liked to. I had no other children. But after Todd left I didn't hear from him again. He might have told his father, but Pete and I had a falling out many years ago and he will barely speak to me now. I don't know if I'll ever see the little boy."

Mrs. Willis was crying openly now. Jonathan wanted to console her, but he didn't see how anything he said would help. He was honestly surprised she had told them this much.

"I guess you think Todd is the accomplice you mentioned," Mrs. Willis said.

"Well," David said, "we don't know where else to look. Unless it's Adam, which we doubt."

"Wouldn't surprise me if it was Todd. If he's alive, I'm sure the drugs have taken him into a very dark place. What I am surprised about is that you had to fly here to find all this out. I thought for sure he would have told you this stuff when he went to see his boy."

"Why would you think that?" Jonathan asked.

"Because he planned to make a new life in Wichita. He was going to meet his son and then reconnect with his old friends. He said it was time to make things right with you boys, but it sounds like he never got the chance."

62

David was back in his squalid hotel room after returning from Corpus Christi. Both Jonathan and Alicia would arrive in the next thirty minutes so they could review what they'd learned today. He poured himself some scotch and took it into the shower, where he stood for a long time thinking about Todd. If you believed Mrs. Willis, her son had returned to Wichita Falls three years ago to meet the child he'd never known and also intended to make peace with his old friends. That Todd had never contacted Jonathan didn't mean a whole lot. It was easy to imagine, in order to function as a father, he had spent time reconnecting with the boy's mother and trying to kick his drug habit. Maybe later he had relapsed, like three years later, which would bring them to the present day. In a compromised state Todd could have decided it was time to make his old friends pay for their childhood lies, a theory that aligned perfectly with the unknown arsonist's chosen targets. David wasn't clear why Todd would have approached Bobby directly and convinced *him* to burn down Lone Star, and it wasn't obvious how he had managed to remain off the grid (and thus unfindable by Gholson), but these were questions David planned to ask Todd when they finally confronted him. Which, if Erik could locate the father, might be tomorrow.

He made himself another drink while he dressed. What he needed now was a plan. He wanted to understand Todd and how he had known about the music. Like the process exactly. Was it something he could effect at will? How clear was the experience? And, of course, was he willing to drop his ridiculous revenge plot and focus on something more productive?

There was a knock on the door. David was pleased to see Alicia had arrived first.

"Hi, there," he said. When they hugged, he enjoyed the warm firmness of her body. It was rare for him to look at a woman on the wrong side of thirty, but aside from a weariness around the eyes, Alicia looked much younger than her actual age.

"I thought Jonathan would be here by now," she said.

"Should be any time. Want a drink while we wait?"

"Sure."

He poured a healthy scotch and invited her to sit with him on the sofa, which was gray and upholstered in an abrasive fabric that had surely been invented solely to cover cheap hotel furniture.

"So Meredith went back to California?" Alicia asked.

"Yeah. I guess you could say we had a fight."

Alicia reached forward and squeezed David's arm. "I'm sorry about that. Are you all right?"

"I'm fine. We've been having some issues."

"Issues?"

"She thinks I'm afraid of commitment. Maybe she's right. Or maybe I'm just not in love with her."

Alicia digested this statement in silence.

In the meantime, David took a drink of his scotch and said, "I'm surprised you're still single. I doubt there are many women like you in this town."

"Well, thank you. I guess the problem is there aren't that many men in Wichita, either. Like I said, I want to move away one of these days."

"Does Jonathan know that?"

"Yeah, we talked about it."

"Would he consider moving?"

"Why do you ask that?" Alicia said. She looked down at her fingers and fidgeted with her cuticles.

"Oh, I don't know. I got the feeling the other night Jonathan might be interested in you again."

"Yeah, I suppose he is."

"And how do you feel about him?"

Before she could answer, there was another knock on the door. Jonathan was there with two pizza boxes in his hand.

"I saw the delivery guy in the lobby," he said, and stepped into the room. "So I just paid for the food there and brought it up myself."

Jonathan set the pizza on the coffee table in front of the sofa where Alicia still sat. He didn't seem pleased to find her here already.

"I see you guys are drinking."

"We are," David told him. "Let me pour you one and then let's dig into this pizza. I'm starving."

David and Alicia remained on the sofa together, and Jonathan pulled a chair up to the coffee table. Between bites the two men recalled their visit to Mrs. Willis: Todd's experiences in Austin, the drugs, the girl from Wichita Falls who recognized him.

"So he turned out to be a musician? I'm surprised he didn't record all his famous songs and get himself a music contract."

David could tell she was joking. It was obvious she still didn't accept the reality of Todd's gift.

"But the big reveal," Jonathan said, "is that he got the girl pregnant. Todd has a son. And she didn't tell him until the kid was like ten years old."

"What? Are you serious?"

"The kid would be thirteen now. Which got me wondering on the way over here: What if he's in one of my classes?"

"Holy shit," said Alicia.

"The other thing," David explained, "is Todd planned to meet with everyone when he came back to town. To make things right, she said. But he obviously never spoke to Jonathan, and we assume he didn't talk to Adam, either."

"If he came back here to be with his son," Alicia said, "he might have decided to focus on that. Like get himself sober and be a father.

Sometime later he could have fallen back into the drug habit again, lost touch with reality, and then here we are."

David was pleased to hear his theory corroborated, and impressed by how quickly Alicia had constructed her solution with the available data. He found himself wanting to have sex with her. Like right this minute he wanted to. It wasn't a matter of pure physical attraction, not when she was pushing forty and could not compete with the nubile skin and raw sex appeal of a young woman like Meredith. It wasn't necessarily the scotch's hold on him and the prospect of an empty hotel bed tonight. The reason David wanted to sleep with her arose from a strange combination of her intelligence and his own desire to take something Jonathan obviously wanted for himself.

David could remember a time when he hadn't been this way. As a kid he had believed everyone treated each other with respect, the way they preferred to be treated themselves. It made no sense for the world not to function in this manner, because no other alternative made logical sense.

But certain life events had corrected these naïve beliefs out of him, and David, being a survivor, being a winner, had adapted to the world as it truly was. If he had learned anything at all from his dad, it was this: Take what you want and let everyone else fight over the rest.

The scotch went down quickly after the pizza was gone. Bladders filled, visits to the bathroom ensued, and eventually David and Alicia were alone together again.

He grabbed the bottle and two paper coffee cups.

"Want to take a shot with me?"

"Shouldn't we wait for Jonathan?"

"He seems a little drunk to me. Don't want to encourage a hangover, you know."

Alicia looked at him doubtfully.

"What about me? Aren't I too drunk?"

"Not yet," he said and smiled. "But we'll get there eventually."

When she agreed to take the shot, and when the scotch went down so easily, David could tell his strategy was working. When Jonathan returned and she behaved as if nothing had occurred while he was away, the plan moved even farther forward.

But there was a break-even point where, beyond it, alcohol would sabotage the effort he had invested in his prospect. So eventually he moved to end their little party.

"We've got a lot to do tomorrow," David explained. "We'll probably know the name of the kid and his mother by then. We may know who Todd's father is. We'll want to visit them, and it's probably not a good idea to do it hungover."

"Yeah," Alicia said. "Plus I have to drive home, and I'm already feeling a little shaky."

"I'll walk you to your car," David said. "I'll call you guys tomorrow when I hear from my friend."

Jonathan shook his hand and hugged Alicia. It was easy to see he was highly displeased, but in this situation, if he were to reveal how he felt, he would come off paranoid and unattractive. It wasn't a fair fight at all.

As David escorted Alicia through the hotel, he felt a twinge of guilt about what he was doing to Jonathan. But he pushed the thought aside. Empathy was dangerous when you were working to secure victory. It could erode your will. The way to win, he'd learned from friends in the military, was to employ sudden, overwhelming force. Often you could subdue your opponent before he ever realized there was a fight.

As the two of them walked out of the hotel and across the parking lot, neither said a word. David could sense reluctance from Alicia, so he chose a subtle angle of attack. When they stopped at her car, he fired.

"Want to grab a drink?"

"Um," she said. "Yeah, sure."

"Does Wichita have any good bars?"

"Let's try Toby's. It's just a few minutes away. Hop in."

No matter how much he achieved, David never stopped being amazed at how easily life came to him.

63

Jonathan knew his suspicions were borne from paranoia. Both Alicia and David were his friends, albeit from a former life and only newly reunited, and there was no way either of them could be so calloused and imprudent. Especially not a second time. Still, he could not shake the feeling that they had been flirting with each other the entire night, communication passing between them in code for which he possessed no key. Who knew what had happened when they were alone together?

Sitting here on the bed of his hotel room, navigating the television menu past $10 pay-per-view feature films and $18 porn, Jonathan was overwhelmed with the bizarre direction his life had taken over the past couple of days. Bobby's death, Fred Clark's murder, his own house being destroyed by fire . . . these were the sort of events that happened to other people, that you saw on the evening news or maybe in a gritty Hollywood drama. But this wasn't a movie. It was his life. His house was gone. His furniture and dinner plates and everything he'd ever written, it was all charred or melted or reduced to ash. Sure, tomorrow he might join David and Alicia on a hunt to find Todd's dad, and if they were lucky, they might eventually understand why someone was attacking them in this way. But what then? What would his life look like a week from now? A month? Could he be expected to go back to teaching like nothing had happened? Maybe he would spend more time with Alicia, or maybe she would take her insurance settlement and move somewhere else like she'd always wanted.

He looked around the room at the cheap bedding and the striped carpet and the air conditioning unit that droned like an in-room lawn-mower twenty-four hours a day and wondered how he would endure this place for the next six or eight months. Alicia was staying with her parents, but Jonathan would never dream of asking his mother to—

Then he remembered the look on David's face when he came to understand, in an instant, that he had misunderstood his father's feelings toward him, and that they would never have the opportunity to reconcile. If there was ever a time for Jonathan to approach his mother, wasn't it now? Wasn't it possible, as Kenny dealt with the loss of his son, that her will might be softened?

The drive to Tanglewood didn't take long, but it was full dark by the time he approached the old house. He sat outside for a few minutes, meditating on the buzz of scotch in his brain, before summoning the nerve to approach the door. When he rang the bell, he felt like an outsider, a stranger to this place where he'd lived almost nine years.

Kenny answered the door.

"Well, hello there," the old man said. Jonathan had not seen him in a few years, but he looked the same as he always did. Tired, haggard, drunk. "Come on in, son."

His mother had moved her wooden rocking chair from the bedroom to the den. She was sitting in it now, idling back and forth, and the sensation of déjà vu was so dizzying that Jonathan put his hand on the sofa to steady himself.

"Look who decided to pay us a visit," she said. A drink of some kind sat on a table beside her chair. She lifted the glass and sipped on it. "We gotta have a death in the family before you come calling?"

"Hi, Mom. Hi, Kenny. I'm really sorry for what happened to Bobby. I know it must be tough on you."

"Thank you much," Kenny said. "Carolyn isn't quite as sympathetic."

"That boy of yours has been drifting since high school. No kids, depressed wife, job going nowhere. It's no wonder his mind flew the coop."

"That's an awfully bleak way you have of looking at things," Kenny told her.

"I'm an awfully bleak woman."

They were both drunk, or close to it. Jonathan wondered if his visit here would turn out to be for nothing. Still, he forged on.

"Kenny, would you mind if I had a few minutes alone with my mom?"

"You can have all the minutes you want. I've had my fill of her this evening."

He walked out the back door, onto the porch, and lit a cigarette.

Many years had passed since the summer he met Todd, since the night Jonathan talked to Alicia on the phone, yet it seemed like he was living that scene all over again. The rocking chair still ticked in a recognizable way, and the look in his mother's eyes was as full of wrath now as it had been that night. Except for the silver in her hair and wrinkles around her eyes and mouth, she even looked the same. The primary difference between now and then, Jonathan thought, was her power over him had diminished, even if its effects had not disappeared completely.

"Mom, the reason I came here tonight is because I don't want us to go through life not talking to each other."

"You're the one who stopped calling on your own mother."

"Yes, but do you understand why?"

She drank from her glass again, this time consuming most of what was left.

"I suppose because you don't care for it much."

"Mom, I get the feeling you couldn't care less about me. That after the tornado you just gave up on everything."

"Such melodrama. Poor ol' Johnny, nobody loves him."

"Make fun if you want. But if you do care about me, you have a strange way of showing it."

His mother didn't respond to this.

"Do you remember, a long time ago, when you heard me talking on the phone to a girl? Her name was Alicia and I asked her to be my girlfriend. Do you remember that?"

"I do. Wasn't my finest hour as a parent."

"Yeah, and what you did stuck with me a lot longer than an hour. I grew up thinking all women were like you. Half the reason I married Karen was so I didn't have to be single anymore."

"Your generation blames everything on their parents," she answered. "Why don't you take some personal responsibility for once?"

Jonathan stood up and turned to leave. "I can see this was a waste of time."

"Johnny, wait."

He stopped walking but didn't turn around.

"I'm sorry for doing that. You have to understand how hard it was when your father died. I didn't see how I could ever raise you alone. Kenny felt the same way when he lost Lynette."

Now Jonathan turned around.

"If that's true, why weren't you closer to me? I was just a kid and you were an adult. I needed you."

"I understand what you're saying. But I needed someone, too."

"But once you met Kenny—"

His mom finished the rest of her drink and looked at him carefully.

"Let me tell you something. I've never told you this and I'll never speak of it again. But the day of the tornado, your father had just closed the biggest business deal of his life. He agreed to terms with a wealthy oil man, and the contract was going to make us a little bit rich ourselves. Your father had worked hard his whole life, and I helped this family scrimp and save and keep our heads above water. The two of us were finally about the reap the benefits of all that sacrifice."

She lowered her voice and looked outside at Kenny. Kenny smiled a sarcastic smile.

"That man came over and ruined everything. If it wasn't for him, your father would have survived the same as we did. And if you want to get down to brass tacks, the reason Kenny showed up at our house that day is because you were friends with his son. So maybe I blamed you for what happened to your father."

"That seems fair. How could I have known about Dad's business? About the tornado? I missed him as much as you did, you know."

"There's no way you could have missed your father as much as me. I loved that man. We shared a bond most people will never understand."

"Isn't there supposed to be a bond between mother and child? Didn't you ever realize his death wasn't my fault?"

His mother raised the empty glass to her lips and tried to drain more liquid from it. Then she reached behind the end table and retrieved a bottle of Smirnoff vodka. She poured herself a shot's worth and downed it in one swallow. It was obvious she was far drunker than Jonathan had realized.

"It's funny," she said. "Usually in a marriage it's the wife who wants children, but in my case it was the other way around. And if I hadn't conceded to your father on that point, he might still be alive. So maybe it's my fault he's gone."

Jonathan stared at her. He couldn't decide if it was the alcohol or simple meanness that produced venom from her mouth.

"Honestly," she said, "this is stupid. You coming here to make amends, me trying to apologize for what I did. Could I have been nicer to you? Sure, I could've. But I wasn't. I had a tough time, you had a tough time, and that's how the world is. There isn't anything we can do it about it, anyway."

"I'm sure that's how it seems when you're a drunk old woman. I came here to salvage a relationship with you, and you seem hell bent on ensuring it doesn't happen."

His mother laughed hatefully. "You must have figured it would be a nice, heartwarming scene, something out of a movie, the two of us reconnecting after all this time. But that's not how the world works. This is all going to go a certain way, and there's nothing you or I can do about it. So let me count the final hours and drink in peace."

Jonathan understood, finally, after all these years, that he'd lost both his parents in the tornado. One had taken longer to die than the other, but he'd lost both of them just the same.

"Go ahead and kill yourself if that's what you want," he said. "You won't see me again."

"The water is freezing, son, and there aren't enough boats. I don't want to be around when the ship finally sinks."

"You've lost your mind."

"Not yet," his mother said. "But I'm doing my best."

64

It was late, nearly midnight, and Daniels had gone home hours ago despite the ominous email that had arrived in Gholson's inbox this afternoon. Daniels' position was there was nothing to be done about such a sweeping threat to the city, and that if he didn't get some sleep he wouldn't be worth shit tomorrow.

Gholson wished he could sleep.

The email was bad news, but he was forced to concede that Daniels was correct: A threat to the entire city was too general to address directly. He had forwarded the email and the contextual information about this week's events to Homeland Security, which was protocol, but he doubted the Feds would elevate the terror threat based on some crazy moron in Wichita Falls. The only tangible action to take at this point was to remind the beat cops to keep their eyes open for anything unusual and hope the arsonist wasn't in possession of a suitcase nuke.

The spiral notebook he'd found in the evidence archive, however, was more than bad news. It was a mystery that rattled Gholson's confidence in himself, in the world at large. He had not yet shared the notebook with his partner because he was afraid Daniels would accuse him of forging it. After all, the content inside was impossible. The lyrics were impossible.

The lyrics for thirty-three songs.

A couple of these tunes had been released to the world when Todd was still a kid, either during or before the summer when he had been apprehended for arson, but the rest of them had been recorded and released after that time.

There were two ways Todd could have known about these songs so far in advance: 1) The kid was one of the most successful (and private) songwriters of all time and had submitted these songs to a number of artists who turned them into popular radio hits, or 2) Todd had known about the songs before they were written and released in some other, extraordinary way.

Option 2 was preposterous, but so was Option 1. When you were dealing with two impossible ideas, and one of them had to be true, it made sense to choose the likelier one.

Right now he was leaning toward Option 2.

Gholson was a Christian man. He didn't make it to church all the time, but he went often enough to believe in the Savior, to be confident in the Lord and all His glory. In fact, the primary reason Gholson had chosen to pinch Crane for information instead of Adam Altman was because Altman was a member of his church, an upstanding, well-known member of the community, and Gholson didn't see any reason to fuck with the guy. Crane did not enjoy the same luxury, so he had been the target of Gholson's confusion.

But Crane was either clueless or knew about the music and was unwilling to talk about it.

There was no question about the reality of the song lyrics. Even though Gholson wasn't a fan of popular music—he preferred old-school country like George Jones and Jerry Reed—he was nonetheless able to use the Internet to pin down the source of the lyrics. They were a varied lot: Don Henley, U2, Depeche Mode, Madonna, Pearl Jam, Coldplay, Nirvana, Alanis Morissette, Def Leppard, and so on.

Gholson had taken possession of this journal in 1983 during the original arson investigation. There was certainly no disputing that fact. And if Option 2 was the correct choice, then the idea of time was different from what Gholson had been taught. An idea like that made you wonder what was real in this world.

An idea like that was enough to frighten a man like Gholson, who preferred his reality old-fashioned, thank you very much.

Was it more important to solve the case or to understand the mystery of the song lyrics? Whoever was sending the emails knew the answer to the mystery, Gholson felt sure, which meant solving the case would likely take care of everything. And the purpose of his job, remember, was to protect the citizens of Wichita Falls by removing criminals from the street. But since the first day of this case, when Alicia Ulbrecht's house had been torched, Gholson had felt a personal connection to the events that transcended police work. He felt like he was meant to be involved directly. A crazy part of him even wondered if the reason he had remained in the same job for this long was so he would be here now to lead this investigation. That was ridiculous, of course it was, but so was the possibility that Todd Willis and Gholson's own wife had suffered at different times from the same rare illness.

If he understood what had happened to Todd, if he could talk to the man himself, would that provide Gholson with more information about Sally's condition? Was it possible to help her somehow?

Gholson didn't know, but he sure as hell was going to find out.

At such a late hour he was the only one left in this part of the station. Many lights were off and his computer monitor was a bright rectangle in front of him. The most recent email was centered in a small window.

EMPTY LAKE, EMPTY STREETS IS WHAT WILL BE LEFT OF THIS CITY WHEN I'M DONE WITH IT. I'M GOING TO WIPE WICHITA FALLS OFF THE MAP WITH A DISASTER OF BIBLICAL PROPORTIONS. I HOPE YOU'RE READY, DETECTIVE.

Tomorrow, Gholson would go talk to his wife again, if for no other reason than to hear her voice. Maybe she would acknowledge him this time. Even if she didn't, it seemed likely something was going to change soon.

He had the feeling something big was coming.

65

Now it was nearly two o'clock in the morning, and Adam couldn't sleep. During the past hour he'd gone into the kitchen for water, peed, watched a few minutes of television in the living room, returned to the kitchen to eat some deli turkey, heated a cup of milk in the microwave, peed again, and was finally headed back to bed. Once he was under the covers he would lie there until either he fell asleep or sunlight peeked through the windows, because distracting himself had clearly done nothing to make him sleepy.

On the way to the master bedroom he stopped to check on Bradie. She had kicked aside her blue blanket, and was now sleeping on her back, arms and legs stretched out as if she were ready to embrace someone. He picked up her favorite stuffed animal—a zebra striped pink and black—and cuddled it against her. Bradie stirred and clutched the zebra, but didn't wake up. He kissed her lightly on the cheek and shut the door behind him.

Adam padded down the dark hallway, opened his bedroom door, and snuck into bed. Rachel was breathing steadily. He didn't want to wake her because over the past few nights his wife had made a point of touching him more than normal, had slept with her arm draped over him and her face near his. Last night she had even kissed him with an open mouth. These physical gestures were signals: The urge to make love was approaching again.

When they were a young couple this urge had lived on a predictable and short cycle, like the rising and setting of the sun. But now that he and Rachel were more mature, the urge had changed into something

like a comet's orbit, an erratic celestial body that appeared rarely, without warning, and then retreated deep into space again.

Which was perfectly fine with Adam. He had never been that comfortable with lovemaking in the first place, and as their encounters grew
infrequent, he became less and less familiar with intimacy. His discomfort for the act itself intensified. These days he dreaded the comet's
appearance.

He lay there, staring at the ceiling, trying to clear his desktop of
open applications. He tried not to think about dirt on his shoes or
flames glowing in the night or exposed concrete foundations divided in
half by deep, shadowy cracks. He didn't think about his parents catching
him with Evelyn and he didn't think about Joe Henreid and he certainly
didn't think about the way his sister's face had been caved in by a blood-
stained brick.

Then something fell against his crotch. Something like a hand. It
reached blindly for his underwear and squeezed.

"Hey, sexy."

There was no possibility of denying her. The argument that
would follow if he didn't indulge Rachel would be far worse than
intercourse itself. So Adam turned and put his hand on her waist,
gently, to give himself the chance to warm up to the idea. But Rachel
pulled off his briefs and jerked on his penis as if she were playing a
video game.

"God, I've been missing you," she said, and rolled on top of him.
Her panties were gone, and she rubbed against him, already wet.

Adam looked up at the shadow straddling him. In this absence of
light he could almost imagine she was someone else, a woman with no
virtue he could justly defile. He imagined meeting her in a bar somewhere. Imagined buying her a drink and going back to her cruddy apartment, pushing her onto the unmade bed, where she would let him rip
off her panties and dive headfirst into the warm and forbidden place
between her legs.

He was stiffer now, stiff enough that Rachel lifted him a little and
slid him inside her. He clutched her waist, and gradually his grip drifted
toward the cleft of her butt.

"Do you like it?" she asked. "Making love to me?"

"Yes," he whispered.

"Tell me you like it," she said in a full voice.

"I like it."

"Make noise. Baby, I want to know you like it."

Adam didn't enjoy being loud during lovemaking. He didn't want to grunt with her, speak stupid, clichéd phrases to her. He had learned to be quiet a long time ago and that's how *he* liked it.

Of course he might have said all kinds of indecent things to some anonymous slut he met in a bar, but he'd never met an anonymous slut in a bar.

The conflicts he felt about sex made Adam wonder if he were mad. He could not resolve his unconditional love for his family, or his special relationship with the Lord, with the pornographic images that spooled out like high-resolution IMAX film whenever certain urges called attention to themselves. It felt almost as if he were two separate entities: a low-brained, dim-witted animal and a loving, spiritual servant of the Lord. He hated himself for fantasizing about sinful sex, for coveting some imagined woman over his own wife, and yet he could not climax otherwise. Often, on nights like this, Adam fantasized about running from the house, screaming into the night, never to return.

"I wish you'd make more noise," Rachel said when it was over. "Or say *some*thing. When you're so quiet it makes me think you're not enjoying it."

"I didn't want to wake Bradie."

"Her room is on the other end of the house. She can't hear us from there. We've talked about this."

"I'd like to hear your explanation one night when we get too loud and she shows up in the doorway."

Rachel turned over, facing away from him. Adam lay on his back and stared at the ceiling. After a few minutes his wife's breathing became deeper and more gradual. She twitched twice and was asleep.

Adam, by contrast, lay there for minutes that swelled into hours, staring into the darkness of the ceiling, not imagining that his life was a great mass of spinning water, a whirlpool swirling into a giant drain, not hearing the shrill sucking sound as the world devoured him alive.

66

Somehow David was both hungover and to a degree still drunk, and he was distantly aware that his phone had buzzed during the night, at least once and maybe a couple of times. Because he hadn't bothered to text or call Meredith since she left, some of the messages were probably hers. And hopefully Erik had texted him with information about Todd's father and son. There wouldn't be much to do today otherwise. Without a plan to locate Todd, he'd be forced to deal with Alicia again, and Jonathan, and suffer through more earnest conversations about the impossible music, about what it all meant.

In David's experience, people who sat around debating the meaning of life usually didn't spend much time living it, and they certainly didn't have much say about how things actually worked. You couldn't get elected to office these days by being a thinker, and you certainly couldn't accumulate the kind of wealth that mattered if you spent much time in existential space. To succeed in life you were required to actually do something proactive, and since everyone was going to end up dead in the end, what was the incentive to consider the point of the journey? This was why David was more interested in partnering with Todd than considering the philosophical implications of his apparent ability.

At the edge of his peripheral vision he saw a foot protruding from under the bed sheet. The foot seemed to be moving, sliding toward him, and eventually made contact with his leg. When it did, a hand also emerged from the sheets and reached for his arm.

"How can you stand it out there?" a voice asked. "It's like below zero."

In a world without consequence, David would have used his own foot to shove the girl out of his ratty bed and onto the floor. Unfortunately, this was no such world.

"I like it cold."

"Yeah, well last night you told me you wanted it hot."

Her hand let go of his arm and reached instead for his dick. David pushed her away.

"What's your problem, man? You some kind of crank in the morning?"

He couldn't remember her name, but that wasn't the worst. Until she pulled back the covers and showed her face, David couldn't be sure what she looked like, either.

The last thing he remembered clearly was sitting at the bar, sharing a drink with Alicia, touching her hand, caressing her fingers. He had expected her to welcome his advance, but instead she had jerked away from him, and a brief but unmistakable flash of disgust passed across her face.

"You know Jonathan is interested in me again," she had said.

"Yes, we talked about this before."

"Then what are you doing?"

"You never said how *you* felt about *him*."

"I don't know yet. But he kissed me last night. It was nice."

"Then what are you doing here?"

"I figured you wanted to talk," she said.

"About what, Alicia? I thought we covered every possible angle in that hotel room already."

"I mean about personal stuff. Like you and Meredith."

"That's bullshit. You knew what I was suggesting when I invited you for a drink."

"I have to hand it to you," she said. "You're subtle."

"And you're a tease."

"Does this honestly work for you? Since you're a billionaire, you just proposition women like they're whores?"

"What's the difference? Pay for it now or pay for it later. Pussy isn't free."

Alicia stood up then, even though she'd barely touched her drink.

"I'm going to chalk this up to you being drunk," she said. "In the morning I'll pretend like it didn't happen. The three of us will probably be together for most of the day, so try to be mature about it, all right?"

"Whatever."

She looked around the bar and gestured in a general way.

"You've got a bar full of women wearing short skirts and too much makeup. Should be no problem for a gamer like you."

Now he remembered. There had been some kind of bikini contest at a different, nearby bar, and the girl he'd taken home had been the

winner. She had curly brown hair and fake tits and a cartoonishly narrow waist. After two vodka Red Bulls and a shot of tequila, they had
called a cab and stumbled their way to his hotel room. He also vaguely
remembered a pouch of green tablets she had produced from her purse.
Ecstasy. They'd taken the first one around 2 a.m. and the second one an
hour or two later.

So what time was it now?

Between the blackout curtains, David could see a thin ribbon of
bright light, so it was at least nine, maybe ten. The alarm clock was
nowhere to be found. He slapped around on the nightstand until he
found his phone and pushed a button to activate the display.

"Fuck."

"What?" asked the girl. "Still cranky?"

"You need to get dressed and leave."

"Why? What's the hurry?"

"It's 1:30 in the goddamn afternoon. I've got shit to do. Get dressed."

David rolled out of bed and looked at his notifications. There
were multiple texts from Meredith, from Erik, two missed calls from
Jonathan, and one from another number he didn't recognize.

"Fuck," he said again.

"What crawled up your ass?" said the girl. She stumbled out of bed
and reached on the ground for her clothes. As she bent over, David
could see anything he wanted to see, and none of it interested him. He
could not, in his entire life, remember feeling this hungover. He could
not believe he had put himself in this position, in this state, considering
the long day ahead.

To alleviate the pain, he poured himself a bit of scotch and choked
it down. The girl saw him drinking it and laughed.

"Starting early today, are we?"

The girl was pulling on her shirt and got it stuck on her fake tits.
Her nipples protruded too far from their areoles and looked like little
pink tubes.

"Would you please get your things and go? Go down to the lobby
and ask them to call you a cab."

He pulled his money clip from last night's pants and held out a fifty
for her.

"Fuck you," the girl said as she opened the door to leave. Light thundered into the room and David shrank away from it. "Asshole."

When she was gone, when the room had returned to the safety of darkness, he poured himself a little more scotch. All he needed was a tiny buzz to pull himself loose from the death grip of this hangover, and then he would stop. Any other time he would have just gone back to bed, but David had a feeling today was the day the pieces of this puzzle would fall into place. He could not afford to be unprepared.

The first thing he needed to do was determine if Erik had delivered the necessary information about Todd's father and son. But when he opened his texts, Meredith's were on top. He couldn't help but read them:

Look, I'm sorry I just took off like that. But you've got to understand that what we have is special, and I can't just sit back and let it die.

I realize you have a lot on your mind, and now isn't the time to reason through this with you. But I can't just give up on us. Can you?

Are you serious? This little time travel game you're playing, this visit to the past, is so important that you're willing to throw away what we've spent a year building? Why won't you text me back? Or call??

Fuck you, asshole.

It was not lost on David that Meredith and the girl from last night had bid him adieu with identical language.

The next two texts, as he hoped, were from Erik. One was an address for Christine Phillips, whose son was named Thomas. The other was for a Pete Willis, who lived in Windthorst, a small town south of Wichita Falls. If both locations checked out, Erik had come through like a champ once again.

Now it was time to call Jonathan, but David was still woefully short on the energy required to convey information or make decisions. He was downing more scotch when someone knocked on the door. The room seemed to be orbiting slowly around him, which made the door seem to move as he approached it. Through the peephole he saw Jonathan standing there.

The light was so bright when David opened the door that even squinting he could barely make out a human form in front of him.

"David, what's up? Are you all right? We called like three times."

"Sorry, man. I went to the bar after we talked last night. Met some girl and we got a little fucked up."

"All right. But did you hear from your friend? I thought we were going to track down Todd's son and his father today."

"Yeah," David said. "I did hear back. I have addresses for both. The kid lives here in town and the father lives in Windthorst."

"Well, that's great! Do you want to go soon?"

"I can be ready in like a half hour. Probably need to get some food. Did you guys have lunch yet?"

"We did. But we're happy to stop."

"All right. Let me shower and I'll call you in a few."

"Okay. Hey, so what's the kid's name? Maybe I've got him in class."

David looked down at his phone and found the relevant text from Erik.

"Says here his name is Thomas Phillips. That ring any bells?"

David's eyes had adjusted well enough to the light that he could make out the features on Jonathan's face. It was clear from his expression that he recognized the name.

"Holy shit," Jonathan said.

"What?"

"That kid is in my sixth period. He's the student who told me about what Bobby did at the restaurant. And he knew somehow we were friends."

"Are you serious?"

"And I bet you he's known about all this the entire time."

67

The sun rose quickly in the summer, and so did the mercury; by lunchtime it had been almost one hundred degrees. Now it was nearly two o'clock and too hot to be playing miniature golf, but Adam was here anyway with his daughter, Bradie, after an earlier confrontation with his wife. It was the first Sunday in more than a year that he'd missed a church service.

Rachel had already been out of the shower and getting dressed when Adam woke up. Most Sundays they attended the ten o'clock service, but by then it was already after nine. He pulled back the covers, afraid he would find red dirt in the sheets, but they were clean. He stumbled to the bathroom and climbed into the shower.

"Honey," Rachel called from the closet. "Better hurry. We're going to be late."

The water was hot, cleansing. He lathered a washcloth and began scrubbing. Scrubbed and scrubbed.

After a few minutes, Rachel said, "Adam? What's taking so long? We're never going to make it."

He shut off the water and wrapped himself in a towel. Opened the door and stepped out.

Rachel was looking at him. "Let's go, honey. No time to stand there."

"I'm tired," he said.

"Yeah, I don't think you've been sleeping well. You're tossing and turning all night. It's been keeping me up, too."

She darted around him, pulling on a blouse, punching in an earring.

"Are you going to get ready?"

"I'm tired, Rachel. I don't mean sleepy. I'm just . . . tired. I don't think I want to go to church today."

She didn't seem to comprehend this.

"I have a lot on my mind," he added.

"Let's talk about it when we get back from service."

"I'm not going to service. And I don't really feel like talking about it, anyway. I just want to rest."

This stopped her, finally. "Well, I'm not surprised you don't want to talk about it, since we never talk about anything anymore."

"What does that mean?"

"It means, Adam, that every morning you take off in that pickup of yours and I barely hear from you all day. And then you're so tired you hardly talk at dinner, and then we just sit there and watch TV. You don't talk to me."

"Rachel—"

"I don't know how it's going with the houses you're building. I don't know how your meeting with the police went. I don't know anything."

"I'm sorry if I don't feel like rehashing all the crap I suffer through every day. I own this firm, Rachel, and ultimately no one is going to make sure the houses go up in time except me. There are a million little details I have to oversee every single day. I'm sorry if I'm working a little too hard for you."

"You don't think I work hard? Taking care of our daughter and cleaning up after your stupid dog and taking care of this house? You think I just sit around on my butt all day?"

Adam could feel his hands balling into fists. Fingernails digging into palms.

"And for Heaven's sake why do you have to cover yourself around me?" she asked him. "Always wrapping a towel around yourself. Are you afraid I'm going to see something I like? That I'll want to make love to you, God forbid?"

"Rachel—"

"What are we doing, Adam? Is this our life?"

"What are you talking about?"

"I'm talking about how you've wrapped yourself into a cocoon and completely shut yourself off from me. We hardly ever make love, we rarely talk, and then when something is really bothering you . . . Ever since your childhood friend went nuts at that restaurant, you haven't been the same, do you know that? And I'm scared to ask you about it. You get up and leave the bed at night, and I keep seeing on the news about these house fires, and I'm scared to death to ask you where you go."

"You think I'm burning down houses?" Adam asked. "The man who builds them for a living, you think I'm burning them down?"

"No, I don't. But don't you think the police might? Already one of your projects was destroyed. What if you're hired to rebuild one of these others? Wouldn't that give you a motive?"

She was crying now, and the sound of her sobs broke his trancelike anger. Whatever else was going on in the labyrinth of his brain, Rachel was his wife. Adam had sworn his life to her. He stepped forward and took her into his arms.

"I'm sorry," he said. "I guess I've been a little freaked out lately. I hadn't talked to Bobby in a long time, but he was my friend once. And now he killed someone, and he's dead, and I guess I'm just a little freaked out. But I am not burning down houses. I promise."

She pulled her head off his chest and looked into his eyes. "Is that really it, that you're shaken up about Bobby? You promise you aren't holding something back?"

How could he tell her the truth, that the past was driving him crazy? He didn't think he was burning down houses at night but he couldn't be completely sure. The red dirt on his feet obviously meant he'd walked outside somewhere. It was also true that whenever he visited the home he was currently building, he became eerily transfixed with the slab of foundation concrete. On more than one occasion he'd found himself paranoid, short of breath, feeling a strange urge to get himself a jack-hammer and break the concrete slab into a billion tiny pieces. Because there was something underneath it. Something in the earth. Something terrible.

"I'm not holding anything back," he said to her. "I promise. I'm sorry if I've been distant lately."

"Please don't abandon me."

"Honey, I'm not—"

"I don't mean physically leave. I mean in here." She pressed her index finger against his chest, over his heart. "I love you so much. Just keep me close, okay?"

"Okay," he said, and kissed the top of her head.

"I can go to service on my own today. Why don't you stay home with Bradie? Or maybe take her to Putt-Putt? She's been wanting to go for a month."

So here they were now, Adam and Bradie playing miniature golf at The Plex. His five-year-old daughter's score was only two strokes worse than his own.

The mini-golf course was a collection of odd shapes and silly challenges. On hole ten you putted up a slope toward three separate, volcano-shaped funnels, and at the bottom of each funnel was a hole that would swallow your ball and spit it out on the lower level. If you hit the center funnel, your ball would exit the pipe and head straight for the cup. Adam putted first, but his ball slipped past the first and second funnels, bounced off the far wall, and fell into the hole farthest away. It shot onto the lower level and missed the cup by two feet. After he tapped in for his par, Bradie hit her putt. Her speed was more accurate, barely slipping past the first funnel and dropping directly into the middle one. From there it disappeared underground, rattled beneath the surface, and then squirted onto the lower level, dropping straight into the cup.

"Daddy!" Bradie screamed. "I made a hole-in-one!"

"You did! You're amazing."

She bounded toward him, blonde curls electric in the sunlight, and stopped in front of the cup. With concentration almost like awe, she reached in and scooped out her ball.

"I made a hole-in-one."

In a situation like this Adam would normally have hugged her, but this time he didn't. For some reason the thought of touching her disgusted him. He had the terrible feeling, if he took her into his arms, the result would be disastrous.

"I'm only one stroke less than you," she added.

"That's right. If Daddy doesn't watch out, he's going to get beat today."

Bradie stepped back and looked at him with suspicion. "That's silly! I can't beat Daddy. I'm only five."

For a while it seemed as if Bradie might really win. She caught him on the next hole with a two against his three, but then made a couple of fives in a row and fell behind again. The heat grew intolerable as they approached the eighteenth hole, and Adam was glad they would be finished soon. Bradie seemed to be doing fine, but he was suffering out here.

And not just from the heat.

His entire world seemed to be coming apart. He found it almost impossible to sleep at night, and when he did sleep it wasn't anything you could call rest. He didn't want to touch his wife, he didn't want to touch his daughter, and every time he looked at Bradie he saw his dead sister. He saw Evelyn, the little girl who had occasioned his fall from grace. He saw Joe Henreid's glowing eyes.

Adam had spent his life trying to make up for his childhood sins, but there was no amount of penance that could erase all the mistakes he'd made. The story was coming to an end, the pages turning ever more frequently, and sometime soon it would all be over. He would be forced to look himself in the eye and confront the reality of his life, of existence as a whole. What choice would he make? Death was inconceivable to him. But so, it seemed, was life.

On the way home all Bradie could talk about was the hole-in-one.

"It went straight in. I can't believe it! It went underground and then straight in the cup!"

Adam smiled at her. "Bradie is my little pro golfer."

"Straight in the cup! Underground and straight in the cup!"

Adam wondered why she was so fixated with the underground part of the equation. You aimed for the middle funnel because it was the only way to make a hole in one. Who cared what path the ball took to get there?

Except lately it seemed like things underground were becoming more important.

"Why'd you do it, Adam?"

He looked in the back seat at his daughter, that antsy little girl staring out the window.

"Honey," he said to her. "What did you just say?"

Bradie looked over. "Nothing, Daddy."

"Didn't you just call Daddy by his real name?"

"Of course not. Is this a game? Are you playing a trick on me, Daddy?"

"I am. Apparently it's a fun game where Daddy hears voices in his head."

Bradie looked at him with her gorgeous blue eyes and laughed. Adam turned away from her and stared at the road.

"It went underground and then it came out again!" his daughter fairly screamed.

But when he looked back at her, Bradie's eyes were focused out the window, watching the world go by. From this angle she looked so much like his dead sister, Christi, that Adam was forced to turn away.

The problem with memory was that it was subjective and imperfect. Memories in your mind—unlike those in a computer—were colored by perception and could be altered chemically. Certain imbalances could create great discrepancies between what you thought happened and what actually happened. Although who could say with any certainty what really happened? Ever?

"It was fun digging the ball out of the cup," Bradie said.

Adam looked back at her.

"After my hole-in-one, it was fun digging the ball out of the cup."

They entered Tanglewood and a few turns later were on Shady Lane.

"Where are we going, Daddy?"

"We're going home."

"But we don't live in Tanglewood, we live in Canyon Trails!"

He passed by the offending house, and stared hard at it, and remembered how this place had looked many years before, when the houses were new, when the neighborhood was still being built.

"You're right, Honey. Daddy was just playing another game to see if you were paying attention."

"*I'm* paying attention. But I think Daddy was off in La-La Land. The place you go when you're crazy."

"What?" he asked her. "What did you say?"

Her smile was brighter than the sun. Her innocence knew no bounds. "I *said*, 'The name of this street is Shady!'"

68

The difference between fiction and reality had never been more aptly demonstrated, Alicia reasoned, than in her experience with David Clark.

It didn't surprise her that he turned out to be an overconfident, misogynistic jerk. She assumed any billionaire might see the world and the humans who populated it as mere playthings at his disposal. But David had arrived in Wichita Falls with such a self-assured, well-groomed manner about him—even his supermodel girlfriend was positioned as a natural extension of himself—that Alicia had not been ashamed to feel awed in his presence. She'd even been flattered by the attention he paid her. Had Jonathan not already demonstrated interest, had he not reinforced that interest when he kissed her in the car, maybe Alicia would have been more open to David's advances. After all, he could with a snap of his fingers turn her wildest dreams into reality. Promote her from the bleakness of Wichita Falls to the sunny luxury of California. Fund better medical treatment for her mother, grant retirement to her father, and end the grind of customer phone calls that were for eight hours every weekday the bane of her existence. No matter where a woman fell on the spectrum of feminism, the allure of such a pampered, easy life was difficult to ignore.

As long as you weren't disgusted by the man providing such a life.

She had sent the wrong message to David by agreeing to have a drink with him, that was for sure. But in the end she was glad how things had turned out, because now she could see the darkness that lay behind David's golden façade. He was a man in serious need of therapy.

The three of them were in David's rented BMW. Jonathan sat in the passenger seat and Alicia had taken the back. So far she had avoided much conversation with David, partly because he wouldn't make eye contact with her but mostly because of Jonathan's fascination with Thomas Phillips, the thirteen-year-old kid who was not only Todd's son but one of his students.

"So the mother has lived at the same address for six years," he said, "but her kid enrolls at my school like three weeks ago? Why?"

"Maybe Thomas lived with his grandparents," Alicia said. "Or was in foster care. Maybe he only just moved back in with his mom."

"That's awfully convenient timing. Two weeks before all this shit goes down."

"Obviously it's related," David said.

"Related how?" asked Jonathan.

"Let's say the kid lived with someone else, like he and the mother didn't get along. Then he goes back to live with her, like against his will, so he acts out."

"So you think the kid is the one who's been attacking us?"

"I don't know. But you're right. The timing is too convenient for it not to be related."

Alicia wanted David to be wrong. Just on principle she hoped his guesses were miles off the mark.

"All this is speculation," she said. "Let's just get there and talk to someone and see what we can find out."

The plan was to visit Thomas' mother, Christine Phillips, first. Later in the day, if necessary, they would visit Pete Willis, who was Todd's father. Alicia couldn't imagine why any of these people would want to talk to a bunch of strangers, but at this point there were no other options available except sit around and do nothing. The longer Detective Gholson took to solve his arson case, the less likely it became that Alicia's insurance claim would ever be settled. Also, a more pragmatic and vengeful side of her wanted to see someone pay for what had been done to her house and her life.

"There," Jonathan said, pointing out the passenger window. He was using his phone to direct them to the correct address. "That house there."

A white Ford Focus stood in the driveway. So someone was home.

"Have we decided what we're going to say?" she asked Jonathan.

"I think it depends on what happens when we knock on the door. For all we know, Todd could live there, too. If it's just her and the kid, we'll ask if she's willing to talk to us."

They stepped out of the car and approached the front door. Alicia walked beside Jonathan and David lagged behind them. They reached the porch and rang the bell.

Alicia could hear rustling sounds behind the door and then it opened just a crack. A woman's face looked out at them. She was very thin. Her green eyes looked exhausted, as if she hadn't slept in days.

"Hello?"

"Christine Phillips?" Jonathan asked.

"Yes, that's me. Who are you?"

"My name is Jonathan Crane. These are my friends, Alicia Ulbrecht and David Clark. This might seem a little odd to you, but we wondered if we might ask you a few questions about Todd Willis. He lived here in Wichita Falls when he was younger and we were friends with him."

Not much of the woman's face was visible through the crack in the door, but Alicia could nonetheless detect alarm in her reaction.

"Excuse me? How did you even—"

"We talked to Todd's mother," David said, and Alicia wished he would keep his mouth shut. He sounded like he was half asleep. And possibly drunk. "She told us about your encounter with him. About your son."

For a long time the woman didn't answer. Alicia expected at any minute she would slam the door on them and the interview would be over.

Instead, she said, "I don't really know much about Todd. I met him in Austin and we had a brief affair that produced my son. I don't understand what you want."

"Ms. Phillips," Alicia said. "We are very sorry to bother you about this. If I were in your shoes, I wouldn't want to talk to strangers, either. But all three of us have suffered terribly from crimes that have been going on in town the past few days. Both Jonathan and I lost our homes to arson, and David's father was killed in another fire that was related. We believe all these things are connected to Todd Willis somehow. Even the smallest thing you could tell us about him might help us better understand what's happening."

"If that's the case," the woman said, "why aren't the cops here instead of you?"

"Government bureaucracy," David croaked. "Takes them forever to do anything."

The woman seemed amused by this.

"If we could just ask five minutes of your time," Alicia said.

"Oh, all right," Christine Phillips said. "Come in if you must. But only for a minute."

It was an old house and the first thing Alicia noticed about it, aside from the creaking hardwood floors and low ceilings, was the drone of a window air conditioning unit.

"Sorry it's not cooler in here," Christine said. "A/C can't keep up with this kind of heat."

She led them to a living area and invited them to sit. Alicia was startled at how thin she was, how fragile she seemed.

"So what do you want to know, exactly?"

Jonathan spoke first. "The most important thing is to find out if you've seen Todd lately."

"No, I haven't. As you probably know, I didn't tell him about his son for a long time. Till the boy was ten years old. After that, Todd came to see us and said he wanted to be a father, but that didn't work out. I knew it wouldn't. You can't count on a man to hang around. Especially not a guitar player. Which is why I was so hesitant to tell Todd about his kid in the first place."

"Do you mind explaining to us what happened exactly?" Alicia asked.

"Oh, it's not any kind of surprise. Todd was excited to be a father when he showed up, but his son was understandably guarded with him. The kid met a couple of the guys I dated over the years and neither cared much for him. He didn't expect Todd to be different. But for a while he was. From what I could tell, Todd really tried to bond with the little guy. But then he got back on the drugs and everything went to shit."

Alicia noticed Christine was intentionally not using her son's name. It was the sort of thing any mother might do to protect the privacy of her child.

"What sorts of drugs?" David asked.

"I don't know. I never caught him using. But he started looking like shit all the time, slept in too late, lost the job he had working in the oilfield."

"Mrs. Willis said you met Todd when he was onstage in Austin," Jonathan said. "Did he ever play around here?"

"No. He said he gave up on music. Which was unfortunate because his son is gifted in that way, too. I bought him one of those nice computerized keyboards, and he can play it like you wouldn't believe. I could see him growing up to become a famous singer."

Jonathan and David exchanged glances then, very obviously, and Christine noticed.

"What?" she asked them. "You think I'm exaggerating?"

"No," David said. His voice was unsteady, unlike his usual confident tone, and Alicia again had the feeling he might be drunk. "If Thomas is anything like his father, he's nothing short of a child prodigy."

"How do you know my son's name?" Christine asked. "I never told Cassandra that."

Alicia couldn't believe it. David was too sharp to have made such a stupid mistake. Had he not been paying attention at all?

"We did a little research," David said. "And besides, Thomas is a student of Jonathan's. He knows all about our past. How do you explain that?"

"Ms. Phillips," Alicia said. "Christine. Please excuse—"

"Are you here to ask about Todd or my son?"

"Both," David said. "Your son may know why my dad is dead, why someone is systematically attacking us and—"

"You need to leave," Christine said. She wobbled as she stood and pointed at David, at all of them. "I let you into my house and you have the nerve to accuse my *son*—"

She stopped then and her eyes saw something over Alicia's shoulder. They all turned to follow her gaze. A teenage boy was standing where the hallway met the living room.

"Thomas," she said in a quiet voice. "Go back to your room. These people were just leaving."

The kid didn't appear to hear her. He looked at the three of them and a strange smile spread across his face.

"Hi, Mr. Crane," he said. "I didn't know you made house calls. Is this like a parent-teacher conference?"

Alicia looked at Jonathan and then back at Christine. Time seemed to slow down and then stop completely. Something was terribly wrong here. The fear in the woman's eyes was unmistakable, and the confident way Thomas was looking at them made him seem anything like a thirteen-year-old kid.

"Thomas," Jonathan said. "Can you tell us what's going on?"

"You leave my son alone," Christine hissed at him. "Get out of my house. Now."

"Mom, it's okay. I told you they were confused. They just want to understand what's happening to them."

Alicia was struggling to believe what was happening. This scene, this moment, seemed to reinforce everything Jonathan and David had been asking her to believe. Thomas' behavior was eerily similar to their description of Todd Willis as a child. And what might that mean? That Todd had passed on some implausible quality of himself to his son, specifically the ability to see the world in an impossible way?

"Thomas," Jonathan said. "You're right. We are confused. Is there anything you can tell us? Is your father acting out against us?"

"I haven't seen him since he left," Thomas said. "He went to visit my grandpa in Windthorst and no one ever heard from him again. I think he's dead."

"In class on Thursday, you asked me some funny questions. You already knew what was going on, didn't you?"

"Well, yeah," Thomas said. "I know all kinds of cool stuff."

The kid looked at David then, as if he were going to say something else, but didn't.

"Then tell us what's going on," Jonathan said. "We've lost our homes, David's dad is dead, our friend Bobby is dead. . . ."

"Your homes were lost anyway. The whole city is lost. This story is coming to an end."

Alicia had forgotten about Christine, but now the woman approached them.

"I want you out of my house. I didn't ask for any of this and I want you out."

"Thomas," Jonathan said. "Tell us something."

David stood and Alicia followed her. Jonathan didn't seem ready to leave.

"Check the weather forecast," Thomas said. "The American weather models have it wrong but the European one is spot on. It's all there for anyone to see."

"Get out," Christine said. "Get out or I'm calling the cops."

Jonathan finally stood up. David seemed unsteady on his feet and was looking at Thomas in a way that made Alicia uncomfortable. The three of them walked toward the door.

"Don't ever come back here," Christine said to them. "I didn't ask for this. Todd is the worst thing that's ever happened to me and now so are you people."

"Christine," Alicia said. "I know you're upset, but we're victims the same as you. We—"

Thomas was still in the living room, and when Christine answered she lowered her voice, apparently so he wouldn't hear her.

"Go see Todd's father in Windthorst," she said. "He knows the answers to the questions you're asking. I can't tell you anything."

She glared at them, and in her eyes Alicia saw overwhelming weariness.

"Thomas won't let me."

69

"**W**hat the hell?" Alicia said. They were back in the car and David was pulling away from the house. "What the hell is going on in that house?"

"I'm telling you," Jonathan said, "that kid has known everything from the beginning. And this isn't just about us. You heard what he said about the whole city being lost."

"He's just posturing," David said.

"Are you out of your mind?" Alicia shot back. "That kid is clearly a carbon copy of his father, who, according to you guys, knew things about the world no one should be able to know."

"Sure, he's a lot like Todd," David said. "But he's not some all-knowing Oracle. Let's be realistic."

"Be realistic? Are you drunk? What part of any of this is realistic?"

David shot her a withering look but didn't respond.

"Should we call Detective Gholson?" Jonathan asked. "Tell him about Thomas and his mom?"

"Tell him what?" David replied. "That a thirteen-year-old kid just threatened the whole city of Wichita Falls?"

"He may be the one sending the emails," Jonathan pointed out. "It would be a lead of some kind."

"He has no probable cause to show up here," David said. "Maybe when we're done in Windthorst, we could share with Gholson what we know. Do you even trust him?"

"I think he wants to understand what's going on as bad as we do, but he's missing information we could provide. If we're not going to talk to him now, I say we do it after Windthorst for sure."

"So we're headed there now?" Alicia asked.

"It's twenty minutes away," David told her.

70

Windthorst, Texas sat on U.S. Highway 281 about twenty miles south of Wichita Falls. It had been settled a little more than a hundred years ago by German Catholic immigrants, who erected a church reminiscent of the homeland on the county's highest point—a building that on a clear day could be seen from miles away. It was still a charming little place—a smattering of homes and barns, Holstein cows, the huge church—perfect, Jonathan thought, if your goal in life was to carve an existence out of the land like the immigrants who settled the town in the 1890s.

The drive from Wichita Falls had been tense and quiet. Alicia and David seemed perturbed with each other, especially when she made the comment about David being drunk, and Jonathan wondered again if something had happened with them the night before. But the evidence didn't support it. Alicia was behaving normally and seemed well-rested, whereas David was clearly suffering from an epic hangover. Jonathan didn't think this would be the case if they had spent the night together. At least he hoped it wouldn't.

He was looking at his iPhone map and watching the road.

"It's just up ahead," he told them. "On the right-hand side. It should be one of these houses. Yeah, I think this is it."

David stopped the car in front of a small house with tan bricks and brown siding. There was a decorative windmill in the front yard, a green Jeep Cherokee in the driveway. And just a few feet away, close enough that Jonathan could nearly reach out and touch it, stood a shiny black mailbox. Metal block letters spelled out a single word.

WILLIS.

Jonathan began to feel a sense of inevitability, as if the scene about to unfold had been scripted to happen in just this way. In a sense it had, because the three of them had taken proactive measures to arrange a meeting with Todd's father. But what Jonathan really felt was some external source of determination, as if their arrival here was not only decided for them but inescapable. That in order for the seconds to continue advancing, the three of them were required to meet with Pete Willis and learn what he knew about Todd. The surreal thing was how the fantastical nature of what he expected to happen did not jibe with the remote location of this small town or the unassuming house that stood before them.

David shut off the car, and the three of them climbed out. Weeds and vines had overgrown shrubs in a flowerbed beside the porch. Jonathan reached the door first, which was flanked on both sides by narrow windows covered by gauzy white curtains. He knocked. After a moment, a pair of thick fingers pulled one of the curtains back a little, and eyes appeared in the opening.

"Who's there?" a man asked.

"Jonathan Crane. Alicia Ulbrecht. David Clark."

The guy didn't answer right away.

"What do you want?"

"To ask about your son," Jonathan responded. "Are you Pete Willis?"

More silence.

Even more silence.

"I don't know where my son is," the man finally said. "He's probably dead."

"What about your grandson, then?" Jonathan said. "We know he's not dead because we just spoke to him half an hour ago."

Now the man threw the lock and jerked open the door. He was a stocky fellow, not quite six feet tall. His hair was gray and receding and too long for his age. He was wearing a plaid shirt and jeans and brown shoes.

"You talked to Thomas?" the man asked, which seemed to certify his identity as Pete Willis.

"We did."

Willis looked away.

"We believe he's been waging attacks on us. He burned down Alicia's house, my house, and a restaurant owned by David's dad, who was killed. You might have seen all this on the news."

"Goddamn son of a bitch," Willis said. "Of course you had to wait till the last goddamned day."

"I'm sorry?" said Jonathan.

"I finally let myself believe it wasn't going to happen, and now you show up at the last minute. Goddamn son of a bitch."

"What's going to happen?" Alicia asked.

"Just come in. Jesus Christ."

Willis opened the door further and they followed him inside. Soon the three of them were sitting on a couch together in a den not unlike the one at Christine Willis' house. In one corner stood a roll-top desk. In another, adjacent to the couch, stood an ancient-looking upright piano. Sunlight streamed through a sliding glass door and painted a bright rectangle on the carpet. David appeared to be shrinking away from it, like a vampire might.

"So how much do you know?" asked Willis.

"We came here to ask about your son," David said. He seemed bored with Willis and their visit here in general, although Jonathan couldn't understand why. "Surely you must know Todd is not like most other people."

"No shit. Why else would you be here?"

"Mr. Willis," Jonathan said. "Obviously we're at a disadvantage. We came here to find out if you know where Todd is, and to ask you about some strange encounters we had with him when we were kids."

"You mean how he knew about music that didn't exist yet?"

Jonathan looked at Alicia to gauge her reaction, but by now she didn't seem surprised.

"It wasn't just the music," Willis said. "That was the part he remembered best, probably because he was so talented that way. He saw other things in there, too. When he was catatonic. I . . . I can't believe this. I can't believe you came here at the last minute like this. Goddamn it."

Willis rubbed his eyes and looked away from them.

"We don't mean to upset you," Jonathan said. "It's just that—"

"We left town that summer because of the trouble Todd caused," Willis explained. "We hoped he could start fresh somewhere else, that maybe he would feel better, but instead he got worse. He had these terrible, crazy dreams where he would see pictures of people he didn't know, or what looked like home movies, or file folders. What other kid has nightmares about manila folders?"

Jonathan noticed David was sitting up now and looking carefully at the old man.

"When Todd was fifteen or sixteen we came back to Wichita for a few weeks and took him to see a doctor at that mental hospital in Lakeside City. The man who first treated him had moved out of state, so a new doctor listened to Todd's stories and put him on medication. But the medication only made things worse. Todd became bored with everything and eventually dropped out of school. He was such a smart boy, but he could not focus on anything. He said it didn't matter if he graduated, that nothing he did mattered because everything was already decided.

"And anytime he got agitated, he would go on about this endless white space where he lived while he was catatonic. He said being there was worse than death."

Willis' hands were shaking. When he looked up again, his eyes were glassy and bloodshot.

"He came back here a couple of years ago, and you could see the intervening time had taken its toll. By then he was a shell of himself. He left some things behind he wanted you to see. At first I didn't look at them—out of privacy, you know—but eventually I couldn't help myself. When you see what he left, you'll understand why I was hoping you wouldn't show up. Hold on just a minute."

Willis left the room through a doorway behind the couch. Jonathan watched him go and then turned to Alicia.

"He's talking like Todd isn't around anymore."

"He sounds frightened to me," David replied. "And maybe a little paranoid."

"Paranoid?" Alicia said. "He says he was expecting us. This should be like your wildest dreams come true."

"You think this is so fucking funny," David said. "If we're so full of shit, why are you even here?"

"Because I've lost everything. If *your* house burned down, you could buy another one the very next day. But Jonathan and I have to live with our parents or in hotels and hope our insurance claims aren't denied by some guy whose job is to deny claims. I don't know if I believe this horror movie stuff, but someone has attacked us, specifically us, and I want to know why."

Jonathan couldn't help himself: He loved watching Alicia being surly with David. And though he disagreed with her assessment of the available evidence, Jonathan hoped Alicia might come to understand that the loss of their homes and possessions, while devastating, might eventually be outshined by what they stood to gain from these events. Namely each other.

Willis returned carrying a cardboard box about the same size as the one Jonathan had brought down from his attic on Friday. He placed it on the floor in front of his chair and sat down to rummage through it.

"This was Todd's when he was younger. It's the first instrument he ever owned and the one he learned to play on."

Willis retrieved from the box a rectangle of white plastic upon which was mounted a row of black and white keys. It was an electronic keyboard. A Casiotone MT-45.

"Wow," Jonathan said. "So that's the one he used to play for us."

"What else is in there?" David asked.

The next thing Willis retrieved was a handheld cassette recorder. He handed it to Jonathan.

"Does it still work?" he asked Willis.

"Give it a try and find out."

Jonathan pressed the play button, and low-fidelity sound burst out of the onboard speaker.

It was a kid's voice, growling angsty lyrics in time with silly, cartoonish notes of the Casio.

"Nirvana?" Alicia asked. "I thought he only knew songs from the 80s. Did he change into flannel when he played this?"

"Is there anything else on the tape?" asked David, who seemed unimpressed. "Maybe something Todd said?"

Jonathan pushed the fast forward button and the cassette recorder whirred. No one said anything while they waited for the tape to advance. The air conditioner clicked on and began to hum.

When Jonathan stopped the tape and began playing it again, he recognized the track at once. It had been popular only a couple of years ago, and as he listened to Todd sing, he wondered if Alicia might finally be forced to accept what Jonathan and David had suspected from the beginning: there was something larger at work here, some force guiding the narrative of these strange events.

> *I remember when, I remember, I remember when I lost my mind*
> *There was something so terrible about that place.*
> *Even your emotions had an echo*
> *In so much space*
>
> *And when you're out there*
> *Without care,*
> *Yeah, I was out of touch*
> *But it wasn't because I didn't know enough*
> *I just knew too much*
>
> *Does that make me crazy?*
> *Does that make me crazy?*
> *Does that make me crazy?*
> *Probably*

"These lyrics," Willis said, "it's like Todd wrote them about the endless white space he was so afraid of, the one he saw when he was catatonic. Except, from what I understand, the song itself was released maybe two years ago with slightly different lyrics."

"Do you still think we faked the tape?" David asked Alicia. "How could he have known about this song twenty years ahead of time?"

Jonathan knew religious friends whose beliefs had been shaped by or borne from what they described as a transcendental event, a connection to the world deeper than what could be attained by everyday experience. This incident, they believed, was the act of God speaking to them. Jonathan did not believe in God, not in the church-going, Ten Commandments kind of way, but if there existed in the universe some method by which Todd or anyone could glean information from a future not yet lived, then it stood to reason that reality was not necessarily defined by the input collected by a human's five senses. That maybe there was some other form of reality out there.

"But honestly the music is incidental," Willis said. "The last time I saw Todd, he gave me this. This is what he wanted you to see."

Willis handed Jonathan a sheet of paper folded in half. On the inside surface of the page were several paragraphs of text that had been produced by an ink jet printer. Jonathan opened it and read from the top.

> If you believe legend, the city of Wichita Falls was doomed from its first day. Erected near a small waterfall on a muddy tributary of the Red River, where white settlers displaced a tribe of Indians known to them as Wichita, the community was officially named on September 27, 1872. Just before sunset, as new landowners celebrated their good fortune, the revered chief named Tawakoni Jim recalled an old Caddo legend about a boy bestowed with the Power of the Cyclone, which enabled him to summon black clouds and bring their powerful winds to the ground . . .

"What is this?" Jonathan asked. He tilted the page so Alicia and David could read it, also.

"Something Todd found. Something his son, Thomas, wrote. Keep reading."

The text comprised a short tale about the genesis of the Wichita Falls community, and a curse that had apparently been cast on the town by an Indian chief. The story sounded like the kind of old wives' tale that a quick search on Snopes.com might easily dispel. But it was the last couple of lines that caught Jonathan's attention, that helped him understand why Pete Willis seemed so disappointed by their visit today.

> What happened in Wichita Falls on June 2, 2008 has been described as "biblical," though Wichita Indians know the Bible had nothing to do with

it. Careful readers of the story that follows, however, will find clues to a mysterious book that *did* contribute to the demise of a Middle American city and a number of characters contained herein.

"June 2?" Alicia said. "That's tomorrow."

"Yes, ma'am," said Willis. "So you can see why I was hoping you folks wouldn't show. It's been two years since Todd brought this to me, and if I could have made it one more day without seeing your faces—"

"So what did he say is going to happen?" David asked.

"The end of the world."

"What does that mean? Were those his exact words?"

"It's been a while, son. But yes, when I asked why he was so upset, all he would say was his son had done something terrible, and your appearance here would mean the end of everything."

"Our appearance here?" David asked. "Like the three of us? Or someone in general?"

"You three," answered Willis. "Jonathan Crane, Alicia Ulbrecht, and David Clark."

"But that's . . . " Alicia said, and then trailed off. "When did you last see him? Exactly?"

"Like I said, two years ago, maybe less. He moved back to Wichita Falls to be near Thomas, but apparently the kid had problems and wanted nothing to do with him. And when Todd found that page you're holding, I think it pushed him over the edge. He showed up here nearly out of his mind. He said the only way to stop his son was to kill him. I said, Todd, no matter what you think is going to happen, you can't hurt that boy. But he wouldn't listen. He explained how you three would show up one day looking for him, that I should give you the letter, and he begged me not to read it. I tried not to, but you should have seen him. He looked like a man on a ten-day bender. Like he was a junkie in need of a fix. After Todd dropped off the letter, he left again for Wichita Falls, but I don't think he ever made it. They found his car on the highway a little south of town. There was a four-inch hole in the windshield right over the steering wheel. Like something had been driven through the glass and into the headrest.

There was blood in the car and a trail of it on the highway, and then it just stopped. Like someone picked him up or he just vanished. No one has heard from him since."

"So he could still be alive," David said.

"If you saw the look in his eyes that day, if you saw what happened to the car, you wouldn't think so. Plus, Thomas is still alive, and I think if Todd had made it to Wichita—"

Willis' eyes were filling with tears again and he stopped to compose himself.

"So his body wasn't found?" David asked.

"No, it wasn't."

"He disappeared and you just assume he's dead?"

Jonathan didn't like David's tone, and apparently Willis didn't care for it, either.

"I believe I've said all I'm going to say about my son. I think it's time you folks leave."

"David," Alicia said. "You're out of line. You owe him an apology."

"No, he doesn't," Willis said. "I only talked to you folks because I promised Todd I would. I've done my part and now I'm ready for whatever's coming."

He stood up and waited for the three of them to do the same. Then he led them toward the door.

"What do you think is going to happen?" David asked as they stepped out onto the porch. "What do you think that letter means?"

"I don't know, exactly. But I've never seen Todd wrong about anything before, so there's no reason to believe he's wrong about this. And if the ship is going to sink, I plan to have my brandy on the deck and take it like a man."

To Jonathan this seemed like a curious thing to say. He felt like he'd heard something similar recently but couldn't remember what it had been.

"Is there anything we can do for you?" Alicia asked him. "Anything at all?"

"You can't do anything," he answered. "At this point I don't think anyone can."

71

David had brought along a flask of scotch to nip from during the after-noon, because there was honestly no other way to function. He'd incurred too much damage the night before, and the only way he would be able to get through this day was with a moderate, ongoing buzz. The problem he faced was that Jonathan and Alicia were with him nearly every single minute. When they stopped the first time, to meet Christine Phillips, he'd managed to sneak a pull while Jonathan and Alicia were climbing out of the car. But since then there had been no opportunity at all, and as the energy from his buzz leaked away, it was replaced by throbbing hangover agony.

But he would be rid of them soon enough, and once they were gone, David would drink more scotch and begin making calls.

He was going after the kid.

The two of them had shared a long moment of eye contact when Thomas walked into the living room, and David was sure they had developed an understanding. And if the kid possessed a gift equal to or greater than Todd's, that made him extremely valuable. Together, he thought, the two of them could do something special.

"David," Alicia said, as they climbed into the car. "You're such an asshole."

He figured he was doing something right if three different women had called him that in less than twenty-four hours.

"Why? Because I, as a father, wouldn't just assume my kid was dead because someone found an empty car?"

"You as a father," she replied. "That's rich."

"The guy was obviously hurting," Jonathan said. "You didn't have to press him."

"We came here to ask him questions, so I asked."

David pulled away from Willis' house and drove in the direction of Wichita Falls. No one said anything for a while.

But eventually Jonathan ruined the silence. "So what do you guys think is going to happen tomorrow?"

"I don't know," Alicia said. "A part of me is never going to accept the crazy shit you guys believe. But two people are dead and I don't have a house or a way to build another one. Neither do you. Let's say something terrible really is going to happen tomorrow? Do we call Detective Gholson and tell him that? What's he going to do with the information?"

This, David reasoned, was what separated people like him from everyone else. Most people took an essentially passive view of the world, a wait-and-see attitude, whereas David was the kind of man who seized opportunity wherever it presented itself. When you were aggressive, you occasionally got burned, but overall the payoff was worth it. And let's be honest: David himself never got burned. Not even singed. Last July he had begun to sell off many of his stock holdings and invested the proceeds into low-risk securities and credit default swaps. This had raised eyebrows in his circle of investor friends, especially with the Dow pushing to record highs seemingly every day, but David's instincts had once again proven to be on the mark. With mortgage lender IndyMac headed for insolvency, as major banks began to buckle under the weight of their mortgage-backed securities, those same friends were now close to panic. Irresponsible lending practices and the toxic investment products built upon those loans were poised to collapse the world economy and no one was sure how the markets would respond.

No one except David. With Thomas at his side, he could wait for the crisis to bottom out in early 2009 and then select financial products that would propel his fortune into the stratosphere on the wave of the stock market recovery. He suspected, in five or six years, he could grow his net worth by a factor of ten. Maybe more, depending on what Thomas could tell him. It was imperative to have the kid flown out of here as soon as possible. All David needed was a little rest, a little time to marshal his resources, and then he would act. If Alicia and Jonathan wanted to fret over what might happen in Wichita Falls tomorrow, that was their business. He was getting the hell out of here.

"Gholson might think we're nuts," Jonathan said. "But he might not. At the very least, if he knew Todd had a son, if he knew where that son lived, maybe he would have someone watch the kid's house. Just in case."

David wanted to reach across the center console and smack Jonathan in the mouth.

Instead, he said, "You think Gholson is going to spy on some kid? Because the little guy threatened to take down the whole city?"

"It's some kind of lead," Jonathan said. "Better to act on something than sit around doing nothing, right?"

"Fine," David said, and reached for his cell phone. "I'll call him."

72

Sally was looking out the window when Gholson opened the door. The way she was sitting there, perched on the chair, she could have been any normal woman admiring the view of Lake Wichita.

But she didn't turn around when he walked in. She didn't respond when he called her name.

"Looks nice out there, doesn't it? Too bad it was a hundred and eight degrees this afternoon."

Gholson had leveraged his badge to arrange a Sunday meeting with Dr. Young, which was unethical behavior and something he would never dream of doing under normal circumstances. But he needed to understand the relationship between Sally's illness and a similar condition suffered by Todd Willis many years ago, and this was the only way he could do so on short notice.

Dr. Young had only seen Todd once, for two weeks in 1986. This information was included in the criminal case file, but the details of Young's treatment were not. If Gholson were here on behalf of the investigation, he would have requested a subpoena to open Todd's medical file. But since this inquiry was of a personal nature, he planned to lean on the relationship he had built with Dr. Young and appeal to the man's good nature.

Gholson wondered what Sally saw when she looked out the window. According to Dr. Young, there was nothing wrong with her ability to see or hear or employ any of her five senses, but once the signals reached her conscious mind there was some kind of roadblock, either in her perception of reality or her ability to render reactions to it.

The more Gholson thought about it, the more his visit here seemed like a waste of time, and yet any moment Dr. Young would knock on the door. What could Gholson possibly say to him? He'd brought along the journal, but what did that prove? Anyone could have written the words on those pages. At any time. The journal proved nothing unless you were confident about the acquisition of the document and its chain of custody.

"I wish you could hear me, Sally," he said. "You have no idea how much I miss you. And the more I learn about this case, about Todd, the more I think there might be a way to save you."

Gholson approached his wife. He knelt behind her chair and wrapped his arms around her shoulders. Sally stiffened ever so slightly, but beyond that there was no further response.

"If you're in there, if you can hear me, I want you to know you are as loved as the day I proposed to you. And if this is the way things are, if I never get to speak to you again, I'll still be here loving you until the day I die. But if there's anything I can do to help you come back, anything at all, I have to try. I just wish you could give me some kind of sign."

Sally turned around and looked at him. It was the first eye contact she had made with him in two or three months, and goose bumps prickled the back of his neck. He waited for her to say something, anything, but instead she turned back toward the window.

"There's got to be a reason all this is happening now," he finally said. "Two people are dead. Multiple structures have been destroyed by fire. And the person writing these emails is threatening the entire city now. I've got the Feds involved and the whole police force is on high alert, but no one knows what to look for. Including me."

"Not long now, Jerry."

At first Gholson didn't realize what had happened. The sound of her voice was so natural to him that for the shortest of moments he forgot about her years of silence.

"Honey? Did you say something?"

She didn't turn around. Her gaze appeared fixed upon some distant point on the water.

"Tomorrow," she said.

The taste in Gholson's mouth was like he had pressed a fresh nine-volt battery to his tongue. His fingers and toes tingled. They burned.

"Honey, what's going to happen tomorrow?"

"He changed the beginning and the ending and now the cyclone is almost upon us."

Gholson was breathless. Whatever Sally was talking about, it wasn't anything like what she would have said in her normal life.

"Honey, are you there? Can you hear me?"

"If you know where to look," she said, "you can see everything. But I don't understand the file system the way he does."

Gholson could hardly believe this conversation was happening. For a moment he wondered if he was hallucinating Sally's voice, if maybe she wasn't really talking to him at all.

"I don't know how to come back, Jerry," she said. "But I wish you could join me in here."

There was a knock on the door. Gholson nearly jumped out of his skin. It was surely the doctor here to speak to him, but if he left Sally's side to answer the door, would she be gone when he returned?

"Join you? What do you mean, Honey?"

"If you stop him from taking the kid, maybe we can make our own ending."

The nine-volt battery was more like ninety volts now. His vision turned red. Warning red.

"Make our own? What ending?"

The door opened, and Dr. Young poked his head in.

"Everything all right in here?"

"Yes," Gholson said. He turned and looked at the doctor. "Sally has been, uh, she's been talking to me. Haven't you, Honey?"

Sally was staring out the window. Her face was a blank page.

"Sally? Tell the doctor how you've been speaking to me."

She didn't respond. Dr. Young looked dubious.

"She spoke to me. I promise she did."

"What did she say?"

There was no point in trying to explain himself. Gholson could see clinical doubt in the doctor's face. Arrogant disbelief. He could already guess how the conversation would proceed if he inquired about the similarity between Todd's and Sally's conditions.

"Or maybe I only imagined it," Gholson finally answered.

73

Adam was chewing on a brisket sandwich, staring out his windshield at the setting sun, when his cell phone rang. He'd just spoken with his foreman about a delivery of flagstones that were two weeks late, and he hoped the foreman was calling back with an update about the flagstones. He was parked in front of the new project again, which yesterday afternoon had become a freshly-poured foundation. Soon there would be a wood skeleton, then sheathing, then a roof, and at some point the ambulance-chasing owner would bring his wife here. The mister would smile and the missus would cry, and they would dream fraudulent dreams, imagine a few pointless memories that might occur inside those walls, and at no point would they think of the pain that would also happen, pain that was as eventual as the rising sun. The pregnant wife wouldn't acknowledge the likelihood of philandering by her husband. The ambulance chaser wouldn't tell her about the hot new paralegal. They were Baptists and pillars of the community, and also hypocrites who enriched themselves at the expense of everyone else while pretending to honor the values of Jesus. He should never have agreed to build their stupid dream home.

They were blasphemous, these thoughts that oozed like motor oil through his mind, but Adam couldn't help himself. He'd almost sworn when his foreman protested at being called on a Sunday afternoon, and now Adam picked up the phone without looking at the Caller ID, ready to threaten the foreman with his job if he wasn't more cooperative.

"Hello? Give me some good news, Danny."

"Hey, Adam," said a voice who was not his foreman. "It's Jonathan."

"I thought we were through with this."

"Just because you didn't want to talk about it, that doesn't mean it's over. Either way, I think we figured out who is setting the fires, and I thought you'd want to know."

The brisket sandwich ceased to be a marginally pleasant fullness in his gut. It became more like a hot slug of lead that was not at all pleasant. Because lately the truth was becoming more insistent. Lately it was waving its hands, whistling, flashing its privates—making all manner of distasteful gestures to call attention to itself.

"Adam?" Jonathan asked. "Are you there?"

"My parents were hypocrites. They blamed everything on me."

"What?"

"But I was just a kid. It wasn't my fault."

"What are you talking about? Are you all right?"

Adam pushed the handset away from his ear. He had the weird feeling he'd never seen a cell phone before. Like it was some kind of futuristic communicator, small and black and shiny. Phones were supposed to be big, plastic, tan things with buttons as big as the tips of your fingers. They were connected to a base by a coiled cord of the same color.

He pressed the communicator back to his ear and said, "So you were saying about the fires. You know who set them?"

"Yeah," Jonathan said. "Todd has a thirteen-year-old son. Turns out he's one of my students and we think it's him."

The relief was immense. Because of the unexplained dirt on his feet, Adam had feared *he* was the arsonist.

"How did you figure that out?" he asked.

"We found the kid and talked to him. We also talked to Todd's dad. It's complicated. We've just left a message with Detective Gholson and now David and I want to meet with you."

Adam could hear music, distant and cavernous. He could hear his parents drunk and laughing with their friends at the silly song.

"I don't think we need to meet," he said. "You figured it out. That's good enough for me."

"Adam—"

"Really, it's no problem. He's just as proud as he can be."

"Listen, when we talked to Todd's father—"

"Of his anatomy."

"Dude, what's wrong with you? What are you talking about?"

"He's going to give us a peek."

Adam placed the handset of his phone onto its imaginary base. He started his truck and drove away from the house.

The atmosphere in his mind was unstable.

The cap was about to break.

74

Adam drove directionless for a while, orbiting the city, trying to decide what to do. Except he already knew what to do. The problem was marshaling the courage to actually go through with it.

He thought about last night, when Rachel had complained he was too quiet during sex. It wasn't the first time she'd mentioned this—it had been an issue ever since their wedding night, when Rachel's first, desperate, animal noises had startled him flaccid. Every feminine bark had chipped away at his concentration; every high-pitched yap had disturbed the well-constructed illusion he'd built to conceal reality. The fiction of their nights together, he wanted to believe, was that no graphic sex would ever be had by anyone. Any possible romantic encounters were to be of the quiet, cable channel, underwear-covering-privates variety, they were to occur in strategic lighting, and they were not to involve fluid or mention of body parts. But Rachel's yapping preempted his PG illusion. The noise overrode his carefully programmed V-chip. Christian woman that she was, Rachel nevertheless felt like consummating their love in a decidedly un-Christian way.

Adam didn't know how to change himself. It didn't feel natural. He had been frightened of intimacy since childhood, and the only sex he'd ever felt comfortable with was the single-player game. Behavior of that sort was necessarily silent. When you were trying to be covert, you couldn't exactly close the bathroom door and belt home runs at the top of your lungs.

You couldn't scream the way his mother had.

Eventually Adam found himself parked in front of his first childhood home. He remembered how the structure had been stripped to its foundation, remembered Christi's tiny arms wrapped desperately around his waist as she begged him to protect her. And he had refused. Not because he didn't love her (he missed her desperately) but because something about him had changed after the encounter with Evelyn. Adam might have blamed his mom for leaving her young children alone as the tornado approached, but even she was merely an imperfect human. No, the real blame for Christi's death, for the devastation to Wichita Falls as a whole, belonged to God. It was He who had conjured the tornado from the volatile atmosphere. It was God who had directed the giant vortex to churn through neighborhood after neighborhood of His devoted children—the worst hit neighborhood was named, in fact, "Faith Village." Why would God send the tornado through a city of devout believers like Wichita Falls and not somewhere comparatively more evil, like Las Vegas or New York City? Why, in fact, were tornadoes most common in the middle part of the country, where God's children were most highly concentrated? This made no sense to Adam. The only way it *could* make sense was to believe God did not love His children. That perhaps for some reason He held them in contempt. Perhaps, of all His children, God detested Adam the most. Maybe that's why He had sent five-year-old Evelyn to proposition Adam in a New Orleans living room so many years ago. Maybe her proposal had been a test he had miserably failed.

Adam's family had been on vacation at the time, which meant his daddy didn't have to go to work and could watch baseball and drink out of metal cans with his friend, Chuck. His mother could lounge on the back porch with the lady named Carla, sipping drinks that were pretty colors like red and green, that were made of ice like a Freezee but didn't smell like a Freezee. And since Chuck and Carla were the parents of a daughter one year older than Adam, it was natural the two children should also play together, should spend much of this time unsupervised. So it happened one night that the mommies and daddies were in the kitchen playing Wahoo—a game of marbles set upon an old wooden board—while Adam and Evelyn entertained themselves in the living room. The mommies and daddies were enjoying their drinks and smoking cigarettes and using words that, at home, under normal circumstances, would have been off limits.

Evelyn was sitting next to the TV, but since there was nothing on the three channels but news, she had turned the set off. Music boomed at them from the living room. Evelyn was wearing a nightgown. Adam was in his green and white pajamas. She was five and he was four.

"Are you a big boy or a little boy?" asked Evelyn.

"I'm young but I'm big for my age."

"Are you big enough to play an adult game?"

"Like Wahoo?"

"No, like Peek-a-Boo."

"That's a game for babies," said Adam.

"Not this game."

She lifted her nightgown. She wasn't wearing anything underneath and he could see a crack between her legs. At first Adam was surprised to see how empty and smooth it was there, but then he remembered that in some important ways girls were different than boys.

"I don't think you're supposed to do that," he said.

"Now you do it. Now you show me yours."

Adam wanted to shake his head, because it was wrong what she was asking. And yet he didn't want to disappoint her. She was five and he was four and he didn't want to look like a baby.

"We could get in trouble," he said.

Evelyn dropped her nightgown, and the fissure vanished. "You're a scaredy-cat, aren't you?"

"No."

"Then show me."

Quickly, before he lost his nerve, Adam hooked his fingers into his pajama bottoms and pulled them down. His little boy bobbed innocently. That's what his mom called it: his little boy. Evelyn looked at it and smiled and he yanked the pajamas back up where they belonged.

"See?" she said. "Nobody got in trouble."

From the kitchen Adam could hear the roaring of his father and the squealing of his mother. They laughed and yelped and coughed like animals. The song on the radio was very strange, and someone kept calling someone else The Streak.

Evelyn said, "You want to do something else?"

"What?"

"I'll put my mouth on yours if you'll put your mouth on mine."

Evelyn smiled. She pulled her nightgown up again.

This time he considered leaving. He could get up, go to the room where his clothes were, where his temporary bed was . . . but then he remembered he was staying in Evelyn's bedroom. She might kick him out. Or she might suggest the game again, in secret, in the dark. He thought about going to the kitchen where his parents were, but his father had already ordered him twice to stay out, and anyway he wasn't a tattletale.

Evelyn smiled at him. It wasn't a mean smile. She just wanted to play a game, a different kind of game. The game was wrong, but if they didn't get caught then maybe it didn't matter. His parents were in the kitchen breaking rules. Why couldn't Adam also break rules?

"Okay," he said to her.

"Okay. But you go first."

Adam looked at the place between her legs. He wasn't sure what to do. There wasn't anything there but a crack. The room seemed to grow quiet as he looked closer. His heart began to beat very fast. He—

And then screaming. Screaming. His mother screaming. Carla screaming. Chuck thundering, his father a tornado that jerked Adam off the ground and carried him upstairs. Screeching and yelling and the medicine smell of his father's breath and his mother's scratchy, smoky coughing, and that night they slept in a hotel.

He could understand, cognitively, that what happened with Evelyn wasn't his fault. It wasn't Evelyn's fault. She was five and he was four, and both of them were young, curious children. If you wanted to know where Evelyn's knowledge of oral sex had come from, you could guess she had seen her parents doing it, or perhaps she'd been molested by someone. In any case, she had not understood the gravity of what she asked Adam to do, and neither had he. If there was human fault to be assigned, it belonged to the parents, who had reacted in a way that frightened the children. And later, as Adam's parents introduced God into his life, they had made sure he felt guilty about every little transgression they noticed. Adam had grown up in a world where he loved and feared God and assumed the same from his parents. But now his mom and dad were divorced, and both of them were shacked up with lovers and had long ago stopped attending church. God had been a fad for them, the solution to an unpleasant problem, and when that problem left home the fad had been forgotten.

But Adam had been raised to believe in the Word of the Lord. Christian morals were the foundation of his value system, and he could not imagine a world where a man such as himself could reason his way out of the consequences of his poor decisions. At the same time, it was God who had sent Evelyn to tempt him, God who steered the tornado into town, and yes, it was God who placed Joe Henreid at the scene of the Driftwood house when they burned it down. In what kind of world could God be allowed to blame Adam for his decisions when it was God who had put him in these situations to begin with?

Not the kind of world where Adam cared to live.

He put his truck in gear and drove himself to the house in Tanglewood, where the victim of his worst crime had been laid to rest. On that night, years ago, there had been no house. Just a plot of red dirt.

There was a gasoline can in the bed of his pickup. Matches in his glove box. He was parked on Shady Lane, and the sun had just dipped below the horizon of roofs and trees.

In the early 80s these homes had been upscale and trendy and symbols of a temporary upturn in the economy. Now paint had faded and peeled, and cracks had appeared in masonry exteriors. Foundations had settled. Roof shingles were peeling and warped. Many years had passed without an injection of capital and the entire neighborhood was sagging under a burden it had never expected to carry.

When Adam was a kid, on a street like this, there would have been children playing and adults chatting and bicycles passing this way and that. Back then, if a stranger was parked at the curb, especially in an unmarked pickup, someone would have stopped to ask who he was and what he was doing.

Tonight, the street was empty. Everyone was indoors watching cable TV or browsing the Internet or both.

Adam didn't want to hurt anyone. He would ring the doorbell and warn whoever was in the house, and once they were gone, once the house had burned to its foundation, the slab would be exposed. This would set the stage for Adam to come back and uncover the evidence of his childhood crime. In doing so he would lose his family, and though he could not imagine leaving his daughter behind, Bradie would be better off without him, anyway.

At 9:29 p.m., Adam removed the matchbook from the glove box. He stepped out of the truck and grabbed the gasoline can. If someone were watching from their window, they might come outside now and ask what he was doing.

No one did.

It was a single-story house. The front porch light was on, but the rest of the house was dark. Actually there was one window glowing yellow on the west side of the structure, what appeared to be a bedroom window with the curtains drawn. Adam stepped quietly past the glowing window and into the backyard. No light was on here. A quarter moon cast the trees and house in muted, silvery tones. He lifted the can and slung gasoline onto the brick wall of the house, onto the roof. Wood siding had been used in place of masonry around the back porch, and he splashed plenty of gasoline there. He orbited the house, spilling fuel into shrubs and flowerbeds, but gave the front door and sidewalk a wide berth. Then he walked back to the pickup and replaced the gasoline can. As dark as it was, Adam was still surprised someone hadn't seen him. He had made no attempt at stealth except to wait for darkness. At any time someone could have looked out their window and confronted him. Or called the police.

No one did.

When Adam approached the house again, the smell of gasoline was choking and humid. He pulled the book of matches from his pants and struck one. He thought perhaps the match would ignite gas fumes and maybe burn him alive (he wouldn't have minded this) but it didn't. He kept waiting and nothing happened, so finally he tossed the match against the house. Before the match made contact with anything there was a *FLOOMF!* and nighttime became daytime. Flames leapt from the ground to the masonry to the roof and raced around the house in the blink of an eye. When Adam had inspected the entire perimeter of his work, he ran to the front door and beat on it as hard as he could. For good measure he rang the bell a few times in rapid succession. Then he walked to his truck, jumped in, and drove carefully away.

75

B y the time they returned to the hotel, and David had said goodbye to Jonathan and Alicia, he was solidly drunk. They'd stopped for dinner at a steakhouse that was abysmal by coastal standards and he used the opportunity to publicly order a couple of drinks. On a visit to the bathroom, in private, he choked down what was left in his flask. This had left him too impaired to make any arrangements where Thomas was concerned, but that was okay because he didn't plan on being awake much longer. Honestly he was pleased to have made it back to the hotel in one piece, and to have fooled Alicia and Jonathan into letting him get behind the wheel.

He discovered a bottle of scotch in the room, still a third full, and poured himself a nightcap. Then he switched on the television and found a documentary about astronomy. Apparently there was a star somewhere nearby that could explode at any time, and if it did, it could wipe out all the modern technology on Earth. That made David think of his iPhone, and how he hadn't set an alarm to wake him in the morning. But when he reached into his pocket, the phone was nowhere to be found, and he decided to take a little nap before going to look for it.

Sometime later David woke up to the phone ringing. In a haze of sleep he reached around on the floor until he found it against the foot of the bed.

"David Clark," he croaked.

"Get your shit together," said a voice in the phone. It sounded like a kid's voice.

"Who is this?"

"Set your alarm. When you wake up, arrange the plane first thing. I'm expecting you at 11 tomorrow morning. So get your shit together and don't be late."

"Who is this?" he asked again. "Thomas?"

"11 o'clock. Don't be late. And get some rest."

76

As a child, Alicia had loved to read about the supernatural and the fantastic, especially in novels where the characters seemed like real people. Vividly-rendered details and imagery made the impossible seem possible and could blur the boundaries between what happened on the page and what was real life. In her adult years she had drifted away from high-concept stories in lieu of serious fiction, since literary novels more closely aligned with her own experience.

Now the boundaries of real life and fiction were being distorted again, this time in reverse. The circumstances surrounding Todd and his son strained credibility, especially the printed page given to them by Pete Willis that suggested disaster tomorrow in Wichita Falls. But her story with Jonathan might have even been more unbelievable. At the moment they were back in his hotel room, buzzing a little after drinks at dinner, and he kept looking at her in a way that left little doubt about his intentions. Alicia wanted to resist him for no other reason than the sheer corniness of the scene itself: two childhood friends reunited because darkness from their past had returned to haunt them again. Could she find any reason to be attracted to him beyond this contrived situation? Like maybe his intelligence? His systematic analysis of their high concept predicament? The lovely, intense curiosity that deepened his eyes whenever he looked at her?

Jonathan was standing at the bar, using his iPhone to Google phrases from the page Pete had given them. Every time he glanced up at her, he was smiling confidently. She was alternatively annoyed and turned on by it.

"It seems this Power of the Cyclone story is a real Caddo Indian legend," he explained. "And the language of the Wichita is based on Caddoan, so the connection makes sense. But I can't find where anyone named Tawakoni Jim ever visited Wichita Falls or placed a curse on the city."

"What about the weather models Thomas mentioned?" she asked him.

Jonathan tapped away on his phone.

"Okay, it looks like that's called the ECMWF. But I don't see anything about a terrible weather event. It's just a bunch of maps I can't decipher. My weather app says we do have a chance of storms tomorrow, though."

"Like tornadoes?"

"It says, 'Windy, mostly cloudy, and turning cooler. Chance of storms in the morning. Some could be severe."

"I should call my dad," Alicia said. "He hasn't chased in a while but I bet he would know what these models are and what they mean."

"Either way it appears we have a chance of severe storms tomorrow. That's pretty significant when you consider the page Pete Willis showed us. As if Thomas knew tomorrow's forecast two years ago."

"So Thomas is the boy bestowed with the Power of the Cyclone," Alicia said, "and tomorrow he's going to wipe out the city with another tornado. Is that what you've come up with?"

"It sounds absurd, doesn't it?" Jonathan approached the couch and sat down next to her. His eyes searched her own. "I don't want to believe this kind of crap any more than you do. But let's say it's true. What would you do if you knew this would be your last night on earth?"

"My last night on earth? That's your best line?"

Jonathan smiled. He wasn't even trying to be subtle.

"You don't seem to be taking this too seriously," she said.

"It is serious. But it's also been a rough week and it might be nice to relax a little. Since we have no idea what's going to happen tomorrow or what we can do about it."

"I guess you're right," she said. "Do you want to go somewhere for a drink?"

He was sitting on her left and facing her directly. His right leg rested against hers. He looked into her eyes and her heart fluttered a little.

"No, I don't want to go somewhere for a drink. Do you?"

"I suppose not," she conceded.

"I don't know what's going to happen tomorrow, but I don't want to regret what I didn't do tonight."

She might have balked at Jonathan's earnestness if he hadn't chosen that moment to lean in and kiss her.

And when he put his hands on her skin, Alicia remembered the red wicker basket, the curious look in his seventh-grade eyes, the sound of his intelligent voice over the phone. She wondered if the years between those childhood moments and tonight could be considered irrelevant space between the pages of her life. As his lips drifted across her face, as they nuzzled into her neck, as she felt the weight of him upon her, Alicia wondered what the next chapter of her life might bring.

The next paragraph.

The next line.

77

Something was wrong with reality. Adam had begun to realize this while he waited for the blaze to be brought under control, while he watched from a distance as the fire trucks packed up their equipment and eventually departed. He wanted to understand why he'd made certain choices over the years, why he had veered so far away from the innocence that was fundamental to every little boy and girl born into the world. But when he closed his eyes and looked back, when he reviewed the anthology of memories that should have composed the story of his life, Adam was alarmed to discover very little in the way of actual content. He could recall several events from the past few days, a few more from the summer when he met Todd Willis, and even the visceral scene of the tornado bearing down upon him in 1979. But the rest of his life, the many days and weeks and moments that should have comprised the bulk of his existence, was nowhere to be found.

He watched the fire trucks drive away, the police cars follow soon after, and eventually Shady Lane returned to its earlier lonely stillness. He waited a little longer to make sure no one had remained behind, like a curious arson investigator or detective. Sure enough, an aging fellow with an impressive beer gut eventually emerged from the trees behind the house. He looked up and down the street, climbed into a government-looking Ford sedan and drove away.

Still, Adam waited another full hour before he moved.

And when he finally walked toward the site of the burned house, carrying an electric demolition tool and an extension cord, Adam began to wonder if the missing scenes of his life could perhaps be uncovered through some archaeological expedition that would reveal heretofore unknown adventures and calamities. Maybe he had once hiked into the Grand Canyon. Or maybe he had taken Rachel on a long-ago vacation to explore the shadowy depths of Carlsbad Caverns. It was even possible, when he was thirteen years old, that Adam had experienced a psychotic break when he realized someone might report him to the police for burning down the house on Driftwood.

If he could not remember most of his life, then it followed that existence itself was nonsensical. Why bother to live each day when only a small fraction of those days could be recalled later? Why worry about the consequences of your actions when you could not be sure what actions you had previously taken?

The pointless nature of things was a kind of liberation.

Adam reached the house, which was a charred ruin, damp and steaming and smoky. He stumbled around the site, hoping for a clue that would help him decide where to dig. But in the end there was no way to locate the exact spot because too many years had passed. Instead, Adam selected a nice, slender crack on the exposed foundation, a spot that could've been the right one. Maybe. He put down the tool and strode toward the adjacent house, spooling out his cord. He found an electrical outlet on the porch and pushed in his plug. Then he returned to the exposed slab.

A few hours earlier, this structure had been divided into living rooms and bedrooms and bathrooms, had sheltered a family's love and life, but now it was reduced to a burnt, hissing skeleton. Adam located again the crack in the concrete and pointed his chisel at it. Threaded his fingers into the grip and pulled the trigger.

The crack opened millimeters at a time. The concrete screamed and squealed.

It sang.

ZONE FORECAST PRODUCT
NATIONAL WEATHER SERVICE NORMAN OK
TXZ086-192200-
WICHITA-
INCLUDING THE CITIES OF ... WICHITA FALLS
942 AM CDT SUN JUN 19 1983

.TODAY ... SUNNY AND HOT. HIGH AROUND 111. WINDS SW
15-25 MPH AND GUSTY.
.TONIGHT ... CLEAR. LOW AROUND 82. SW WIND 15-25
MPH.
.MONDAY ... SUNNY AND VERY HOT. HIGH AROUND 112.
SOUTH WINDS 20-30 MPH.
.MONDAY NIGHT ... CLEAR. LOW IN THE LOW 80S. SOUTH
WINDS AROUND 25 MPH.
.TUESDAY ... SUNNY AND VERY HOT. HIGH NEAR 113.
.WEDNESDAY ... SUNNY AND VERY HOT. HIGH NEAR 114.

78

On the day after they burned down the Driftwood house, the sky was unreal, like puffy white clouds painted upon fierce blue marble. A day so beautiful was punishment to Adam, a way to remind him of the terrible thing they'd done the night before. With the sun so bright and the wind only a whisper, the black skeleton of the house was rendered in exquisite detail. Adam walked by again and again, unable to resist looking at it, and finally on his last visit he saw Joe Henreid watching him from the edge of the woods. Surely this was not the reason he had been drawn to the ruined house, on the chance he might run into the boy who held Adam's future in the palm of his hand?

He stopped walking and stared at Joe. Even from this distance he could see a predatory look in the kid's eyes. At thirteen, Adam was old enough to understand that his entire life would be defined by how he handled this situation, but he was not mature enough to know how to proceed. As he approached Joe, however, he began to hear a voice in his mind. Whispering something to him. Probably he was just imagining this voice, but there was also the chance that someone was trying to direct his actions in this scene, someone offstage that he could hear but couldn't see.

Finally, Adam reached Joe and they walked into the woods together, as if both of them understood what would happen next.

"Just so you know," Joe explained, "I went there to help you guys. You told me to do something for you, so that's what I tried to do. But then you ignored me."

"We didn't know you were there until we were leaving. We were caught off guard and didn't know what to do. How did you even know we would be there?"

"I watched you guys earlier. When you were drinking alcohol. You burned the house down to hide the damage you did."

"So you were spying on us."

"I was trying to do what you guys asked. I was trying to be part of your club."

The voice in Adam's head was growing louder. It was explaining in crude language how the selfish little brat wanted something from them. The voice was saying things like *the little fucker is trying to EXTORT you, force you into making him a member of the club, the little COCKSUCKER.*

"I won't tell anyone," Joe said. "If you make me part of the club, I won't be able to tell, because then I would get in trouble, too. Since I was there and all."

On the surface this sounded like a great plan, but Adam feared it would never work. The only way to keep something secret was to never tell anyone. Joe was asking for club membership now, but what would stop him from asking for more favors later? *He will keep asking and in the end he will TELL ON YOU, ANYWAY. He has NOTHING to lose while you have EVERYTHING.*

The problem was there was no good way to stop Joe from telling whoever he felt like telling. There were only ugly ways.

"All right," Adam said. "Let me talk to the other guys. I'm sure they'll agree. So what you should do is meet us here, at the fort, at two o'clock tonight. That way we can initiate you."

Joe beamed like the sun. "Initiation! Cool. I can't wait!"

Adam went home and all evening his mom and dad talked about the fire, and all evening he heard the voice reaffirming his plan. The voice became so loud that he could barely hear his parents when they got into a fight about who was spending more money and whose fault it was they couldn't pay the mortgage and how unlucky it had been that it wasn't their house that burned down.

Finally, two in the morning arrived, and the stars were so pure and bright that Adam felt he could almost touch them. Crickets screeched and owls hooted and the voice in his head explained how to silence Joe Henreid. The idea was so horrific and described in such intricate detail that it could not possibly have come from Adam's own mind, so it seemed there really was a voice offstage somewhere, directing him. All Adam had to do was follow instructions and the story could go on.

After a time, Joe crept into the trees, and Adam snuck up behind him with a rope.

He wrapped this rope around Joe's neck. Pulled it tight and held it firmly.

Joe kicked. Choked. Clawed at Adam's face.

But eventually he stopped moving.

Per instructions, Adam dumped Joe into a wheelbarrow and pushed him through the woods until they emerged by the west end of Shady Lane. The street was new and only a few houses had been built, so no one saw him. He wheeled Joe to a lot that had just been graded, that was waiting for the concrete foundation to be poured. The dirt was easy to dig up. He made a hole three or four feet deep and dropped Joe into it. Adam also threw in the rope so it couldn't be used later to obtain forensic evidence. Then he shoveled dirt on top of Joe, made the grade smooth again, and any leftover dirt he tossed into the wheelbarrow. He dumped this extra soil near some other piles of moved dirt. Later, of course, he would wash out the wheelbarrow.

The stars overhead were brighter than Adam had ever seen. He imagined each star was a person in another world watching him. Judging him.

Any day now, concrete would be poured over the burial site. Soon after that a house would be built on this foundation, and probably no one would ever think to look for Joe there. With no body, the police would be unable to say for sure that the kid was even dead. It would be the perfect crime, the fire would remain their secret, and Adam's life would proceed as it had been written.

Except for one little problem.

When he was done burying the body, when he was ready to walk away, Adam heard something in the dirt.

A voice calling to him. Yelling for him. Screaming for him.

He had no idea what to do. What if Joe clawed his way out of the hole?

Adam stood there, uncertain. Finally he walked away, through the woods, all the way back home.

But he could still hear Joe's voice.

The next day Adam returned to the graded lot. Construction workers were already there and he was mortified: What if they had found the body?

But the men were already pouring concrete, which should have made everything okay, but it didn't. Because Adam could still hear Joe screaming. He didn't understand why the workers couldn't hear it, because Adam could, loud and clear. He thought of the tornado and how it had stripped his house to the foundation, and there seemed to be a kind of symmetry involved, it couldn't be a coincidence, all these slabs of concrete. The only answer he could think of was the director had arranged things this way because it made for a better story.

That night, as Adam lay in bed, unable to sleep, he wondered what it was like offstage, where the director lived. He wondered what made that world different than his.

What about the director himself? Was he being directed by some more distant director even further offstage?

And if so, who was directing him?

ZONE FORECAST PRODUCT
NATIONAL WEATHER SERVICE NORMAN OK
TXZ086-022200-
WICHITA-
INCLUDING THE CITIES OF ... WICHITA FALLS
814 AM CDT MON JUNE 2 2008

... TORNADO WATCH IN EFFECT FROM 930 AM UNTIL 300
PM CDT ...

.TODAY ... MOSTLY CLOUDY WITH WIDESPREAD
THUNDERSTORMS. STORMS LIKELY SEVERE, WITH DAMAGING
WINDS, LARGE HAIL, AND STRONG TORNADOES POSSIBLE.
HIGH IN THE MID 80S WITH TEMPERATURES FALLING
THROUGHOUT THE AFTERNOON. WINDS SW 25-35 MPH EXCEPT
HIGHER IN THUNDERSTORMS. CHANCE OF RAIN 90 PERCENT.
.TONIGHT ... CLOUDY AND TURNING COOLER. LOW AROUND
45. WINDS NW 25-35 MPH. CHANCE OF RAIN 20 PERCENT.
.TUESDAY ... PARTLY CLOUDY. HIGH IN THE UPPER 60S.
NW WINDS 10-15 MPH.
.WEDNESDAY ... MOSTLY SUNNY AND WARMER. HIGH IN THE
UPPER 70S. WINDS LIGHT AND VARIABLE.
.THURSDAY ... SUNNY AND MILD. HIGH IN THE LOWER
80S.

... TORNADO WATCH IN EFFECT MONDAY FROM 930 AM
UNTIL 300 PM CDT ...

... THIS IS A PARTICULARLY DANGEROUS SITUATION ...

A CLASSIC TORNADO OUTBREAK SETUP IS DEVELOPING
ACROSS NORTHWEST TX AND SOUTHWESTERN OK AS DISCRETE
TORNADIC SUPERCELLS APPEAR LIKELY THIS MORNING AND
EARLY AFTERNOON. STRONG LOW LEVEL AND DEEP LAYER
VERTICAL SHEAR ... COMBINED WITH A MOIST AND UNSTABLE

AIR MASS ... WILL POSE A DANGEROUS RISK OF STRONG/
VIOLENT AND POTENTIALLY LONG-TRACK TORNADOES.

HAIL TO 5 INCHES IN DIAMETER ... THUNDERSTORM WIND
GUSTS TO 100 MPH ... AND DANGEROUS LIGHTNING ARE
ALSO POSSIBLE IN THE WATCH AREA.

80

G holson was at his desk, waiting for his visitors to arrive. He'd called Crane about an hour ago, who promised to show up at the station this morning with Clark and Ms. Ulbrecht in tow. Adam Altman was in custody after having been caught at the site of last night's house fire.

Altman refused to answer questions, and in fact the only time he spoke was when he asked to talk to Crane. He did not specify what he planned to say, but at this point Gholson would take any steps necessary to understand the mystery of what was happening in this town. He was no longer directing a law enforcement investigation. He was looking for a way, if such a thing was possible, to recover his wife.

The words Sally had spoken yesterday, the fires and crimes of the past week—Gholson was sure it was all related somehow. But was he looking for patterns that weren't really there? Maybe his wife was wrong and nothing special would happen today. Perhaps weeks or months from now he would wonder if she had really spoken at all. But who could examine the strange circumstances surrounding this case—the song lyrics, the sudden onset of arson events, the bizarre behavior of Altman at the scene of last night's fire—and not expect something extraordinary to happen?

Crane and Ms. Ulbrecht arrived together a little before ten. Clark was not with them.

"Thanks for coming on such short notice," Gholson said to them. "Is Mr. Clark not coming?"

"He didn't answer his phone or the door of his hotel room," Crane said. "He had a few drinks last night so he might be sleeping it off."

"A few hundred," Ms. Ulbrecht joked.

"Well, it's too bad he couldn't make it," Gholson said. "Your friend Mr. Altman threw us a curve ball this morning."

"What exactly happened?" Crane asked. "Has he said anything since you brought him in?"

"Nothing except when he asked to speak to you. And as I said on the phone, we believe he burned down a residence in Tanglewood last night. We found him there later, after the fire crews had left, apparently trying to dig something out of the foundation. He was using an electric breaking hammer."

"Why would he do that?" Crane asked.

"I'm hoping we'll find out when you talk to him. Why don't we go do that now?"

He led them down a long hallway and into a room with no window. Altman's hair was pushed back from his head and speckled with black flakes of soot. He was wearing a T-shirt that may have once been white but was now streaked with stains of gray. His eyes appeared to be looking at something that wasn't in the room with them, and they barely moved. They could have been glass.

"Adam," Crane said. "What happened, man?"

No response.

"Adam?" Crane asked again.

"He was there to help us," Altman said.

"Who was where?"

"You know. You saw him. Joe Henreid."

"What?" said Crane. "What does any of this have to do with Joe?"

"Don't play dumb. We all know that kid was in the house with us. He showed up out of nowhere and we freaked."

Crane seemed to consider his response. He glanced at Ms. Ulbrecht and then at Gholson.

"Okay," Crane finally said. "So Joe was there. But his parents still found his clothes the next day. The ones that smelled of gasoline. He didn't die in the house."

"Yeah, but he would eventually have told someone what we did."

"So you boys have been lying to me," Gholson said. "Joe Henreid didn't set any fire when you were kids."

"Yes," Crane admitted. "We burned down the house. Joe showed up in the middle of it and we had no idea why he was there."

"He wanted to be in our club," Altman explained. "He followed us around and saw us destroy the inside of that house. When we decided to come back that night and burn it down, he showed up with gasoline to help us."

Gholson looked separately at both of his visitors. Crane appeared stricken. Ms. Ulbrecht looked confused. Altman was still staring into space, his expression no different than when he had first arrived at the station hours ago.

Crane said, "Adam, please tell me you didn't hurt Joe because you thought he would tell on us. All that poor kid did was show up at the wrong place at the wrong time."

Altman's voice was rote, almost robotic, as if someone had programmed him to paint the story by numbers. He turned his head in Crane's general direction but still didn't make eye contact.

"I saw him in the trees the next day. He promised not to tell anyone what we did if we let him into the club. So I agreed."

In less than a minute, Altman described how he lured Joe into the forest that night, strangled him, and buried him on a graded residential lot. Halfway through the story, Crane put his hand over his mouth. Ms. Ulbrecht wouldn't even look at him.

It should have been startling for a case that bothered Gholson for so many years to be solved in seconds, that his working hypothesis on what happened to Joe Henreid was almost exactly what had transpired. But by now nothing surprised him. Every related event that had occurred since the moment Gholson received the first arson call on Monday had simply been a step in the direction of a final outcome that felt moments away. Like scenes in a movie, each event had pushed the plot forward toward an inevitable conclusion. The only questions left were to determine what the ending was, when it would come, and if he could find a way to get back to Sally.

Altman said, "You think I regret killing him? I don't. Because there is no point to anything. For twenty years I've tried to deny it. I've pretended like there was a god out there watching over me, over everything, that my actions on earth would grant me access to Heaven or banish me to Hell. But I'm thirty-eight years old and I've barely lived any life at all. The only actions that could be used to judge me are terrible ones. And now that we've reached the end, the only thing left is for me to explain things you should already know."

"Adam," Crane said. "Just shut up already. You're not making sense. You shouldn't say another word until you call an attorney."

"I can still get the death penalty, right? I can be tried as an adult? I strangled an eleven-year-old kid."

"Adam!"

In any other interrogation, Gholson would have assumed a far more directive role than this. But in this case he was content to sit back and consume information until he knew, hopefully, what to do about his wife.

"There's a storm coming," Altman said. "You all know this. Even the detective knows."

"Like a tornado?" Ms. Ulbrecht asked.

"Not just a tornado," Altman answered. "The end of the world."

Gholson wasn't sure how to proceed. He required more information to act on Sally's behalf and yet didn't know what questions to ask. Or to whom. But his mind was fixated on something Altman had just said, something that seemed to capture how he felt now, how he had perhaps always felt.

I'm thirty-eight years old and I've barely lived any life at all.

He could sense the reality behind this statement and it was terrible. Unspeakable.

"Mr. Altman," he said. "We know you burned down the house in Tanglewood last night. But what about the other fires last week? Did you set those, too? Did you have an accomplice?"

"I had nothing to do with those events. But I think those two know who did."

He gestured in the direction of Crane and Ms. Ulbrecht.

"You guys found Todd's son, isn't that right?" Altman said. "You think he's the one who burned up your houses?"

Gholson looked at Crane.

"We called you about this yesterday," said Crane.

"Who called me?"

"David, Alicia, and I. After we left Windthorst. You didn't answer so we left a voicemail."

"Are you sure you left it with me?" Gholson said.

Crane looked at Ms. Ulbrecht and then back at Gholson.

"Actually," he said, "David placed the call. So you didn't receive any message?"

Sally had mentioned a kid. She'd warned Gholson not to let someone take him away from Wichita Falls. Who might do that? Someone who didn't live here in the first place? Someone with the resources to extract him without leaving a trace?

"Where did you say Mr. Clark was?" he asked Crane.

"We assume he's back at the hotel."

Gholson approached Crane and lowered his voice.

"Let's talk outside," he said. "I need to understand exactly what happened when you talked to this kid. I have a feeling Mr. Clark might—"

"You don't have to be so covert," Altman said.

Gholson turned around and saw the suspect was finally looking directly at him.

"Isn't it obvious?" Altman said. "What if you could see stock prices instead of hear music lyrics? How do you think that would turn out for David? And for the rest of us?"

81

The midmorning sky was a hot, hazy blue, and the air was so humid it had taken on a physical quality you could almost reach out and touch. David, who years ago had become accustomed to the temperate climate of the California coast, was suffering in a way he wouldn't have believed possible for a conscious human being. The amount of alcohol he had consumed over the past couple of days, combined with a gross deficiency of sleep, had reduced him to a state barely above pure survival, and this was timing of the worst kind. If there was any day when he required full access to his mental and physical resources, today was it.

It was a huge risk, what he was planning to do with Thomas. Despite the kid's assertion that he would be waiting for David, there was still a chance the mother would complicate matters. But the potential reward for a successful extraction was almost without measure, and even Thomas himself seemed to understand this. So they had to try.

Once David took possession of the kid, even if the mother was unaware of this or neutralized somehow, David knew law enforcement could eventually become involved. If anyone saw or suspected foul play, an AMBER alert might be issued, and there was also the problem of Jonathan and Alicia deducing his intentions. Right now they were both with the detective, and if any or all of them suspected where he was and what he was doing, David might find the whole police force waiting for him at the airport. That was why he had called his Gulfstream pilot first thing and ordered him to depart Wichita Falls immediately. Hopefully they would all believe David had been on that plane. The plan now was to drive to a smaller airport near Thomas' house, where David's friend, Jim Thain, promised to deliver a jet before noon. Apparently someone in Houston owed the guy a favor.

Once David was in the air, and specifically once he was back in California, he could hide Thomas somewhere. As long as the mother wasn't home when he picked up her son, there would be no proof of what had happened. David had no prior criminal history of any kind, and he had always generously supported California law enforcement. The only possible reason Gholson or anyone could give for David taking the child was based on an idea no sane person would take seriously. If he could just get out of Wichita Falls safely, he would probably be in the clear for good.

There was a part of him, hidden somewhere in the blinding haze of his hangover, that was asking the pesky question of why he was bothering with all this. Yes, he might make more money, a lot more, but what, exactly, would he do with it? Like Meredith had been happy to point out, David had fathered no children who could inherit his fortune, and he couldn't spend the money he'd already earned without catastrophically wasting it. He supposed the answer was encoded in his character. All life on Earth was programmed to survive, and humans in particular had learned to maximize this instinct in different and intelligent ways, but David and men like him had learned to leverage their incredible achievements to generate runaway success. It was not in his nature to earn only the amount needed to survive and share the rest. He was a doer, a decider, a creator. He was a king.

Or was he?

Surely the motivation that drove him to amass unspendable wealth wasn't something more personal, like for instance revenge. Or pride. Surely his life hadn't been written as a hackneyed son character whose entire adult life was a bid for his father's approval.

Surely not. Definitely not.

David put his father out of his mind and drove to the kid's house. He was relieved to see the mother's car was not in the driveway, which meant at least the first step of this process would proceed smoothly.

He found Thomas on the porch, waiting for him, a strangely confident smile on his face.

The kind of smile David liked to see on his own face.

82

To Jonathan it felt like the world was coming apart. He was sitting in the front seat of Gholson's police cruiser, watching out the window, and everything seemed out of focus. The sounds he heard might have been drenched in static, like he was tuning into the world with an AM radio. Alicia was in the back. All Jonathan could think about was what Adam had said before they left the police station.

I'm thirty-eight years old and I've barely lived any life at all.

He should have known what that meant. It was related to something Todd had told them many years ago, right before they burned down the restaurant. Something strange and amazing and horrifying about the world. Whatever the truth was, it had touched every day of his entire life. It had been driving all of them toward a conclusion that felt moments away. He imagined he could hear the energy of the end as it approached, like the whooshing sound of a tornado directly overhead.

"The mother didn't answer," Gholson said, putting away his mobile phone.

"If David picks him up," Alicia said, "then what?"

"I'll put out an APB on the rental car. We could issue an AMBER alert, but not until we have confirmation the kid is missing. We could be chasing a wild goose here."

"By then David could have taken him anywhere," Alicia said. "Can't you call backup? Wouldn't there be a cop closer to their house? This shouldn't be up to just us."

"Call backup and tell them what?"

"Anything! Shouldn't we save Thomas first and worry about explanations later?"

"We don't even know for sure he's going after the kid," Gholson said.

"We're talking about a little boy's life, for God's sake."

"A boy you seem to believe has committed some pretty serious crimes. That's not any kind of boy I'm going to put in front of my career, no offense. And anyway we'll get there in time. You'll see."

Soon they had left the city proper and were driving south on its perimeter. Thomas' house was only a couple miles away, and Jonathan watched the road for David's rental car.

Something caught his eye on the right, out the passenger window, and Jonathan turned his head in that direction. To the west and south he saw a tall cloud. A thunderhead. The base of it was wide and dark, but the rest was a large, white tower, stretching high into the sky like stacked popcorn.

"That's a supercell," Alicia said. "The kind of thunderstorm that produces tornadoes. I'm going to call my dad and see if he knows anything."

She reached into her purse and keyed a number into her cell phone.

The tower seemed to grow even as Jonathan watched it, erupting into the atmosphere as if shot from a gun, as if it had previously been held in place by some invisible barrier and had only now managed to break through. As they neared Thomas' house, he could tell the thunderstorm was strengthening and leaning toward them.

"No answer," Alicia said. "Shit."

"It looks like it's coming this way," Jonathan said.

"Yes, it does. It'll be over the city before we know it."

David's rental car was not parked in the driveway of Thomas' house.

"What if he already left?" asked Alicia. "What if he's already got him?"

Gholson nodded. "Let's knock on the door and find out."

He steered his car into the driveway and jumped out. Jonathan and Alicia followed. The detective pounded on the door.

"Thomas Phillips! Christine Phillips! Are you inside? This is the Wichita Falls Police. Please open the door!"

As they waited, Jonathan noticed the daylight had dimmed. He could see high, wispy clouds blotting out the sun. The storm was approaching quickly.

Someone unlocked the door. It was Christine Phillips. Eyes bloodshot, entire face flushed, cheeks shiny with tears.

"Ms. Phillips," Gholson said. "I'm—"

"He's gone," she cried. "Your friend drove up in his car and my son just climbed in. Like he knew someone was coming to take him away."

"What?" Jonathan asked. "He left voluntarily?"

"Please," she said to them, to Gholson specifically. "My son is sick. He doesn't know what he's doing. Can you please get him back for me?"

"Do you know where they went?" asked the detective.

"He said he was flying far away from here and never coming back."

"We have to do something," Alicia said to Gholson. "Can you call the airport?"

"Ms. Phillips," Gholson said. "I will get your son back. I need you to go back inside and call 9-1-1 and tell them what happened."

"He told me not to do that. He said he would hurt me if I did."

"Who? Mr. Clark?"

"No. My son. This morning he drove my car into a ditch and wrecked it so I couldn't follow them."

Jonathan, Alicia, and Gholson all looked at each other.

"You call, anyway," the detective said. "Go back inside and call. I will get some backup and we will stop your son before he leaves town. Do you understand?"

"I am so scared," Christine said.

"Just go inside. Let me take care of it for you."

On the way back to the car, Detective Gholson said, "I'm calling this in now. We'll enter the data into NCIC and then I'll ask my sergeant to contact the airport and ground all flights. His plane is at Municipal, correct?"

"Yes," Jonathan said. "I flew in it with him this weekend."

They reached the car and Gholson got on the radio. Outside, the sky was growing ever darker, and Jonathan could hear the rumble of thunder. Except the sound of it was constant and growing ever louder, which wasn't like thunder at all, which was more like the sound of a jet airplane.

Jonathan threw open the car door and ran out into the yard. The sound was even louder now, so immediate that the jet couldn't have been more than a mile away and flying low, much too low to be safe. Unless . . .

He ran back to the car.

"Isn't there another airport around here?" he asked Gholson. "Like a small one?"

The detective was barking information into the radio about Municipal Airport. But it was all wrong. David was two steps ahead of them.

"You mean Kickapoo?" Gholson finally said. "It's on the other side of the highway. Like right there. But what—"

"David wouldn't try to take the kid out on his own plane. He would expect you to be looking there."

"So then what—"

On the radio, a male voice said, "Detective, a Gulfstream jet departed about an hour ago. Appears to be the plane you're looking for."

"Is he gone?" Alicia shrieked. "Did they already fly away?"

Raindrops began to hit the windshield. They were loud and fat. Jonathan walked around the house and looked west, in the direction of the airport. The storm was almost on top of them, its underside gray and blue and black. In the foreground, just above the treetops, Jonathan saw what looked like a small private plane flying parallel to the highway. It dropped out of sight. A moment later he heard the high-pitched shriek of tires skidding against asphalt.

"Let's go," he yelled at Gholson. "A plane just landed at that airport. It's for David. It has to be."

On the radio, the male voice was yelling. Gholson reached forward and switched it off.

"If Clark left on his plane," he said. "It's all over. Let's hope that was some kind of misdirection and go find this other plane."

"This is awful," Alicia said. Jonathan looked into the back seat and saw her skin was the color of plaster. "Not only is David trying to steal a child, but look outside. We read about this, Jonathan. On that fucking paper Pete Willis showed us. Thomas knew about this. He knew about it *two years ago*."

Gholson drove back onto the highway. At the intersection with Southwest Parkway he turned west, and then took an immediate north. On their right Jonathan could see white buildings made of corrugated steel. Plane hangars. The airport was that close.

"Over there!" he said, and pointed.

Gholson turned down a narrow asphalt road and soon they reached a chain link gate. The gate was closed.

"Now what?" asked Alicia.

Gholson backed the car up, across the narrow road, until a fence would allow him to go no farther. Then he threw the car into gear and pushed the accelerator to the floor.

"Oh, shit!" Alicia cried.

"Hold on," Gholson said.

Jonathan didn't think they were going to make it. There wasn't room to generate enough speed. He braced for impact as they hit the gate, expecting to feel the seatbelt grab him across the chest, but it didn't. Instead his ears winced from the deafening screech of metal on metal, the sound of it like monstrous fingers being raked across a giant chalkboard. Gholson jerked the car right to avoid a white airplane hangar, and Jonathan could see a flat plain of grass where the runway surely was. In the distance, a private jet had just landed and appeared to be slowing down. Closer to them, about fifty yards ahead, stood a silver BMW SUV.

83

As Gholson watched the aircraft taxi slowly toward them, he wondered exactly when he would understand what to do. Sally had known about the kid, Thomas, and she had apparently known about the impending tornado. She also had suggested he could change the ending of something. But he did not understand what he was supposed to do or how to do it.

Crane and Ms. Ulbrecht obviously knew things he didn't. If he was going to pick the right course of action, he would have to trust them. Share what he knew and hope they would do the same.

"Let me tell you something," he said to Crane. "I knew you were lying to me from the first time I interviewed you. I knew you were hiding something. But I couldn't act upon my suspicion because the thing I knew wasn't something I was willing to share, either."

"Detective Gholson—"

"I know all about Todd. I have a journal of his with song lyrics in it. Lots of songs. And though this began for me as a law enforcement investigation, now it's become personal."

"You have a journal?" Crane said. "What else does it say?"

"If there was anything else useful in it, I would tell you. But listen to me: My wife is in a mental hospital. Over there by the lake."

When he pointed out the window, it looked like he was gesturing at the storm, which was approaching from the same direction.

"She's sick. She suffers from the exact same condition Todd Willis did, and she hasn't been able to speak to me in three years."

"That's terrible," Ms. Ulbrecht said. "But—"

"At least not until yesterday. Yesterday she came out of the coma long enough to tell me something I think you two ought to know."

Gholson imagined he could hear a clock somewhere, ticking off measured seconds one after the other. He imagined he could watch the scene unfold before him in slow motion, frame by frame, could hear the gears of a great film projector turning, pushing the aircraft forward, dragging the thunderstorm toward them.

"She told me the cyclone was almost upon us, which I suppose means this storm. But she also said a kid had changed the beginning and the ending. I don't know what she meant by the beginning, but I assume the ending means this. Right here and now."

Crane turned and looked at Ms. Ulbrecht. Then he looked back at Gholson again.

"We found a sheet of paper," Crane said. "Like a page from a book manuscript. Apparently Thomas wrote it. Maybe that was the beginning."

"What did it say?"

"That readers of the story that followed would find clues to a book that helped destroy Wichita Falls. On June 2, 2008. Today."

"Do you know what that means? This book he was talking about?"

"We don't," Crane said. "But I think we're about to find out."

Rain was still falling, the drops few in number but large in size. The wind strengthened to an intensity Gholson had seen only one other time in his life. He looked out his window, to the west, and a childlike sense of fear washed over him. The sky in that direction was a shade near black, and the clouds were moving in ways that didn't seem real. The ragged base of the storm looked almost as if it were squatting upon the ground.

Ahead of them, the aircraft had reached the end of the runway and appeared to be turning around. The BMW began to move. It rolled toward a road that joined the concrete driveway with the runway proper. Gholson followed.

"What are they going to do?" asked Ms. Ulbrecht. "Just get out of the car and into the plane as if we aren't right behind them?"

"I will put a stop to it if they try," Gholson said.

Clark's BMW reached the runway and turned left. It rolled toward the aircraft. Gholson followed and pulled closer. Finally both vehicles reached the end of the runway, where the aircraft had completed its turn and was now pointed in the direction opposite from which it had landed.

This was it. The whole story would be decided in the next couple of minutes. Gholson had been smart to ask what his passengers knew, because now he understood, as unbelievable as it sounded, that everything Sally said had been correct. He suspected the beginning and ending Thomas had altered was to destroy the city while he flew away to

California or wherever he planned to go. Which meant Thomas was behind everything. The fires he set, the damage he caused, the men he killed—all these crimes had been committed to set in motion a chain of events that would lead to this ending. Fred Clark's death had brought his wealthy son to Wichita Falls and now Thomas would use David to escape just before the city was destroyed.

But apparently the moment they were living now had not been intended as the original ending. And if it could be changed once, as Sally had suggested, maybe it could be changed again.

In order to take Thomas Phillips from here, Clark would be forced to exit the vehicle. When he did, Gholson would intervene.

They all watched the BMW carefully. There appeared to be motion inside. When Gholson looked at the aircraft again, he saw a door open and a staircase emerge.

The large drops of rain slowed and stopped.

Everything seemed to stop.

The driver's side door of the BMW opened.

84

The kid wouldn't talk and it gave David the chills.

It was strange enough that Thomas had called him the night before to make sure the plane was ready, that he had instructed David to arrive at a specified time. But to watch the kid climb into his rented SUV as if he'd been waiting on a bus, this was surreal. He had spoken two words then and none since:

"Let's go."

David was short on time because Jim had instructed him to be ready to board as soon as the plane was on the ground. Even so, he couldn't quiet his curiosity.

"So I guess I understand how you knew I was coming for you. But how *long* have you known?"

Thomas answered him with a withering look but declined to elaborate.

"What do you want from all this?"

For a while David was content with the silence that followed, willing to drive to Kickapoo Airport and wait for the plane while Thomas sat next to him. It was a hell of a lot easier than what he had feared, that the mother would be there to put up a fight and oblige David to neutralize her.

But his mind wandered as they waited for the plane to arrive, and he began to consider the kid's position more closely. If Thomas could know the details of David's idea, if he was voluntarily willing to comply, that meant he wanted out of Wichita Falls as badly as David wanted it. It meant he had his own reasons for leaving. His own plans.

Was David using Thomas to improve his fortunes or was Thomas using *him*?

The implications of the answer were staggering and David's head swirled with questions. He remembered the page Pete Willis had showed them. The page that implied Wichita Falls would be destroyed by a tornado today. That text had been written, according to Willis, at least two years ago.

Two *years* ago.

He looked over at Thomas. Thomas didn't look back.

"How far away is the plane?" David asked him. "How much longer before it lands?"

The kid said nothing.

It was clear by looking out the window that a storm was on the way, presumably the one Thomas had written about, and David wondered how the plane was going to land and take off again if the storm arrived first.

"Is the plane going to arrive on time? I mean, look at that storm."

The kid still said nothing.

They were parked inside the airport gates on the road bordering the runway. David watched the storm approach, an apocalyptic sky gathered over the flat and barren prairie, and was consumed by a loathing for his hometown. He hated the iron-rich soil that stained everything red. He despised the ever present wind and heat. You could be driven mad by looking into the hollow eyes of the overworked and underprivileged citizens, by sensing their resentment and despair. And if not for that day in the forest, if not for the storm that had changed the lives of everyone in Wichita Falls, he might be one of them. Instead, he had been selected for a different fate. On a late afternoon day in the spring of his tenth year, a day that looked a lot like this one, something had happened to him as he ran through the trees, as he dodged hailstones large enough to kill him.

I can see you. . .

David remembered it clearly now. He had slipped in the mud, fallen to the ground, and the world seemed to flip somehow. For a moment he thought he heard a guitar. He had bumped his head and when he looked up, the opening bars of a song he shouldn't have known were floating through the trees above him.

Don't look back, you can never look back. . .

What happened when he fell to the ground? In one moment he had been a normal, frightened kid and in the next he had been blessed (cursed?) with the ability to hear things other people could not hear and see things others could not see.

Did Thomas know how all this worked? Or was he simply trying to make sense of the world? David recognized (finally) that he had maneuvered himself into an unfamiliar position: He didn't want to simply use the kid. He also wanted to help him.

A low, droning sound approached from the south, a sound that could only belong to a jet engine. He looked up and could see the plane just ahead of them, low and wobbling in the wind. Rain was beginning to fall, large drops that sounded like marbles hitting the roof of the car. Spray kicked up from the runway as the plane touched down, and David watched for any sign the wheels might begin to slide. But the landing was perfect. The plane slowed quickly, clearly under control. As it reached the end of the runway, David put the car into gear, and that's when he heard a loud crash behind him. In the rearview mirror he saw another car appear, a blue sedan he was pretty sure belonged to Detective Gholson.

The BMW creaked on its hinges as the wind pushed it like a giant hand. He switched the windshield wipers on, to push aside the few raindrops that were falling, and began to roll slowly toward the plane. Fuck Gholson. Fuck Jonathan and Alicia and whoever else. What could they do? Shoot at him while he walked the kid to the plane? No way they would do that.

The plane had turned around now and was pointed back down the runway in the direction from which it had come. A door opened in the fuselage and the airstair emerged.

"Thomas," David said. "It's time to go. Are you okay to walk? You haven't said anything since you got in the car, so I'm not sure what you're going to do when we get out."

"We don't have much time," Thomas answered. "I'll get out on your side so the cop doesn't try to shoot you."

David nodded and pushed his door open. He was about to step onto the runway when something slammed into the hood of the BMW. The sound of it was deafening. He shrank back into his seat.

"What the fuck was that?" David yelled. "Is he shooting at us?"

Another detonation hit the roof of the car, as if someone were launching mortar shells at them.

"Oh, shit," he said. "Those are hailstones."

By now the sky had turned as black as night. A terrible idea occurred to him, blinking like a siren in his mind: *What if I die out there? I'm not ready to die!*

Behind them, Gholson's sedan was inching closer. There was no choice. They had to go now.

The hailstones were falling sporadically and spaced widely apart. David thought they could reach the plane without getting hit, but he wasn't completely sure.

He turned toward the kid again.

"Are we going to make it?"

"There aren't any goddamn hailstones," Thomas said. "You're confusing the ending with the beginning. Get out of the car and let's go."

David didn't understand. He could hear the hailstones falling around them. But now they had no choice. They had to go, hail or no hail.

He stepped out of the car and Thomas followed. It was a sprint of fifty or so yards to the airstair. David took Thomas' hand and they ran.

A flash of light turned the sky to fire. Deafening thunder shook the ground. David knew a direct hailstone strike could be fatal, and he tried to move them faster. He ran for their lives. From behind them he thought he heard footsteps. He imagined he could hear his dad's voice coaching him, cheering him on. *Don't look back, you can never look back.*

But he couldn't help it. He had to look. And when he did, David found Gholson only a few steps behind him. The sneaky fucker.

"Stop!" Gholson yelled. "You are not taking that child! I will shoot you!"

David drew Thomas close to him and wrapped his arms around the kid's chest, like a bear hug from behind.

"Leave us alone!"

"Just tell me which eye you'd rather me shoot and let's get this over with."

Gholson was bluffing. He had to be. David saw movement behind the detective and realized Jonathan had climbed out of the car. Alicia was right behind him. They were all against him now. The common folk hated him for what they didn't have. For what he had earned and they had not.

"David," Jonathan called. "Come on, man. This is crazy."

"Go home," David replied. "You're out of your league."

"That poor kid has a mother," Alicia said. "He's got a life here. Why do this? Why do you need more than you already have?"

"How do you know what I have or what I need? And anyway it doesn't matter because Thomas came with me of his own free will."

"Free will," Thomas whispered to him in an amused voice. "I like your sense of humor."

The hailstones seemed to be increasing in number and David began backing toward the jet. He didn't understand how all of them could stand there and not worry about being hit. He wondered if the plane would be able to take off under this sort of duress.

"Mr. Clark," Gholson growled. "This is your last chance. Let the kid go."

A volatile, spiraling network of black clouds approached them. The runway shined brightly. Emerald green sunlight lit David's view in mystical hues. The clouds were ragged, low to the ground.

He wasn't stealing Thomas. He was protecting him. How could they not see this? How did they not understand the boy needed a real father in his life?

"I'm out of here," he said as he reached the airstair.

But he could see Gholson was serious. Gholson was going to pull the trigger.

And then above him, there was a loud, sharp report. The spreading wave echo of gunfire. David, to his surprise, was still vertical.

Gholson collapsed to the ground.

At the top of the stairs, a man David didn't recognize gestured to him.

"Bring the kid up here. We have to get off the ground. Now."

David was disoriented and confused, but he obeyed the order. He shoved Thomas onto the stairs and pushed him forward, upward. In moments they were on the plane. The unfamiliar man stood before them.

"Move out of the way," he said, reaching for the airstair controls.

David guided the kid away from the door, but not before he turned and looked briefly outside. Jonathan and Alicia had knelt above Gholson and were apparently trying to stop a bleeding leg wound. David couldn't believe they weren't more concerned about the falling hail. And then he noticed with some bewilderment that he could see no hailstones on the runway or anywhere.

"What the hell?" he finally said to the unfamiliar man. "Who are you? Why did you shoot the cop?"

"I'm Special Agent Paulson. I'm here to facilitate your safe departure. We have an extreme weather situation and must depart at once. Please take your seats."

The plane was a Lear and far smaller than his own Gulfstream. It was outfitted with eight seats in two groups of four. David guided Thomas to the seat next to him, which faced the front of the plane. Paulson took the opposite seat.

"Jim didn't say anything about a federal agent," David said.

Paulson replied, "We intercepted communication between you and your friend, Mr. Thain. As for Erik Lehman—who has been providing classified and other sensitive information to you—he has been relieved of duty. His contributions to your abduction of this child will likely land him in jail. In the meantime, this situation has been deemed important to national security. The child will accompany me to a safe location at Ford Meade in Maryland."

"What? On whose authority?"

The roar of the engines grew louder. David was pinned to the back of his seat as the plane began to accelerate.

"As a matter of national security, sir, I can take whatever means necessary to protect the nation. Not to mention, your claim to the child is not exactly legal. Either way, you better hope our pilot can outflank that tornado. I don't think I've ever seen anything like it."

David was seated on the starboard side of the plane. He raised the window screen and looked outside.

What he saw turned his blood cold. There was no chance they were going to make it.

85

Jonathan had never received formal medical training and it appeared Alicia hadn't either. Gholson's wound was in the thigh, which had not seemed all that critical when Jonathan first saw it, but now blood was pouring out of it at a rate that didn't seem possible. The detective would be dead in minutes if they didn't figure out how to stop the bleeding. Even pushing as hard as he could against the wound, blood still oozed between his fingers, warm and urgent and smelling metallic.

Gholson's eyes fluttered in a state between open and shut. He tried to say something but only managed to choke on fluid in his throat. His tongue quivered. Spittle trickled down his chin.

"Sally," he finally managed. "You're so beautiful. Everything is beautiful."

Around them, the world seemed to be ending. The sky was so dark it could have been eight in the evening instead of eleven in the morning. The wind, which slowed to a whisper when the rain stopped, had picked up again, and was increasing with each beat of time. It whistled in Jonathan's ears, it growled. Something terrible was going to happen.

"I think the bullet hit an artery," Alicia said. "I don't know if we can do anything."

Jonathan couldn't believe what David had done. He couldn't believe the man on the plane had shot Gholson. Whoever would come here and steal a young boy from his mother and his hometown, whoever would shoot a police officer working to stop this travesty, these were the kind of integrity-free antagonists you found in mindless action films but never expected to encounter in the real world. Jonathan couldn't believe David had sunk so low.

He pulled off his shirt and tied it around Gholson's thigh, but the leg was so thick there, and the wound so deep, the cotton material was soaked almost immediately. Blood began to drip out of the shirt and Jonathan realized Alicia was right.

"Jonathan, we have to get out of here. If we don't, we'll never outrun the storm."

He looked upward, over Gholson's car, and felt all the strength drain out of him. The storm was a wall of spiraling black, and at the base of it, little cloud fingers were on the ground, dancing around each other. Sometimes there were two fingers. Sometimes there were six.

Fear washed through him. He was nine years old all over again. The storm was bearing down upon them again. But this time he would not cower as he had before.

"That tornado," Alicia said, "it must be two miles wide, Jonathan. It's like across the entire horizon."

"We have to get out of here. But we can't just leave Gholson behind."

"He's dead already, Jonathan. We really need to go."

Jonathan looked down at Gholson and realized Alicia was right. At some point the detective had stopped breathing. His eyes were open, but whatever he was looking at was something Jonathan couldn't see. And it looked almost like he was smiling.

Jonathan climbed into Gholson's car and sat behind the wheel. The engine was still running. When Alicia shut her door, he put the transmission in gear and floored the accelerator. For a terrible moment he thought he was going to run over Gholson, but he jerked the car to the right, missing him by inches, and drove onto the runway. The tornado was approaching from the west, and there was no road headed east. Beyond the runway there was only red pasture and weeds, and a highway in the distance. Rain had turned the dirt into mud and they wouldn't be able to drive through it without getting stuck.

The only way to exit the airport on a paved road was to head west, and he could not imagine driving toward the tornado. They were trapped.

"Jonathan!" Alicia screamed. "Get us out of here! I don't want to die!"

Outside the car, the wind continued to increase. It shrieked around them, tugging on the car, urging it toward the storm. Jonathan looked around, hoping to see something, anything, any sort of escape route that might save them. Just a little north and east of the runway stood a FedEx building, and though there was no road connecting the facility to their location, the amount of open field they would need to traverse to reach the other side wasn't more than fifty or sixty yards.

Jonathan punched the accelerator and made a run for it, knowing if they didn't find asphalt before the car bogged down in the mud, both of them would die.

86

The plane was listing. David was sure of it. And it seemed to be slowing down, which was an alarming sign for an aircraft working to gain altitude. His right hand gripped the seat armrest hard enough to nearly puncture holes in the leather. His left held Thomas' own hand.

Across from him, Paulson looked as alarmed as David felt. The agent unbuckled himself and lurched toward the cockpit door, which was closed but apparently not locked. When he threw the door open, David could hear a buzzing sound, oscillating like a car alarm. Some kind of warning.

Paulson's voice was loud and commanding, but so was the pilot's reply. Then David heard something that turned his heart to a lump of ice in his chest.

It was the sound of a gunshot.

Thomas unbuckled his seatbelt and stood up quickly.

"What in the hell?" he yelled, apparently to himself. "This is not supposed to happen!"

"Son!" David said. "You have to sit down!"

Thomas ignored him. He tried to walk toward the cockpit, but the plane was listing so hard to the right that he couldn't keep his balance. And then someone emerged from the cockpit. It was not Paulson.

"What the hell are you doing here?" Thomas yelled at the man. "You're supposed to be dead! What are you doing?"

"Son, this is wrong."

"Wrong? The whole world is wrong! Why do you care what *I* do?"

David's eyes were reporting the appearance of Todd Willis, the boy who twenty-five years ago had emerged from his walking coma no longer a boy. This version of Todd was a wiry man with receding hair and tired eyes, but David might not have believed what he was seeing if it weren't for the look on Thomas' face.

"Just because you lucked into the ability to tilt the world in your favor doesn't mean you should actually do it."

"I didn't luck into anything," Thomas said. The plane was veering at an absurd angle and the kid nearly fell down. "I figured this out. I earned it!"

"You were born with it," Todd explained. "And rather than give back to a world that has been so generous to you, you just want to keep taking more."

"Anyone in my position would do the same thing. It's how the world works!"

David's stomach lurched as the plane turned obscenely, as it was dragged backward and toward the ground. This was it. He was going to die. They were all going to die.

"We don't have to be prisoners to our impulses," Todd said. "We can choose. And I'm choosing to end it here. No one should be able to control the world this way."

Thomas tried to reach out and strike his father but fell down instead. Out of sight.

"What's out there?" David asked Todd. "Wherever you go, is it really that awful?"

There was a piercing, human scream, and suddenly David's seat-belt was crushing him. Then it released. Then the world seemed to turn upside down, and the last thing he heard, as everything went dark, was Todd's answer.

"You would love it there."

87

Alicia had heard the story many times. Her father told it at parties and family holidays. When he had a few drinks he would even tell *her*, for the nine millionth time, how the first tornado he ever chased almost became his last. How his tires couldn't gain traction on the dirt road. How he had given up on his car and dove into a ditch. The tornado had passed almost directly over him and sent tree branches through the windshield and the radiator.

Now, Alicia was reliving the scene twenty-nine years later. Jonathan was attempting to cross a short stretch of mud so they could reach the FedEx parking lot, and she didn't think they were going to make it. But finally they did. Their tires gripped the asphalt and the car shot forward. Jonathan swerved through the lot until they reached a small two-lane road. Before he turned east, she watched in horror as the swirling mass stretched across her entire vision, a storm that surely dwarfed the tornado she had seen in 1979.

The road was wet, the headwinds hurricane-force, and she knew they would never outrun the supercell. They had to locate some kind of shelter, and quickly.

"This is how my dad almost died," Alicia cried. "We've got to get out the car and find shelter. Get below ground. Something."

Jonathan pointed ahead of them. "Look!"

Alicia looked and saw a set of buildings beside the road. It appeared to be some kind of church. A driveway connected the buildings to the road, and a concrete culvert sat in the drainage ditch where the driveway crossed it.

Jonathan slammed on the brakes. The car slid toward the drainage ditch. The horizon tilted. The car slipped off the shoulder.

Now Jonathan threw open his car door. He seized Alicia's arm and she scrambled over the center console. They climbed outside and Jonathan pointed toward the culvert, which for now would double as a human-sized shelter made of concrete.

"Go," he yelled. "Now!"

Alicia went.

88

Sally's face was angelic. When she smiled at him, Gholson thought of that windy Friday in 1976, the day after Thanksgiving, when the two of them had shared their first kiss as husband and wife. He remembered thinking how Sally had altered his entire world view, how she had helped him see life not as a series of obstacles to overcome, of miseries to endure, but rather a long journey on open road, a journey with an uncertain but hopeful conclusion.

Over the years, as Sally's health declined, as she became more distant and reclusive, Gholson had clung desperately to the optimistic feelings she taught him to embrace. Even when she stopped speaking completely, he had never given up on her.

And now here Sally was, her beautiful face young again, her eyes bright and lucid and shrouded in a field of white.

She was at home in here. She was alive.

Sally took his hand and together they flew at a silent, extraordinary speed. The field of white gave way to rectangles of color: golden folders, photographs, moving pictures, organized grids of numbers, executables, blocks of code, and long, written documents that might have been stories written by someone. Books written by someone.

"Where are we going?" he asked her.

"Anywhere you want. Just say it and we'll go."

Gholson smiled.

"Do you remember," Sally asked, "what we asked the minister to include in our vows?"

"'Until death do we part," he said. "And even in death we shall not part.'"

"And just look at us now," Sally said, and smiled again.

89

The spiraling tornado stretched across the horizon as far as Jonathan could see. The air began to vibrate, to tremble; he could feel the sub-sonic rumble of the storm even in his bones. There was a dark mass above him and a swirl of browns and reds before him. Black, wispy scud clouds were being sucked toward the funnel complex at unfathom-able speeds. Mesquite trees leaned at blasphemous angles, waiting to be uprooted as the tornado approached. With no shirt on he was suddenly freezing. The roar of the storm was organic and deafening.

Jonathan had always believed, when death was imminent, that he would experience fear as a white and incomprehensible void. But as he directed Alicia into the culvert, her hair whipping him in the face, Jonathan was instead buoyed by a sense of purpose that he pictured as a paragraph of narrative and descriptive text. Such a paragraph would reveal how death, while terrifying, was a fair price to pay to save some-one else's life.

Alicia was almost fully inside the culvert. She was pushing up with her hands as Jonathan pressed forward on the soles of her shoes. The wind threatened to suck him backward. He turned around briefly

don't look back you can never look back

and saw the leading edge of circulation was no more than two hun-dred yards away. By now it had swallowed the airport. Multiple hori-zontal funnels orbited the main circulation. These vortices looked like spiraling elephant trunks or octopus legs. Debris was raining down around him. Mesquite tree branches, an airplane propeller, and papers, papers, everywhere. The sound of the tornado and the crashing debris was overwhelming. Alicia was inside the culvert and now Jonathan knelt to follow her. The opening was barely tall enough for him to fit inside, and using his arms to propel himself forward was nearly impossible.

The concrete surface grated his chest and he barely noticed the pain. He wiggled and shimmied and tried to use Alicia's ankles to pull himself forward. He was only halfway inside. It was dark and he could barely see Alicia even though she was inches away. Something landed on his right calf, punching a hole in him, and Jonathan screamed through gritting teeth.

"Are you okay?" Alicia cried.

"Something hit me. I have to keep moving and get inside before I lose both my legs."

He wiggled forward and tried to push with his toes. His chest was bleeding. His right calf was slick with blood.

There was nothing in the world but the sound of the tornado, the growl, the rumble, the shrieking debris flying through the air and crashing into the ground. Jonathan had just pulled his feet into the culvert when the world became black. The tornado was on top of them. He could feel the rumble of it in every cell of his body, as if he were plugged into the energy of the world somehow. Alicia's feet were centimeters from his face. She was trembling.

"Are you all right?" he yelled.

"Jonathan I'm scared! I'm afraid we're going to get stuck in here and I think there's a spider crawling up my leg!"

"Just close your eyes! It'll be over soon!"

He hoped that was true, because the shrieking, animal growl seemed to go on forever.

But it didn't.

And after the storm, sunshine.

ZONE FORECAST PRODUCT
NATIONAL WEATHER SERVICE NORMAN OK
TXZ086-031000-
WICHITA-
INCLUDING THE CITIES OF ... WICHITA FALLS
314 PM CDT MON JUNE 2 2008

.REST OF TODAY ... MOSTLY CLOUDY WITH FALLING TEMPERATURES. SCATTERED SHOWERS. WINDS NW 25-35 MPH. CHANCE OF RAIN 40 PERCENT.
.TONIGHT ... CLOUDY AND COOLER. LOW NEAR 45. WINDS NW 25-35 MPH. CHANCE OF RAIN 20 PERCENT.
.TUESDAY ... PARTLY CLOUDY. HIGH IN THE LOWER 70S. NW WINDS 10-15 MPH.
.WEDNESDAY ... MOSTLY SUNNY AND WARMER. HIGH IN THE UPPER 70S. WINDS LIGHT AND VARIABLE.
.THURSDAY ... SUNNY AND MILD. HIGH IN THE LOWER 80S.
.FRIDAY ... SUNNY AND WARM. HIGH IN THE MID 80S.

Fantastic and horrific video images glued the nation to its collective television set for days afterward. The Weather Channel reported its highest Nielsen ratings of all time and quickly revised its advertising rates to reflect the new audience. Major networks set up makeshift television studios. National morning shows interviewed hundreds of survivors, who reliably cried on cue. Al Roker predicted a return to sunny skies for Wichita Falls and then passed the baton to local weathermen who informed everyone else how the weather would fare in their neck of the woods.

Final tally: 9,351 dead. 51,249 injured. An estimated 85,000 homeless.

The 1979 tornado had cut a mile-wide swath of destruction through Wichita Falls, had destroyed entire neighborhoods with its core of 260-mile per hour, F4 winds that flattened almost every structure in its path. The tornado of June 2008 carved a spiraling path of EF5 damage *four* miles in diameter through the heart of Wichita Falls, and its powerful center of circulation opened a corridor two-thousand yards wide where nothing—no structure of any kind, no debris, not even foundation concrete—was left behind. Meteorologists, unable to estimate wind speeds in this area with the normal method—by analyzing debris patterns left behind by the storm—instead resorted to video footage and radar data, which revealed wind speeds in excess of 400 mph. These measurements certified the June 2008 tornado as author of the most powerful winds in recorded human history.

But before all this, there was tragedy still to be lived. Like Adam Altman in a jail cell, watching out his barred window as sirens and people screamed. Debris swirled and shrieked, the sights and sounds of hard materials in conflict. For a while Adam could detect no visible funnel, just a chaotic cloud of black and brown and red, but then swirling vortices finally emerged, closer than he had expected, and he stood tall in defiance of the storm. He prayed for the safety of his wife and daughter (who did, in fact, survive). He begged God to take him instead. God's answer was a blinding crash of stone on metal, a growl of wind, and when Adam looked down again he saw a street sign sticking out of his thigh. Blood poured out of the wound, coating the white letters, but as Adam faded away he thought he saw the word "Shady."

Storm chaser Jeff Piotrowski was on the tornado from its formation near the town of Holliday. "The base of this supercell was the largest I've ever seen," he said in a later interview with CNN. "You could see from the beginning it was going to be a monster. Typically you have the parent thunderstorm, and a wall cloud hanging beneath it, and then a funnel or tornado poking out of the wall cloud. With this storm the wall cloud *was* the tornado, at least for a while. But then the entire storm seemed to squat on the ground. I've never seen anything like it. My wife and I followed it on Highway 1954, well south of town, and even from that distance we knew people were dying. The tornado covered basically the entire city limits, like it was trying to smother everyone who lived there. I even saw the storm swallow an airplane, what appeared from our location to be a private jet. We would have gone into town sooner, to help anyone we could, but then we would have died, too. And the worst thing is the town's history. All storm chasers know the story of the '79 tornado in Wichita Falls. It was the event that introduced people my age to the kind of devastation these storms can do. So when my wife and I finally drove into town, ready to render aid," (here Piotrowski stopped to compose himself) "I tell you, what I saw will haunt me until the day I die. I've seen destruction. I've seen people's lives ripped apart. But I don't think I've ever seen the sort of despair I saw that day. The people of Wichita

Falls didn't even seem surprised. It's like they knew it was coming. It's like they had been waiting on it for twenty-nine years."

92

In the weeks that followed, Wichita Falls leaders designed a predictable campaign to once again bring the city back from disaster. Thousands of FEMA trailers formed a temporary living area south of the city that resembled an oil drilling boomtown. But even though the program ultimately succeeded in clearing debris and reviving infrastructure, most of the affected families finally gave up and moved away. A 2009 interim census survey estimated the city's population at 36,000, down substantially from the official 2000 count of 104,120. Two of the departed were none other than Jonathan Crane and Alicia Ulbrecht.

93

For several months they lived together in one of the FEMA trailers. Unmarried citizens were asked to share living spaces in order to maximize the rescue effort, so it made sense for Jonathan and Alicia to split one rather than be put with someone they didn't know. Alicia's mother and father had died in the storm, as had Jonathan's mother, and for the first few weeks the trailer was mainly silent. There was no television or cell service for many days, and Alicia spent much of her time away from the trailer, walking up and down highways south of the city. One day the two of them took a government bus to Dallas, where they picked up some new clothes, and where Jonathan purchased an inexpensive laptop. After some searching, he managed to find a copy of *The End of the World* buried in his email Sent folder, but upon reading this manuscript again he discovered he hated every word of it.

He decided instead to write a novel about what had happened to Wichita Falls.

The project would be a high-concept narrative that blended fiction with fact and ended with the vividly recreated, real-life disaster that destroyed a Texas town. Jonathan suspected the project would be an easy sell, and in fact, before he had written even a quarter of it, one of the agents who rejected him long ago actually called him on the phone. In what was surely the most bittersweet conversation of his life, Jonathan explained his story idea, and the agent suggested he could sell the project while Jonathan was still writing it. Three days after reading Jonathan's first seventy pages, the agent had called again with news that an auction for the partial manuscript had netted a high six-figure offer from Random House. Now there was a film agent involved, and Jonathan could expect to hear something from Hollywood in the next couple of weeks, if not sooner.

For reasons both kind and selfish, he kept this information to himself for a while.

94

Alicia's grief felt gratuitous considering the tragedy that had befallen the city of Wichita Falls was nearly without measure. How could she spend weeks mourning her parents, her friends, when so many entire families had been lost? The living arrangement with Jonathan was awkward, to say the least, but he was sensible enough to give her space. Alicia had expected Gholson's partner, Daniels, to come around sometime and question them, but he hadn't. With so much carnage and bloodshed, Gholson's gunshot wound had probably gone unnoticed. Maybe his body had been so badly deformed that the wounds had not been visible. Maybe his body had never been found.

She also didn't understand who had arrived on the plane. David had arranged for Thomas to be taken away, obviously, but Alicia thought he had been surprised by the gunfire. Like maybe the people who showed up weren't exactly who David had called. And once the plane had been inhaled by the tornado, there was no way to know.

On their third bus trip to Dallas, Jonathan bought himself a car, a 60's-era Ford Mustang convertible. When she inquired about the money it cost, the effect such a purchase might have on his finances, Jonathan offered an oblique answer about his upcoming insurance settlement and a savings account. Something had been different about him for a while now, though she couldn't quite say what. He walked more upright, he spoke with more authority in a slightly deeper voice, and he smiled a lot. He made plenty of jokes, too, even in a climate that was not friendly to humor.

After signing paperwork for the car, Jonathan had taken her to an expensive steak dinner, and then in a bar on lower Greenville, while they sat watching golf in a dark corner, he had kissed her like he meant it. Alicia hadn't been surprised. The eventuality of their relationship had colored every moment of her time with him since the tornado. She wondered sometimes what would happen if she walked away from the trailer and didn't return, if she stuck out her thumb next to the highway and let some man drive her to a distant, unknown destination. Would Jonathan come looking for her? Would she eventually surrender and find her way back to him? She remembered how miserable she felt when she went away to college, and how the pain had vanished the moment she returned to Wichita Falls. Did that mean she was never meant to leave this place? Or had her presence been required, as she had come to suspect, for some larger plan that was now complete?

As it turned out, Jonathan's kiss at the restaurant pleased her deeply, and later, in a downtown hotel room, she had welcomed his hands on her. His large and confident hands.

A few weeks after the car purchase, Jonathan announced his intention to move to Austin.

"Why Austin?" she asked.

"I want to be involved in the art community. I want to feel like part of something greater than myself, and Austin's the only place in Texas like that. Maybe someday it would be cool to live in California or New York, but for now this is a good start. I just can't handle living in this trailer anymore, and I don't think I want to rebuild my house, anyway."

It was no coincidence, she supposed, that Jonathan's plan resembled the kind of escape Alicia had dreamed about for years. How else would one have expected their story to end?

"Have you looked for jobs there?" she asked him. "Austin is more expensive than what we're used to."

"I think we can work something out."

And though Jonathan's easygoing confidence had become his most attractive quality, it was natural to question a seemingly arbitrary decision to move. Under more typical conditions, Alicia might also have asked how he planned to fund such an adventure. But this particular narrative, she predicted, had answered that question before she thought to ask it.

"You said 'we,' didn't you?"

"I did."

It was lovely how Alicia could know Jonathan would eventually ask her this and still be floored by the reality of it. Her heart fluttered in her chest.

"Are you asking me to go with you?"

"I already did that. Now I'm waiting on your answer."

"I would love to go," she said. "But I don't know how we're going to make it with no jobs. Even if you have savings—"

"That's the other thing I need to talk to you about. I have some news."

Jonathan grabbed a stack of printed pages from their makeshift kitchen table and handed them to her.

"What is this?" she asked, and looked at the opening page.

The day was electric, charged with possibility. Bobby Steele could feel it in the humid air and freshening wind, the power of the world. Ahead of him the sky was a gathering darkness. He was ten years old and had the strange feeling something important was about to happen, something that would alter the course of his life forever. At the moment Bobby was headed south toward Jonathan Crane's house, and by the time he crossed Midwestern Parkway it was barely five o'clock.

His feathered hair bounced against his head, blonde and thick and sculpted by the wind. His smile was magnetic. It was the second day of Spring Break and his mom didn't expect him before dark. She would have let him stay out longer if it weren't for his dad, Kenny, who was unreasonable when it came to Bobby spending time with Jonathan. . . .

"It's a novel I'm working on about what happened here," he said, and winked at her. "Like a fact-meets-fiction story."

There was a moment, post-wink, when Alicia believed Jonathan's awareness of their reality matched her own. If he had written something like this, especially after seeing the opening page Thomas had composed, surely he must be in on the joke. But the moment passed without comment or change of expression.

"So you're going to use real names?" she finally asked.

"Oh, I'll change that when it's done. But somehow, when I sit down to write, it just flows out of me this way. Like I already wrote it in another life, or someone else wrote it. It's hard to explain. But it comes to me so naturally that I don't want to mess with it, you know?"

Alicia found it difficult to believe he could say these things with a straight face. His childhood experiences with Todd, and all that had happened this week, should have made it clear what was really happening.

"You know," she said, "we've never really talked about David and Thomas and the detective. Like what was really going on. How Todd and his son knew the things they knew."

"I know. And I realize there is something about the world we don't understand. But even if we knew the answer, what would we do about it? We still have to live our lives no matter what the reality of the world is."

Jonathan had a point. There was nothing to be done with the knowledge she'd acquired, especially since it wasn't some supernatural force that might further complicate their lives. Still, now that her eyes were open, she could not imagine them closed. And she wondered: Why did she perceive the events of the past week differently than Jonathan? Did proximity to Todd limit his understanding somehow?

Or maybe the truth would be revealed to Jonathan at some later time. In the next chapter of their lives, for instance.

"Every day it seems a little less important to me," Jonathan continued. "I don't want to spend the rest of my life obsessing over something I can't control and don't understand. I want to focus on the things I *can* and *do* understand. That I care about a great deal."

Alicia smiled. She saw love in his eyes, and she hoped he could see it in hers, even if that love would not be translated into words for a while.

"This could really work," she said, looking again at the manuscript page. "With all the press coverage from the tornado, I bet you'd get a lot of interest."

"Actually, that's what I wanted to talk to you about."

Three days later, as they approached the Austin city limits, cruising along I-35 with the top down and sunglasses on, Alicia looked into the adjacent lane and spotted an 80s-era Cadillac that had been recently and lovingly restored, its bright blue paint accented by chrome spoke wheels and bright whitewalls. As the driver passed them, Alicia marveled at the long tailfins and chrome bumper, and when she saw the sticker there, a simple black-and-white design labeled with the word *Deadhead*, she looked over at Jonathan and laughed. After a lifetime of waiting for something extraordinary to happen, for the fairy tale to begin, Alicia finally understood the truth.

She had always been living it.

ZONE FORECAST PRODUCT
NATIONAL WEATHER SERVICE NORMAN OK
TXZ086-041000-
WICHITA-
INCLUDING THE CITIES OF ... WICHITA FALLS
1143 PM CDT SUN JULY 3 1983

.TONIGHT ... CLEAR. LOW AROUND 82. WINDS S 10-15
MPH AND GUSTY.
.INDEPENDENCE DAY ... SUNNY AND HOT. HIGH AROUND
110. SOUTH WIND 15-25 MPH.
.MONDAY NIGHT ... CLEAR. LOW IN THE LOW 80S. SOUTH
WINDS AROUND 10 MPH.
.TUESDAY ... SUNNY AND HOT. HIGH NEAR 111.
.WEDNESDAY ... SUNNY AND VERY HOT. HIGH NEAR 114.
.THURSDAY ... SUNNY AND VERY HOT. HIGH NEAR 116.

95

T he five of them stood in a rough circle between three barbecue pits. It was a little after two o'clock in the morning, and the city was asleep.

Todd smiled dreamily, his eyes far away, as if he were enjoying a movie only he could see.

"Tell me again," Adam complained. "Why do you want to burn down your own dad's restaurant?"

"Because he's an asshole. I caught him having sex with some woman who works here. He cheated on my mom."

"But if he loses his business, you guys will go broke."

"He pays for insurance," David said. "Just like the people who owned the house we torched."

Adam didn't seem to appreciate this answer, but at least it shut him up.

Todd said, "We can't use gasoline because we did that last time. But David tells me there's a way to set these barbecue pits on fire with left-over grease."

"You bet there is. I do it every Monday and Tuesday to clean these stupid things. Or at least I used to. After I caught my dad with that woman, I stopped working here."

David opened the doors to the barbecue pits and explained the process to his friends just as The Turk had relayed it to him 322 pages ago. The plan was to set fires inside the pits and then prop open the building doors to provide easy egress for the flames.

"We'll splash grease everywhere as if it were gasoline," Todd said. "I'm sure half the place will burn down before the fire department shows up."

"How do you know?" Jonathan asked. "The building is made of cinderblocks. Maybe it won't burn at all."

"I just do," Todd said. "I read it already."

"What do you mean you read it?"

"You know that place I saw when I was asleep? The empty white place?"

Everyone nodded or murmured agreement.

"Well, I probably shouldn't tell you this, because it's not the sort of thing anyone should know. But if I don't tell you now, I won't ever be able to."

"What is it?" Bobby asked.

"The things I saw and heard when I was asleep were real. But they weren't any kind of reality we know. There's some other world out there."

He gestured upward as if that would somehow explain what he meant.

"Other world?" David said. "What do you mean?"

"These songs I play for you guys aren't mine. How could I write 'The Boys of Summer?' I'm just a thirteen-year-old kid."

"So who wrote it, then?" asked Jonathan.

"I don't know who he is. But I heard those songs when I was in the coma, and it wasn't just songs. I also saw pictures of some guy's family, and home movies he made, all kinds of stuff. Even books he wrote. One of those books was about Wichita Falls, and now I remember I read the whole thing while I was in there. While I was asleep."

"You sound like a crazy person," Bobby said.

"Maybe I am crazy. Or maybe not. Because this story I read, it was about us. Bobby and Adam and Jonathan and David and me. And Alicia. And some police detective named Gholson. We were all in there. I read it. Someone wrote a book and it was us."

"That's just weird," Adam said. "You dreamed all that while you were asleep. There's no such thing as some other world."

"Maybe you're right. But if *I'm* right, then we're all just characters in a book."

"This is bullshit," Bobby said. "Let's set these pits on fire and get the hell out of here before we get caught."

"We're not going to be caught. But a long time from now some of you are going to remember what I told you tonight. And you aren't going to handle it well. And neither is my son."

"In this book you have a son?" Bobby asked. "Now I know you're full of shit."

"Yeah, and he figures all this out before I do. In fact, he figures out how to rewrite the ending so it works out better for him."

"He *rewrites* the *ending*?" Jonathan said, and laughed. "What kind of a story would it be if a character could step outside of it and change the ending?"

"Laugh all you want," Todd said. "But I had to figure out a way to get in there and change the ending back, because in his version, the bad guys win."

"So now who wins?" asked David.

"Come on, dude. I can't tell you the ending."

"I hate all that suspense when I read a book," David explained. "I usually read the last line and then work my way back up to it."

"That's a shitty way to read a book," Jonathan said.

"Maybe so, but that's how I like it."

"That's all you want to hear?" Todd said. "The last line?"

"One sentence isn't going to spoil it, right?"

David had a point. One sentence wouldn't spoil anything.

So Todd grabbed a match from the box he was carrying and struck it alight. His eyes felt magical and alive with fire.

Then he spoke the last words any of them would ever hear.

"It ends like this."

© Kimberly Cox

Richard Cox is the alleged author of three previous novels: *Thomas World*, *The God Particle*, and *Rift*. He claims to lives in Tulsa, Oklahoma, and is hard at work on his next novel. Then again, you shouldn't believe everything you read.